ZANAIKEYROS

SON OF DRAGONS

BY TESSA DAWN

BOOK ONE

PANTHEON OF DRAGONS

Published by Ghost Pines Publishing, LLC http://www.
ghostpinespublishing.com

Volume I in the Pantheon of Dragons Series by Tessa Dawn

First Edition Trade Paperback Published October 31, 2016 10 9 8 7 6 5
4 3 2

ISBN-13: 978-1-937223-21-2

Printed in the United States of America

Author may be contacted at: http://www.tessadawn.com

This is a work of fiction. All characters and events portrayed in this novel
are either fictitious or are used fictitiously. Any resemblance to actual
persons, living or dead, business establishments, events, or locales is
entirely coincidental.

 Ghost Pines Publishing, LLC

Credits and Acknowledgments

Ghost Pines Publishing, LLC., Publishing
Damonza, Cover Art
Damonza, Layout
Reba Hilbert, Editing

Pantheon of Dragons

BEFORE TIME WAS a recognized paradigm, seven dragon lords created a parallel primordial world for their glory…and their future offspring. They harnessed seven preternatural powers from seven sacred stones and erected the *Temple of Seven* beyond the hidden passage of a mystical portal that would lead back and forth between Earth and the Dragons Domain. And finally, they set about creating a race of beings—the Dragyr—that would exist on blood and fire, and they gifted their progeny with unimaginable powers, unearthly beauty, and immortal life.

For all of this, the dragon lords required only one thing: *absolute and unwavering obedience* to the *Four Principal Laws…*

I.   Thou shalt pledge thy eternal fealty to the sacred Dragons Pantheon.
II.   Thou shalt serve as a mercenary for the house of thy birth by seeking out and destroying all *pagan* enemies: whether demons, shadows, or humans.
III. Thou shalt *feed* on the blood and heat of human prey in order to reanimate your fire.
IV.   Thou shalt propagate the species by siring *dragyri* sons and providing The Pantheon with future warriors. In so

doing, thou shalt capture, claim, and render unto thy lords whatsoever human female the gods have selected to become *dragyra*. And she shall be taken to the sacred *Temple of Seven*—on the tenth day, following discovery—to die as a mortal being, to be reborn as a dragon's consort, and to forever serve the sacred pantheon.

And so it came to pass that seven sacred lairs were erected in the archaic domain of the dragons in order to house the powerful race begotten of the ancient gods, each lair in honor of its ruling dragon lord:

Lord Dragos, Keeper of the Diamond
Lord Ethyron, Keeper of the Emerald
Lord Saphyrius, Keeper of the Sapphire
Lord Amarkyus, Keeper of the Amethyst
Lord Onyhanzian, Keeper of the Onyx
Lord Cytarius, Keeper of the Citrine
& Lord Topenzi, Keeper of the Topaz

While a *dragyri* may appear to be human, *he is not*.
While a *dragyra* may appear to belong to her mate, *she does not*.
While the Dragyr may be fierce, invincible, and strong, they are *never* truly free...

Chapter One

DEEP INSIDE THE Sapphire Lair, concealed in the Dragons Domain, Zane Saphyrius leaned back against the plush leather cushions of the soft copper sofa, placed his feet up on the sturdy coffee table, and stared at his anxious housemate, waiting for Axe to speak. "Well, Axeviathon?"

Axe snarled beneath his breath. "Don't use my consecrated name."

Zane, whose given name was Zanaikeyros, snickered conspiratorially. "Understood. What did Valen have to say when he called?"

Axe cocked an eyebrow. "He said Lord Ethyron finally lost his patience with Caleb."

Zane blew out an anxious breath. "And?"

"And he had him brought to the temple last night... for punishment."

"Really," Zane spat, his voice thick with disgust. His spine stiffened, and his feet hit the floor as he leaned forward in his seat. "What kind of punishment?"

Axe just frowned and shook his head.

"*Axeviathon*, what kind?"

"Spiked lashes. Fifty, I think."

Zane brought a clenched fist to his mouth, released his fangs, and sank them deep into his fingers, imagining the wicked, jagged lash and how much skin Caleb must have lost before the male passed out. *If he passed out.* As Zane's temper flared, he fought to rein it in before his *fire* sparked and he burned his hand. "What for?" he growled.

Axe paced to a nearby window, stared out at the picturesque landscape—a cascading cliff-side waterfall, flowing out of a towering set of jagged rocks—and popped his neck to relieve some tension. "He got distracted on a mission." He pressed his palm against the glass and then absently cleared some dust from the windowsill with his forefinger.

"Pagans?" Zane asked, inquiring about the assignment.

"Nah," Axe replied. "Humans."

Zane shook his head in antipathy. "The Society?"

"Yep." Axe turned around to face his roommate. "The kid Caleb was supposed to protect, the one who got mixed up in a gang? He died before Caleb could dispatch his rival enemies."

"Damn," Zane whispered, as the picture grew increasingly clear: Among the human population, there were several secret societies that still worshipped the primordial dragons of old. The fellowship typically consisted of ordinary humans living ordinary lives, many of them being inconspicuous members of the community who just happened to be involved with a cult. Some were harmless; some were not. And occasionally, one or more of these followers would pray to the dragon lords, petitioning them for favor, asking for anything from prosperity to protection—from justice to vengeance. On even rarer occasions, one of the dragon lords would feel benevolent enough to respond, and despite the fact that humans weren't really their thing, the lords would get intimately involved.

Lord Ethyron, Keeper of the Emerald Lair, had a larger ego than most, so he was fairly susceptible to praise…and to prayers.

He tended to either lavishly reward or harshly punish the human interlopers from time to time. And, of course, that meant sending a mercenary to do his bidding, sending a member of the Dragyr to get down and dirty with the humans.

In this case, he had sent his servant Calebrios—*Caleb*—to

provide protection for a two-bit gangster: As far as Zane understood it, the youngest son of a middle-class family had gotten mixed up with drugs and joined a local gang, and one night, while he was high as a kite, he had sexually assaulted the girlfriend of a rival gang member. Needless to say, the rival gang had put a price on his head, and they were gunning for him, pretty hard. Having heard about it through the grapevine, the kid's father had made an offering of incense and precious oils to Lord Ethyron, beseeching the dragon lord to intercede on his son's behalf—to keep the boy alive. And for whatever reason, Lord Ethyron had been inclined to grant the favor. Although Zane didn't know all the details, he imagined Lord Ethyron had instructed Caleb to either extinguish the family's enemies or scrub their minds free of the incident—make the hit go away.

And, apparently, Caleb had screwed up.

He hadn't acted swiftly or definitively enough since, according to Axe, the kid was dead.

Zane rolled his eyes.

It was absurd for Lord Ethyron to get involved in mortal affairs to begin with, especially at such a petty and distinctly human level, something Lord Cytarius or Lord Topenzi, the most noble of their kind, would never—*ever*—do. Each lord had his own preferences and values, and some were more honorable than others, but Lord Ethyron ruled the house of Emerald, Caleb's house, and Caleb should have known better.

He should have known his master's temperament by now.

He should have known the cost of disobedience.

He should have handled the gangsters right away.

Still, the very idea of having one's flesh peeled from one's bones—from the back, buttocks, and thighs—made Zane sick to his stomach.

"How is he?" he finally asked, bringing his thoughts back to the subject at hand. "Caleb, that is?"

Axe frowned and shook his head.

"That bad?" Zane said.

Axe leaned back against the window frame and crossed his

arms over his chest. "Guess it could've been worse. Lord Ethyron could've had Caleb's amulet removed."

"Shit," Zane mumbled, understanding the implications. "You think?"

The only way to kill an immortal dragyri was to remove the amulet that kept him tethered to The Pantheon, the sacred gemstone that infused him with life, the *permanent* talisman he received at his formal induction into his adulthood lair. And the only way to get it off his neck, since the cord wouldn't break, was to first remove his head—a pretty severe punishment for a fairly insignificant crime…

Then again, they were referring to Lord Ethyron, and there was only one dragon lord who was worse—

Lord Dragos.

Zane instinctively clutched the sapphire ornament that hung around his neck, raised it to his lips, and pressed a kiss of reverence against the sacred stone. For the first time in a while, he was genuinely grateful that he belonged to the Lair of Sapphire, that he was subject to Lord Saphyrius and not one of the other dragon gods. As the third deity of the sacred pantheon, within the venerable Temple of Seven, Zane's ultimate master displayed characteristics of both light and shadow, but he wasn't that bad. The dragon could be both generous and brutal, merciful and unforgiving, but he was generally fair, just so long as he was given his due; and he loved his immortal offspring as much as any father loved a son.

Lord Dragos, on the other hand, the first deity of the sacred sect, the one who ruled the Diamond Lair, was by far the worst of the lot. Had Caleb belonged to him, he would have surpassed Lord Ethyron's cruelty in the same situation—hell, he would have had Caleb placed in a cauldron and boiled until his skin blistered and strips began to float in the water. And even then, he might have considered removing his amulet…

Once again, Zane shook his head to dismiss the morbid thoughts.

That wasn't his problem.

That wasn't his ruling lord.

Thank the gods.

"Not to sound insensitive," he said, "but why did Valyntheros call *you*?" Like Caleb, Valen was also a member of the Emerald Lair, so it only made sense that Caleb's punishment was Valen's concern—but Axe was *Zane's* pantheon brother, a fellow member of the Sapphire Lair, and he kept his relationships closer to home. It just seemed odd that Valen would have called Axe.

Axe sauntered away from the windowsill, strolled to an antique rolltop desk in the corner of the room, and retrieved a piece of parchment from the upper right-hand drawer. Turning to face Zane, he said, "You do know that Levi and Caleb are thick as thieves, right?"

"Yeah," Zane said, waiting for a deeper explanation. Levi was a member of their lair as well, their sapphire *brother* for all intents and purposes, and every member of the house was connected by a bond as true as blood. While they didn't say it often, the Dragyr revered each other. Since a male could only father *one* offspring—a son—they did not have blood siblings, which made their house-mates even more significant. Despite occasional spats, they would go to the mat for a member of the lair—hell, they would die if they had to—for a *brother*.

Axe blew a loose strand of dirty blond hair out of his eyes and met Zane's stare with a blazing sapphire gaze to match his own. "Those fifty lashes were supposed to be a hundred."

Zane grimaced, but he didn't speak right away. *Shit, a hundred lashes would flay all the skin off a dragyri's bones.* And the worst part was that Lord Ethyron would not allow Caleb to regenerate the damage quickly. In fact, he'd probably have some willing human servant mete out the punishment, just to add insult to injury. "Yeah, so he went light on him—what gives?"

Axe smiled, but the expression was absent of mirth. "Lord Saphyrius knows that Levi and Caleb are close," he explained, "and he wanted to spare Levi the anguish of watching his friend suffer as he slowly healed. So he offered up one of his own to appease Lord Ethyron's ego, to mitigate the damage."

Zane closed his eyes. *So, Lord Saphyrius had tried to appease*

Lord Ethyron for Levi's sake... He blinked them back open. "In exchange for the last fifty lashes?" he asked, understanding just how the deal had gone down.

"Exactly," Axe said.

"So, you're going to finish off the gangsters for Lord Ethyron—give the family vengeance to make up for the failed protection?"

Axe shook his head. He paced to the sofa and dropped the parchment in Zane's lap. "Nope, my brother. You are."

Zane sank back into the cushions and lifted the paper, quickly perusing three cursive names: the identities of the rival gangsters, those who had killed the petitioner's son. "What were the exact orders?" he asked.

"Execute them," Axe said.

"All three?" Zane asked.

"All three," Axe confirmed.

"And their souls?"

"Rotten to the core," Axe said.

Zane nodded, understanding.

Whether it was a code between gods or just common sense, even the Dragons Pantheon knew better than to take the life of an innocent soul, one that belonged to another race, to another set of deities: Humans had their religions; dragons had theirs; and never the two should meet. And while feeding on prey was one thing—even lions fed on zebras; after all, nature was nature—getting involved in the immortal journey of another species' souls was, well, considered off limits. The dragons were both allowed and expected to dispatch the wicked—demons, shades, and morally depraved humans, a trait which the Dragyr could discern—but they left the pure of heart alone when they could.

"And my deadline?" Zane asked.

"Friday at midnight," Axe replied.

"So tomorrow..." Zane sat back and chuckled. Lord Ethyron didn't play around. Apparently, he wanted these bastards dead, like yesterday, and Lord Saphyrius had made the call...for Levi.

He gave the paper a second, cursory glance and committed the address to memory: It was the name of a local hangout in Denver, the Two Forks Mall, a place where gang members often gathered after dark to see what kind of mischief they could get into. Zane could easily slip through the portal at twilight, stake out an advantage before the sun went down, and mete out the required executions before the clock struck midnight. He folded the paper and slipped it into his pocket. "Very well," he grunted, putting his feet back up on the coffee table.

The way he saw it, the night would go off without a hitch.

Three human gangsters—that was child's play.

However, it had been a really long day already. Bottom line: If he was going to execute the criminals in the next twenty-four hours, he needed to catch a little shut-eye.

Chapter Two

"DISTRICT ATTORNEY'S OFFICE; this is Jordan." Jordan Anderson twirled her mechanical pencil between her thumb and forefinger and tapped the eraser impatiently against the desk. It was Friday night, only five more minutes until quitting time, and she *really* didn't want to take another call.

"Is this Jordan Anderson?"

She rolled her eyes. Being that the call had been put through on her private line, and she had just given the caller her first name, who else could it be? "Yes, it is. How may I help you?"

The voice on the other end of the phone dropped to an eerie, demented purr. "Do you know what happens to witches in Salem, Jordan?"

Jordan held the phone away from her ear and stared blankly at the receiver. She cleared her throat and pressed it back to her lobe. "Uh, no, I don't. And since this happens to be Denver—and the twenty-first century—I can't say that I'm really interested." She was just about to hang up, perhaps deliver a few choice words to her secretary for putting the call through, when something made her pause: All day long she'd had the oddest, sinking feeling in her stomach, like something major in her life was about to change, like the axis she had always stood upon was about to shift beneath her feet, and she had no idea where the feeling was coming from. Perhaps this call was somehow related; the vibe was oddly the same.

When the caller began to chuckle in a crass, deranged chortle, she shivered. "Well, you're about to find out," he said.

"Who is this?" Jordan demanded.

He whistled the introductory tune to *The Twilight Zone* in the receiver. "It's your death calling."

Now this grabbed Jordan's full attention. She leaned forward; pulled the base of the phone closer, toward her keyboard; and hit a small red button to begin recording the call. "I see. And does my *death* have a name?"

"Yeah," he sneered. "Former inmate number 28765. The innocent guy you put in prison."

Jordan swallowed convulsively, even as she scribbled the number down on a Post-it. She wasn't sure if it would help at all, considering the fact that he might be lying, and every guilty perp she had ever put away believed he or she was innocent. She would need a better clue. "And what did I put you in prison for?"

"Sexual assault." He laughed, as if the very term was somehow funny, and her stomach clenched in response.

"Well, Mr. 28765"—she pronounced each number with heavy sarcasm—"I think you should be advised that you are threatening an officer of the court, and that happens to be a felony, not to mention a parole violation. Furthermore—"

"Oh, it's not a threat," he interrupted. "It's a *promise*. And frankly, I don't give a damn who you think you are, you haughty skank." Before Jordan could reply, he taunted, "I know where you live, and I watched you last night." He groaned. "You were sitting oh-so-cozy in your red silk pajamas, eating popcorn in front of your big-screen TV. What were you watching, *witch*? *Salem's Lot*?"

Jordan frowned, chewing on her bottom lip, as she tried to remember what she had been wearing last night…

A pair of red silk pajamas.

And she *had* been eating popcorn on the sofa.

She sat up straight in her chair. "How long did you spend in prison, Mister…"—she paused—"what did you say your name was again?"

He laughed. "Oh, it's not going to be that easy. In fact, it isn't going to be easy…or enjoyable…or quick at all. But it is going to be soon."

Jordan tried to home in on his voice. He had a faint South American accent, perhaps Cuban or Colombian, and he sounded like he was in his late teens or early twenties, definitely no more than twenty-five. Since she didn't deal with juvenile cases, he had to have been sentenced in the last seven years. "Look, Mr. Whatever-Your-Name-Is: I don't know how you got my direct number or what you've been doing outside of my apartment, but it ends right now. Do you understand? I am going to report this call, as well as your recent activity, to the proper—"

"Yessss…" He practically hissed into the phone like some kind of reptile, some kind of slithering snake. "Yes, it ends now. See you soon, Jordan." With that, he hung up.

Jordan sat back in her chair and bristled as the hairs on the back of her neck stood up. *Great, just great,* as if she didn't have enough to deal with at the moment: Her current caseload was monstrous; her best friend Macy was about to have abdominal surgery; and her grandmother had recently passed away, leaving her, for all intents and purposes, without a family support system.

Now this?

What else could possibly go wrong?

She brushed her long auburn hair behind her shoulder and sighed. She was tired of dealing with everyone else's chaos, tired of constantly swimming upstream. She was tired of fighting for a secure place in a sometimes-hostile world, and honestly, she was growing weary of dealing with the scum of the earth on a daily basis, just to make a living.

Something needed to change.

And perhaps that was what all her previous unease was about.

Not being one to get mired in self-pity, she swallowed her trepidation and hit the intercom button on her phone. "Janice?"

"Yes, Jordan?" her secretary replied immediately, her cheery, sing-song voice playing through the speakers like a merry tune of light.

"I need you to place a trace on the last call you sent through."

"Is everything all right?" Janice asked, her gaiety instantly fading to concern.

"No, not really," Jordan said. "The guy on the phone was a real creep, a disgruntled ex-con, and I think he's been stalking me. We're going to need to file a report." She sighed, betraying her exhaustion. "Oh, and while you're at it, would you pull up all the files we have from the last seven years of sexual predators who we've successfully prosecuted, then cross-reference them for those who were recently paroled with an inmate number 28765—the number might be bogus, but check it just the same. It could save us a lot of time. Also, look for males between the age of nineteen and twenty-five, those who might have a South American accent."

Janice paused for a moment. When she finally spoke, her tone was unmistakably somber. "Sure, Jordan. Sheesh…I'm sorry."

"Yeah," Jordan said. "Me, too." She disconnected the call, not wanting to focus any more energy on gloom and doom. And then she picked up her cell and texted Macy: *Hey, M. I'm gonna need a rain check on dinner. Something came up. I can probably still do coffee a little later, maybe meet for cinnamon buns at the Two Forks Mall, instead??? Does 8:30 work for you?*

Macy texted right back: *Sure, J. Hope everything's okay. See you at 8:30.*

Jordan smiled in spite of her current concerns. Not unlike her secretary, Macy was always a bright light in Jordan's occasionally dim world, and it was very important for Jordan to keep their engagement—Macy was going into the hospital on Monday for laparoscopic surgery, to have a benign tumor removed from her abdominal wall, and the last thing Jordan wanted was to leave her best friend hanging, especially when Macy's nerves were already frayed. The girl had always been there for her, and she intended to return the favor. She would be damned if some psycho and his drama, legitimate threat or not, would keep her from supporting Macy. The latter just wasn't an option.

The intercom buzzed in her office, and she hit the neon-green button. "What've you got?"

"I'm still working on the trace," Janice said, "but I've already found twelve files, all convicted sex offenders, all sentenced in the last few years, and all with Latin surnames—I'm going to have to call corrections to check on the inmate number, but I'll send them through to your email. Let me know if you want me to cross-check CDIC or NCIC, just to see if there's anything new, especially if the guy has been released since we archived the files." She tapped away on her keyboard and double-clicked her mouse, the familiar sounds echoing through the speakers. "Oh, and Detective Jacobs is on his way over to take your complaint."

Jordan smiled. She couldn't help it. Janice was an excellent assistant, and Detective Mike Jacobs? Well, he was just an excellent cop. Not to mention, a really good man: a hard-nosed investigator who had a crazy sixth sense when it came to sniffing out a lowlife. If anyone could get to the bottom of this—quickly, efficiently, and with aplomb—make sure that Jordan was safe, it was Mike. Besides, there was no point in jumping the gun or freaking out, ruminating about all the morbid possibilities at this juncture: whether the caller was a talker or a doer, whether he just wanted to scare Jordan witless, or whether he was actually capable of acting out some sick, demented fantasy, going further than just peeping through her ninth-floor window with a pair of binoculars.

Either way, Mike would figure it out, and in the meantime, Jordan would do her due diligence and keep her energy positive for Macy.

Bad things had happened before, and evil people existed in the world…

They always had.

But the good ones were all that mattered.

One way or another, Jordan would handle the situation. She always did. And more than likely, Mike would have the crackpot in custody before she finished having coffee with Macy, especially if the idiot was dumb enough to give her his real inmate number.

Opening her email, Jordan clicked on the link Janice had just provided and began to download the files.

Chapter Three

JORDAN SAT ACROSS the table from Macy in the Two Forks Mall, Cinnamon Café, and slowly licked her lips, savoring the last sticky bite of her cinnamon bun. "Oh my gosh," she groaned, "that was heavenly."

Macy smacked her lips and smiled. "Almost as yummy as a naked man with hard abs and a huge...smile."

Jordan chuckled.

"So, did you take care of that business, whatever had you tied up earlier?"

Jordan shrugged one shoulder with indifference. "Yeah, pretty much." She had given a full report to Michael Jacobs, and they had narrowed down potential suspects to three possible men: a Cuban named Carlos Blanco, who had been convicted of stalking a pre-teen girl; a Colombian named Javier, who had spent four years in the state penitentiary for aggravated sexual assault; and a loser named Alonzo, who was in and out of prison every couple of years, as if he had the routine set on a revolving schedule. Detective Mike was looking into all three cases, waiting to see if one of their inmate numbers matched, and he had offered to send a patrol car by Jordan's building at regular intervals throughout the week—or at least until they got to the bottom of it. As she had surmised, the caller may have been set on vengeance, or he could just be a creepy cuckoo-bird, hell-bent on scaring a pretty young attorney.

One way or the other, they would put a quick end to it.

Jordan slapped her hand down on the table in an abrupt change of subject. "Enough of that. We're not here to talk about me. How are you doing? How are you feeling? Are you ready for Monday?"

Macy sat back in her chair, considering Jordan's words. Her eyes darted around the café in a sudden bout of *people-watching*, and then she abruptly slapped her hand on the table, mimicking Jordan's gesture. "Enough of that, too!" she exclaimed. "We are only here to talk about frivolous things—nothing heavy." She ran a finger through a clump of cinnamon, sugar, and butter, the gooey concoction left over on her plate, and sucked it off her finger, smiling. "Let's look for hotties."

Jordan threw her head back and laughed. "Oh, Macy, a one-track mind, as always." She checked her watch and smiled. "As much as I would love to stalk the mall with you, trying to find a rare, delectable hunk, I can't." She frowned in apology. "I have to get back home. I have a case in Judge Stanley's court on Tuesday morning—jury selection—and I'm not ready." She raised her eyebrows. "Can you forgive me?"

Macy stuck her lip out in a playful pout. "Well, you're no fun."

"None at all," Jordan agreed, hoping for mercy. She batted her large hazel eyes at her friend. "But you still love me, right?"

Macy sighed. "I guess." And then she rolled her eyes.

"What?" Jordan asked.

Macy practically glared at her. "Nothing."

"What?"

Macy harrumphed. "It's just that I'm really getting tired of spending weekend after weekend home alone. Batman movies no longer really do it for me."

Jordan furrowed her brows. "Okay…so what does that have to do with me?"

"Oh, please," Macy chided.

"What?" Jordan repeated, sincerely puzzled.

Macy leaned forward in her chair and gave Jordan a cross look.

"*You* are the eye-candy, the guy magnet, the one that draws the hotties in like bees to honey."

Jordan smirked. "Yeah, or more like flies to shit."

Macy laughed. "That, too," she teased. "But it's just that I need you to find me a man—just for the month of June, at least. Okay?"

Jordan scrunched up her nose and scoffed. "Oh my gosh. *No.* Even if you weren't having surgery on Monday—which means you couldn't really entertain a man right now, anyhow—you know that I am not into matchmaking or dating. Right now, I'm just focused on my career."

"A career you hate," Macy supplied, eyeing her meaningfully.

Jordan flicked her wrist as if shooing the topic away. "Maybe, but I thought we agreed: We aren't having any heavy discussions right now."

Macy nodded. "Right. Okay. But just as a quick aside, I'm only going to say one thing: I don't care how much money you spent on that fancy law education. You hate it. You're miserable doing it, and life is too short to spend rolling around in the muck with criminals."

Okay, so Macy was going to go *there,* despite their agreement to keep it light. "Who's rolling around in the muck?" Jordan asked.

Macy cocked her eyebrows. "You understand what I'm saying. You're a gifted artist, Jordan, and you're never happier than when you're painting. So what if you don't get to live on the top floor of a high-rise apartment or drive an eighty-thousand-dollar car; wouldn't you be better off doing what you love?"

Jordan tried to shrug off her annoyance.

So much for a quick aside…

Macy had a way of oversimplifying things and then occasionally caging them in the most unattractive way possible, even though she meant well. "First of all," Jordan said, "I live in the high-rise apartment because I love the view of the sunset over the mountains, and I've earned it." She winked conspiratorially. "It's an artist's thing. And I love my car because *I love my car,* not because of the price tag. And besides, I'm not married to any of those material things. What I am married to is having some sort of security and stability in my life, knowing that I can take care of myself, even past retirement."

And there it was again…

That sinking feeling in Jordan's stomach like something global in her life was shifting.

She thought about Macy's words, the fact that she was bringing all this up now, and tried to dismiss the significance: Following her parents' death, Jordan had been raised by her aging grandmother, and growing up on a fixed income had not been easy—life had been one constant struggle after another, and Jordan had made herself several promises at a very early age. One, that she would never go hungry again. Two, that she would always be in a position to take care of herself, no matter what. And three, that she would be the captain of her own ship, even if she steered it into a veiled cluster of jagged rocks, and she had always done just that—captain her own ship, that is. So why did she feel like someone else…*something else*…was about to take over the helm?

She quickly dismissed the thought and sighed. "I'm trying to be independent, Macy, because I have to be. Besides, I still paint on the side." It was a cursory but adequate explanation. Well, either way, it was all Macy was going to get.

Macy eyed her dubiously. "When was the last time you did a scenic? A mountain range, a meadow, a waterfall? *Anything?*"

Jordan frowned. "Fine. Point taken." She searched for a playful way to change the subject. "Is there anything else you would like to say about my life before I go? Perhaps I should change my hair color, join a new religion, or take up yoga?"

Macy sneered in jest. "No, I guess not." She immediately perked up. "Although I have heard that yoga really improves your flexibility." She winked at her and sighed. "All I'm saying is that you need to take *total* care of yourself—emotionally, spiritually, that kind of thing." She hesitated, chewing on her bottom lip. "Maybe even consider getting back together with Dan someday."

Jordan bristled, and Macy immediately held up both hands, palms forward, in a placating gesture, before the prosecuting attorney could snap her head off.

The assistant district attorney of the 2nd Judicial District, Dan Summers, had been Jordan's one true love: handsome, charismatic, and amazing at his job—the man had never lost a single case. And he had also been the one to break her heart in a thousand pieces by conveniently failing to mention that he was married when they first met. While he may have truly fallen in love with Jordan during their short, six-month affair—and while he had eventually left his wife after they broke up—the fact that he had lied to her, day in and day out, that he had taken the moral choice away from her, as if she didn't have an opinion on the matter, had been utterly and irreconcilably devastating to the twenty-seven-year-old prosecutor. While Jordan did not consider herself the single most virtuous human on the planet—every now and then she struggled with a petty thought here or there, like anyone else—she had never been the type to date a married man. She would have never chosen to disrespect another woman so selfishly. And that's what Dan never got: It was more than the lies and the deception; it was the lack of regard, his willingness to make Jordan's choices for her. And ever since, he had been trying to find a way back into her heart—and back into her bed—but that door had been summarily closed.

Indefinitely.

Macy's tenacious voice interrupted Jordan's thoughts. "You're way too young, way too smart, and way too beautiful to live your life all alone or in a job you don't enjoy. That's all I'm saying."

Jordan blinked several times, and then she nodded crisply, not wanting to encourage the conversation any further. "Thank you, Macy," she said softly. "And I do—I will—take better care of myself." She plastered a congenial smile on her face. "Honestly. I promise."

Macy seemed satisfied with that answer. *Thank God.* "All right then," she said, sounding like someone's mother. "Will you come see me on Monday at the hospital, before I go into surgery?"

Jordan nodded emphatically. "*Of course.* I'll be there before you arrive. I can still take you if you want."

Macy shook her head. "No. My mother is insisting on the honor. She wants to make sure I follow all the pre-op instructions to the letter, like I might suddenly lose my mind and drive through a Starbucks on the way, drink a gallon of coffee and choke under anesthesia."

Jordan chuckled. That sounded just like Karen Wilson. She glanced down at her watch and gasped. "Oh my gosh: It's already 10:15! I really do have to go."

Macy followed her eyes to the watch and sulked, playfully extending her bottom lip. She stood up, gathered her purse, as well as the extra cinnamon bun she had ordered for later, and brushed a few crumbs off her blouse. "Are you parked in the font lot?" she asked, apparently hoping they could walk out together.

"No," Jordan answered. "No spots when I got here. I'm parked right below the furniture gallery in the garage. I'll just take the exterior stairs down—my car is close." She gestured toward a pair of glass doors that led to an outside balcony and staircase, pushed back her seat, and stood to give her friend a hug. "I'll see you later, then. Monday for sure." Giving Macy an extra hard squeeze, she added, "Oh, and if you start to get nervous or worried before then, you know you can call me. Doesn't matter how late it is."

Macy's voice softened with appreciation. "I know. And thanks."

"All right, I'll see you later then."

"Yep. See you on Monday," Macy said. "Love you, girl."

Jordan smiled. "Love you, too." She was just about to walk away when Macy reached out and took her hand. "Hey, you be safe, okay?"

Jordan started, a bit unsettled at the unexpected directive. *Where in the world had that come from?*

Knowing Macy to be more intuitive than was natural, she shivered, and then she shrugged it off. "Of course," she said, "always."

With that, she turned around and headed for the stairs.

❧

Zane Saphyrius locked his arm around the gangbanger's chest from behind, drew him backward, off his feet, and slowly sank into the shadows, dragging his prey along with him.

The youth spat out a curse and tried to wrench free from his hold. "Get your nasty-ass arm off me, punk! You have any idea who you're messin' with? I swear: My posse is gonna jack you up!"

Zane seared a harsh, unerring mental compulsion into the idiot's brain, demanding immediate compliance: *Shut up and stop moving.*

The gangster froze, and a bead of sweat trickled down his brow. He opened his mouth to speak, but his voice wasn't working—nothing came out.

"That's better," Zane hissed, feeling his fangs press insistently against his gums. He'd rather not feed on the likes of this human trash, but the urge was almost irresistible. Stepping further back into the shadows, until the two of them were safely masked behind a thick cement pillar in the dimly lit garage, he called on his inner dragon.

As the heat rose in his chest, radiating outward toward his limbs and infusing his muscles with power, he reveled in the near-orgasmic sensation. The pulse of his inner-fire was sweltering. The pain was invigorating. And the feeling was akin to having the full powers of the cosmic universe at his fingertips. He growled deep in his throat, even as the fingers of his right hand curled inward, and his claws slowly began to extend. "Lord Ethyron sends his regards," he drawled in that unique, unfamiliar accent that all the Dragyr males shared. And with that, he drove his clawed hand through the gangster's back, clutched his heart in his fist, and ripped it from his chest, along with a two-inch-thick gold chain that just happened to come along for the ride.

Dropping the organ and the chain to the ground, Zane cocked his head to the side in a feral, serpentine motion, and slowly exhaled a scorching orange flame.

He needed to release some heat.

The fire consumed the gold in seconds, leaving the heart untouched, while charring most of the precious metal to ash. It was an exercise in precision, a way to refocus Zane's beast before his hunger got the best of him. As the ravaged body slumped to the ground, Zane caught it by the elbow and quickly retrieved the male's cell phone from his pocket before he let him fall: He would need to cross-reference the phone numbers for the other two gang members in order to get their addresses. They hadn't been at the mall.

Staring down at the limp, lifeless body now slumped at his feet, he paused to consider what to do with the corpse: to burn it, bury it, or leave it. He didn't think he could incinerate it without drawing the attention of other humans, and that would mean he would have to control all their minds, erase their memories, redirect them away from the scene, and tie up loose ends, more trouble than the situation was worth.

Snarling at the unpleasant nature of the duty, he squatted down, picked up the heart, and stuffed it back into the gaping chest cavity. He drew regenerative power into his forefinger and began to reattach the organ—not enough to reanimate it, but just enough to reseal the severed chambers—make the whole scene appear a little less gruesome, point the authorities toward a rival gang, rather than a supernatural intervention.

Hell, let the medical examiner try to figure it out.

It was only a human, and a soulless one at that.

Wiping his hands on the dead man's shirt, Zane sanitized his own flesh with more silver fire and then slowly stood up and glanced around the garage.

No one had seen him.

Of that, he was certain.

He would have heard them, sensed them, *smelled* them.

Rolling his head on his shoulders to release some tension, he kicked the corpse further into the shadows with his steel-toed boots, straightened his duster around his shoulders, and headed toward an outdoor stairway that led into the mall. While there were few delicacies in the human world that appealed to an immortal dragyri—and virtually no luxuries that The Pantheon could not provide in greater quantity and substance—Zane was a sucker for red licorice! Twizzlers, to be exact. And while the Dragyr only consumed human food for pleasure—they fed on the blood, heat, and the *essence* of humans to survive—he may as well pick up a couple bags before heading out to finish the remaining two gangsters, before traveling back through the portal.

He glanced at his watch to check the time: It was 10:15 PM, and he needed to get a move on. He had less than three hours to find and dispatch his remaining quarry, lest he fail to meet Lord Ethyron's deadline and end up like Caleb Ethyron—on the receiving end of a spiked lash, whipped for a minor offense.

Chapter Four

JORDAN GATHERED THE lapels of her lamb's wool coat, clutched them in her fist, and hurried down the narrow cement stairway, trying to avoid slipping on the steep, polished stairs. The night was cool; the air was crisp; and it reminded her of a late autumn evening, rather than the middle of June. As her two-inch heels clicked against the pavement, she gripped the rail with her free right hand and slowed down to maintain her balance.

She absently glanced to the right, and her eyes locked with a stranger's: a huge, imposing man ascending the otherwise empty stairway. She couldn't help but notice that he was strikingly handsome—in a rugged, medieval sort of way—his hair was as dark as night; he was naturally tan; and there was something almost savage in his bearing. His ethnicity was odd...curious...indefinable... impossible for Jordan to place, and she shivered involuntarily, thinking immediately of the caller, the guy who had threatened her earlier, the one who had called her a witch.

She quickly dismissed the connection.

First, she would remember the likeness of a guy she had sent to prison, and second, she would never forget this particular man's face.

Realizing she was staring, she nodded politely in greeting and planted another foot on another cement stair—and then she drew back in surprise.

He was practically gaping at her!

Staring straight through her.

His piercing sapphire-gold eyes were locked, like lasers, on hers.

As gazes went, it was both terrifying and ominous, as if he could see into her soul, as if he were seeking the same…

She licked her bottom lip in a nervous gesture, even as she consulted her common sense: *Get a grip, Jordan. It's just a curious glance, a fleeting intersection of eyes, the kind that happens a dozen times a day.* She forced a good-natured smile and quickly glanced away, hoping to pacify his curiosity—to dismiss his attention—and to remind him of common courtesy.

As expected, the stranger followed suit.

He continued to take the stairs, two at a time, until he had passed her without incident, and then he suddenly stopped in midstride and spun around to face her.

She sensed it more than she saw it.

She could literally *feel* his domineering presence behind her, and despite her immediate impulse to *run*, she turned to face him, instead.

The stranger tilted his head to the side and emitted some strange, feral sound. It was almost like a snarl, and Jordan's heart began to race. They locked eyes a second time, and she almost let out a yelp: He was glaring at her now, like she had stolen his first-born child, his dark, sculpted brows creased into a frown.

She unwittingly took a step back, clutched the rail, once again, for stability, and stifled a terrified gasp. Determined to appear calm, she stuffed her free hand into her pocket, hunched her shoulders in some instinctive, submissive gesture, and slowly backed away, feeling carefully for each stair beneath her.

He took a casual step toward her, and she almost bolted.

He halted, almost as if he dared not frighten her any further, and then he did the oddest, most animalistic thing: He inhaled deeply, sniffed the air, and he *groaned.*

Whether it was a groan of annoyance, impatience, or anger, Jordan had no idea, but that was the final straw—she had no intention of sticking around to find out.

Releasing the rail, she spun around in a whirl, leaped the four remaining stairs—almost twisting her ankle—and took off running for her car, all the while digging frantically for her keys as she ran. She could hear the stranger's footsteps behind her, and she cringed at the stupidity of her choice. *Why hadn't she screamed or tried to push past him? Headed back in the direction of the mall, to the safety of other people?*

Rounding the corner of the parking garage, she eyed her forest-green, metallic BMW, only five spaces away, and rotated her key-fob in her hand, pressing the *unlock* button over and over, just to be sure it opened. She glanced over her shoulder to judge the distance between herself and the stranger, and gasped, her feet skidding to a sudden halt.

He wasn't there.

Even though she could have sworn she'd heard his footsteps, just moments ago, the man was no longer behind her.

She pressed her hand to her heart and fought to catch her breath, feeling a curious mixture of both relief and embarrassment. She scanned the garage in all four directions, making sure she hadn't overlooked his presence, that he wasn't hiding behind a nearby post or a vehicle, and then she started once again for her car.

Angry tears filled her eyes as she finally reached her BMW, yanked on the door handle, and bent to climb inside.

"Stop." An *invisible* hand snatched her by the arm, slammed her door shut behind her, and pressed her back against the driver's-side panel. And then, just like that, the stranger was standing, once again, in front of her.

What the hell!?

She jolted in surprise, dropped her keys on the ground, and opened her mouth to scream; but the sound would not come out. Her eyes grew wide, and her heart constricted in her chest, beating so frantically that it pulsed in her ears. The dangerous, imposing male pressed both hands flush against the hood of her car, and caged her in like a trapped, helpless animal, framing her shoulders between two taut, muscular arms.

She dropped down, tried to duck beneath his right bicep, but it was all to no avail. He simply followed the movement of her body with his arms.

And then she foolishly tried to back up, to escape him with a twist, but once again, there was nowhere to go—the solid panel of her car was behind her. Her heart thundered in her chest, and she gasped for air. "Get away from me!" she finally bit out, shoving hard at his iron chest. *Good lord,* the man had to be six-foot-four, and his chest must have been made of iron, because he didn't budge an inch. She clutched his wrists and tried to wrench his arms free from the hood of her vehicle. "Let me go!"

He leaned into her, pressed his forehead to hers, and his dark, silken hair fell forward, shrouding them in an intimate midnight curtain. "Shh," he whispered softly. And then he pressed a finger to his lips to demonstrate the command as he slowly shook his head. "Be at ease."

Be at ease?

Did he just say, *Be at ease?*

As if!

What the heck was that supposed to mean, anyway?

Jordan suddenly felt sick to her stomach. She wanted to scream—she had tried to scream—but it was like the scream was trapped in her throat. It simply would not come out. Her eyes clouded with angry tears, and she scanned the parking garage for a Good Samaritan, praying someone—*anyone*—would come her way. The mall didn't close until midnight, and there was still a scattering of parked cars—they couldn't *all* belong to employees.

She choked back a sob and forced herself to meet the stranger's penetrating sapphire gaze. *Dear God, he was frightening,* and not even in a criminal way—his demeanor went so far beyond that. He was like fog rising off the sea, or that large spiderweb, unseen in the corner: mythical, ethereal, and a part of the shadows themselves.

And suddenly she knew…

This was what she had feared all day, the cause of that deep, uneasy stirring in her belly, not some two-bit criminal who wanted to pay her back for a perceived, wrongful conviction, not the caller who had threatened to burn her like a witch, but *this man*, the one standing directly in front of her.

She summoned every ounce of courage she possessed, suddenly realizing it was vitally important that she get away.

Now.

"Who are you?" she whispered. "And why are you doing this?"

He reached out to grasp her by the jaw, and she instinctively slapped at his wrist. "Don't touch me!"

His fingers were like an iron vise, welded to her chin, permanent and unmovable. His shoulders stiffened, and he encircled both of her wrists with his other hand, locking them in a flesh-and-blood handcuff. "Do not fight me, angel," he drawled, as if he fully expected her to comply.

Oh shit, she thought, as her knees grew weak. She hoped she hadn't just ticked him off.

It was already clear he was crazy.

Jordan tugged at her hands, trying to wrench them free, but they wouldn't budge; and he refused to release her.

"What is your name?" he asked.

She nearly swayed in place.

Was he serious?

"Anna," she finally croaked out, hoping to talk her way out of the terrifying situation.

He frowned. "Your name is not Anna. *Try again.*"

She swallowed hard and stared over his shoulder, her eyes still scanning the garage, her soul still praying that someone might come and save her. "Look, I don't know what you want, but trust me, you don't want to do this."

"I want you to look into my eyes," he said, his voice dropping in both pitch and timbre so that it sounded like a haunting chime of bells.

She gaped at him in disbelief, even as she locked her gaze with his.

He released her wrists and clutched at a deep blue object that was hanging around his neck, some sort of gemstone attached to the end of a leather cord, like an amulet. And then, all of a sudden, the object began to glow, and she thought she smelled burning flesh. He winced in pain and released it, muttering beneath his breath: "*Dear gods of The Pantheon…*" His expression flashed with the strangest hint of…*recognition?*…and then he placed his hand in her hair; caressed a lock of her thick auburn curls; and slowly let the strands slide through his fingers. His eyes practically glowed with a reflection of ownership in their depths as he reached out to trace her bottom lip with his thumb. "Gods, you're beautiful," he whispered.

Jordan visibly trembled, all the while wishing she had the courage to bite off his thumb.

Yet and still, she couldn't scream.

She. Couldn't. Scream.

As it stood, all she could do was stand there and gawk…and tremble…as her palms began to sweat. By all that was holy, he was the most strikingly handsome man she had ever seen, and the most frightening creature she had ever encountered. His deep sapphire eyes, with their pale pupils of gold, practically smoldered with ferocity; his harsh masculine features belied a barely leashed lethality; and his unseen aura radiated all around him in a dozen tangible waves, projecting dominance, power, and possession. For lack of a better description, he didn't seem altogether human—why weren't his irises white?

She shivered, trying once again to find her voice.

Why couldn't she scream?

Jordan Anderson was a strong, educated woman. Hell, she was a prosecuting attorney, and she had spent years arguing with scumbag lawyers, reading the riot act to bad guys, and besting other, much more experienced counselors in court. She knew how to handle herself in a tight situation, but it was as if her will was no longer her own, as if this man—*this being*—had captured her voice and locked it away in a vault, allowing her words, but refusing to *let her scream.*

She knew it didn't make any sense, but what other explanation was there?

Swallowing her fear, she tried to summon her reason and collect her wits. She tried to think like a lawyer. "Look," she said, in as firm a tone as she could muster, "I don't know what's happening here, who you are, or what you think you want with me, but you have to know that I'm a criminal attorney, an officer of the district court; and that means what you're doing right now is a felony." She quickly shook her head and held up her hand to appease him. "But it's okay...*so far*...nothing has happened that can't be reversed. You can still walk away. You can still let me go. This can still end in your favor. If you would just take a few steps back, I would be happy to forget this ever happened. I'm sure we can come to an understanding." She tried to soften her eyes as well as her voice. "What do you say?"

The corners of his mouth turned up in a parody of a smile, but it didn't reflect any mirth. In fact, the gesture was curiously sad. "Ah, my sweet, sweet angel. You are trying so hard to alter something that is older than time, something so much bigger than you or I. Indeed, we must come to an understanding...very soon. There is much we need to work out." He lowered his hand and absently brushed the backs of his knuckles over her lower belly, rotating the digits in a slow, methodical circle, and she thought she might just die of fright.

"Please," she whispered, her knees nearly knocking together. "Don't."

He took a slow, careful step back. "I cannot do this right now, my dragyra. It is less than two hours from midnight." He scrubbed his hand over his face and then glanced around the garage, almost as if he were at a loss as to what to do next. "Alas, I would like you to go home and wait for me."

Jordan stifled a nervous chuckle, even as a small spark of hope ignited in her heart: If, in that moment, a little pink pig had flown by the windshield and oinked, Jordan would not have been a bit surprised. This terrifying, insane man wanted her to go home and wait for him.

Yeah, because that was really going to happen.

Still, this might be her only opportunity to get away.

She nodded her head and forced a hospitable smile. "Absolutely. I can do that. If that's what you think is best, for us to *talk later*, I think that sounds reasonable." She held her breath and prayed.

He chuckled, deep in his throat, the sound a cross between a snicker and a growl. "Mm, you are a lawyer, aren't you? As clever as you are sweet. As determined as you are beautiful." He cupped her cheeks in his hands, let out a long, drawn-out sigh, and bored his faint golden pupils into hers. "Look at me," he commanded her again, only this time, his voice was as pure as the driven snow, as dark as the endless night, and as compelling as a hypnotic tone. "Tell me where you live."

She couldn't believe her ears.

Was he crazy?

She had to stifle a nervous titter at the absurdity of the question; and then her eyes grew wide, her lips began to tremble, and she had to bite down on her tongue to keep from doing exactly what he'd asked—she was about to give him her address!

Her real address.

What the hell?

She quickly thought of a viable alternative before her tongue could betray her, the address of her ex-lover and the assistant district attorney, Dan Summers. "My address is 591 Elkhurst Lane. It's in Pine Hills."

He nodded. "You will wait for me, then? You will do as I bid?"

Her head felt cloudy; her stomach turned over in small little waves; and she felt like she was falling into his eyes. She nodded. "Yes. I will. *I promise.*" Her mind was sorting a dozen thoughts per second—reminding her to call Dan and let him know she had given this predator his address; calculating just how quickly her ex could set up a sting; and wondering what it would feel like to know that this man had been apprehended...in the case that he showed up at Dan's.

She reined in her random, racing thoughts, lest she get too far ahead of herself. "I will," she repeated, waiting...

Hoping.

Praying that he would just walk away.

He stared at her for what felt like a millennium, and then he cocked his head to the side and frowned. "You are not easily enthralled," he said. "That's amazing." He folded his hands together as if considering other options. "Very well, then I will find you, instead."

She nodded. "Of course." *Whatever.* Just so long as he let her go, right now.

He took her hand in his and raised it to his lips, like he was planning to kiss her knuckles in some old-world, seductive gesture, and then he rotated her arm, instead, exposed her wrist to his mouth, and bit her right in the center of her radial artery.

She gasped at the pain.

Hell's bells, it felt like the man had fangs!

As he took several deep, dragging pulls from her vein, Jordan staggered in place. Her arm grew unbearably cold; *frost* began to settle on her skin; and for the first time that night, she began to wonder if she would make it out of this alive. She choked out a muffled sob and grimaced.

Who was he?

What was he?

And why was he doing this?

He moaned, as if in great pleasure, and then he slowly withdrew his fangs, blew warm air over the wound, and watched as a thin, bluish flame healed the lesions.

Jordan hiccupped, but she was well beyond speaking.

When his eyes met hers once more, they were infused with light, and the sapphire irises were glowing amber. Rising to his full, intimidating height, he drew back his lips and snarled.

The man actually snarled.

"Know this, *Jordan Anderson*: If you contact your lover, Dan, I will rip out his throat with my teeth and spit out his spine at your feet. If you run, I will retrieve you. If you continue to lie to me, you will make this far more difficult than it has to be. *Who am I?* I am Zanaikeyros Saphyrius, but my brothers call me Zane. *What am I?*

I am the son of a dragon, consecrated to the lair of Sapphire, born to the sacred pantheon; and you are my *dragyra*, my *fated*. *Mine*. And I am doing this because I must. And you must."

Sensing her rising terror, he took a judicious step back and sighed, his voice returning to its normal silken purr. "Jordan," he cajoled, "I will not die in order to appease you, but know this: I will not harm you, either. I will *never* harm you. I am sorry this is all I can share right now, but all will be explained to you soon."

Jordan inched back until her legs scraped against the car. She opened her mouth to speak...or cry...but, once again, nothing came out. He was absolutely, certifiably insane, and she had no idea what this maniac was planning to do next. Finally, when she felt like she could at least croak out a sound, she tried to plead with him for mercy. "Zane..." Her voice was a mere whisper of her terror. "Please, just let me go. I'm not lying, playing any games, or trying to trick you, not anymore. I'm just...I'm begging you: Please, let me go."

"Oh, angel..." He bowed his head and his eyes flashed with something akin to deep regret in them. "I cannot do what you ask. Who can reverse what the gods have decreed?" He stepped forward and leaned in—pressed a chaste kiss on her forehead—and sighed. "Go home, Jordan. We will meet again soon."

And with that, he simply vanished from her sight.

Zane stood in the garage for a few moments longer—invisible—watching as Jordan climbed into her car, quickly engaged the locks, and rested her head against the steering wheel, trying desperately to breathe.

So this was her.

The woman the dragon lords had chosen for him upon his inception.

The one who would share his life and one day bear his son.

She was beautiful and smart—that was for sure—and he was still shocked by the fact that he couldn't enthrall her, that he couldn't compel her to do his will, with nothing but his voice. She had a very strong mind, to be certain.

He sighed, thinking of the challenge before him.

None of that mattered, really.

In ten days, he would present Jordan Anderson to the seven dragon lords, and she would kneel in the sacred temple before The Pantheon, offering herself for consecration…to be reborn…

To become Zane's eternal mate.

And it was his job to make sure that it happened.

He hated the way the whole thing had played out, but there was little he could do to change it. Normally, he would have just taken her back to The Pantheon and dealt with the consequences there, taken some time to acclimate her to her new surroundings, but he still had a job to do for Lord Ethyron.

And he had to get it done before midnight.

Chapter Five

ZANE STROLLED BRAZENLY into the backyard of the two remaining gang members.

They were lounging on the front porch, listening to music, throwing up gang signs to the dark, pulsing beats, and passing a forty-ounce of what looked like Old English back and forth between their limited crew. The moment they saw him approach, the smaller of the two, a poorly dressed teenager with some sort of upside-down symbol shaved into the side of his head, pushed off his perch against the railing and sauntered to the top of the stairs.

"Yo, fool! Wassup with that shit!" he barked, trying to make his voice sound hard. "How you gonna stroll into someone else's yard like you own the place—you high or somethin'?" He reached across his waist with a bent wrist, allowing his hand to hover over the butt of a pistol, protruding from his pants. The gesture was clearly meant as a warning.

"Nah," his partner said, rising lazily from his deep sprawl in a rickety chair. "I think your boy just has a death wish." The second banger was massive. He looked like some kind of gladiator with huge, steroid-enhanced biceps and two prominent gold teeth, right in the front of his grill.

"For real," the first guy groused. He took several paces forward and strolled languidly on purpose, his body swaying in an exaggerated side-to-side swagger. "Wassup then, bruh?"

Zane rolled his eyes, but he held his tongue. He had no time for this inane banter. In a matter of moments, both of these idiots would be dead. He walked straight up to the first gangster, laughing as the miscreant drew his pistol and angled it sideways, in the most nonsensical way to point at a target, at least if you wanted to hit it.

Before the banger could even register that Zane had moved, Zane slapped the gun out of his hand, sending it flying across the yard; placed both hands on the sides of his jaw; and snapped his neck like a twig, leaving him lying at his feet as he turned toward the other gangster.

"Oh, shit!" the golden boy exclaimed, instantly swelling up with adrenaline. He drew an automatic weapon from the back of his waistband and held it forward, upright. This human wasn't playing around. He intended to hit his target.

As he got off ten successive rounds, Zane held up his hand to catch the bullets. When the spent shells were scattered along the ground, he growled and lunged at his opponent.

"What the hell are you?" the gangster shouted, sounding curiously like a girl in his panic.

"Your mama," Zane growled, and then he hurled a bolt of fire from the tips of his fingers, instantly melting the gun along with the gladiator's hand, and he grasped at his throat with fully elongated fangs. Just as he was about to sink his teeth deep into the gangster's flesh, something landed on his back, and *son of a dragon*, the impact felt like he had been hit by an oncoming train.

Zane released his prey and grunted in surprise. He arched his back, dropped into a squat, and spun around in an attempt to dislodge this new assailant. The dark, murky attacker dropped at his feet, his reptilian features gleaming in the moonlight as he landed between Zane and the injured human. Zane stepped away and sniffed the air. The strong scent of sulfur permeated *everything*, and the night grew ten shades darker. As if that weren't enough, there were two more silhouettes rapidly advancing toward the porch: two hulking creatures slinking in the grass, eager to join their comrade.

Zane grew deathly quiet as he analyzed the threat and enumerated his enemies.

One human, still alive, and three *pagans* in total: the demon on the porch, a demon in the grass, and a shade, slithering off to the right, in the yard…

Zane immediately locked on to the Sapphire Lair's private bandwidth and sent a telepathic call to two of his brothers, the two he knew were hanging out this night. *Levi! Axe! It's Zane. I've got some trouble with a couple of pagans, not sure if there's more around. Find me.*

Pagans were not easy prey to take down, and while Zane figured he could handle two or three, he wasn't about to take any chances. His fate was now tied to the pretty attorney's, the human he had cornered at the mall…

Jordon.

And now that they had made contact, the ten-day clock was ticking. If the female wasn't at the temple before her time ran out, she would die that final night in her sleep, and Zane's amulet would be removed. Jordan was no longer free to remain mortal—one way or another, she belonged to The Pantheon.

Sensing the demon behind him rising, and knowing that his lair-brothers would first have to come through the portal before they could transport into the yard, Zane decided to deal with the pagans first—they were a far greater threat than the gangster, and he could simply maim the latter with one swift action and deal with the human later. He hurdled the pagan on the porch; threw a wicked-hard elbow into the jaw of the banger, and shattered his two gold teeth. *That ought to slow his roll*, he thought as he spun around deftly, reached for the demon's crotch, and dislodged the family jewels, leaving the creature a eunuch. The injury wouldn't kill him, but it would sure as hell keep him at bay for the next couple minutes.

Buy Zanaikeyros some time.

The second demon, approaching from the yard, was now

coming up the stairs. He stopped on the landing, about five feet away, and snarled, "Ah, I thought I smelled the stench of a dragon's son. Look what we have here." He turned to regard the shadow behind him, and wasn't that just a hell of a combination? A demon and a shadow, hanging out together—*what the heck was going on?* The demon shrugged an indifferent shoulder. "Greetings, Zanaikeyros Saphyrius. I see your puppet master has let you out of his sight." He snickered. "How is Lord Saphyrius?"

Zane rocked forward onto the pads of his feet, dropping into a nimble squat as he sidestepped away from the demon on the porch, who was still cupping his groin and moaning, and gathered a lethal amount of fire in the palms of his hands. "Demon," he barked, acknowledging the second fiend's presence. "What the hell are you doing in gangland?"

The pagan cocked his head to the side. "A little of this. A little of that." His lip twitched in anticipation, even as the tendrils of his inky-black hair began to slither and coil about his head like a band of mating snakes. His rotten breath assailed Zane from across the modest distance, making the dragyri's stomach roil, and then the demon simply disintegrated, his body collapsing like a pillar made of salt, and all the tiny particles transformed into dark, black-hearted beetles, instantly sprouting wings.

"*Shit*," Zane grumbled beneath his breath. Those tiny bugs were deadly. They carried enough venom to stop the heart with a single bite, and their little feet contained miniscule, parasitic pincers that latched onto the skin and would not let go. Not to mention, they dripped some sort of acidic goo as they crawled, and on rare occasions, they could transmit messages to the pagan underworld. Now he had about half a million to contend with. Speed and agility was the name of the game.

Priming his reflexes for a preternatural tennis match, where the balls would fly back and forth faster than the eye could see, Zane swiftly transformed his skin into scales, to toughen his outer shell; he converted his pupils to electric lasers; and he began to listen for the high-pitched shrill that would function as an internal radar, identifying the trajectory of the rabid bugs. His hands moved in graceful circles, rotating lithely to the left and the right with incredible dexterity as he prepared to block, swat, or incinerate everything that came his way.

And of course, the eunuch was finally rising behind him.

With no time to spare on the wounded demon, Zane sent an imperious command into the mind of the toothless gangster, the one with the melted hand—the one who was still in shock and whimpering like a baby: *Kill the demon on the porch, the one behind me. Punch him. Gouge out his eyes. Go for his throat. Do not stop, and do not waver. Do not let go. You can't feel pain. You don't care if you live or die. You only know that you must kill the demon…now.*

Zane knew the pagan would make quick work of the human, but again, it might buy Zane a little time.

As the ghoulish beetles attacked with force, Zane countered each strike with a defensive maneuver. Between the beams shooting from his eyes and the fire pulsing from his hands, the front porch lit up like a cosmic light show, transforming the night into an interstellar dance of red and yellow rays, punctuated with macabre sparks, sizzles, and pops. As a horde of beetles all rushed at once, moving like a slithering pile of oil along the ground, Zane drew back his lips, opened his mouth, and scorched the earth before him with a blistering hot red flame. The beetles squealed as they died, the demon inside of them groaning.

And then the remaining shadow, the one in the yard, leaped over the staircase and lunged at the dragyri. The shadow's skeletal hands extended like branches as he sought to affix them around Zane's throat.

Zane had no choice.

He had to forget the beetles.

He turned his attention away from the bugs, reached up to block the pagan, and swore beneath his breath as a score of vermin attached to his arm. A high-pitched whir sliced through the air from somewhere behind the shadow, and the pagan's head fell from his neck, dropping to the deck like a heavy stone. A pair of giant hands, belonging to Axeviathon Saphyrius, wrenched the shadow backward by the shoulders and tugged the corpse away from Zane, even as the brutal, blond warrior smiled. He had beheaded the shadow with a lance, and now, he was making exceptionally quick work of incinerating his translucent body before the pagan could rise again.

Levi bounded on the porch with a thud. He grasped the head of the human gangster in one hand, the head of the eunuch-demon in the other, and slammed both skulls together with so much force that the craniums exploded as one, and then he spun around to come to his brother's aid. "Did they bite you?" he growled in a husky tone, glaring at Zane's tormented arm.

"No," Zane bit out, peeling the bugs from his flesh; then, "yeah, shit, just now," he added, as he felt a pair of mandibles sink into his skin, just above his inner elbow, where a beetle had managed to crawl between his scales.

Levi snatched Zane by the collar of his shirt, drew him upright from his squat, and slammed him against the house, along the back side of the porch, in a desperate attempt to gain quick, easy access to his fully exposed torso. All the while, Axe continued to incinerate the remaining bugs.

"Damn, Levi," Zane snarled, more out of instinct than displeasure.

"Be still," Levi barked. He released his fangs, bit Zane just above the elbow, in the exact same spot as the bug, and began to pump counteractive venom into the wound, hoping to neutralize the demonic substance before it could reach Zane's heart.

Zane sucked in a sharp breath of air. The dragyri's venom stung like a dozen scorpions biting into his flesh at once—it was far more painful than the demonic poison injected by the bug. He continued to peel off the remaining beetles, those still crawling on his arm, crushing them in his palm before they could bite, while simultaneously regulating his breath in an effort to slow down his heart.

He was trying to give Levi a hand.

Retracting his fangs, Levi spit out a gob of toxic venom and rose languidly to his feet, all the while watching Zane like a hawk.

Zane followed suit. He straightened his spine, brushed off his pants, and shook out his hands, checking the front of his body, just to be sure. Nodding at Levi, he sighed in relief. "Thanks, brother. I think we got 'em all."

"No problem," Levi said, backing away to survey the yard.

And then, just like that, another beetle bit Zane—this time, in the ass.

Zane clenched his lower cheeks and snarled, cursing in the ancient Dragonian language. He stuffed his hand into the back of his jeans, grasped the obnoxious beetle, and crushed it in his palm, groaning with disgust.

"What?" Levi asked, staring inquisitively at Zane's tortured expression.

"Another bite," Zane answered as his chest began to seize. *Son of a demon!* That bug had been strong. He would have said it out loud, but his throat was starting to close.

"What the hell?" Axe said, making his way toward his lair-mates.

"I think another one just bit him in the ass," Levi replied. He touched the tips of his fangs with his tongue and grimaced, staring at Zane's backside warily. "Damn, brother," he moaned. He planted his palms on his narrow hips and shook his head rather slowly. "I mean, I love you and all, Zane; but dang—I'm really not trying to suck venom from your ass."

Zane stooped forward and braced his hands on his knees. The porch was beginning to sway beneath him, and the yard was going all topsy-turvy, spinning in dizzying circles.

Axe shook out his hair, as if he were still creeped out by the bugs. "Ah, hell," he grumbled. "Strip him."

Levi took one hard look at Zane, who was now beginning to struggle for breath, and shrugged his powerful shoulders. "Sorry, brother." He stepped forward, and with a lightning-quick series of motions, he eviscerated the male's clothes in an instant, leaving only his athletic socks and his steel-toed boots intact.

Zane turned around and spread both legs, about shoulder's width apart. *What a helluva night.* He braced both arms against the side of the house, giving his lair-brothers an up-close-and-personal view of everything he was packing from behind, and waited.

Axe sidled up behind him, stopped a few feet short of touching Zane's hips, and then got straight down to business. He bathed the afflicted dragon in silver-blue fire from head to toe in an effort to heal, cleanse, and incinerate any remaining toxins from the outside in.

Zane grit his teeth as the healing flames got to work.

Burning was nothing new to a dragon.

Not after centuries spent in the Dragons Domain with the feral lords, but it still hurt like a mother when it happened, healing flames or not.

Zane held his breath, waiting for the remedy to take hold, grateful that it was only silver-blue flames assailing him. Orange—*or gods forbid, red*—would have dropped him to his knees, had him pleading for mercy like a sycophant.

Like a little girl.

When at last his breath had returned, his heart had settled down, and there wasn't a beetle, gangster, or pagan left in sight, Zane cupped his hands over his privates and slowly turned around. He gestured toward the inside of the house with his chin. "Clothes," he muttered. "Someone?"

Levi chuckled, vanished from view, and returned with a pair of oversized black silk pajamas and a plain white tee. "Sorry," he murmured. "Best I could do."

Zane took the clothes and donned them with appreciation, and then he finally stepped down from the porch. "Thanks for the backup," he said to no one in particular. The yard was already clean. Axe must have incinerated everything he saw, right down to ash, because all that remained were several inky spots where bugs had once been, and a couple of piles of cinders where the bodies had once lain.

"You good?" Axe asked, following Zane from the porch into the yard. He chuckled as Zane squatted down to strap his steel-toed boots beneath the silken black pajamas. "Nice combo."

"Ha. Ha," Zane mocked, flipping Axe the bird. "I'm glad you're getting some humor out of all this."

Levi smiled broadly then, meeting the other males on the grass and tilting his head to the side to gaze longingly at Zane's derriere. "I dunno, brother; the way you were bent over on that porch"—he drew a slim hourglass circle with his hands in the air—"for a second there, I thought, damn, Levi. I know he's not exactly a woman, but what the hey. Maybe you should just go ahead and—"

Zane's feral, baritone snarl cut him off midsentence. "Very funny, Levi."

Levi's deep, melodious chuckle filled the chilly air. "Seriously, though, I hate when they unleash those beetles."

"Must've been an ancient," Axe said. "Not many demons have that kind of power."

A companionable silence settled amongst them, until finally, Zane cleared his throat. "Make sure Lord Ethyron knows that his business was handled," he said, meeting his brothers' eyes, each one in turn.

"You're not coming back with us?" Axe asked.

"Nope," Zane said. "Can't just yet."

"Why?" Levi asked.

Zane bit his lower lip and decided to just go for it. "I made contact with my dragyra. Earlier."

Axe narrowed his sapphire eyes and raised his thick upper lip in a scowl. "Come again?"

"You heard me," Zane said. "In the parking lot, at the mall."

"You sure?" Levi asked.

"Oh yeah," Zane insisted. "I passed her on a staircase, and her pretty hazel eyes turned glowing sapphire in an instant. I had to do a double-take. Then later, when I *made her acquaintance* once again in the garage, *when I touched her,* my amulet heated up." He grasped the sacred talisman encircling his neck with his fist, and he lifted it from his chest, knowing that both lair-mates would immediately see the dark maroon scar where the amulet had burned his flesh. "She's mine, all right."

"Whew!" Axe whistled low, beneath his breath. "So…" He

hesitated, as if searching for just the right words. "So, you're bringing her back, tonight? To the lair?"

"Nah." Zane shook his head. "No idea how I'm gonna play this yet." He shrugged. "But I am gonna find out where she lives, make sure I leave a compulsion to *stay put*, wait for me, while I figure it out."

Levi ran his left hand through his thick golden-brown hair. *"Zanaikeyros..."*

The formal address brought Zane up short. "Yeah?" He gave his brother his full attention.

"What do you need?" The male's even, sonorous voice was heavy with resolve. "Whatever it is, just name it."

Zane nodded in a show of appreciation. "No idea, yet," he answered truthfully, and then he turned to place a light hand on Levi's shoulder. "By the way, how's Caleb?"

Levi frowned. "Lord Ethyron made his point," he said sharply, careful to bite back the full extent of his disdain.

Zane looked away.

There was no upside in speaking critically about the dragon lords, not any of them. They were their fathers. They were their gods. And they kept the sacred amulets imbued with life force. In other words, to speak against the Dragons was akin to defying one's own soul. All Zane knew was that Calebrios would heal—*or not*—in time. Meanwhile, Zane had ten days—really, nine, now—to claim his mate, try to break through her resistance, and get her to the sacred temple as an offering to The Pantheon. Not counting what was left of this night, he had nine more days to solidify a connection with the only female he would ever have a chance to mate in an eternal lifetime. "So I'll catch you later," he said, eyeing each of his brothers in turn.

Levi nodded, understanding without the need for a further exchange of words.

Axe crossed his arms over his chest and held Zane's vulnerable glare with a matching stare of both intensity and color—they all had sapphire eyes. While they may have been born with irises the shade of their pupils, those irises changed the day they were consecrated to their permanent lairs, the moment they were pledged to Lord Saphyrius. Axe then swept his gaze across the yard, indicating the earlier battle with the subtle gesture. "Be careful," he intoned, reminding Zane of the constant need for vigilance. "You never know where the real danger is going to come from."

Zane inclined his head in formal acknowledgment of Axeviathon's words, and then, without pause or preamble, he vanished from the yard.

Chapter Six

ZANE FLASHED INTO view in a dark, empty alley—it was as good a place as any to quiet his mind, collect his thoughts, and tune into Jordan Anderson's unique vibration. He had taken her blood earlier in the parking garage at the mall, when he had pierced her wrist with his fangs and tasted her delectable essence; and that was all he needed to find her, to track her and stake his claim.

He tuned everything else out and concentrated on those microscopic platelets, the blood that now moved through his own veins, and slowly, one by one, fragments of information began to emerge: a memory; Jordan pulling into an underground garage beneath a high-rise building, an impression; Jordan walking through the front door of a comfortably appointed living room and dropping her keys into a nearby basket on a decorative iron-work stand, and an address; Jordan filling out a credit card form—no, a shipping statement—for an online purchase, an expensive pair of earrings.

Yep, that was it: *2496 East Haley Avenue* in the Skyline Mosaic subdivision, *unit 905* on the top floor. *So she had lied about her address*—smart. He took bits and pieces of the layout, internalizing the blueprint from random scattered images and other disconnected impressions, and he committed them to memory.

It was enough to go on…for now.

Zane took a deep breath, solidified his determination, and then shimmered out of view.

It was 11:45 PM, still day one of the mandatory claiming; he wouldn't stick around to get to know the female better. Rather, he would simply materialize inside her room; place a fixed compulsion inside her head while she slept, perhaps weaving the command into a dream; and then he would head back through the portal to the Dragons Domain, where he would prepare the sapphire lair for a new arrival.

∽

Alonzo Diaz stuffed the large, sloppy end of the mop into the heavy plastic bucket and pushed the contraption forward, stepping out of the service elevator. Three months of cleaning up after spoiled, rich white people who'd been born with silver spoons shoved up their tight derrieres; three months of shining chrome and sanitizing toilets in the public lobby so stuck-up African-Americans could look down their haughty noses at other, ignorant black people; and three months of polishing mirrors in the common hallways so his own kind, other Latinos who thought they were white, could pass by the glass and forget where the hell they came from: This job was bullshit, and he hated every minute of it.

But—and wasn't there always a *but*—he had done it for a reason.

To bide his time and get close to Jordan Anderson, close enough to wrap his strong, tattooed hands around her skinny little throat and end her pathetic life, but not before he used her in every way imaginable. Oh yeah, Jordan was gonna learn a thing or two about *sexual predators*, up close and personal. Enough of watching her from across the veranda, from the top of an adjacent building with a pair of cheap binoculars. Enough of cleaning up her pristine building's halls.

Alonzo pushed the mop to the end of the corridor, came to a stop—just outside of door number 905, Jordan's luxury apartment on the top floor of the high-rise—and he smiled like a Cheshire cat. Damn, he had waited a long time for this. He stuffed his hand into the oversized pocket of the dark blue jumpsuit—*and why the hell did they dress janitors like prisoners, anyway?*—and felt for the master key. *Damn right*, he had a copy of the master key, and all it took was a bottle of tequila, a couple of sleeping pills, and a late-night card game with the superintendent to get his hands on the original and make the copy.

Done and done.

Now glancing at his watch—it was 11:45 PM—he slipped the key out of his pocket and laughed. He had all night long to play his wicked game.

Chapter Seven

JORDAN ANDERSON SAT up abruptly in bed. She stiffened and angled her head to the side, trying desperately to listen. She thought she'd heard footsteps in the hall, a soft but steady *clomp, clomp, clomp* heading in her direction. Her heart began to race as she struggled to clear the cobwebs, force her brain to come online, and will her senses to awaken.

What time was it anyway?

One glance at the soft blue LED lights glowing on the nightstand clock answered her question: 11:50 PM, almost midnight. She tossed the sheets aside, bounded from the bed, and pressed her back against the wall, beside the closet doors, still listening. Those were definitely footfalls, and she needed to act quickly.

The phone; she should call 911.

The security alarm; why hadn't it gone off?

Protection; she needed a baseball bat or a knife or a—

"*Jordan.* Oh pretty Jordan. Here, witchy witch. *Here, witchy witch.* Come to papa."

She gasped, her heartbeat accelerating to double time. *Oh, shit.* That was him. *The creepy guy.* The one who had called her office earlier, threatening her life. The sexual predator she had helped put away. *What in the world was he doing in her apartment?* And how the hell had he gotten in? Didn't Mike have patrol cars surveying the building?

None of that mattered right now.

Her LC9 was on the other side of the room, safely tucked away in a gun safe with the loaded clip resting *beside* the revolver—safety on, chamber empty—and she didn't think she could make it across the room in time, around the bed and to the safe, let alone punch in the four-digit code quickly enough to retrieve the weapon. Some home protection that was. She made a quick dash to the nearby nightstand, instead, snatched her cell phone, and ducked into the closet, trying to close the heavy wooden doors as quietly as possible as she swiped wildly at the cell phone screen, trying to turn it on.

Emergency login.

Bypass security code.

Go straight to 911.

Her hand shook as she tried to work the buttons, and then a large, clanging boom wrenched an unbidden scream from her throat as the closet door slid open with a violent thud.

"What are you doing, witch!" His voice was positively maniacal, and she dropped the phone, immediately switching to another, more primal instinct: *survival!*

Jordan kicked at the towering frame hovering above her, coming at her, her heel taking aim for the center of his thighs. He immediately blocked his groin, and she went at it with a fury, pedaling, kicking, trying to obliterate his crotch like a wild thing. Stomp. Thrust. Kick-kick-kick. One foot after another, trying frantically to lodge his gonads all the way into his pelvis.

He backed out of the closet and snarled.

She spun around in the dark, feeling for the phone, but he came at her again, this time with a knife.

She reached for her nearest shoe, a heavy black snow-boot with a three-inch wooden heel, and swung it at the proffered blade.

This wasn't happening.

This was not happening!

Some irrational part of her brain kept insisting that she should just turn back the hands of time, go back and get it right, do it over and take proper precautions—make all the right moves, next time.

This simply could not be happening.

And then he dove on top of her, closing the distance between them, eliminating the use of her feet, and knocking the boot aside. She screamed again, this time fighting wildly with her hands: scratching, gouging, punching, trying to force him...*off!*

He butted his head against hers, knocking the sense right out of her, and while she was still reeling from the pain and disorientation, he scrambled backward on his hands and knees, grasped her by the ankles, and tugged, yanking her out of the closet.

She tried to flip over and crawl.

She tried to kick back at his face.

She tried to wrench free from his hold, but nothing seemed to work.

Good Lord, why was he so strong?

In an instant, he grasped her by the waist, lifted her from the floor, and tossed her onto the bed like she was nothing but an insubstantial rag doll!

Noooooo!

This could not be happening!!!

Fight, Jordan. Fight!

Tears of angry frustration stung her eyes as she vacillated between utter disbelief and panic. And there was moisture, thick, viscous liquid, trickling into her eyes—*was that blood?* Had he opened her skull with that head-butt?

And then, all at once, the most terrifying sound Jordan had ever heard reverberated through the room: A deep, feral hiss grew into a deafening roar, causing the furnishings to shimmy where they stood, as if from a terrible earthquake.

Jordan sucked in air, her eyes darting this way and that, trying to identify the primal sound and its source. And the convict, the vile, criminal piece of crap that was climbing on top of her, spun around as well, trying to confront the unexpected threat.

He was no match for what hit him.

In the blink of an eye—without any preamble or warning—the

convict's back, chest, and arms lit up in flames; and the sudden blaze of fire singed the clothes from his body, melted his skin like wax, and created a thick, molten residue that clung to his flesh like tar. He screamed in agony as a long set of—*claws?*—reached around his burning shoulders, dug into his neck, and opened a virtual geyser of arterial spray.

Oh shit, oh shit, oh shit!

Jordan let out a primordial cry that was beyond identification. It wasn't a shout, or a scream, or a whimper—it was a horrifying bellow for mercy.

And she was so outta there!

She dove from the bed, landed awkwardly on the floor, her ankles still caught in the comforter, and then shimmied forward on her elbows, like a soldier in a low-crawl exercise navigating an obstacle course, hoping to gain forward momentum any way she could. She scrambled to her feet and bolted for the door, just as she heard a deafening whir whiz past her. It was the convict's head, flying from his shoulders and ricocheting off the wall. The *thing* had wrenched it from his shoulders.

Holy mother of mercy!

Jordan's feet had never moved so fast as she sprinted for the front door of her apartment, desperate to get away. She didn't bother to look behind her. At last, she reached the familiar six-pane panel and grasped at the bolt, flipping it to the left in one furious twist, while yanking it open at the same time.

A huge, powerful hand slammed the door shut. "Stop."

She spun around, pressed her back to the door, and stared at the titan before her, and then her jaw hung open in shock. She knew him. Well, she didn't know him, but she'd seen him before, earlier, in the Two Fork's garage.

She began to hyperventilate.

"Breathe," he rasped, placing his hand gently against her throat.

Her eyes bulged like balloons. "Please," she whimpered. "Oh God, oh God...*please.*" She hated herself for her weakness—she knew better than to show fear to a predator—yet the tears fell freely, despite her best intentions. "Oh, please, don't hurt me."

The man—*no, the male*—took a cautious step backward, his piercing sapphire eyes glowing golden in the centers, and slowly nodded his head. "You are safe now. Just breathe." He lowered his hand from her throat, and curiously, the air was flowing more freely through her windpipe.

Jordan swallowed, almost convulsively, as she eyed him warily from head to toe. His dark, chestnut-brown hair was drenched with blood; his lips were still curled back in a snarl; and his canines were far too long for comfort, two razor-sharp points descending well beyond his taut, angry lips. He looked like death on two feet, the grim reaper in pants—pajama bottoms, to be exact. She blinked rapidly and stared at his clothes: He was wearing a white Haines T-shirt that stuck to his powerful frame—molded to every muscle, bulge, and sculpted mass like a second skin—and a pair of black silk pajamas…over hard, steel-toed boots.

What the hell?

He looked down at his attire, presumably following her gaze, and jacked up one shoulder in a shrug. "Yeah…it's…it's been a long night."

Jordan shook her head in disbelief and absently raised a hand to her own mouth to point at her teeth. "Your…your…teeth."

He shut his eyes, and his fangs slowly retracted.

She recoiled, wishing she could step right through the door, out into the hall, and into the next, neighboring country. "What are you?" she whispered, warily.

He didn't hesitate. "I already told you."

She furrowed her brow. *What? He'd already told her?* And then it all came back: *I am Zanaikeyros Saphyrius, but my brothers call me Zane. I am the son of a dragon, consecrated to the lair of Sapphire, born to the sacred pantheon; and you are my dragyra, my fated. Mine. And I am doing this because I must. And you must.*

She wet her lips and tried to focus. "Zane," she whispered.

"Yes," he grumbled.

"You're a…dragon." Her voice sounded hoarse.

"No," he corrected her, that deep, otherworldly legato evoking a fearful quiver. "The son of a dragon, a member of the Dragyr race…I am a dragyri."

She nodded, feeling all at once light-headed. "Right. And I'm…you think I'm a…*dra-gyr-a*, like…a daughter of a dragon?" Her tone betrayed her distress.

He chuckled then, the sound emerging from deep in his throat, as if any part of this was funny. *Crazy?* Yes? *Psychotic, delusional, and positively terrifying?* Absolutely. *But funny?* Not so much. "You are not a dragon," he drawled, way too slowly, reaching up to stroke her jaw with his thumb. "You are human enough." And then he withdrew his hand and locked his sapphire gaze with hers. "What you are…is mine."

Jordan wet her lips again. At this point, it was a nervous tic. She opened her mouth to reply, then thought better of it and closed it. What in the world could she say to that? This man, if he was a man, was clearly insane. Yes, he had set her attacker on fire—that sounded like something a dragon—*a son of a dragon*—might do. And yes, he seemed to have claws and fangs and supernatural powers, but…but…

The walls were shifting position.

"Jordan?" His deep, melodic cadenced strummed against her thoughts, much like a pair of satin knuckles rapping on a door. *Hello? Is anyone home?*

"Can I go now?" she asked, feeling like it was the only truly relevant question.

"No, angel." He shook his head.

"Why not?" She thought it sounded stupid; but really, they were a bit beyond that.

"The police will be here soon. I need to clean the apartment, deal with the humans, and you—you need to be made to understand."

It wasn't exactly a threat.

He hadn't said: *You need to die; you need to be made to submit… or obey; or turned into a charcoal briquette.* But just the same, it was the last straw: Of course, he needed to clean the apartment, deal with the police, and probably take a shower, considering all the blood and gore. And she needed to…*understand*…something way beyond her purview.

She nodded. "May I get a glass of water?" Again, another really stupid question, but honestly, at this point, there was a deep, thickening fog surrounding her brain—everything was drifting into the ether, becoming less and less real, more and more hollow. The apartment, his voice, everything that had happened was simply… drifting away…disappearing behind an irrational fog of cerebral self-protection.

Why not ask for a glass of water?

He rotated a powerful shoulder, angling it slightly to the side as if offering her a safe, unobstructed lane from which to make her exit, and she took two hesitant steps toward the kitchen, ducking around his body.

And that's when she hit the floor.

Jordan Anderson had never passed out before—not once in her twenty-seven years of life—but apparently, there was a first time for everything.

Chapter Eight

ZANAIKEYROS CAUGHT JORDAN just before she hit the carpet, grimacing at his horrible—and wonderful—luck. Horrible, because what a way to reacquaint himself with his dragyra, while executing her attacker. And wonderful, because *dragon lords protect them all*, if he had been just five minutes later, the human excrement would have raped Zane's woman; and Zane would have been utterly incapable of restraining his beast, the inner spark, the primordial furnace linked to Lord Saphyrius that burned like molten sapphire. He may very well have scorched every living thing within a ten-mile radius, and wouldn't have that just made the news: Crazed serial killer tosses woman over his shoulder and terrorizes the Skyline Mosaic subdivision, leaving a trail of gorged and bloodied bodies in his wake.

Not to mention, the dragon lords would have shown no mercy had the deviant human killed her, had Zane failed to protect his *fated*.

They would not have let Zane off the hook.

Now, hefting her up in his arms, he made his way to the light beige sofa, where he gently laid her down, healed her head wound with a cooling exhale of blue fire, and placed her head on a soft, square pillow. He was just about to check her vitals, assess her pulse, and measure her breath when he heard a brisk knock on the door.

"Police! Open up!"

Oh, great.

Just great.

Could this get any better?

This was exactly what Zane needed—*not*—a bunch of humans interfering in the middle of this mess, especially when there was an incinerated body in the back bedroom—missing a head, no less—and an unconscious woman on the couch. "Hold on," he barked in an angry, no-nonsense tone, and then he hightailed it to the door, placed his palm on the panel, and tried to read the impressions of the humans on the other side.

There were two distinct sets of heartbeats pulsing through the panel, which meant two officers on the other side of the door, and by the acrid smell of fear, mixed with the pungent aroma of anger, he could tell they were hyped up on adrenaline. More than likely, their guns were already drawn.

Perfect.

Just perfect.

The human on Zane's left whispered something to his partner on the right, but he more or less mouthed the words with very little air escaping his lungs. Zane couldn't make out the sounds. No matter. He was probably telling the deputy to be ready for anything.

Anything, indeed.

Including a dragyri?

Probably not.

Zane snatched the handle to the door and yanked it open so quickly it caught the officers off guard. The men backpedaled where they stood, pointed their weapons forward, and started to squeeze their respective triggers. And that's when Zane took control.

The guns went flying first, a simple feat of telekinesis, and then Zane reached out, snatched the first officer by the collar with his left hand, the second with his right, and dragged them both into the apartment, slamming the door behind them with his mind.

Oh hell.

The guns.

He switched into lightning-fast mode, moving faster than a human eye could trace, reopened the door, flew through the threshold to retrieve the weapons, and quickly reentered the apartment, all in the space of two heartbeats. He started to tuck both .45 caliber weapons into the waist of his jeans, realized he was wearing pajamas with a flimsy elastic band, and tossed both firearms into the corner, instead, after first removing the clips.

The humans were still in shock.

"W…w…what the hell!" A tall red-headed officer stuttered, spinning around in a dazed, wobbly circle while searching the floor for his gun.

"John, behind you!" the second officer warned, reaching toward a small black clip on his waist, attached to a thick leather holster, to unlock a canister of pepper spray—or was he reaching for the stun gun?

Again, it didn't matter.

Zane cleared his throat and shook his head, commanding both officers' attention. "I wouldn't do that if I were you," he said to the hesitant blond, whose hand hovered—and hesitated—above the holster.

The blond blinked two times and measured Zane from head to toe, his gaze lingering on the liberal sprays of blood soaking the once-white T-shirt. His jaw tightened, and his fist twitched, almost as if he were priming a pump, and he took a measured step backward. His hand shifted from the backup weapon to the narrow, hand-sized radio as he slowly depressed a button. He intended to call for help—hell, to bring half the force as backup.

Zane pierced his mind in an instant, retrieving his thoughts with ease, as well as his name. "I wouldn't do that, either, Ryan. Why don't you just relax."

Ryan's thumb fell away from the button even as his jaw dropped open. "Look," he said, surveying the apartment with a wary, hurried glance—he caught a glimpse of Jordan, still unconscious on the couch, and his entire body tensed. "One way or another, this…*this*…this jig is up. Whatever you had planned, it's not going down." He cast a sideways glance at Jordan and slowly shook his head. "Dispatch will send backup in a matter of minutes if we don't call in, and there is no way we're letting this…scene… continue. So my advice to you—"

Zane waved a dismissive hand, cutting him off in midsentence. He narrowed his gold-and-sapphire gaze into two vertical slits, much like a cat's, and locked on to Ryan's pupils. "So here's what you're gonna do." He leveled a quick, passing glance at the other officer, as well—at John—just to bring him into the fold. "You're gonna pick up that radio, real nice and steady, and you're gonna call in, in a relaxed, natural voice—tell them it's all clear, there was nothing unusual going on, and then you're both going to leave this apartment." He dropped his voice nearly an octave. "You saw nothing. You remember nothing. The call was uneventful, and no one is to follow up. Are we clear?"

Ryan's nose wrinkled in confusion, and he ran his tongue over his top front teeth, as if he were trying to get a bad taste out of his mouth—then he nodded slowly in acquiescence. "Uh, uh, yeah." His voice sounded uncertain.

"Are we clear?" Zane repeated, making sure the compulsion would hold.

Ryan nodded more enthusiastically this time. "Yeah, sure, we're clear."

John was a little less certain, possibly because Zane had only held his gaze for an instant. "Wh…what about the lady on the couch. Is she okay?" the unsteady officer asked.

Zane swept his gaze over Jordan. Oh, hell, she was probably anything but okay, at least with the situation, and he was going to have to mend some fairly damaged fences in order to make things right, but that wasn't what the redhead was asking. "She's perfect," Zane replied, searing his gaze into John's. "Right as rain and taking a nap."

John angled his body toward the couch and took a second, hard look at Jordan as if judging for himself.

Not good enough.

"Right. As. Rain," Zane repeated, this time clipping his words.

The officer spun back around and shivered, the compulsion rattling his befuddled brain. "Yeah, yeah," he muttered quickly, shuffling toward the door. "Everything seems to be in order here—sorry we bothered you."

"Not a problem," Zane said. And then he splayed his fingers, pointing two of them toward the clips; rotated his wrist until his palm was facing up; and crooked those same two fingers inward, drawing the ammo into his hands. He repeated the motion with both guns, in turn. "Your weapons," he said congenially, shoving the magazines back into the firearms.

The officers looked momentarily confused, but the enthrallment was deeply set. They each retrieved their weapons, Ryan smoothed his shirt, and they mindlessly made their way to the door.

"Wait." A feeble female voice.

Oh, hell, not now.

Zane did not want to do anything else to Jordan against her will. *Hell's bells*, he had already traumatized the wits out of the woman, and he needed her compliance within the next ten days, technically nine, since it was after midnight—dragyras could not be forced to kneel before the dragon lords at the sacred Temple of Seven.

They either submitted of their own free will, or they died that night in their sleep.

And it was up to the female's dragyri to set that ball in motion, make sure the consecration happened.

"Jordan," he said in an alluring, placid voice. "Baby, these men were just leaving." He didn't put a full compulsion into his voice or his eyes. Rather, he surrounded his words in a mild cloud of confusion, coated them in fog, so to speak, so they would sort of drift around her, neither sticking or landing, but just causing an obstruction. Her mind would be cluttered and confused.

It would buy him a few extra seconds.

"Out, now!" he barked at the officers, staring fixedly at the door in warning.

The men shuffled quickly, like obedient sheep, even as Zane

held his breath. When, at last, the door slammed shut behind them, he let out a long, exasperated sigh.

Jordan was sitting up now; her knees were pressed to her chest; her arms were wrapped around her shins, and she was crying like a baby.

Trembling.

Keening.

Damn near whimpering…

Zane ran his heavy hand through his unkempt hair, tucking several errant wisps away from his face, out of his eyes, and slowly made his way toward the couch.

"Angel of mine," he whispered softly. "Please, don't cry."

Chapter Nine

AXE AND LEVI Saphyrius bounded up the side of the hill, taking the natural-stone steps two at a time on their way to the Sapphire Lair. It was one o'clock in the morning; both dragyri males were eager to take a shower and get to bed. And the sonorous, ambient echo of the sixty-foot waterfall flowing out of the nearby rugged cliffs and flanking the back of the lair called to their nocturnal impulse: Time to get some sleep.

Levi stopped at the dual heavy wooden doors bordered in rough, native stones of sapphire and white, and reached up to retrieve a missive affixed to an iron bracket.

Axe came to a halt behind him. "What's that?"

Levi shrugged his muscular shoulders. "Looks like it contains an official seal."

Axe peeked over his lair-mate's shoulder, caught a glimpse of the red wax-dragon melted on the fold of the page, and curled his lips into a scowl. "The temple?" It wasn't that he had anything against the gods—or receiving a missive from the seven—but Caleb's recent punishment was still on everyone's mind; so the idea of the sacred temple, and anything that came from within it, wasn't exactly a welcome sight. They could all do without the reminder. "So?" he pressed, waiting as Levi broke the seal and silently read the missive.

Levi grunted, his sapphire-and-black eyes scanning the page. "So, it looks like the message is for Zane."

Axe frowned. "What now? I mean, he did Lord Ethyron's bidding, right? So everything should be copasetic."

Levi nodded distractedly. "Yeah, yeah. Nothing to do with that. It's a summons. The lords want to see all of the Genesis, the firstborn sons, at the temple on Sunday, by twilight."

At this, Axe harrumphed. "Hmm. Does it say what for?"

Levi tucked the missive in his front hip pocket and leaned against the door, staring off into the distance, toward the waterfall. "Nope. But whatever it is…bad timing for Zane."

"No doubt," Axe said, copping a lean of his own against an adjacent stone pillar that supported the roof of the porch. "Wonder what this is all about."

It wasn't very often that the Genesis got together, mostly because the males identified more strongly with their lair-mates. Just the same, they had a special bond—and in a way, a special purpose—that set them apart from the rest: From the beginning of time, as far back as the Dragyr could remember, the dragon lords had always been—they had always existed.

They simply were.

Seven omniscient gods with the powers of creation, life and death, and immortality entwined in their natures. But their existence had been lonely, without a greater purpose.

According to legend, they had created the Dragons Domain and the Temple of Seven. They had hung the sun and the moon, created the seven sacred stones and the seven consecrated lairs; but that hadn't been enough. They had needed more. They had wanted sons and daughters.

After centuries of trying to procreate with human women, learning how to modify and mask their dragon forms in order to mate with another species, they had almost given up: Their seed rarely planted successfully; the few pregnancies that resulted usually failed; and the handful of infants who were actually born died shortly after birth.

They simply could not procreate with human women.

And so they had called upon their collective magic, and their boundless powers, to approach the matter from a different tack: to clone their own ancient reptilian DNA in shells, like eggs, and see if the vessels would hatch in the temple, to add human DNA to the specimens to see if their offspring might, at last, possess the ability to propagate...for them.

The experiment had worked to a degree.

The lords had successfully created over a thousand eggs, but only forty-nine had hatched: seven from each of the aboriginal gods, representing each of the sacred stones and each of the consecrated lairs. And of that subset—over time, many pagan battles, and natural attrition—only seven of the original hatchlings remained: Blaise Amarkyus, Brass Cytarius, Ghost Dragos, Jagyr Ethyron, Nuri Onyhanzian, Ty Topenzi, and their own lair-mate, Zane Saphyrius. All original sons—made, not born—of the dragon lords.

All one thousand years old.

Luckily for the dragons, each of the forty-nine hatchlings had contributed to The Pantheon before the unfortunate forty-two had passed away—they had done their duty and propagated the race— although it soon became clear that this first generation could only produce sons, and their fertility extended to only one offspring, born of a chosen dragyra: a human female chosen by the gods at a time and place of the dragon lords' assignment.

Axeviathon sighed.

He knew the heavy weight the Genesis carried, and that Zane would gladly relinquish the privilege if he could. They were bound more tightly to the dragon lords, as the gods often saw them as appendages of themselves—hell, Ghostaniaz Dragos had been named "Ghost" because the darkest of the seven lords, Lord Dragos, considered the male a mere phantom of himself—and their continued existence was as vital to the gods as breathing. Each one was the last remaining progeny of their virginal DNA, like some sick, egocentric extension of their minds, their self-images projected in flesh and blood, scales and fire, power and fangs.

In fact, over time, the patriarchal competition had gotten so out of hand that the wiser, more noble gods, like Lord Topenzi and Lord Cytarius, had acted to rein it in. On a male's eighteenth birthday, he left his father's lair and was consecrated to one of the alternate seven's—he became an abiding, lifelong member of another god's den and the eternal responsibility of another deity. His irises changed color; his permanent amulet was affixed; and he would forever pledge his fealty to the lord of his lair; thus, ending any chance that the Dragyr would be divided, or conflicted, by genealogy.

Yet and still, there was one glaring exception to this rule: the original, genesis seven. Each of the embryonic sons still belonged to his maker's lair, and that included Zane...

Axe rocked forward onto the pads of his feet, stepped toward the dual front doors, and tugged on a thick, heavy panel, holding it open for Levi to enter. "Brains before beauty," he grunted, waiting as his lair-mate stepped inside. "You should put that missive on the refrigerator door, make damn sure Zane sees it when he gets in."

Levi nodded as he sidled past Axe into the elaborate foyer. "And if Zane's not back by then?"

Axe shook his head. The poor male was probably somewhere he didn't want to be; sweating like a pig, to put it in human terms; trying to cajole his dragyra, who was probably shocked and scared out of her wits, into giving him a chance. "Well, if he's not back by tomorrow afternoon, then we intervene, give him a mental nudge."

"Yeah," Levi said, already heading in the direction of the kitchen. "When the lords call..."

"We jump," Axe supplied.

⚜

Drakkar Hades, king of the pagans, sat back in his opulent throne in the pagan underworld and sneered at his chief counselor and principal sycophant, Killian Kross. "Tell me this again: You got *what information* from the beetle?"

Killian Kross, a full-blooded shade—or shadow-walker, if one preferred the term—flicked a piece of lint off his black satin jacket and stepped closer to the dark lord's throne. "The Dragyr murdered three pagans in the yard of a human, earlier this night, two demons and a shade: Rafael, Malandrix, and Alexian. But before Rafael died, he dispatched a thousand beetles, and while the three dragyri thought they'd killed them all, they were sadly mistaken."

Drakkar drew in a deep, ragged breath, trying to marshal his patience as he stared at his long, pointed fingernails and tried not to twitch. Killian had a never-ending flair for the dramatic; he tended to talk in circles, all the while evading the main, essential subject; and he was loath to ever get to the point. Drakkar gritted his teeth and forced a smile. "Sounds like a lovely evening was had by all, but now that we have the numbers—and the names—do get to the point. Tell me what you learned from the beetle. *Please.*"

Killian sat on the arm of the throne, leaned in, and took one good look at Drakkar's scowl, then quickly stood back up, smoothing out the velvet arm in apology. "A-hem." He cleared his throat. "As I was saying, the Dragyr extinguished all the beetles, save one, and the creature was crawling in the bushes, unseen, as the warriors talked. As programmed, the insect recorded what he heard and broadcast it back to the castle."

Drakkar closed his eyes and counted backward from ten to one.

Yes, yes, yes…

Demons could turn themselves into nasty, lethal beetles, and the beetles could act as transmitters, recording and projecting all they saw and heard in telepathic waves that broadcast throughout the underworld, thus, acting as supernatural beacons of a sort. As the singular high lord and king of the entire pagan realm, Drakkar understood the nuances quite freakin' clearly. So then what the hell did the beetle transmit?

Before he could dress his counselor down, Killian assuaged his anger with a pair of pertinent facts. "In a nutshell, one of the dragyri was a Genesis Son, and earlier this evening, he met his dragyra."

Now this caught the king's full attention. "Which one? The male?"

"Lord Saphyrius' progeny."

"Zanaikeyros?"

"One in the same."

"Excellent. *Excellent.*" He narrowed his gaze on Killian, studying his dark hawkish eyes, his thin, reedy lips, and his translucent, skeletal features—the shadow needed to feed. "Please tell me that you have done some modest research, that my congress has done some basic exploration, and you are up to speed with all the facts."

At this, Killian smiled: dark, sinister, and wily. "Indeed, my liege. I would not approach you with the information otherwise." He brushed a thick lock of his long, white, baby-fine hair out of his eyes and bowed his head, infinitesimally. "The female's name is Jordan Anderson—the beetle pulled it out of the dragyri's mind— she is a prosecuting attorney in the Denver DA's office, but that is not the most intriguing tidbit."

The king leaned forward in his throne. "Go on."

"We did our own little investigation, which led to the Two Forks Mall and their internal security cameras, and it would appear that Jordan has a close friend named Macy Wilson, who is scheduled for abdominal surgery on Monday with one Doctor Kyle Parker at Denver Exploratory Medical Center."

Drakkar licked his lips—the possibilities were just too delectable. "Ah," he commented, laughing as he made a thoughtful tent with his hands. As king of the pagans, he knew all his subjects intimately: their comings and their goings; their rapes and their kills; their twisted, demented souls; their every dark, malicious thought. Their very lives streamed into his mind like endless loops of video, audio, and sonar, even when he slept.

And this meant he was aware of many aberrant humans as well.

After all, there were only two kinds of pagans: demons and shadows—also known as shadow-walkers or shades—and Drakkar was equal parts of both. The former, demons, were considered sin eaters because they thrived and *fed* on human sins: pride, envy, lust, and the like. And the latter, shadow-walkers, were often known as soul eaters because they thrived and fed on human souls. It didn't matter if the souls were good, neutral, or evil—as long as they were sentient, the shadows grew stronger by ingesting their anima. The essence was all they needed. But the demons? No, their appetites were a bit trickier. They had to catch sinners in the commission of sins and feed on the base depravity in order to survive. Dr. Kyle Parker was hungry for power and promotion, for national recognition in his field, and that hunger had grown beyond wanting, desire, and ambition into something altogether malevolent. He would lie, cheat, or steal for a golden opportunity, and *that* had caught the attention of a powerful, ancient demon by the name of Salem Thorne. To put it succinctly, Salem had been feeding from Dr. Kyle and bolstering his power-lust for months.

And that meant Dr. Kyle was already under the demon's influence. He could be manipulated by the pagans and used to their nefarious ends.

"Where is Salem this night?" Drakkar asked, assuming Killian could follow along. The pagan was annoying, not stupid—he was counselor for a reason.

"He's resting in his chambers," Killian replied, referring to one of the castle's upper five floors, and the demons' residential wing.

Drakkar nodded. "And I assume, after all these centuries, he is eager to rise up in our ranks. He would have no objection to sharing his prey: We want Dr. Parker to get closer to Macy; we want Macy to keep in close contact with Jordan; and of course, we want nothing more than to use these relationships for our own delicious gain. Assume for a moment that Salem could reduce his essence into *just one* beetle—I believe he is ancient enough to do so—and our ambitious Dr. Parker could transfer that beetle to Macy…

"All our illustrious demon would have to do is enter Jordan's purse, travel with the dragyra through the portal, and voila—just like that—we have an inside agent in Dragons Domain." He slowly licked his lips. "Now multiply that by twenty—say, twenty ancient demons, all in singular beetle form, waiting like a Trojan horse, nestled inside a birthday present or a box of Valentine's chocolates—perhaps a housewarming gift—whatever the hell a human dragyra enjoys—we could conceivably usher an army of prehistoric pagans into the foreign realm. We could strike at the Genesis Sons as they sleep, in their own protected beds." His voice turned devilish and cold. "I have waited a thousand years to get my claws on an original son, to destroy a beloved Genesis. Would it be a major sacrifice to send our oldest and our best? Of course, but the ruin would be worth the risk." His eyes rolled back in his head as if he were enraptured in ecstasy. "Yes, my dear, esteemed counselor: Dr. Parker may very well be the opportunity we have been waiting for, if he can solidify a relationship with Jordan's best friend, and the latter can lead to Zanaikeyros. Lord Saphyrius' last living hatchling would be an unimaginable prize."

"Indeed," Killian said, his own voice growing somber and thick. "And I'm already several steps ahead of you. Requiem Pyre, your chief sorcerer, has already cast a seeking spell, and he has, consequently, divined Macy's soul. She is weak when it comes to romantic encounters, desperate for attention and love, and our power-hungry doctor is as handsome as he is rich. A nudge here, a prod there, and we believe the not-so-good doctor will take the bait. Should Salem suggest it, Dr. Parker will make Macy Wilson his whore."

Drakkar smiled. "Very well." He rested his hands in his lap, as if he were suddenly filled with tranquility. "Then set a plan in motion—let's see if we can't get a demon into the Dragons Domain. If Zane met his dragyra prior to midnight, then he only has nine days remaining to get her to the Temple of Seven." He shook his head in earnest. "And we cannot have that." Musing aloud, he added, "Once she's consecrated to the dragon lords…"

"Her female powers of intuition will grow decidedly strong," Killian supplied. "She may detect the presence of a pagan from ten blocks away, and she'll be much more difficult to manipulate."

"Precisely," Drakkar murmured. And then he stared off into the distance; gazed into an arched, stone fire-pit that housed a blazing fire; and let his dark, demonic soul get lost in the dance of the flames…

Dr. Kyle Parker could finally lead them to Zane—

Zanaikeyros Saphyrius, son of dragons…

A Genesis Son!

Oh yes, the fates were definitely—*finally*—smiling upon the Pagan Horde.

Chapter Ten

JORDAN ANDERSON SCOOTED as far back as she could on the couch, trying to escape the chaos. She pressed her spine into the overstuffed cushions, tried to crawl inside the fabric, and begged any higher power that would listen to render her invisible. She wanted to vanish from the room. She wanted to stop breathing, stop living, stop existing—to somehow, *someway*, just remove herself from the clutches of the monster, the one who had killed Alonzo and banished the police, the one who had filled her mind with cotton, making all of her thoughts so muddled, so foggy, that it had been impossible for her to reason or think...

Or act in her own defense.

She could hardly even speak.

The one who had simply waved his rugged hand in an arc, high above the couch, and detained her where she sat, like an unchained prisoner: She could scoot forward. She could lean back. But she couldn't get up or leave. He had caged her like an animal, taken over her body and her mind, rendered her helpless and defenseless, with the mere sweep of his hand. And to her way of thinking, he was probably going to kill her—devour her heart as a late-night snack—once he had finished doing *heavens-knew-what* in her apartment and possibly toying with her like a cat with a mouse.

Jordan had been crying, off and on, for the last sixty minutes, helpless to do anything else, while the terrifying male had made himself at home, taken a shower in her bathroom, and cleaned up his mess, the mess he had made when he had murdered—*and beheaded*—a rapist.

And now…

And now?

She didn't have any tears left.

Where the hell was Alonzo's body? And what was Jordan going to do? What in heaven's name did this man, this thing—*this dragon?*—want with her now?

The last thing he had said—and it had to be a fairly good sign—was "angel of mine, please, don't cry." *Okay.* That was kindness, right? That meant he had a heart, or at least some sort of conscience.

But what the hell!

As if!

As if she could control her tears…

Or her terror.

As if she was a part of his plan, or his friend, or his acquaintance, let alone his angel.

Blessed Saint Michael, what in the world was going on?

After first determining that the whole thing wasn't just a terrible dream—a horrible nightmare or an REM terror—Jordan had tried, really hard, to exercise reason, to remain lucid and calm. She had pinched herself, half a dozen times, just to be sure she wasn't sleeping or hallucinating, but her senses and her reflexes confirmed the truth: The nightmare was real.

Nonetheless, she had to be going stark raving mad. Her sanity and her reason had to be slipping away, because none of this was possible. It simply wasn't happening.

Monsters did not exist.

Yet and still, the dude had cleansed the blood from the floors with flames.

He had sanitized the apartment with silver fire: vapors that did not singe the carpets, heat that did not melt the tiles, and blazes that shot forth from his throat. *His throat!* And he had moved from room to room like an agile predator—smooth, limber, and vulturine—with an unnatural, animal grace. And he had even, somehow, healed the wound on her head, perhaps while she was unconscious.

So, unless she was sleeping or crazy, then Jordan had to conclude that Zane might just be what he said: a dragon, a beast, and a monster. Only, that would make him some kind of supernatural being, some kind of prehistoric creature, and that just didn't jibe with any orthodoxy, science, or paradigm she knew. Not to mention, he didn't look like any kind of dragon she had ever seen—not on TV, not in a book, and not in some New Year's Day parade—so maybe, just maybe, she was going insane, a few beers short of a six-pack.

She sniffed and rubbed her eyes.

It had to be at least 1:30 in the morning, and the ordeal was still unfolding.

No, no, no!

He was coming back down the hall, heading her way, moving like a lithe, stealthy jaguar—*in boots and pajamas*—approaching the sofa once more. Maybe he would just pass through the living room, saunter out the door, and she could crawl back through the rabbit hole she'd fallen into and get back to her ordinary life.

"How are you?" he asked. "Are you feeling any better?" His voice sounded like ground-up shards of glass trundled in a roll of sandpaper: rough, raspy, and way too domineering for her liking.

She sucked in a harsh breath of air, straightened her spine, and clenched her fists. Even if she wasn't feeling brave, she could always fake it. She would rather go down fighting. "How am I feeling?" she snarled, watching as he sauntered to the couch, stopped a couple feet shy of her perch, and squatted down in front of her, his massive shoulders blocking her view of anything—but *him*: his broad, husky shoulders, his rock-hard chest, and his acutely defined biceps bulging at his sides.

God, give her strength.

"No," she added, irritably. "I'm not okay. And why are you wearing pajamas with boots? What kind of a…dragon monster… does that?"

His mouth curved upward in a sly, quirky smile, and she almost came unglued. This wasn't funny. Yes, her question was asinine at best—in fact, she sounded moderately unhinged. And yes, her nervous energy was taking its toll, but still, it was a valid and somewhat reasonable question. "Answer me," she prodded, trying to sound more brave than she felt.

He looked down at his white Haines T-shirt, his black silk pajamas, and his heavy, steel-toed boots, the former being items he had washed while he'd showered, and he grimaced. "I got into a little trouble earlier, and I had to borrow some clothes. The boots are mine."

"Trouble?" she pressed. "What kind of trouble?"

He cocked one shoulder in a dismissive shrug. "The kind that's been taken care of, the kind that will never breathe again."

"Oh." An awkward silence passed between them, and then Jordan breached an even scarier subject: "And the man who attacked me, the guy in the apartment…you aren't going to ask me who he was…why he was here? You aren't even curious?"

Zane's shoulders stiffened, and he closed his eyes—but when he blinked them back open, he looked perfectly calm. "No, not really," he muttered. "The way I see it, the *whys* don't matter. That problem is solved, is it not?"

Jordan swallowed her antagonism and froze.

She might be two cans shy of a six-pack, but she had just sobered up, real fast. This guy was not someone to toy with. She relaxed her fists and nodded, curling her shoulders inward. "Yes, I would say that it is."

He hung his head, and that thick curtain of dark brown locks fell into his face, framing his angular features. Then he raised his chin and held her gaze, but he didn't utter a word.

Jordan shifted nervously on the sofa, praying she hadn't ticked him off. She wet her lips in a fearful gesture and unwittingly cleared her throat. "Yesterday, in the parking garage, what happened?" This time, her tone emitted more respect. "I tried to scream, but I couldn't. And tonight, while you were cleaning…the mess…while you were showering, I kept trying to get off the couch. I wanted to leave, but I couldn't. What did you do to me? And how did you do it?"

Zane brushed his hand through his hair, ostensibly to sweep it away from his eyes, but once again, he didn't speak. He just searched her gaze with lethal, unsettling intensity.

Jordan shuddered, her stomach roiling in uneasy waves. "How did you find me?"

He swallowed hard, and his Adam's apple bobbed up and down, drawing her attention to the dense, muscular cords along his throat, his smooth, flawless skin, and that rich, unidentifiable complexion, the faintest golden-brown. "What…what's your ethnicity?" It was *ridiculous question number two,* especially when one considered the situation, but since he refused to answer anything serious, it seemed like a safe-enough probe. In truth, she wanted to keep him talking about anything that didn't include murder or killing or beheading.

The corner of his mouth quirked up in another half-smile. "Dragyr."

A single word.

That foreign, cryptic term…again.

"My ethnicity is Dragyr."

"Right," she whispered. "You're a dragon: I forgot." She didn't forget—*how could she?*—but she was so rattled by his proximity, and she was growing increasingly angry…again.

"Not dragon, angel. Dragyr…or dragyri." He extended his right arm toward the couch, palm facing up, and Jordan flinched at the sudden movement.

"Shit!" she exclaimed beneath her breath, and then she immediately exhaled, relieved that he hadn't flown off the handle and smacked her.

He frowned, as if he'd read her thoughts, and then he gestured at her fingers with his chin. "Give me your hand," he whispered.

Jordan shook her head. "No."

"Angel," he drawled, "give me your hand."

She shook her head again. "Why?"

"I want to show you something, put this subject to rest."

She sat there—they sat there—enveloped in silence for what felt like forever, until finally, she extended her hand. "Don't hurt me," she murmured, "please."

His shoulders twitched, like she had just offended him, but he didn't utter a verbal reply. He simply nodded, took her hand in his, and grasped it with exquisite gentleness. He pressed his thumb against the center of her palm; caressed it like they were lifelong lovers; and then slid the digit along her middle finger until he was holding the tip of her joint. His fingernail began to elongate until it formed a pointed claw, and he pressed it against the pad of her finger.

She yelped and tried to tug her hand away, but he strengthened his grip, refusing to release her—his grasp was like an iron vise. "Just a little prick," he said in a deep, soothing voice. "Just a small drop of blood, Jordan; I won't ever harm you, my love."

Jordan tensed and wrinkled her nose, practically holding her breath. Why did he need a drop of her blood, and why did he just call her *my love*?

Oh…God.

She was going to be sick…

She bit her bottom lip, stared down at her hand, and nodded.

What else could she do?

He moved so quickly, so efficiently, that she never saw the nail puncture her skin, and the momentary twinge of pain was as short-lived as it was incidental—he applied immediate pressure beneath the wound. "You good?" he asked.

She felt her face flush.

"Breathe," he instructed. "Your fear is getting the best of you."

She closed her eyes and concentrated on her breathing: one deep breath in, one slow breath out, repeating the process several times. He was right: It wasn't the prick to her finger; it was every-thing—*absolutely everything*—else.

"That's it, baby," he mumbled, watching, presumably, for her color to return.

This time, it was Jordan who refused to answer: She wasn't his baby, and she wasn't his love, and while she appreciated the concern, she would much rather he just leave her alone.

And drop the terms of endearment.

Without hesitation, he squeezed both sides of her finger to extract a droplet of blood. "Child of fire; daughter of flames. More than a woman; more than a name. Born from the soul of The Pantheon." The dark red droplet on Jordan's finger began to glow like a crimson light, and then the light turned from blue to aquamarine…from aquamarine to sapphire. With a sudden sizzle, it erupted into a single white flame that burned at the tip of her finger.

Jordan shrieked. She yanked her hand free and tried to shake out the flame, to smother the fire with her other hand, but the radiance would not go out. "Make it stop," she pleaded in a quivering voice. "Please, I don't like it." There was something too peculiar, too unsettling—too *familiar*—about the enigmatic flame, and it rattled her to her bones.

Zane bent his head to her finger, swept his tongue over the flicker, and the mystical fire went out.

She stared at him like she'd just seen a ghost, a phantom that would haunt her for the rest of her life. Reaching deep inside for a rational explanation, she mumbled, "I…I don't get your point. So you obviously have some kind of mystical power—you're some sort of magician—what does that have to do with me? We already knew that. I already knew that…about you." She sounded so desperate, so piteous, even to her own distrustful ears.

Zane shook his head. "The only power I am wielding now is the power of truth." He grasped her hand a second time, pricked the same finger before she could see it coming, and held her gaze in an iron stare. "You say it."

"Say what?" she snapped.

He frowned. "Say it."

She averted her eyes. "I don't remember the words…whatever it is you said."

He shook his head in earnest. "You do."

Jordan felt like she was drowning, being swept away by a wave of madness, slowly pulled under by a spell. And everything in her independent nature rebelled: how arrogant, how pompous, how rude! And screw him for being such an insolent bastard because, God help her, it was true: She did remember the words.

Almost as if she had known them all of her life.

She stared down at her finger and shivered, helpless to resist. "Child of fire; daughter of flames. More than a woman; more than a name. Born from the soul of The Pantheon."

Light.

Sizzle.

Fire.

Once again, the blood coalesced into sapphire, and the sapphire became a white flame. Only this time, Jordan didn't panic. She simply extended her hand to Zane, held it beneath his chin, and waited for him to extinguish the blaze with his tongue.

"You do it," he said, once again seeking to make a point.

Jordan cut her eyes at him, then looked away, training her gaze on her finger. She already knew what would happen. Raising her hand to her mouth, she brought her finger to her tongue and slowly licked the flame.

As expected, the fire went out.

Her eyes clouded with moisture, and she shuffled further back on the couch, needing the extra space. "So what does it mean?" she asked, defensively.

He sighed. And then much to her surprise, he abruptly changed the subject. "Do you have a large family, Jordan? A lot of relatives?"

Jordan frowned, but she was grateful for the sudden shift in topic. "No," she answered honestly. "My parents passed away when I was just a child, seven years old, and I was raised by my grandmother—she passed away three months ago. I don't have any brothers or sisters."

Zane nodded. "I'm sorry about your grandmother." A faraway look flashed through his sapphire eyes, but only for a moment, and then he briskly changed the subject. "Daughters of The Pantheon are almost always alone in the world until they find their dragyri." He softened his voice. "The room across the hall from your master, the spare bedroom, it's full of paintings: easels, canvasses, and oils. You're an artist?"

Jordan wrinkled her nose. She didn't know if she would go that far—it was more of a hobby. "Yeah, sometimes."

His golden pupils lit with interest. "The waterfall—how old is it?" He quickly held up his hand before she could answer. "How many times have you painted it?"

Jordan shrugged, not understanding his line of questioning. "It... I..." She shook her head in frustration. "What difference does that make? I like landscapes, especially water. What does that have to do with anything?"

Zane reached into the collar of his boot and slid two fingers inside the lining, opening a hidden flap that was sealed with Velcro. He retrieved a compact silver cell phone and raised one shoulder in a casual *what can I say?* gesture. "We don't have much use for these where I come from—we pretty much communicate with our minds—but when in Rome, or on the other side of the portal, we do as the locals do." He let his explanation linger while he opened the phone, swiped a couple of bars, and scrolled through a screen full of pictures. When, at last, he came to a landscape, he selected a photo, expanded the image, and rotated the phone so she could see it more clearly.

It was a gorgeous photograph of a magnificent waterfall, at least sixty feet in height, flowing out of a grand, enormous canyon, and fringed by autumn-colored trees; and every single detail in the picture—from the rugged, towering rocks behind the falls, to the V-shaped crevice at the water's peak, to the serene sapphire sky that arced above the ravine—was an exact, errorless match to Jordan's oil painting, a landscape she had painted at least a dozen times.

An unwitting tear escaped her eye, and the hairs on the back of her neck stood up. "Where is that?"

Zane glanced at the picture and sighed. "It's the waterfall behind the Sapphire Lair. My home. The home of the dragyri warriors, those consecrated to Lord Saphyrius. Your home, Jordan."

Jordan shook her head insistently. "No. *No!*" She tried to backpedal away from him on the couch, only to realize she had nowhere to go. She was as far away as the cushions would allow. She crossed her arms in front of her, instead, creating a worthless barrier.

Zane's eyes missed nothing. He noticed her defensive posture, but he still pressed on. "I am the son of dragons, Jordan." He repeated the claim, so matter-of-factly, and then he held out his arm, turned it over, and coated his flesh in scales: hard, reptilian, immaculately layered scales. He rose from his squat on the floor, took three generous steps back, and stretched both arms to the sides, like an eagle about to take flight. With a punch and a pop, a pair of satin dark-brown wings shot forth from his back and fluttered gracefully behind him. He closed his eyes for the space of two heartbeats, and when he reopened them, they were glowing crimson red.

"Enough!" Jordan shouted, now trembling from head to toe. "That's enough!"

Zane dropped his arms to his sides, relaxed his brawny shoulders, and the wings retracted—they simply disappeared. He pumped his fist, and the scales vanished. He blinked three times, and his eyes once again became sapphire and gold.

"Angel," he murmured tenderly, "this is not a game. And I am not a madman. Nor am I a human. Listen to your heart." He took those same three steps forward, swiftly closing the distance between them, and knelt again in front of the couch. "You saw the waterfall and the fire in your blood, and you recognized my words. You already knew them." He reached out to brush his thumb against her cheek, and then he cupped her jaw in his hand. "I know you're terrified, but listen to your soul, dragyra. What is it telling you? About yourself? About me?"

He leaned toward her, and God have mercy, for a moment, she was absolutely convinced he was going to try to kiss her. His mouth hovered perilously close above hers as he whispered: "What did you dream of as a girl?"

And then he did it.

He kissed her.

Softly.

Gently.

Just a feather-light touch: his thick bottom lip grazing hers, his firm top lip pressing tenderly.

"What have you wished for all your life?" He nuzzled her neck with his cheek and whispered in her ear: "What freedom? What justice? What security? Are you more at home on the beach or in the mountains? Are you afraid of heights, or do you seek them out?" He glanced over his shoulders, toward the stunning row of floor-to-ceiling windows, ignoring the presence of the closed pastel curtains. "How much do you pay each month to live on the top floor of this building, for the amazing view, just to glimpse the purple sunsets? Why do you need that…so much?" He pulled back, just a small increment, and searched her eyes.

Jordan reached up to tuck a thick spiral of auburn hair behind her ear—it was a nervous gesture, and her hand was trembling.

Zane took her hand, held it in his, and applied gentle pressure until her fingers stopped quivering. "You are no longer alone, my angel." He spoke each word with deliberation, and then he traced the pad of his forefinger along the contour of her upper lip. "Jordan…"

"Stop!" She practically barked the word, so great was her terror, so strong was her desire to escape his ministrations. "Please… *Zane*…I need you to stop."

He backed away, rose to his full, intimidating height, and strolled across the living room to the nearest chair, where he sat down gracefully, seemingly unperturbed. The chair looked miniscule beneath him. "You are a lawyer," he said in a seamless change of subject. It was more of a statement than a question. "Tell me about your life, your job, your work, your immediate responsibilities and obligations."

Jordan drew back in surprise at the new line of questioning. Her eyes shot briefly to his, but his stare was too intense, too intimate…too discerning, and she had to look away. It was like he was peering into her soul. "I have a job," she croaked. "A job that I like…that I need." She swallowed her fear and tried to sound more confident, more self-possessed. "A job that I'm good at, and it gives me purpose." She had no idea why she had said that—why she had told him so much with those four little words—but she almost felt as if she had to justify her existence, explain her occupation, argue for her right to continue with her life as it was.

He smiled, albeit faintly, and his rugged, flawless features were so incredibly handsome that it almost stole her breath. "I don't think you like it, but I do think you're good at it." His brow furrowed, and he narrowed his gaze, as if to emphasize his point. "And Jordan, you no longer need it. Your future, your well-being, your livelihood is secure. You will never want for anything again."

She gasped. "I didn't ask you to take care of me. I've never asked anyone to take care of me." As her anger rose, her words became clipped. "And I don't want…whatever this is. You have no right. *No right.*" This time, she met his stare head-on, raising her chin and locking her gaze with his in defiance.

He seemed to become even more serene, his dark, sculpted brows relaxing above his unusual, thoughtful eyes. He sighed, and his chest rose and fell in time with his breath. "Does a doe ask to be a mammal? Does a fish ask to swim in water? Does a bear choose to live in the woods?" He frowned. "No one asks, Jordan. It just is." He sat forward in the chair, braced both elbows on his knees, and leaned in her direction, his eyes never straying from hers. "I didn't ask to be born Dragyr; to be a Genesis Son of the gods, a male fated to one day find a dragyra that he must claim and make his own. Why was I born to The Pantheon and not to the Pagan Realm? Why were you born to a human family when you possess a dragyra soul?" He leaned back again in the chair, this time crossing one leg perpendicular over the other. "We can talk about these things until the sun rises and sets a dozen different times, and we will never know the reasons *why*; but—and you must hear me, Jordan, because as I've said before, this isn't a game—our time, *this time*, may be more wisely spent exploring pertinent questions and answers. What does this mean? What do I want? What has to happen next? Right now, I am wanting to hear from you, to learn from you—to know who you are, what you desire, and how to make this…less difficult—but at the end of the day, I have pledged my fealty to the dragon lords, the seven gods of The Pantheon. And I am not going to let you die, nor am I going to relinquish my life in order to make this easier."

His voice grew thick with conviction. "I'm sorry…because I know this is not what you wish to hear, but it is the truth. Yesterday, in the parking garage, when you tried to scream, I controlled your voice with my mind. And yes, I did the same tonight, in order to keep you on the couch, to stop you from escaping. How did I find you? I took your blood in the parking garage, and then I traced your DNA, much like a homing signal, like a GPS. As for my ethnicity—*your ethnicity*—it is as ancient as time itself. We are born of magic, power, and mystical elements—we are born of the substance of gods. And I am no freer than you are, Jordan, at least not when it comes to The Pantheon, but—"

He held up his hand to assuage her terror, almost as if he knew how badly he was freaking her out, how alarming each and every word he said had to be. "But the life that I live—the one you will live—can be far freer, far more beautiful than the one you have lived until now. Those things you value, your work or your friends, they don't have to go away. We move in and out of the portal almost every day. Those things you have learned or mastered, the law and the arts; there is no reason you cannot continue to practice them both…to exercise your crafts on behalf of The Pantheon. There is much you need to learn—and we don't have a lot of time—yet how we choose to spend it, how you choose to make use of it, is completely up to you."

He glanced at the front door and frowned. "We cannot stay here, Jordan. I can only oblige you for a day, maybe two, perhaps until tomorrow…Sunday at the latest. It isn't safe, dragyra. I have enemies that you cannot even imagine. And the gods; they have laws." This time when he sighed, he sounded truly weary, completely drained by the entire ordeal. "Ask me anything, my angel, and I will answer with the truth. Take this time I give you, to listen and to learn—to teach me what you wish—before we have to go. When I first entered your apartment, when I materialized through the walls, I only had one goal: to place a strong compulsion in your mind to *stay put* so I could come back and retrieve you later.

But the human male who was here—the one who is no more—changed everything. Now there is no way I will leave you alone… unprotected. And I am offering you this time, in your own world, in your own familiar surroundings. Use it as you see fit."

The room fell deathly quiet, and the ensuing silence permeated the atmosphere like dew on the morning grass settling after a light summer's rain. It coated everything around them, within them—*between them*—with a light, ominous mist. Jordan wasn't sure if her heart had stopped beating or if the silence was all-pervasive, but she felt that familiar tightening, that pit in her stomach, the same one she had felt on Friday. Only this time, she knew without question that the sense of foreboding truly portended a major life change: the beginning of a journey, the end of an era.

What was going to happen on Sunday when the sun came up?

What was going to happen tonight?

She glanced around the apartment and cringed: *This was her home.*

She blinked back tears and tried to think like a lawyer: Where was Alonzo's body? What had Zane done with it? And how was that supposed to work out, going forward, if he allowed her to come back through the…*portal*? After all, Jordan Anderson was a prosecuting attorney, and she had told a lot of people about the ex-con's threats. Murder was not exactly an appropriate—or legal—response.

And Macy!

Macy was having surgery on Monday, and Jordan had to be there.

She had to!

What was this man—this creature—saying?

Her thoughts were like scattered, chaotic tumbleweeds tossing in the wind, and her head felt muddled and cloudy for reasons that had nothing to do with the dragon's power. She was simply and utterly overwhelmed.

Folding her knees beneath her and staring blankly into space, she thought she heard her own voice, as if from a distance, as she posed the single most pertinent question: "Where will you take me?"

Zane rose from his seat, and her pulse began to race. She didn't want him near her. His presence was just too daunting, too powerful, too intimidating. "Come here," he said as he knelt before her, crowding her on the couch.

She wanted to withdraw from life itself, to cringe and recoil, but she didn't move a muscle. She didn't say a thing.

"Shh," he murmured softly, as if crooning to an injured mind. "It's okay, dragyra of mine. *It's okay.*"

No, she thought vehemently. *Nothing is okay.*

He raised his hand and fingered her hair—as if he had the right—cradled the back of her head in his palm, and gently drew her forward, until her forehead rested against his chest and she could hear his beating heart. And then he wrapped those massive, lethal arms around her and held her like a child.

And that's when Jordan fell apart.

Sobbing in his arms.

She was entirely helpless to say...or do...anything else.

"To your waterfall, dragyra," he whispered into her hair. "I am going to take you home."

Chapter Eleven

DOCTOR KYLE PARKER glanced at his expensive designer watch, turned up his lip, and frowned. What the hell was he doing at the office at two o'clock on a Saturday afternoon, and on a rare weekend off, especially when he could be at the country club making important connections with other influential surgeons and enjoying eighteen holes of golf?

He stared at the thin manila file lying on his desk, and simply shook his head.

Macy Wilson.

Twenty-seven years old.

In otherwise good health, with the exception of a benign growth attached to her abdominal wall. She was scheduled for routine laparoscopic surgery on Monday, the thirteenth, to have the growth removed—nothing particularly ground-breaking, interesting, or even challenging there—the surgery was expected to be mundane.

His sex stirred in his pants, and he bit down on his lower lip.

And just what the heck was that all about?

Last week at his private practice, he had met with Macy briefly in order to go over the ensuing operation; to examine her one last time; and to have his staff provide her with all the necessary pre-op instructions. As far as he knew, nothing about the average woman had stood out, not the color of her eyes or the texture of her hair, not the curve of her ass or the shape of her breasts. So why had he woken up in the middle of his sleep, late last night, with a raging hard-on tenting his satin sheets?

Why had it taken three rounds of…self-relief…to make that same raging hard-on recede?

And why couldn't he get the brown-haired, brown-eyed, seemingly average woman out of his mind…all day?

He opened her chart, scrutinized her records, and studied her medical history: Maybe there was something there, something about her, something that appealed to his medical mind…something he wasn't seeing. His erection jerked in his pants, and he shifted uncomfortably in his seat.

Nope.

There was nothing scientific about this sudden obsession with Macy Wilson.

It was purely salacious in nature.

He sat back in his chair and sighed.

Well, hell, this was a fine twist of fate.

Kyle Parker knew himself well, and he knew that when he latched on to a new prurient interest, he was a lot like a dog with a bone—he wasn't going to let it go until he chewed it down to the marrow and spit out the gristle: He would have to approach Monday's surgery in a completely different manner, with a completely different style. He would have to give Miss Wilson a whole lot of personal attention, couched in an adoring bedside manner, without coming across as a lecher.

One way or another, he would have to get Macy into the sack.

But the funny thing was this: He didn't just want to seduce her and leave—to hit it and run, so to speak—he wanted to possess her heart, devour her soul, take control over her life, her thoughts, and her choices.

He wanted to dictate her very musings.

He wanted Macy Wilson on her knees before him, eager to do his bidding, in every way imaginable; and honestly, that just wasn't like him. He wasn't the obsessive-stalker type.

He rubbed his forehead to relieve some tension, and then he powered up his PC. For reasons he couldn't possibly articulate, he might be a canine in heat, but he wasn't anyone's fool. Whether he was handsome, rich, or not, Macy Wilson was not going to respond kindly to one of the top surgeons at Denver Exploratory Medical Center successfully managing her surgery, then humping her leg in the bed while she recovered.

He entered his administrative password in the white rectangular box, brought up his browser to search the web, and then typed in the name of the nearest local flower shop, where he perused the most expensive, extravagant bouquets they sold: pale green and violet lilies, purple and white roses, all dotted with baby's breath; the entire arrangement housed in an exquisite crystal vase—two hundred ninety-five dollars.

Son of a bitch, what a racket!

He made his selection and entered his credit card information, choosing midday on Monday as the delivery date and time, and then he entered the hospital's address and Macy's first and last names, since he didn't know the number of her recovery room.

It was undeniably inappropriate, indisputably unethical, and risky as hell, at best. If someone turned him in for pursuing—let alone, harassing—a female patient, he could lose his freakin' job, but he couldn't think about that now.

The urge was too strong.

The need was too great.

Besides, no one on the surgical floor—and certainly, no one employed in his private practice—would dare defy Dr. Kyle Parker. He was too up and coming in his field.

At least he hoped.

He closed his eyes and sighed.

His head hurt, and he felt like he was losing his mind.

Why take such a foolish chance, and for such a plain, average woman?

Especially when he could have anyone he wanted?

He printed out the receipt, tucked it into his wallet, and shut down his desktop, prepared to go home.

What the hell.

It was what it was.

"I'll see you on Monday, Macy."

§

Assistant District Attorney Dan Summers ducked beneath the yellow crime-scene tape and made a beeline to Detective Michael Jacobs' side. He had come to the Two Forks Mall garage for two very different reasons: the first, because he had to see the gruesome scene for himself: a local, low-level gangster mutilated and left for dead in a way that didn't make any sense. His thoracic vertebrae, his lungs, and a chunk of his liver had been eviscerated, as if someone, or something, had tunneled through his back, tried to yank out his heart, and punctured the entire cavity in the process; but the wounds were inconsistent with any weapon they could identify, and the aorta was still intact.

Furthermore, next to the corpse, on the deck of the garage, were the remnants of a very thick chain, probably eighteen-karat gold, but the entire area was scorched, as in blackened and burnt to a crisp. Who the hell would burn four thousand dollars' worth of gold, instead of taking it, hawking it, or giving it away? And who the hell strolled through a parking garage in the middle of the night, with a blowtorch in one hand and *god-knows-what* in the other, something large enough and heavy enough to eviscerate a grown man's entire upper back in one targeted thrust? And why leave the body for the cops to find, unless you wanted to send a message to a rival gang, strike fear in the hearts of one's enemies. Either way one turned it, this was too brutal, too gruesome—*too exact*—for some low-level victim, some unknown gangster. This was a Mafia-style hit. It was meant to instill terror; and it was carried out to send a message—

To someone important…

But the homicide was just an excuse: The real reason Dan had come to the garage was all about Jordan Anderson, his ex-lover.

Late last night, around 10:45, Dan had received a surprising email from Jordan, completely out of the blue: something about meeting a real creepy guy in the Two Forks Mall parking garage, being cornered by her car for a time, and giving the guy Dan's address instead of her own when he had insisted on knowing where she lived. She didn't go into a lot of detail—the message was simply meant as a heads-up. In fact, she had insisted that everything was all right; she had managed to get away; and she did not want to reopen any lines of communication with Dan—*please don't respond to this message*. She had just wanted to make him aware. It had taken all his self-control not to reply.

Then again, earlier that morning, Dan had received a text from a gal he knew at dispatch, informing him about a call that had come over the radio later that same night, just after midnight: Apparently, Alonzo Diaz, a lowlife ex-con who was gunning for Jordan, had threatened her at work on Friday, and the threat had been material enough for Jordan to take action. She had met with Michael Jacobs early Friday evening, and the detective had dispatched a patrol car to watch her house. Clearly, the threat was substantial, and while Dan knew Detective Jacobs would keep an eye out for Alonzo, Dan's inside source had told him about a follow-up report, some kind of dust-up at Jordan's condo.

According to the dispatcher, Officers Ryan Gaines and John Pacheco had responded to a possible domestic disturbance at Jordan's address, shortly after midnight, and Dan wanted to know—*no, Dan needed to know*—if Mike had more facts.

What the heck was going on?

Was Jordan in any real danger?

Was she doing okay after both questionable incidents?

Heavens knew, she would never reach out to him—not again, not anymore—and he had no one to blame, but himself.

"What's up, Mike?" he called, approaching the gruesome scene.

The burly detective turned around and snorted. "Shit. This must be a peculiar homicide if the DA's office is on the scene within fifteen hours of the crime."

"What've you got?" Dan asked, ignoring the comment while he scanned the mutilated body still on the floor of the garage. He grimaced and covered his nose. "Holy shit," he grunted. "Why hasn't the coroner removed the remains yet?"

"Forensics," Mike said. "This one's too bizarre. We need to be careful with the on-scene evidence."

"Hmm," Dan intoned. "What do you know about the victim? I heard it was Daryl Smith, a peripheral member of the North Side Posse. Far as I know, the guy was into petty theft, running heroin— maybe some crack—and he may have recently escalated to GTA, but it was all standard, low-level shit. What kind of enemies could he have made? Who the hell would take him out like this, want to leave this kind of message? And why burn most of the chain, but leave the body? Why go for the heart, then leave it intact?"

Detective Jacobs shrugged. "I see you've still got your sources." He smirked and continued, "Truth be told, we don't know. Not yet. It *is* Daryl Smith, and there was nothing— *absolutely nothing*—the vic was into that explains this shit. One of the weirdest hits I've ever seen."

"And you're sure it was a hit?" Dan asked. "Not some other kind of trouble, an unexpected run-in with a rival gang member, something else the kid was mixed up in?"

Detective Jacobs furrowed his brow. "I'll tell you this much: It looks like a professional job, not just some run-of-the-mill confrontation; but what we don't know is whether or not it was a paid assassination, an act of retaliation, or some strange-ass ritualistic deal. We're gonna have to dig a little deeper on this one."

Dan studied the outline of the fallen body and winced. "Ritualistic?" he parroted. "What do you mean?" His lower abdomen tightened, and the hidden tattoo on the nape of his neck, just above his hairline, began to tingle.

The detective turned to face him and sighed. "So it's looking like we've got a couple more missing gangsters, all members of the North Side Posse, and here's where the shit gets weird: The posse was at war with a rival gang—again, some everyday, petty bullshit; nothing that explains this mess—but one of the families of the rival gangsters was into some pretty strange shit."

"Like?" Dan prompted.

"Like some kind of occultist nonsense, devil worship or something. We don't know the details yet, just that the vic's father belonged to some bizarre dragon sect. Ever heard of the Temple of Seven?"

Dan scrunched up his features in a *what-the-hell* gesture and immediately shook his head. "Can't say that I have."

At that, Detective Jacobs gave him a cursory once-over, almost as if he was reading his posture, analyzing his body language for cues, and then he drew back and frowned, slowly shaking his head. "You're not here about the victim, are you?"

Dan felt his chest constrict, and he tried to play it off. "What do you mean?" He chuckled insincerely. "I'm the assistant DA—whoever did this shit, we'll be prosecuting the guy."

"Or gal," Detective Jacobs interjected.

Dan gestured toward the butchered corpse and smirked. "*The guy*. Maybe guys."

"Yeah," Detective Jacobs conceded. "No doubt." He paused for the space of two heartbeats and then he cut straight through all the minutia. "But since you only prosecute appeals, the case won't come to you. So, what are you really here for, Dan? What do you *really* want to ask me about?" He planted his hands in the pockets of his pants and gave the attorney a no-nonsense stare. "You still carrying a torch for Jordan Anderson?"

Dan dropped his head and stared at the ground.

Well, shit.

Was it really that obvious?

Chapter Twelve

JORDAN FOLLOWED ZANE in absolute silence as they left her apartment early Sunday morning, locked the door behind them, and headed to the elevator carrying several duffle bags packed with her things. Zane had said they could retrieve more items later; The Pantheon could purchase or provide whatever she might need, and she could always come back for more.

He had said he would bring her back.

It was all that was keeping her sane.

As it stood, she felt like a card-carrying member of the Stockholm Syndrome club, aiding and abetting in her own capture, participating in her own abduction, following the lion to his den, but for the life of her, she didn't know what else to do.

The male was real.

The situation was extremely real.

And there didn't appear to be an easy way out: a fact that had become ever-more tangible over the past thirty-three hours...

During that time, Jordan and Zane had talked as best as they could, considering the circumstances. They had co-existed in silence when talking was too much—or too hard—and they had suffered through one and a half, long sleepless nights of him stirring restlessly on the couch, and her tossing wildly in her bed.

And during that time, she had wished—more than once—that she could just jump out the window and make the nightmare end.

She had felt like a captive bird.

Both day and night.

Thirty-two hours, fifty-five minutes, and thirty seconds ensnared in the palm of his hand as they trudged through the history of the Dragyr, the culture and religion of The Pantheon, and Jordan's own mundane human calendar, the imminent things she still had to do: Macy's surgery on Monday, Jordan's jury selection on Tuesday, what had to be addressed right away versus what could be moved.

For now—*right now*—all she could do was "go along to get along," try to learn as much as she could about Zane and the Dragyr, do her best to appease the terrifying male, and try to figure this out with the hope that somehow—someway—an opportunity would present itself for her to escape. As it stood, Zane did not seem intent on harming her—if taking her to some creepy temple to give her to a bunch of ancient gods didn't count as "harm"—so that was what she had to hold onto, what she had to keep reminding herself. So far, he had not tried to abuse her, physically or sexually, and he wasn't carrying her off in chains.

At least that was something.

She watched as he pressed the button to the lobby and the elevator began to descend to the ground floor. Her head virtually swam with all the information Zane had shared with her over the past day and a half, all the bizarre but necessary questions she had asked, and all the frank yet terrifying answers he had supplied.

Zane had explained that he wasn't a shifter, as incomprehensible as the concept had been to digest. He had told her that only the dragon lords could fly through the skies or traverse the lands as enormous primordial beasts: creatures with fully formed scales, spiked, leathery backs, and long, lance-like tails. The dragyri, themselves, were almost a separate race. They were vampiric in nature and imbued with the powers of their dragon lords—telekinesis, mastery of fire, mind control, superior speed and strength—and yes, they also needed to *feed* on the blood, essence, and heat of humans to reanimate their inner fires. But they didn't turn into actual monsters, and they didn't grow horns on their heads. They could, however, make use of scales for armor and wings to fly, so to Jordan's way of thinking, it was a matter of degrees, a purely semantic argument.

And, honestly, that wasn't the most troubling revelation: The sacred Temple of Seven had left her quaking in her metaphorical boots: Zane had tried his best to explain the history of the dragyra and the role the human females played in the domain, the fact that he had ten days from the date he met her to take her to this sanctuary, offer her to these gods, and perform some heathen consecration—some barbaric, ancient ritual—that would result in her *rebirth*.

Her rebirth.

What the hell did that mean?

She didn't want to know—it was more than she could take.

All she'd truly understood, all she'd really been able to digest, was the fact that she would be changed, forever, somehow made immortal. And as for the sacred, driving purpose of it all? Well, that was even worse. Jordan's purpose, at least as she'd understood it, was to bear Zanaikeyros Saphyrius a son; to provide the dragyri with an heir; to bestow upon the dragon lords another mercenary... a future servant for the domain.

It was primitive, savage, and insane.

Yet to Zane, it had all seemed so commonplace, so matter-of-fact.

The thought made Jordan's knees begin to buckle beneath her, and she leaned against the elevator wall to keep from collapsing.

Zane immediately turned to regard her. "Are you feeling faint?" he asked.

She stared at the floor and shook her head. What was the point in telling the truth? It wouldn't change a thing. "I'm fine," she mumbled dryly. "So where is this portal? How far do we have to walk...or ride?" Hell, she didn't know. Was she expected to fly with him, carried in his arms?

Zane shook his head and stared straight ahead at the elevator doors—he had already learned when to give her some space, if only with his body and his eyes. "We won't have to go far," he answered plainly. "Just to a private space." He clutched the enigmatic amulet around his neck—the one, as she had learned, that gave him power and sustained his life—and cast a reverent glance at the jewel. "The portal is inside the gemstone; it's not an actual place. As long as we are carrying your bags, and I'm touching you, I need only clutch this amulet, visualize the temple, and draw on the powers of Lord Saphyrius. The portal will open through him. The only restriction is—we must be outside, somewhere in nature, not in the confines of a building."

Jordan winced. She couldn't help it. The last thing she wanted was to arrive in the Dragons Domain in the presence of some ancient, bestial god.

"You won't," Zane offered, easily reading her thoughts. He swore he didn't do it on purpose—read her mind, that is—it was just the fact that her emotions were so strong...so raw. According to Zane, Jordan projected words from her mind as clearly as if she were shouting. He would have to be psychically deaf not to hear her at times, but he swore he would work on dialing it down, muting it as best as he could. "The portal will take us wherever we envision—*wherever I envision*—when I call upon the stone." He shrugged as if he knew the explanation was paltry. "It's an acquired skill, not as easy as it sounds, but after so many centuries, it's second nature by now."

Jordan blinked several times. "Several centuries?" She practically recoiled. "How old are you?"

Zane pursed his lips together and briefly shut his eyes. "I'm just over a thousand years old."

She gulped, started to speak, then quickly closed her mouth. *Another time.* "So where are we going, then? Straight to your...lair?"

"Yes," he answered bluntly, punctuating the inevitability with silence.

Jordan followed suit.

Sometimes silence was golden, and it had become a language unto itself between the two of them: Jordan's way of saying, *I've heard enough; I can't digest any more*; and Zane's way of, well, being Zane.

Powerful.

Mysterious.

Always in control.

Intimidating, whether he intended to be, or not.

Jordan ran her hands up and down her arms to stave off a sudden chill. So that was that, and this was real. In a matter of minutes—maybe ten, maybe twenty—she would be standing in an alternate world, on the other side of some mysterious portal, surrounded by savage males who were neither human, nor men, vampire, nor dragon, but some cryptic combination of the four.

She would be alone in a foreign, terrifying world.

A world that was ruled by actual dragons.

"Baby…" Zane's deep, rugged voice cut through the tension.

Jordan met his seeking gaze and tried not to tremble. She was so tired of being afraid.

"I've got you," he whispered huskily. "It *is* going to be okay. You are not the first dragyra ever born, nor claimed, and you won't be the last. I am not going to let anything harm you, and this"—he swept his arm around the elevator to indicate the building and the car, even as it came to a smooth, even stop—"this isn't going away. You will be back on Monday to see your friend Macy; you will still attend the jury selection on Tuesday; and your life will go on. We will build a bridge between our worlds, not an impassible chasm. I know it's impossible to see right now, from where you stand, but this is the beginning, not the end—and I am your protector, not your enemy." His voice dropped to a sultry purr. "And in time, I wish to be your lover…and your friend."

Jordan held both hands in front of her in a *cease and desist* gesture: *Stop, just stop.*

It was way too much information, and since she really didn't have a choice, there was no point in litigating her purpose. She didn't need to hear it spoken aloud.

As the elevator doors slid open, Jordan followed Zane into the lobby; and as those same metal doors shut behind them, she watched as her life, as she knew it, came to a close.

Chapter Thirteen

A FIVE-MINUTE WALK TO a nearby park.

Sixty seconds beneath the low-hanging branches of a cottonwood tree.

Thirty seconds clutching his amulet while he reached out to take her hand, and Jordan and Zane were in the Dragons Domain.

Just like that.

An overwhelming wave of vertigo assaulted Jordan's senses, and she reached out to steady herself against the nearest wall: Her palm struck a large, rugged pillar, constructed from organic white-and-sapphire stones, each individual brick possessing its own unique shape and contour, seamlessly woven together by packed, translucent clay. The lighter stones were pearlescent; the darker stones were an unalloyed, deep blue; and the utter vibrancy emanating from the rocks shone like a living band of color, pulsating in visible waves of energy.

Jordan squinted and covered her eyes, trying to adjust to the supernatural light, and Zane immediately set down her bags, sidled behind her, and placed the pads of both fingers on the sides of her temples, where he applied a gentle, circular pressure. "Your eyes will adjust quickly, my love," he murmured.

Jordan cringed at the term of endearment. "The light. It's too bright." She felt hopelessly lost and extremely disoriented.

"You're fine," he reiterated, rotating his fingers in small, soothing circles. "Open your eyes again."

She blinked several times, slowly reopened her eyes, and took
another glance at the stones…at the lair. This time, her vision was
clear, unimpeded, and she couldn't help but notice that the archi-
tecture was magnificent. In fact, she had never seen such expert
masonry in her life—she had never beheld such vibrant colors, not
even in her dreams. And then, all at once, the ambient symphony
echoing all around her rose to a thunderous crescendo, almost as
if the adjustment to her vision had amplified her hearing as well.
Water roared all around her; electricity swelled within her; and her
heart began to pound, like the steady pulse of a bass drum, beating
in time with the rhythmic flow.

"Come," Zane whispered, taking her by the hand before she
could utter a protest. She tried to draw back, but Zane's grasp was
firm. Seemingly unaware of her hesitation, he led her across the
wide wood-and-stone deck to the far end of the lair and came to
a halt before a waist-high terrace wall. "Look to the right, behind
the lair."

Jordan instinctively turned her head and gasped.

Flowing like a crystal surge of raw, liquid power was the most
brilliant waterfall she had ever seen. Six or seven distinct channels
of white-capped, vertical streams flowed out of the apex of an
enormous, resplendent cliff, the entire fall capped by bountiful,
flowering trees in every shade of autumn, each organic cluster of
foliage rising straight out of the rocky bluff. She had never seen
anything like it.

"It's beautiful," she murmured, unable to conceal her awe. She
spun around to face him and immediately drew back. His eyes were
glowing with liquid heat, perhaps in appreciation, perhaps from
something else: some base, primordial emotion brought about by
his close proximity to his lair. Either way, she was immediately
reminded of where she was and the unthinkable fate that awaited
her. She took two healthy steps back, away from the stone-work
ledge, and stared out across the vista, suddenly feeling the urge to
run.

A low, barely audible growl rose in Zane's throat, and he slowly shook his head. "Jordan, do not."

That was all he said, but it struck her heart with terror: *Do not…what?*

Do not fear me?

Do not defy me?

Do not think of running away?

"Do not lose your courage now," he supplied. "You are a guest in a strange land; there is much to see, much to learn, and you will grow accustomed to my dragyri nature."

She shuddered. "Why did your eyes glow just then? When I said the waterfall was beautiful? What was that…emotion?"

His tongue snaked out to lick his bottom lip in a primitive, serpentine gesture, and he shook his head again, this time letting her know that he'd rather not answer her question.

She felt her skin cool, and she knew her complexion had just turned ashen. Then it was satisfaction…or ownership…or lust. She swallowed a lump in her throat and glanced along the length of the porch until her eyes came to rest on her duffle bags, the gear she had packed for her stay in this strange, new land. "Don't hurt me, Zanaikeyros," she whispered in a tentative tone. "Remember your promise." Meeting his eyes once more, she added, "I am completely at your mercy here."

He sighed. "Ah, dragyra. If you only understood…" He took two confident steps forward—there was no hesitation in his approach —slid his hand around her lower back, and tugged her against his chest, pulling her into his embrace. "I wish only to please you, my frightened little bird. Only to make you happy. I will not harm you, dragyra. I will never…ever…harm you."

She shivered, but she didn't pull away.

If he wanted to be her protector, that was fine.

It was better than the alternatives—her captor, her master, her conqueror.

Standing still for what felt like forever, she tried desperately to gather her courage, all the while keeping her head lowered to avoid his eyes, those unsettling blue-gold orbs. "Inside the lair, where will I stay? Will I have my own space...my own room?"

He cupped her jaw in his hands with exquisite gentleness, raised her chin to force her gaze, and stared intently into her eyes, as if he could read her very soul in their depths. "I have my own suite, on the upper level; it has every comfort imaginable. Until your consecration, you will stay there, with me. After that, we can make any adjustments that you wish: redecorate the space to fit your style, move to another floor, find another wing that is more to your liking. But we are only one voice in a chorus of five—I cannot live separately from my lair-mates, nor would I wish to. At the least, it would offend Lord Saphyrius. At the most, it would offend my brothers."

Jordan bit down on her lower lip to keep it from quivering. She immediately consulted her memory, relying on analytical thought to replace vulnerable emotion. "Axe, Levi, Noki, and Jace?" She rattled off the names, and he smiled.

"Axe, Levi, *Nakai*, and Jace," he corrected. "You have an excellent memory, Jordan."

She started to say *thank you*, but the words wouldn't come.

It was all just too much, too soon.

Sensing how deeply her courage was waning, Zane withdrew his touch from her jaw, took a generous step back, and reached for her hand. "Come, dragyra," he drawled in that curious, unidentifiable accent of his kind. "The sooner you meet them, the less you will fear."

When the door to the lair swung open and Zane and Jordan walked in, one could have heard a pin drop from a dozen yards away.

All eyes shifted in their direction.

Four massive males came to a sudden halt, each in the midst of some mundane task, and an enormous warrior with dirty blond hair and irises, identical to Zane's, raised his thick upper lip in a semi-snarl and grunted more than he spoke. His pitch-black pupils narrowed, making his visage primal, if not downright savage.

Jordan drew back in surprise.

"Zane," the fearsome warrior barked, his deep voice pure grit and gravel.

"What's up, Axe," Zane replied casually, instinctively placing a protective hand against Jordan's lower back.

The blond gestured casually, raising his head in an infinitesimal nod, and then he fixed his piercing gaze on Jordan.

He said nothing, and Zane filled the silence. "Brothers, this is Jordan Anderson. My dragyra."

Jordan gulped. Talk about straight to the point. She still wasn't sure if she was on board with the whole fated dragyra thing, but now was not the time to voice her objections—or to show her fear. That is, if she could help it.

The pitch-black pupils softened. "Nice to meet you."

Jordan forced a weak, insincere smile. "Axeviathon, right?"

"Just Axe."

She repeated the same forced smile, trying to stretch it out, make it broader. *"Axe."*

Feeling like a rare specimen under a microscope, she immediately looked away and scanned the room, instead. Like the outside of the structure, the Sapphire Lair was a stunning work of construction. The front room, presumably a great room, was arched by huge cathedral ceilings, which were crisscrossed by thick, wooden beams. There were floor-to-ceiling windows everywhere, showcasing some of the most magnificent views Jordan had ever seen. And the detailing—the iron-work, the ornate wooden trim, the massive perpendicular fireplace which separated the great room from the hall—was made of those same odd blue-and-white stones set into the outside pillars. The effect was positively splendid.

At the back of the room, there was an enormous pool table and a bar—definitely a bachelor pad of sorts—and off to the right of the game area was an enormous foyer flanked by dual rounded staircases trimmed in intricate iron and wood. There appeared to be a gourmet kitchen off to the right, on the other side of the staircase foyer, but Jordan couldn't quite get a glimpse—the only thing showing was a portion of a huge granite bar. If it was the kitchen, she surmised, then it spanned the entire length of the house on the opposite side of the hall.

Her attention was drawn back to the great room as two... *dragyri*...stood straighter beside the pool table, and angled their intimidating bodies toward hers.

The first male, about six-feet-two, sinewy, but strong, locked his gaze on hers, and his warm sea-green pupils nearly burst with light. "Jacepheros Saphyrius," he said, "but you can call me Jace."

Jordan nodded. She was about to force another smile, but gave up—the joy just wasn't there. "Hi, Jace," she mumbled, sounding more like a child than a grown, accomplished woman.

His smile made up for both of them. It was breathtaking and kind, and talk about your perfect, immaculate teeth. Odd thing to observe, she thought.

The second male actually raised his hand, not so much in a wave, but in a flick of his wrist. "Leviathon Saphyrius," he said in a pure, melodic voice. "Levi for short." His smile spoke volumes, as did his sapphire-and-indigo eyes. This one had a deep reservoir of calm beneath him, as well as an endless pool of mirth; and both insights were at odds with his powerful, almost brutish-looking hands.

Jordan shook her head, quickly dismissing the thoughts. "Nice to meet you, Levi," she said. And the Stockholm Syndrome had just been cemented. *Holy mother of mercy*, what was she doing? Where was she standing? How was any of this real?

The third male in the great room had been lounging on a plush leather couch, the color of copper in autumn leaves, and he rose from his perch, took five generous strides forward, and actually extended his hand. "Welcome to the Sapphire Lair," he said softly, although his voice was as masculine as the rest.

Jordan took his hand, more gingerly than usual, and shook it lightly, noticing that he had light-brown pupils within his sapphire irises, and a small, strange, archaic tattoo over his otherwise smooth left temple: something that looked like a winged cross etched inside a flowing circle. She tried not to stare too hard. "And you are?"

He released her hand and clutched his amulet, and that's when she made the obvious connection: Each and every male, when he spoke his given name, unwittingly clutched his sapphire amulet. Was this on purpose? By design? Or just some unconscious habit? "Nakaitheros Saphyrius," he said.

She stumbled over the ten-gallon word. So, he didn't use a shortened version? "Na...kai...ther...os." She tried it on her tongue.

"Nakai," he supplied, letting the name linger before he turned his attention to Zane. "Brother, you got a missive from the Seven. It's on the—"

"The two of you are brothers?" Jordan interrupted, immediately cringing at how rude that was. Holy hell, she was just so nervous! Defensively, she thought, *Well, shit, what do they expect? I'm here against my will!*

Zane tightened his hand against her waist, and then he slowly rotated her body until she was facing him.

Why did he do things like that? she thought.

Take such casual liberties with her body?

Did he want his lair-mates to think the two of them were intimate? They weren't!

"We are brothers of the lair," Zane replied, seeming indifferent to the rudeness of her interruption—or the content of her thoughts.

Jordan swallowed her angst and continued with her original line of questioning; at least it was a distraction. "But not by blood?" she asked.

Zane tilted his head back and forth in a measured gesture. "Well...sort of." He looked off into the distance as if searching for just the right words. "I am a Genesis Son, so Lord Saphyrius is my maker—my *father*." He immediately amended the word. "But my brothers were consecrated to his lair when they turned eighteen, so they also share his spiritual essence."

"We're brothers in the only sense that matters, here in Dragons Domain," Nakai supplied.

Jordan blinked her eyes. Okay, so she sort of got it: Axe, Jace, Levi, and Nakai all had different biological fathers—probably males who had found their dragyras—but they had been more or

less adopted by Lord Saphyrius and ushered into a common lair...
into his service.

"Exactly," Zane said aloud.

Jordan huffed. "You're doing it again."

"Doing what?" Zane asked.

"Reading my mind."

"You're projecting," he whispered.

She sighed. "Stop it...please."

He smiled. "I'll try."

The short exchange seemed to humor Nakai, and he chuckled
softly. "Well, now that we've got that straight, back to the missive
from the Seven?" He posed it as a light-hearted question, and
Jordan felt like a heel, once again, for interrupting earlier. On the
other hand, she sort of felt like slapping the dragyri for bringing it
back up.

"I'm done," she whispered, shrugging the subject off.

Nakai politely turned his attention back to Zane, started to
speak in a strange, foreign language, and then immediately cut
it off, switching back to English. "You've been summoned to the
temple...at twilight...along with all the Genesis Sons. No idea
what it's about."

Zane's eyes shot immediately to Axe's, and he raised his brows
in a subtle question.

Axe shook his head. "No idea," he repeated, punctuating the
words with a shrug.

Hmm, Jordan thought. So were Zane and Axe closer than the
rest? Did they have a special bond? Why had he looked to Axe for
information? She knew she was overanalyzing everything—her
mind churning a mile a minute—it was just what she did when she
felt out of place.

Zane nodded slowly, then released Jordan's waist and reached
for all three of her bags. "I'll check it out after I show Jordan to
our room."

Jordan felt her face flush, and she wasn't exactly sure what she
was feeling.

Embarrassed.

Angry.

Or humiliated.

He was going to show her to *their* room—like she was his.

She bit down against her lower teeth, raised her jaw, and drew back her shoulders in defiance. It was petty; it probably showed her insecurity; and it did nothing to elevate her status amongst these fearsome men—*these fearsome males*—but it was all she had at the moment.

Zane studied her features carefully and frowned. "Dragyra..." he whispered.

But that was all he said.

Ushering her forward by raising the duffels in the direction of the stairs, he nodded in the same direction and began to walk away.

Feeling lost, alone, and oddly tired, she followed him to the dual staircase.

What else could she do?

Chapter Fourteen

Six hours later

SINCE THE SAPPHIRE Lair was located within the highland region of Dragons Domain, on the western end of the
province, Zane headed due east across the mountains on his
way to the sacred temple. He was careful not to veer too far north,
toward the Dragonian River or the Onyx Lair, lest he wander into
the Garden of Grace, the final resting place of Dragyr souls: a cluster of seven white-clay mountains littered with gemstone statues,
each one an eternal pillar erected from the soul of the dead.

He shuddered as he thought about the implications.

Considering the fact that he had just found his dragyra, the
idea of the garden hit a little too close to home. If, for whatever
reason, Zane failed to bring Jordan to the temple on the tenth day
of their mating—to be consecrated by the dragon lords and reborn
into the sacred pantheon—not only would she perish in her sleep
that night, but Zane would find himself on that terminal mountain, a permanent fixture, erected as a pillar of sapphire stone.

He would find himself next to Jaquar...

Nothing would remain of his life but a perfect stone likeness,
a sapphire sculpture raised in his eternal image. His amulet would
be removed by Lord Saphyrius, and he would join all the souls that

had perished before him, whether made by the gods, slain by an enemy, or born of a dragyra's womb.

He brushed the back of his hand over his eyes, absently clutched his amulet, and turned his attention to the matter at hand: the summons he had received from the Seven, the reason he was heading to the temple.

Hells fire, it had been some time since he had gathered with his genesis brothers, and while he'd just as soon avoid the reunion, a part of him was always curious to see their faces, connect with their lives, and judge for himself how the males were evolving through time. After all, they had known each other for a thousand years.

As he climbed an especially steep incline, he thought of each Genesis Son in turn: First, there was Ghost, and gods bless the poor soul because he couldn't help being the progeny of Lord Dragos, the darkest of the dragon lords. Since the time Ghost was consecrated, the male had been a fearsome, if not terrifying, force to be reckoned with, for sure. With irises the color of diamonds and pale, phantom-blue pupils, the male's stare alone could send a heart into arrhythmia—it was like staring into the eyes of a Siberian husky, and the soul that leaked out beneath those ghostly peepers, well, it was dark, haunted, and *angry*.

Just one heartbeat away from brutality or madness.

And, frankly, who could blame him?

When Lord Dragos ordered the dragyri of the Diamond Lair to slay enemies on his behalf, he wasn't satisfied with the mere consumption of blood, the natural act of draining a prey's essence—consuming their fire and heat. He expected his soldiers to dine on their victims' hearts. A dozen or so centuries of that, and yeah, crazed was the appropriate term, as well as the inevitable consequence.

And then there was Jagyr, made by Lord Ethyron, a Genesis Son of the Emerald Lair. He was a badass dragyri from the days of old, quick-tempered and hot-headed; but, thank goodness, he was quick to cool. Like Ghost, he had dark, almost-black hair, but he wore it in random, slicked-back layers and kept it rather long. His emerald eyes were offset by jet-black pupils, and he wasn't crazy, per se. As the son of the second-most depraved dragon lord, he was just amped up, a bit too feral. He had a dark, crimson fire burning at his core, and a hair-trigger fuse attached to that flame.

Blaise Amarkyus was the fourth, after Zane, and he was consecrated to the Amethyst Lair. The most one could say about Lord Amarkyus was that at least the dragon was fair—he wasn't dark, and he wasn't light. He was somewhere in the middle, and Blaise walked that same tempered edge.

Nuri Onyhanzian was a son of the Onyx Lair, and his maker was honorable, but too eager to punish those who crossed him. Consequently, the dragyri could be ruthless, with very little cause. One did not cross Nuri Onyhanzian if one had any sense. Still, with his golden-blond hair, his onyx-and-midnight blue eyes, and his classical good looks, the male was the first to crack a joke or play a prank on another warrior. He was decent, loyal, and a prime choice for backup in a fight.

Brastonian Cytarius and Tiberius Topenzi—Brass and Ty—were the final two Genesis Sons, belonging, respectively, to the Citrine and Topaz Lairs. As the sixth and seventh dragon gods of The Pantheon, Lord Cytarius was generous and kind, and Lord Topenzi was downright noble: wise, righteous, and just. He was the kind of god a warrior would gladly bend a knee to and seek out for guidance or counsel. Needless to say, both Brass and Ty were fairly easy to get along with, just so long as one didn't get it twisted—make no mistake, a dragyri of any shade was a primordial, savage beast at heart, all instinct, dominance, and untamed heat. All the males gave each other a healthy dose of respect and a wide berth when it was called for, and no one went out of their way to provoke another Dragyr.

They tried to live in harmony, brother to brother, lair to lair.

Zane rounded the last of the remaining mountain peaks, angled due south toward the entrance to the temple, and began to make his descent. After all these years, he didn't give much thought to where he stood in the whole pantheon hierarchy, as the son of Lord Saphyrius. The dragon was the third god of The Pantheon, and that placed him two steps above Lord Dragos and one step above Lord Ethyron in terms of his immortal soul. Lord Saphyrius could be harsh, without question. He could be both kind and unforgiving; however, he had one thing in his favor, something he never let Zane forget: Lord Saphyrius loved his dragyri children—all of them—and that was evident to the entire Sapphire Lair.

If nothing else, Zane could reason with his master, petition him for leniency, on the basis of nothing more than his love. After all, he was the dragon who sought at least a small semblance of justice for Caleb by loaning Zane out to Lord Ethyron to extinguish the gangsters.

Zane only hoped that this meeting had nothing to do with that night.

He had done the gods' bidding, and the matter was closed.

Now, as he approached the awesome white-marble staircase that led to the font of the temple, flanked by seven enormous, opulent pillars, he took a deep, cleansing breath, tried to bank his inner fire, and drew upon a healthy dose of humility.

He needed to cleanse his hands in the sacred fountain before he entered the sanctuary, and he needed to remember to avert his eyes in the presence of his lords. The difference between breathing—and burning—was often a matter of degree, reverence versus even the slightest hint of disrespect.

He retrieved the summons from his front hip-pocket and glanced at the missive one last time: Yep, it was just about twilight. The native sun was ebbing, the horizon was darkening, and the dragon moon was rising in the glorious crystal skies.

Zane was right on time.

&

Jordan's eyes darted nervously around the enormous suite—*Zane's room*—as she took a deep breath to calm her nerves and tried to come to grips with her situation.

She was alone…at last.

Granted, she was in a strange room, in a strange home, in a strange and distant land, one she had entered through an enigmatic portal. So yeah, there was that. But the air wafting through the open windows was crisp, cool, and refreshing; and the ambient sound in the background—the glorious waterfall behind the lair, flowing into a rushing river that winded beneath the lair—was as enchanting as it was beautiful to look at. And she and Zane had a direct view from the bedroom windows.

She and Zane...

Had she lost her mind?

There was no she and Zane!

And she needed to keep her focus.

Surveying the structure and contents of the suite once more—the enormous iron-and-wood bed that sat on a center platform and frankly made her shiver; the unobtrusive kitchenette against the rear, northeast wall that also sported a stocked mini-refrigerator and bar; and the plush but comfortable seating area in the northwest corner that housed a large flat-screen TV, mounted on a 360-degree swivel arm so it could face the sofa or the bed—she wondered at the luxury, technology, and obvious wealth possessed by these...dragons. After all, weren't dragons supposed to be an ancient, barbaric species?

She rolled her eyes at her own inner discourse—she had truly lost her mind. Dragons weren't supposed to exist. They were myths, fairy-tale creatures, the stuff made of nightmares and fantasy. She stared at the dual French doors that led to the wraparound-deck, followed the wall of thick glass windows that snaked along the porch, and tuned into the soothing sounds of the river below, forcing herself to readjust her thinking...

No, Jordan; dragons are real.

This is real.

Brushing her arms to stave off a chill, she stiffened her spine and strolled quietly to the corner desk, opposite the kitchenette, on the other side of the room. She had already made note of a yellow legal pad of paper and a container of expensive blue ink pens. And what she was thinking about doing—what she knew she had to do—was as dangerous as it was seditious.

But she was determined to go through with it, just the same.

Somehow...someway...she had to change her fate. She had

to get some help from the outside. And the only thing she could think of—the only person she knew would fight to the death to save her—was Dan Summers, her ex-lover. Yes, the one who had broken her heart.

But what if…just what if…she could somehow manage to get a message to Dan, an SOS of sorts? What if Dan could marshal the forces or come up with a plan…find a way to rescue her, return her to her life?

She had to try.

As she reached for a blue ink pen, scribbled on the pad to make sure it was working, and bit down on her lower lip in trepidation, she slowly began to organize her thoughts:

Dear Dan, I need your help—

She dropped the pen and shivered.

Good lord, if Zane found out—if he found the letter…

What would he do?

Would he lock her up in this room, refuse to let her go back through the portal?

Would he chain her to the lair…or the bed?

Her stomach turned over in shallow waves of nausea.

Or would he punish her somehow…actually hurt her… kill her?

No! she immediately reasoned. He wouldn't.

He couldn't!

His future was tied to hers; he needed her to produce an heir… another mercenary…a future servant for the dragon lords.

At least, that was what he had said, perhaps in softer terms.

Steadying her trembling hand, she reached for the pen once more, flipped the pad to a fresh, new page, and began to draft her letter:

Dear Dan,

I know I have insisted on maintaining silence between us, so this must come as a surprise, but I'm in trouble. Real trouble. And I desperately need your help…

Chapter Fifteen

ZANAIKEYROS SAPHYRIUS CHECKED his watch, just to be absolutely certain, as he traversed the outer platform of the temple, entered beneath a high, open-arched doorframe into the inner foyer, and slowly approached the sacred, cleansing fountain.

Yep, it was 6:50 PM, ten minutes before sunset, and honestly, after living in Dragons Domain for a thousand years, the internal clock was built into his DNA: Regardless of the seasons or the day, the sun always rose at 7 AM and always set at 7 PM in homage to the gods.

He ignored the eerie echo of his boots against the solid diamond floor of the foyer, even as he found himself captivated by the light reflecting through the magnificent, priceless platform; padded his way across the plush, multicolored ornamental rug situated beneath the sacred fountain; and dipped his hands in the lukewarm basin. Not unlike the Oracle Pool of pearlescent water that ran along the northern end of the inner sanctuary, the cleansing fountain contained living water, full of undulating currents—diamond, emerald, sapphire, amethyst, onyx, citrine, and topaz waves—all swirling in a luminescent pool of amalgamated power.

His hands hit the water, and he immediately felt the tug on his essence: his heat, his soul, his dragon's inner fire.

The gods were feeding from his core.

Purifying his essence.

And registering his presence…long before he entered the actual sanctuary.

No one—absolutely no one—could ever sneak up on the gods. If one tried to enter the temple without first cleansing their hands, the handles on the doors would singe their unclean flesh, burn it to the bones. If they somehow managed to open the mammoth doors anyway, they would perish the moment their foot crossed the threshold into the sanctuary—they would simply drop dead.

The gods used the cleansing process to feed from, purify, and welcome their guests, and there was no getting around it.

Zane shook off the unsettling feeling that came over him as the lords drew from his essence: the shiver that ran up his spine as his temperature plummeted; the frost that collected along his finger-tips as his heat was expunged; and the uncomfortable sensation of spiritual dispersion, the feeling of another being stirring within his soul. And then he simply withdrew his hands from the fountain, shook them out to dry, and took a deep, steadying breath as he approached the stone sanctuary doors, each one standing twenty feet high. Neither could be opened by a mere mortal.

"Eyes down." He reminded himself of temple etiquette, prefer-ring not to get scorched, and then he opened the door on the right and strolled into the inner sanctum.

Bright prisms of light immediately assailed his vision, but he was accustomed to the short transition, and the temporary effect it had on the eyes: The magnificent glass floor beneath him was crowned by a high coffered ceiling, which was gilded in multiple layers consisting of the seven jewels, each one refracting their light, their very essence, onto the highly absorbent floor. The effect was a stunning, blinding reflection.

In the center of the room, which was built to face the eastern wall of thrones, was a raised dais, set upon an octagon platform, made of gemstone tiles, and it was often the center of activity. At a glance, Zane noticed five of his genesis brothers—everyone but Ghost—already standing on the platform, facing the seven empty thrones; and as his eyes swept forward, a few yards in front of their feet, to the dual anchored handholds bolted to the ground—the bars Jordan would be expected to grasp as she kneeled before the Seven, awaiting the fires of *rebirth*—he shuddered deep inside.

Hell, that was one conversation he was not looking forward to having: telling Jordan about the conversion, the ceremony in the temple, exactly *how* the dragons would claim her for The Pantheon…

Her consecration by fire.

He strolled confidently toward the dais, pushing the thoughts out of his mind—he would cross that bridge when he came to it.

As Zane joined his brothers on the platform, the pearlescent pool on the northern end of the sanctuary shimmered with renewed vitality. The seven gemstone pillars along the western wall—each one mirroring an opposite jeweled throne in the east—practically thrummed with rising energy. And the seven empty thrones, each one constructed from its ruling lord's essential gemstone, radiated light and heat.

"What's up," he barked to all five Genesis Sons. "Where's Ghost?"

Jagyr, Blaise, Brass, and Ty all grunted in reply; whereas, Nuri angled his head and bit out a curse in Dragonese. "He'd better get his ass here soon," he snarled.

Before any of the Genesis could reply, the doors to the sanctuary flew open, and in strolled Ghostaniaz, his raven-black hair mussed in several places, despite the shorter length; his phantom-blue pupils, stark with intensity against his pale, diamond irises; and his heavily muscled arms flexing beneath the sleeveless black tee he was wearing. Heavy boots pounded the tile as he made a beeline for the center dais.

"Miss me?" he growled in that deep, caustic voice, taking his rightful place across from the center diamond throne—the throne of the first dragon lord, Lord Dragos.

Taking the warrior's hint, the other Genesis shuffled into place, until each was standing opposite their ruling lord's throne, facing an opulent gemstone cathedra that matched their governing lair.

"Cutting it pretty close, aren't you?" Jagyr snarled, the amped-up male being true to form.

Ghost didn't balk. He just cut those cold, brutal eyes at Jagyr, turned up his lip, and brushed some lint off his tee. "What the hell is this about?" he asked, speaking to no one in particular.

Ty, the peacemaker, shrugged his shoulders and exchanged a glance with Brass, another male who was easy enough to get along with. "No idea. You?"

Brass shook his head. "Might have something to do with Zane."

Zane stiffened at the mention of his name. "Me? What makes you figure?"

Brass furrowed his brows, as if thinking it over. "You found your dragyra, right?" He posed it as a question, but he already knew.

Guess news traveled fast…

Zane nodded. There was no point in trying to keep it a secret. Everything that happened in the Dragons Domain affected all of the Dragyr—his genesis brothers had a right to know. "I did," he said succinctly. "Friday night."

At this, Nuri's harsh but chiseled mouth curved up into a sly, mischievous smile. "What's her name?"

"Jordan," Zane supplied, not liking the quirk in Nuri's top lip—it was too insinuating.

The jokester licked his lips. "Pretty?"

Zane snarled reflexively. "Off limits," he replied.

Nuri laughed out loud. "Ah, then she is pretty…very pretty."

"She's smart," Zane countered. "Very smart." Of course she was pretty—stunning, actually—but Nuri didn't need to know that.

Sensing that Zane's dragon was rising, Nuri immediately backed off. He was all about the pranks and jokes—though it was never a good idea to cross him—but at his core, he was also loyal and decent. Respect was the name of the game when seven dragyri males gathered together. "Well, I'm glad that you finally found her," he said in an even tone of voice. "A thousand years is a long time to wait."

The comment did not fall on deaf ears.

Other than Tiberius, better known as Ty, none of the Genesis had met their *fated* yet, and it was a sore subject among the aboriginal crew. The Dragyr were high-strung by nature; they needed a calming influence to counterbalance their primitive natures, and loneliness was a whole other issue—there was something to be said about having a mate.

Before anyone could comment, the partition behind the seven thrones began to sway, to undulate from the kinetic power of the dragons stirring behind it—

The lords were about to take their thrones.

As was custom in the temple, Zane and the other Genesis immediately bowed their heads, dropped to one knee, and clutched their amulets in their right hands. They would remain in that position until their lords released them.

Consequently, Zane felt—more than he saw—the presence of the dragons as they took their respective seats, in the order of their rank, settling from the center outward. He knew by experience that they would be in amalgamated form—they would not appear as giant beasts with scales, pointed ears, and jaws filled with wicked teeth, but as bright prisms of light reflecting the hues of their primary stones, their bodies outlined as human, yet translucent and ethereal to the touch. In short, they would appear as a combination of the two species: clearly dragon in nature and silhouette, but human enough to perch on their thrones.

The suspense of their entrance having subsided, the sanctuary grew deathly quiet, and Zane knew the lords were in their rightful places...watching...waiting...observing the males.

The Genesis didn't move a muscle.

"Sons." Lord Dragos spoke first, as was proper, and the dark, malevolent cast of his voice echoed through the hall and reverberated in the rafters.

The males genuflected in reply, their heads dipping lower in obeisance.

"Rise," the dragon commanded.

And they did.

Each dragyri male in order, opposite his master's throne: first

Ghost, in the center; then Jagyr to his right; then Zane to Ghost's left and Blaise to Jagyr's right... On and on, the Genesis stood, facing their makers' cathedrae, until all were standing at their full, proud heights.

Ghost was the first to speak, from the center of the line. "Greeting, my lords; how may we serve you?" Despite the homage inherent in the words, his tone was unmistakable: *What's up, you overbearing monsters—and what the devil do you want?*

That was just Ghost's way.

And all had come to expect it.

In fact, the lords either excused it, or they no longer noticed it—he was Lord Dragos' progeny...enough said on the subject.

Lord Topenzi spoke next, and his noble, gentle spirit filled the hall like a light summer's breeze on a hot, scorching day, refreshing the males as one. "Thank you for coming." His affection was tangible. "We will try to make this brief so you can be on your way." He then eyed each male, one at a time, and crooked his fingers inward. "Enough with the peripheral vision. You may release your amulets, and you may regard our eyes."

Hmm, Zane thought as he dropped his hand to his side and allowed his gaze to take in the visage of the dragon lords, face-to-face, eye to eye, subject to lord. *Well, that's a first.*

A sudden tinge of pain tightened Zane's chest, and for a moment, it felt like there was a fist squeezing his heart. And then he both felt and heard the voice of his ruling lord—his father, Lord Saphyrius—speaking in his mind. "Guard your thoughts, son. This is no time to be careless...or sarcastic."

Zane didn't acknowledge the admonition, but he took note of his master's warning, and the sensation immediately eased.

"Now then," Lord Dragos bellowed, startling them all to attention with the tremolo of his voice, "you have been summoned as a result of a growing concern."

Zane glanced askance at Ghost to see if the dragyri might give anything away—after all, he dealt with Lord Dragos more than the rest—but his face was a mask of indifference.

"The other night, when Zanaikeyros traveled through the

portal on Lord Ethyron's business," Lord Dragos continued, "he was beset by two demons and a shade." He cleared his throat, ostensibly for effect, as dragons didn't suffer physical anomalies…of any kind. "The incident sparked a discussion amongst the Omniscient about the safety of our sons. As you well know, there are only seven of you left, seven of the original embryos."

Zane almost blanched—*original embryos? Wow, that was endearing*—but then he caught himself, reined in his thoughts, and turned his attention back to the dragons.

"What Lord Dragos is trying to say"—apparently Lord Topenzi caught the insensitive reference as well—"is that your lives are too invaluable, far too important, too rare to risk. We must consider the incident as a serious threat, and we must address it going forward."

A black stain, like sludge, projected outward from Lord Dragos' aura, and he sneered at Lord Topenzi, his amalgamated upper lip taking the momentary form of a dragon's snout as he flashed a row of barbaric, treacherous teeth. "I know exactly what I meant to say, Lord Topenzi," he snarled. "I do not require an interpreter."

Lord Topenzi merely declined his head and linked his hands in his lap, unruffled.

And that's when Lord Saphyrius took over. "Zanaikeyros…"

Zane's eyes swept to his ruling lord and fixed on his seeking gaze. "Father."

"Friday night, as I was divining shadows in the Oracle Pool, I saw a glimpse of the night's event. Is it true that you were bitten, not once, but twice, by one of the demonic beetles?"

Zane nodded, reluctantly. Was his ass going to be the topic of discussion? "Yes, milord; it's true."

Lord Saphyrius frowned, and Zane winced.

My bad, he spoke in his head.

A bright blue band of light streaked through the air, as if conjured by Lord Saphyrius' emotion. "You could have died, my son. Right then. Right there. In an instant. I could have lost you."

Zane heard the concern—and dare he say, the tenderness—in Lord Saphyrius' words, and his throat constricted…just a bit. He fidgeted with his amulet as he sought to formulate a respectful reply. "I'm fine, Father. I am. Levi and Axe were there, I did not take any unnecessary risks, and all was well in the end."

"Yes," Lord Saphyrius acknowledged. "Levi removed the toxins with cleansing fire, but that does not allay my concerns—our concerns—for the future." He pressed the tips of his diaphanous fingers together in a thoughtful, contemplative gesture. "If the Pagan Horde has grown so bold, if they would attack a Genesis on the front lawn of a human's home, knowing full well the war they could start should one of you be harmed—the decades of battle that would inevitably ensue—then perhaps they have grown truly arrogant. Perhaps it is time for us—for you—to take greater precautions."

Zane furrowed his brow. "What kind of precautions, milord?"

Ghost visibly smirked, but he stopped short of rolling his eyes. Everyone knew the dragyri was as suicidal as he was homicidal—the last thing he cared about was safety.

This time, Lord Cytarius took the lead, even as he leaned back in his throne. "You are not to travel through the portal alone, not anymore." He eyed each Genesis in turn. "None of you."

Blaise Amarkyus blinked in surprise and frowned. "If I may," he said, cautiously, "how is that going to work?" He shuffled forward, a couple of feet on the dais, avoiding an arrogant stride. "I have several missions I've yet to complete, and Zane—he just found his dragyra. I'm certain he's going to need to go back and forth. How are we to honor your wishes, complete our directives, if we can't travel alone?"

Lord Dragos shifted on his throne and began to study his nails, looking curiously bored. Then he raised his jaw, angled his head to the side, and growled like a hungry lion. "Carefully," he mused. "Deliberately, and with planning."

Lord Amarkyus narrowed his gaze on his offspring and spoke in a gentler voice. "Son," he intoned considerately, addressing Blaise, "Lord Cytarius is right. What happened to Zane, though it turned out fine, is not something to take lightly...or to overlook.

It could have been you." He drew back on his throne and swept his gaze across the line. "It could have been any of you."

"We've all been attacked before," Ghost grumbled in a brazen challenge befitting of his lineage. "Hell, we've all been beaten half to death. We've all looked mortality straight in the eye, and yet we somehow manage to come home. It's part and parcel of who we are...what we do—why is this any different?"

Lord Dragos rose from his throne, and his almond-shaped diamond eyes narrowed even further with contempt. "And yet, you are immortal beings, are you not?" he purred wolfishly. "And as for being beaten half to death, are you referring to Calebrios?" A puff of smoke wafted from his nose, and Zane knew the hostile dragon lord was this close to roasting his genesis brother.

Ghost, he spoke on a private, telepathic bandwidth. *Dial it down, brother. Shit!*

Mind your own business, Ghost shot back.

Zane shrugged.

"Speak to each other again, and I will scorch you both," Lord Dragos threatened.

Lord Cytarius held out his hand in a calming gesture, hoping to bring the temperature down a few notches. "Ghostaniaz," he said, politely, "it is true; you have all battled valiantly in the past, and you have all faced your share of danger, of lethal enemies—but this was a routine assignment, and our enemy *is* growing bold. Therefore, there will be no further discussion. Consider it a decree for all the Genesis, required as fealty under the *Four Principal Laws*: From this day forward, if you travel outside the portal, you travel in pairs."

Zane shut his eyes, even as he cursed beneath his breath.

Silently, of course.

Great, just great, Jordan was going to love that: having to bring Axe or Levi, or someone else with them when they went through the portal. As if she wasn't terrified enough...

Yet and still, a decree was a decree.

The next male to open his mouth would be barbeque.

"As you wish, milord," Blaise acquiesced, speaking for the entire group.

"Is that all?" Ghost grunted, apparently ready to end the session.

The blast of fire that shot from Lord Dragos' throne was so fast and furious, so hot and fevered, that it traveled as a light-blue streak of light and whirred through the air, exploding with a sonic boom as it struck. The impact hit Ghost square in the chest, landing like a freight train, and he flew backward off the dais, falling into a heap. Luckily for him, Lord Topenzi stretched out his ethereal hand and sent shards of ice hurtling from his fingertips, coating the cringing dragyri in frost. "Brother." He spoke to Lord Dragos cautiously. "Forgive me if I overreach."

Lord Dragos paused as if thinking it over, and then he shrugged a casual shoulder and sauntered back to his diamond throne, where he sat, looking bored.

Zane glanced over his shoulder, dreading what he knew he would see, but unable to restrain the impulse: Ghostaniaz was curled into a ball on the floor, vomiting in pain, and his entire six-foot-five, powerful frame was trembling in brutal agony. Yet the male didn't make a peep: not a grunt, not a groan, not a whimper. He wouldn't give the dragon the satisfaction. He wouldn't give his father the play.

Zane shook his head, wishing there was something he could do, and praying Lord Dragos was done with the flame-show.

Why couldn't Ghost just let it go?

Why did he always have to rebel?

It was no great secret that the male hated his father with a passion that defied common sense, and he was as defiant as he was dangerous, broken to the core. And one of these days he was going to get his deepest wish—Lord Dragos was going to kill him, and then his whole piteous existence would be done.

Zane glanced toward the back of the sanctuary at the soothing, pearlescent pool of life and slowly shook his head.

That's all it would take.

One dunk in those sacred waters.

Simply immersing Ghost in that powerful stream.

And the dragyri's wounds—his blisters, his scarring, and his internal pain—would all be healed instantly. Lord Topenzi would offer the pool out of conscience. Lord Cytarius would offer it out of generosity—hell, even Lord Amarkyus and Lord Saphyrius would be moved by the sound of Ghost's retching and the stench of his burning flesh—but not Lord Dragos.

He would revel in Ghost's suffering…at least for the rest of the night.

Zane turned back around to regard the wicked dragon on his throne, and just as he suspected, his hideous mouth was turned up in a smile.

Chapter Sixteen

JORDAN WAS STANDING outside on the terrace, wearing jeans and a taupe, sleeveless blouse, gazing at the waterfall when Zane returned later that night. The dragon moon hung low in the bottomless, dark sky, the air was cool and crisp, and her beautiful auburn hair reflected in the moonlight like a mirror of the crystalline stars.

Zane inhaled sharply as he strolled further onto the deck. "Evening," he said, trying to pitch his voice in a deliberately gentle cadence to avoid startling her.

It didn't work.

She spun around, placed her hand on her heart, and gasped. And gods be merciful, but in that moment, she was the most beautiful sight he had ever seen. He told his beast to heel—this wasn't an invitation to pounce. "Sorry." He spoke softly. "I didn't mean to frighten you."

Jordan shivered involuntarily. "You didn't." She lied. And then she wrung her hands together in a nervous gesture, paced backward until she bumped into the terrace railing, and leaned back against the iron banister, trying to appear at ease.

Zane stopped about five paces away; no need to crowd the woman. "So, how was it? Your time in the lair? Are you feeling any better about being here?" Now that was a loaded question, and he was probably opening a can of worms—but hell, they only had seven days left, and she had to enter that temple of her own voli- tion. They didn't have a second to waste. They didn't have time to play games.

Jordan stared at the planks on the deck nearest to her bare feet, ostensibly to avoid making eye contact. "It was fine," she said, surprising him with the brevity of her answer.

He nodded. "I see. Did you have a chance to explore the lair, spend any more time with my brothers?"

She swallowed convulsively—once again, betraying her nerves. When her eyes finally met his, she couldn't hold the contact; they darted to the left and the right. "Um, yeah," she murmured. "I mean, you already gave me a cursory tour, so I didn't feel the need to check anything else out. But Levi was kind enough to take me to the library—I grabbed a couple books."

Her demeanor was almost edgy, Zane thought.

Cagey.

Sure, she was uncomfortable and afraid—*who wouldn't be?*—but she almost seemed to be hiding something. He quickly dismissed the thought. After all, what could she be hiding? Her cell phone wouldn't work inside Dragons Domain—they had little use for cellular towers and Wi-Fi when they could communicate telepathically, even across a distance—and the signals wouldn't cross the portal anyway, unless they were enhanced by a jewel, in this case, by a special sapphire sphere. Something he wasn't going to tell Jordan…just yet.

Better to turn his attention to something that could move the conversation forward. "So, you tried out the library? What did you think? What kind of books did you grab?"

Damn, that sounded like an interrogation.

Oh well, at least it was a start.

"Oh," she said, smiling weakly, "well, you know me." She shut her eyes, shook her head, and took an obvious, slow breath. Raising her chin, she amended the statement: "Well, you *don't* know me, not at all; but if you did, you would know that when I'm…when

I'm unsure about something…I always choose analysis first. I gather information."

Zane cocked his eyebrows. "And?"

"And…I thought the library was very nice, very well appointed, and obviously stocked to the gills. And I grabbed three books."

He studied her hazel eyes, wishing he understood that guarded undercurrent, wishing she could relax just a bit. "So, you didn't grab a novel or a cookbook, I take it?" He forced a congenial smile, and she pressed her back harder against the rail.

"No," she said quickly, and then she actually turned around, rested her forearms on the railing, and pretended to view the falls. In other words, she gave him her back. "I grabbed an atlas of your territories, a volume about the customs of the Dragyr, and another journal—the genealogy of the Sapphire Lair."

Zane strained to hear her clearly.

It wasn't like he didn't possess supernatural hearing, but with the waterfall flowing, the fact that she was mumbling, and his proximity being ten feet away, he had to concentrate on each of her words. *Screw this*, he said to himself, closing the distance between them and sidling up behind her.

She instantly stiffened, but that didn't deter him.

He placed his right hand on the curve of her exposed shoulder and brushed lightly against her back with his chest. Yes, she would feel crowded, maybe even pressured, but she would also sense his warmth…his presence…his nearness. The fact that she wasn't in this alone. "Tell me about the atlas," he breathed in her ear, giving her something neutral, safe, and linear to concentrate on.

She shivered, but she didn't brush his hand away. Rather, she tilted her head slightly to the side to make her words more audible. "Um, I…I thought it was interesting…the territories, the way the domain is laid out."

"Mm. Hm."

She squirmed. "I was surprised to see the different regions, um, the mountains in the west, the desert in the east, the flatlands in the south, and what looks almost like a massive body of water, an ocean, in the north…the way the lairs are positioned, like numbers on a clock, more or less surrounding the temple in the center. The domain is bigger than I thought."

She arched her back slightly to ease away from the contact, and Zane absently rotated his thumb along the slope of her shoulder. "It's a beautiful land, Jordan. The colors are brighter here, the sounds of nature are almost lyrical, and everything grows to perfection—it's almost like a garden of Eden. I think you will come to love it."

She practically writhed, rotating her shoulder to escape his touch.

He removed his hand and brushed the back of her cheek with the backs of his fingers, instead, just a soft, gentle slide of his hand. "Dragyra," he whispered. "What can I do to assuage your fears?"

She stiffened. "You can stop touching me for starters."

He grimaced. "No, I cannot. Your fear is drawing me in like a moth to a flame; your unease is distressing my dragon. He can hear your heartbeat racing in your chest; he can smell your terror drifting on the breeze; and he can sense your pulse, the way your blood rushes in your veins. And all of it...*all of it*...awakens his protective instincts. I can't...not touch you." He lowered his head, rested his chin in her hair, and inhaled her feminine scent. "Breathe for me, Jordan. Slowly, in and out. It will help us both."

At that, she seemed to bristle. "That's an excuse, Zanaikeyros." *Wow*, she used his given name. "You've brought me here against my will, you're invading my personal space, and you're using the fact that you're a dragon to do what you please." To his utter surprise, she wriggled out beneath his touch, faced him head-on, and squared her shoulders in defiance, her eyes remaining locked on his. "If you're going to do something—and make excuses to do it—then just get it over with and stop playing games." Her jaw was rebellious, but her mouth was trembling.

Zane took a generous step back. "Just what do you think I'm going to do?"

It was a stupid question.

He knew what she feared.

It was written all over her face.

"Jordan," he intoned in a deep, husky rasp, trying to conceal his frustration. "I am not going to harm you. And I am not going to force myself on you—not now, not tomorrow, not ever."

She visibly sighed with relief. "You aren't?"

"No." His tone left no room for argument.

She looked away, staring at an unidentifiable point beyond his shoulder. "Then your dragon doesn't want...he doesn't feel...he doesn't have the impulse to—"

Zane chuckled aloud. He couldn't help it. "Oh, don't get it twisted, pretty lady. My dragon is fully male, and you..." His voice grew hoarse with conviction. "You are an amazingly beautiful woman, Jordan Anderson. Every instinct in my body is...aware. But neither I, nor my dragon, is a rapist." She literally turned a pale shade of green, and Zane thought she was about to hit the deck. "Angel," he said soothingly, reaching forward to frame her face in his hands, "look at me."

She glanced at his mouth, then his nose, then the side of his face, fidgeting in discomfort.

"Look at me."

Her beautiful hazel eyes met his, and they were moist with the onset of tears.

"If you were standing on a street corner, and you saw a child about to step out in front of a car, what would your impulse be?"

She drew back and frowned. "To stop her...of course."

"Yes," he agreed, "but what would it *feel* like...in that moment? Would you think it over? Would you weigh the implications—*where is her mother; where is her father; do I have the right to intervene?*—or would you possibly gasp, feel a surge of adrenaline, and dive for the kid without thinking?"

Jordan shrugged. "I would grab the kid on an impulse."

"Yes," Zane said, "because it isn't a thought—it's an urge. And in that moment, it is all-pervasive." He brushed his thumbs over her cheeks in the gentlest of caresses. "Your fear is like that car. Your heartbeat speeds it up. Your dread provokes a surge of adrenaline in my dragon. He doesn't think. He doesn't reason. He only knows he must act—place himself between the danger and his dragyra, and that's why he reaches out. It is not something I can easily restrain. But the impulse to mate—the desire to take you in my arms and make you want me, make you need me, make you *mine*—that is more like a hunger. It gnaws at my gut, but it doesn't demand immediate action."

Jordan blanched.

She opened her mouth to speak, but nothing came out.

She closed it and pursed her lips together, and then stood there—just stood there—frozen like a statue.

Zane smiled. "Jordan, I have the power to help you with my mind. I can slow your heartbeat for you, if you'll let me. I can even control your breaths. Let me hold you, dragyra, just for a time. I know you are not ready to accept this new reality—and you certainly don't understand it—but there is a single flame that burns in your heart...and mine. That means there is a spark between us, however concealed or dormant, because the gods put it there. It will awaken on its own if you'll let it. Let me hold you, Jordan. And let tomorrow take care of itself."

⤢

Jordan's head was spinning.

Zanaikeyros was as smooth, polished, and hypnotic as he was terrifying, and she wondered if he wasn't using his power...already.

An errant cluster of chestnut-brown hair had fallen into his sapphire eyes, and between that and his flawless, angled jaw; the soft, smooth complexion of his skin; his words...his demeanor... his oh-so-gentle touch; it was all clouding her brain.

And she didn't like it.

Not one bit.

She had questions she wanted to ask, but she couldn't even imagine bringing them up, like *to hell with tomorrow, what about tonight?* Did he expect her to sleep in his bed? Like what about the consecration, this date she had with the temple—what exactly was involved with *rebirth?* It wasn't in the books she had read, and he hadn't gone into it at her apartment.

And worse, there was that thing she had done earlier.

That thing in her purse.

That thing she didn't dare think of, lest the dragon was reading her thoughts.

Lest she was projecting again…

But he was right about one thing: Her fear was consuming her—it was practically making her sick. She couldn't breathe, she couldn't think, and if it got any worse, she could hardly function going forward. She would give anything to feel calm, to be back in control, to even embrace the illusion of self-determination.

If only for a moment.

And so she went out on a limb and slowly nodded her head, trying desperately not to tremble.

Zane immediately took the cue. He pressed forward to close the small distance between them, dropped his hands from her face to her waist, and gently tugged her forward. As her body gave way to his momentum and strength, he braced her lower back with one hand, encircled her shoulders with his arm, and pulled her against his chest…into his embrace.

There.

It was done.

More or less.

He was holding her, and she was letting him.

So why did she feel like she was about to panic?

"Shh, little one," he whispered in her ear, and a strange, peaceful warmth poured into her. It traveled along the canal of her ear, down her neck, and into her shoulders, where it spread out in light, pulsing waves and enveloped her chest.

She took a slow, deep breath, and even that felt like a summer's breeze wafting through her chest, delivering a powerful sedative throughout her body.

He rotated his hand on the small of her back, and the same thing happened there: Her hips, her thighs, her knees relaxed, and her body folded into his.

She felt like she was floating on a cloud.

He caught her up in his arms, and she didn't protest as he traversed the deck in five long strides, entered through the large

French doors, and made his way across the suite to the raised platform, laying her down on the bed. "No fears, precious angel," he reassured her—though she was too relaxed to care. "Only serenity and sleep," he added, and she felt a current of lethargy pulse through her. "I will sleep in the chair beside you," he whispered. "And in time, we will talk about the temple and your *rebirth*. No worries. Not now. Only peace."

Ah, she thought absently: So he had been reading her mind.

As her eyelids fluttered shut and she sank into the mattress, she had the sensation that he was drawing a blanket over her, and she sighed.

"Ah, baby," he whispered, sounding curiously sad.

"Hmm?" she tried to reply.

"What did you put in your purse?"

My purse? she thought, unable to catch his words…

And then the entire world went dark.

Chapter Seventeen

Monday ~ the next morning

JORDAN ANDERSON SHOT straight up in bed, her eyes darting to the nearest clock in a panic.

What time was it?

Had she missed Macy's surgery?

She was met by a deep, gravelly voice and a strong, steadying hand on her forearm—Zane, perched in an armchair beside the bed. "Whoa there, angel. You're in Dragons Domain with me...in the Sapphire Lair. You're safe."

She glanced at the tall, muscular male and rubbed her eyes. "I know that. I remember, but what time is it. I have to—"

"It's six AM," Zane interrupted. "From what you told me on Saturday, Macy's surgery is at nine, and she has to check in at seven. We still have plenty of time."

Jordan drew back, trying to process Zane's words through her sleep-fogged brain. *It was six AM?* "You remembered all that?" she mumbled.

"Of course I did," he replied.

She sat up in bed, leaned against the massive iron-and-wooden headboard, and tried to collect her thoughts. Tried to remember the night before.

She immediately peeked beneath the thick cotton blanket still covering her body and sighed in relief, noticing that her clothes were still on. "You put me to bed?" she asked, still a bit confused.

"I did. You needed the sleep."

She nodded. "Yeah...*yeah*...I sort of remember that. I just"— and then her eyes caught a glimpse of her purse, situated on the nightstand, and the entire memory slammed into her like a freight train. She swallowed a lump of anxiety. "Last night...my purse..." *Oh dear God...*

His voice turned solemn. "I didn't rifle through it. I figured that would be wrong...disrespectful." He leaned in toward the bed, and his severe sapphire-and-gold eyes met hers. "I wanted to wait so you could tell me yourself."

Jordan folded her hands in her lap and stared at her thumbs. "Tell you what?" She decided to play stupid.

He chuckled, but it was a humorless sound. "What's in your purse, Jordan. What didn't you want me to find?"

Well, that was a fine wake-up call, she thought. And holy hell—what could she say?

His expression grew impassive. "Look, I know the situation is awkward, and neither one of us chose this fate, but here it is. Here we are. The way I see it: The only thing we have going for us, this far, is honesty. It's the only way we're going to work this out." A dead calm settled over him, and he modulated his voice. "What's in your purse, Jordan."

Jordan shut her eyes.

She needed to think.

On one hand, he was right: They were facing a bizarre, untenable situation, and honesty always helped—hadn't he been brutally honest with her? But on the other hand, she was committed to something far more basic, more primal, than working things out with Zane. She was committed to her own survival, intent on her own escape. There was no way—no how—she was going to become the consort of a dragon and live in some foreign domain, and he was batshit crazy if he thought otherwise...no matter how congenial he was being.

No matter how deceptive she had been.

I mean, let's just get real, she thought.

"I photocopied a page from the atlas," she said, diving in with both feet.

"Come again?" he prompted.

She fiddled with the hem of the blanket. "In the library, when Levi took me, I used the copy machine to photocopy a page." She prayed that the copier she'd seen actually worked, or the jig was up.

He furrowed his brow, and his striking, enigmatic eyes grew more intense. "What page? Why?"

She let out a slow, deep breath. This just might work. "Um, one of the pages in the back—it showed the whole of the territory." She winced, feigning a measure of guilt. "I'm not sure why I took it. I guess...I thought I might be able to use it, maybe find a portal, maybe find a way to escape."

Zane didn't react, at least not visibly. If there was something going on in that dragyri heart, it was very well concealed. "I already told you, the portal is in here." He brushed the pads of his fingers over his amulet and frowned. "And where in Dragons Domain would you possibly go? You know nothing about this realm."

She nodded and met his gaze. "I know. I can't say it was rational. It was just...I just...what if I needed to escape, to run...from you? I just took it, okay?"

Zane studied her eyes, far too keenly, and then he slowly nodded his head. "And you thought that would anger me? That I would be upset if I knew?"

She pivoted like a lawyer. "Aren't you?"

He smirked, clearly catching her ploy. "I am...concerned... that you don't trust me, not even a little, not yet. We are running out of time."

And there it was again: the metaphorical elephant in the living room: *six more days until the temple...*

She pivoted again.

"You said you would tell me more—everything—about the ceremony in the temple, the thing you call *rebirth*. The thing you expect me to do."

Zane nodded, appearing contrite. "And I will...when we have

more time. When you're ready to hear more about our lives, our kind, to listen with an open mind." He glanced at the digital clock beside the bed. "But right now, it's already 6:15. You still need to get dressed and eat breakfast. And we still need to travel through the portal if you want to meet Macy at the hospital at seven, to be with her throughout the pre-op." He leaned back and raised his eyebrows. "It's up to you. I won't deny you if you insist on talking now."

Well, wasn't that just an impossible decision—keep her word to her best friend, or finally hear the details of her date with destiny.

With doom.

Any other time…

She glanced toward the pocket door that led to the en suite bathroom and frowned. "I need to be there for Macy."

Zane stood up, and the sudden shift in his position, the stealthy, animalistic way he moved, the slumberous yet predatory rise to his full, intimidating height made her heart lodge in her throat. She was in the presence of a slayer, no matter how charming he could seem, and she needed to remember that.

"Your duffle is in the bathroom, and the shower panel is self-explanatory—the way you work the jets, whatever heads you choose. I'll meet you downstairs in the kitchen—Jace is already preparing the morning meal."

Jordan's heart retreated from her throat, sank in her chest, and dropped lower…to her stomach. That was all she needed, next: to sit at a massive, mission-style table, surrounded by four more predatory dragons, and try to swallow food. She'd be lucky if she didn't spew in her plate.

Still, she wasn't about to tell that to Zane.

The sooner he left the room—and she could breathe again—the better.

"I'll be down in twenty minutes," she said, marshaling her courage. Her eyes darted to the elegant French doors, and then the floor-to-ceiling windows that illuminated the deck, almost involuntarily. Every instinct in her body told her to run, to flee, to dash out the doors or climb through a window and sprint as far…and as fast…as she could. But Zane had been right when he had reminded her that she was in a foreign land. She didn't know the topography—hell, she didn't know what strange or dangerous animals might be lurking in the trees, behind the bushes, crawling out of the waters, poised and ready to pounce—and she didn't want to know.

Today was all about Macy.

That was it.

That was all.

And she needed to remain focused.

Besides, she had to get a text off to Dan.

Someway.

Somehow.

She had to keep her cool.

⸙

Salem Thorne, a venerable pagan, stood at the edge of the surgeon's bed in the doctor's expensive, modern condominium, and he watched as Kyle Parker tossed and turned on his satin sheets.

And why wouldn't he—feel fitful, that is?

His peaceful, then later erotic, dreams had turned quickly into nightmares, and Salem had orchestrated it all.

It was true: He could have met the surgeon face-to-face, demon to human, and demanded his obedience, spelled everything out in clear, unambiguous terms, but unlike the multitudes of human servants who willingly served the Pagan Horde—or even the Temple of Seven—the man did not possess the stamina for the confrontation.

He didn't have the balls.

He would have taken one look at a true, immortal demon, and his pristine, perfectly layered black hair would have wilted on his head; his baby-blue peepers would have grown wide with fright; and that lion's heart, which he incorrectly believed he possessed, would have instantly stopped beating from the fright.

No, Kyle needed to be approached in the typical, more subtle manner: manipulated through his dreams.

And so, Salem had spent the last two hours weaving all manner of symbols and fanciful tales. First, he had shown the aspiring surgeon his potential greatness: ceremonies in his honor; awards embellished with his name; lucrative, important promotions. Then he had interrupted those grandiose dreams with erotic scene after erotic scene—Dr. Parker sharing his most hidden, elicit sexual fantasies with Macy Wilson: the pretty blonde dropping to her knees in eager anticipation; a pair of handcuffs slipping around her wrists; and a red silk tie…placed in her mouth. Oh yes, Dr. Parker had been adequately aroused.

And then the dreams had changed.

A barren wasteland teeming with snakes.

A medieval dungeon filled with spikes.

A vile of poison being poured down his throat as he choked on the bitter concoction.

He had been shown every manner of personal agony, unbearable cruelty, and torture; and the nightmare had made it clear: There was only one thing that stood between Dr. Parker and suffering such horrendous pain—the need to give Macy a pin.

Yes, a simple gold-and-ruby pin.

Fashioned in the shape of a beetle, attached to the post and card, inserted in her flower arrangement, following her successful surgery: a gift from the doting doctor. *Just give Macy this gift, and you will escape all the torture you've seen.*

You will be rewarded with fame…and complicit sex.

Would the malleable surgeon remember the dream?

No.

Would he make a linear connection between the pin on his nightstand, where it had come from, and his overwhelming desire to place it in Macy's flowers?

Not even for a minute.

But then, he didn't have to.

All he had to do was do it.

Salem bent low, over the bed, and sniffed Dr. Parker's hair—for the sake of all that was unholy, the narcissist shampooed with scented oils.

Whatever.

The demon's groin hardened, and for a moment he wondered if he could enjoy lying with a man—hell, the guy's hair was still perfect, even as he tossed and turned on his fluffy pillow, and his long, sinewy body…that lush, pouty mouth…

Nah.

Salem preferred young girls, preferably in their teens: helpless, virginal, and adept at screaming. The louder, the better.

But he needed to focus.

He let his head roll back on his neck, his arms fall, extended, to his sides, as he embraced the darkness within him, connected to his master and lord: the venerable Drakkar Hades, often referred to as Drak—and wasn't that just a fitting term of veneration, considering Bram Stoker and all…

As his lethal claws extended from his hands and his gums began to ache, the demon began to chant—the words too ancient, too vile, too cryptic to pronounce without guttural grunts.

And then his body began to morph.

It did not splinter apart like a collapsing pillar of salt, because his orders had been clear: He was not to release a thousand beetles; he was to become…only one.

Just one.

One that he would still occupy.

One that he would still possess.

His spine crackled and popped as it bent inward; his ears began to bleed as they formed into antennae; and his head throbbed like it was going to split open as it gave way to frontal and pronotol lobes…emerged as vermin horns.

The pain was as delectable as it was unbearable, and he gave himself over, fully, to the transformation, allowing his member to rise. Soon, it too began to change, growing dozens and dozens of spikes. Salem chuckled inside: The male Bruchid beetle actually punctured the female's reproductive tract during sex, causing heavy and permanent injuries to her system, preventing her from mating again.

How utterly exquisite was that?

He stopped laughing when his rib cage broke and his outer wings emerged—when his legs spouted into femurs and began to grow spurs. In fact, he may have whimpered a time or two before he buckled down and focused, narrowing all his concentration: *Transform your eyes to rubies, Salem; transform your abdomen to gold.*

Concentrate.

Harder…

Just a little bit more…

Ah, and there it was.

He let his newfound body fold inward, drawing down in size until a perfectly formed ornamental bug landed on the doctor's nightstand.

Still as the night.

Lethal as sin.

Waiting to reanimate…once more.

Chapter Eighteen

JORDAN LACED THE last of five crisscrossed back-straps on the airy, pale-green summer dress she was wearing, looked at her reflection in the mirror, and cringed. Other than the one-inch-wide shoulder straps, her arms were basically bare. The neckline was too low, showing the rise of her modest breasts, and the waist was too form-fitting, showing the dip in her stomach and the curve of her hips. In other words, the dress was way too revealing. She had grabbed it on the fly because it was lightweight and easy to pack—it didn't take up much room—but now she wished she had grabbed a turtleneck instead, something that covered every exposed inch of skin, despite the fact that it was almost mid-June.

She slipped on her sandals, waved her hand under the motion sensor to turn off the bathroom lights, and began making her way down the sturdy stairs. She could have taken the elevator at the back of the hall, which she had been told stopped on all five floors, but she needed an extra minute or two to calm her nerves and clear her mind.

Breakfast.

She could do breakfast.

In fact, the sooner they were finished, the better—the sooner she would be headed back, through the portal, to her familiar earth-dimension, and one step closer to flagging Dan for help.

As she descended the base of the left-side staircase, she raised her chin and drew back her shoulders for courage, and then she softly padded beyond the large gourmet island, across the modern, well-appointed kitchen, and to the front of the house—the eating nook, surrounded by floor-to-ceiling windows and housing a massive mission-style table.

The males were already seated and throwing back a feast of what looked like bacon, eggs, sausage, pancakes, and fruit. Her stomach did a little flip—there was no way she could eat.

Zane patted the seat of the chair beside him, at the far end of the table, and Jordan slowly nodded her head.

The other dragyri fell silent.

Great.

Just great…

Make her feel like a laboratory specimen.

She kept her eyes straight ahead as she took her seat, scooted forward, and stared at the empty plate. Zane—or someone—had already set her place. "Do you always eat such a large breakfast?" she asked, glancing up at him through her peripheral vision.

His entire countenance softened. "Pretty much," he said. "We take meals pretty seriously around here, even though it's not our primary sustenance."

She cringed at his reference to *feeding*, but she didn't murmur a word.

Someone at the table snickered, and then Axe, who was sitting on the opposite side of the table, lifted a platter full of pancakes and offered it to Jordan.

"No, thanks," she said politely. "I think I'll just have fruit."

Zane reached over her, forked a giant pancake off the platter, and dropped it on her plate. "You're gonna need more than that."

She bit back an insolent retort. *Okay.* So he was making her food choices for her now?

"Don't want to hurt Jace's feelings," Levi said.

"Excuse me?" Jordan asked, meeting the handsome dragyri's eyes and making note of the fact that there was a lyrical quality to his otherwise masculine voice. "Did Jace cook all this?" She stared at the bounty of platters before her.

Jace smiled, and it was a grin laced with pride. "Yep. These other heathens try to cook from time to time—or they rely heavily on human servants, cooks and maids—but I think there's an art to culinary preparation, and just getting it done, heating it up, isn't good enough."

Zane rolled his eyes. "Jace is a pansy."

"Next thing you know," Nakai cut in, "he'll be arranging flowers and placing them...*just so*...all around the lair."

The whole table chuckled.

"Yeah, all right," Jace said in a counterfeit surly tone. "And who's the better marksman, Nakai?" He leveled his gaze at Zane. "And last time we sparred with Katars, who got their ass kicked?" he chided.

Zane's top lip quirked up in a mocking smile. "Good thing my weapon of choice is a battle axe, right?"

"What's a Katar?" Jordan whispered to Zane, losing ever more of her appetite.

"It's a fancy word for dagger," Zane said.

Hearing the conversation perfectly, Jace chimed in: "It's a very specific kind of dagger, a push blade with an H-shaped handle—it originated in India—very easy to thrust and wield with your wrist. Its original name was Kattari, then later Katara, before the British shortened it to the Romanized version, Katar."

"And you just made our point," Nakai taunted. "Damn, let the woman eat breakfast." He cocked his eyebrows and goaded him some more. "*History of the Katar*—by Jace Saphyrius." He reached for a nearby link of sausage and speared it with his knife, but when he started to place it on his plate, Jace flicked his wrist, extended his pinky, and a bright orange flame shot across the table, incinerating the chunk of meat.

"Then cook the shit yourself," Jace snarled, eyeing the charcoal-colored dust now dotting the dragyri's plate.

Jordan jerked back in her chair and gasped.

More raucous laughter echoed around the table before Zane

cleared his throat and projected his voice. "Hey!" He had the room's immediate attention. "Take it down a few notches—you're scaring my dragyra." He leveled his gaze at Jace before eyeing the entire room. "And watch your language…all of you."

More laughter began to ensue, when all of a sudden, it was simply cut off.

Like someone had pressed *mute* on the nook's remote.

All five males stirred in unison: scooting back their chairs, standing to their full, domineering heights, and stepping gracefully to the sides of their seats. Then they each fell to one knee, bowed their heads, and clutched their sacred amulets.

Jordan's mouth dropped open.

Was this some sort of archaic, over-the-top, caveman apology? *Was it meant for her?*

Surely not.

She absently glanced toward the head of the table, and she immediately knew what all the fuss was about.

Her heart nearly seized in her chest.

Standing like a giant prism of sapphire light, his presence utterly filling the room with kinetic energy, was the outline and ethos of a terrifying man, flanked by the silhouette of a ferocious dragon. And without being able to explain how she knew, Jordan was absolutely certain: The beast in the background—the mirrored soul hovering in, around, and atop the semi-human form—was only a fraction of its true, colossal size.

His power radiated outward.

The temperature in the room increased by several degrees.

And the light reflecting from the depth of the dragon's core virtually undulated in waves, making curious, ambient sounds, like whales in the depths of the ocean, or ancient pterodactyls screeching in a prehistoric sky.

It wasn't particularly loud.

It was eerie.

It was haunting.

It was petrifying.

And Jordan wanted to crawl through her chair, melt into the floor, and become one of the travertine tiles.

"Sons." The fearsome lord spoke only one word, yet the power in his otherworldly voice rocked the rafters and shook the chandelier, causing the seven dimly lit globes within it to radiate sapphire light.

Jordan's hands trembled uncontrollably.

She didn't know what to do—should she kneel on the floor with the rest of the Dragyr; bow her head in homage to the fearsome god; or apologize for being in his lair? She had a sinking sensation that she was a heartbeat away from the end of her life, a mere twinkling from being scorched into dust…just like Nakai's link of sausage.

"Father…" The dragyri males spoke the word in unison—did they choreograph this stuff? And why *Father*? Why not *lord*…or *my god*? Jordan shook her head—she thought Zane was the only biological son.

"Rise," the dragon said.

And all five males stood up.

"How may we serve you, Lord Saphyrius?" Axe said next, and Jordan nearly quaked in her sandals.

She crossed her arms over her chest, hugged her midriff snugly, and stared down at her lap—she honestly didn't know what else to do.

"The dragyra," the dragon lord said. "I wish to meet my daughter."

Oh, no-no-no, she thought as she swayed in her chair.

Zane reached out to steady her back with the palm of his hand, and then he placed his fingers beneath her elbow and nudged her gently upward, directing her to stand. She couldn't do it, not on her own volition, and he had to give her a tug.

"Jordan Briana Anderson"—*how did Zane know her middle name?*—"I present you to Lord Saphyrius, third deity of the sacred Temple of Seven, ruler of Dragons Domain, creator of the dragon sun, the dragon moon, and the Dragyr race, and keeper of the sacred sapphire. God of my pantheon, father of my heart—*and my blood*—and master of the Sapphire Lair. Honor him with your silence."

Holy shit...

She gulped.

Then she curled her lips inward and bit down with her teeth, determined not to make a sound. The fearsome lord—and his shadow-dragon—began to draw nearer; and like light switching from one source to the next—one candle extinguishing, another igniting—the outline of Lord Saphyrius, the "man," faded into the background, while the silhouette of the dragon grew stronger... more detailed.

More ominous.

The dragon drew back like an ocean wave retreating from a sandy shoreline, and then his neck craned forward in a creepy, meandering motion. His massive head, festooned with haunting, almond-shaped eyes, traversed the expanse of the table and came to rest, eye to eye, with Jordan. Her knees knocked together, but she was too hypnotized, too beguiled, too terrified to even blink.

The dragon's scaly nose wrinkled as he *sniffed her*, and his eyes grew disturbingly narrow, blazing with sapphire flames in their depths, as he appeared to search her soul, much like Zane had done the first night she had met him.

Don't flinch; don't flinch; don't flinch, she told herself, but despite her best efforts at self-control, Jordan drew back her head and cast her gaze to the side, unable to meet his eyes.

Lord Saphyrius regarded her circumspectly, for what felt like a thousand years, and then he simply meandered backward—recalling his dragon and reclaiming his mostly human form—and nodded his regal head. "Welcome to the Sapphire Lair, my daughter"—he practically purred the words—"I am pleased that you are home."

Zane exhaled an audible sigh of relief, and that worried Jordan even more.

What the heck had just happened, and what had Zane expected?

She swallowed her angst and searched Zane's expression for

some sort of direction: Was she supposed to remain quiet...or respond?

Zane inclined his head, and she took it to mean: *Answer him.*

"Thank you," she said in a whisper, though she didn't really mean it.

"Milord," Zane prompted softly.

Jordan frowned. And then she got it. "Thank you, milord," she repeated.

Lord Saphyrius clasped both ethereal hands behind his back and smiled, a warm, tender acknowledgment. And then he turned his attention to Zane. "Who will you be taking with you through the portal?" he asked, his voice, now, matter-of-fact.

"Axeviathon," Zane answered. He didn't appear to be afraid.

The lord nodded, demonstrating his approval, and then—just like that—his essence withdrew from the room. He swirled upward and inward, and the dragon vanished.

Jordan plopped down in her seat and fought to catch her breath. After several pregnant moments had passed, she let out a tormented groan. "Does he do that often?"

Zane regarded her...strangely, like he'd never seen her before; and in that odd, cryptic moment, his golden pupils were filled with such raw, unfettered possession, Jordan almost jumped up and ran.

"Not that often," he said huskily. "Are you okay?"

Jordan winced as she thought about his words: *Was she okay?*

She was lost.

She was entrapped.

And she was reeling from shock.

No, she was definitely not okay.

She blinked back the moisture of a pressing tear. "Will I ever be okay again?"

✥

The words continued to echo in Zane's mind as he ushered Jordan out of the lair, stepped onto the porch, and stood next to Axe, preparing to open the portal.

Will I ever be okay again?

He didn't know how to answer that question: not when she'd asked it, and certainly, not now.

Centuries of dragyri had claimed their dragyras, and in the end, the race had always gone on. The women found their place in a strange new world, and the males adapted to the presence of the women. The dragon lords continued to rule, commanding the lot of them, together, and through it all, more sons—more mercenaries—were born.

The cycle seemed as old as time, certainly as old as the Dragyr, and it was all Zane had ever known. But now, as he felt his dragyra's alarm, he was beginning to doubt the entire paradigm.

The responsibility he felt—the overwhelming weight on his shoulders—was so enormous: Jordan's heart, her sanity…her sense of well-being; all of it was in his carnal hands, and he had no idea how to teach her.

How to reach her.

How to love her.

How to interpret her perception of *right versus wrong* from her curious, human perspective.

He only knew that he cared more deeply than he had anticipated—he didn't expect to feel this much, this soon—and the entire situation made him feel off-balance.

Levi stepped out on the porch, providing a much-needed distraction. He said something to Axe in Dragonese, to which Axe merely grunted in reply, and it reminded Zane of some unfinished business: He still had a question for the youngest member of the Sapphire Lair.

Levi—he pushed the telepathic call into the dragyri's mind on a private bandwidth—*I have a question for you. Act natural.*

Levi leaned against one of the blue-and-white stone pillars and crossed his arms over his chest, looking out into the distance like he didn't have a care in the world. *Shoot*, he said.

Yesterday, while I was at the temple, you escorted Jordan to the library, correct?

Correct, Levi said.

Did she use the copy machine before she left—did she photocopy any pages from a book?

Levi paused for a couple of seconds, clearly thinking it over. *No,* he finally muttered.

Zane sighed. *Are you absolutely certain?*

Yes, brother. I kept a careful eye on her the entire time, mostly out of duty and instinct—I knew she was nervous, and I was trying to make her feel more comfortable. I saw everything she did.

Zane resisted the impulse to nod. *Very well. Thank you.* He closed the communication and turned to Axe. "Ready, brother?"

Axe placed his hand on his amulet and shifted his attention to Jordan. "Ready when she is."

Zane extended his hand to his female, trying to conceal his disappointment. "Are you ready, my *dragyra?* Do you remember what to say?" It was an unnecessary question—Jordan had a mind like a steel trap. Just the same, they needed to keep their stories straight in the presence of other curious humans.

Jordan nodded soberly. "Ready as I'll ever be."

And with that, Zane raised his free hand, clutched his sapphire, and opened the portal.

Chapter Nineteen

MACY WILSON SNUGGLED beneath the heated white blanket that Patty, her friendly nurse, had given her. She glanced at the IV taped to her inner arm and felt grateful that the preliminaries were over. Macy detested IVs, actually needles of any kind, but Patty had been pretty good at inserting it, and now the worst part was over.

Feeling more bored than anxious, she stared at the large white clock on the wall and frowned. It was already 7:45 AM, and Jordan wasn't there yet.

What in the world was going on?

Not only had Jordan failed to call her that morning, but she hadn't responded to any of Macy's texts over the past twenty-four hours, and Macy was beginning to worry: It just wasn't like Jordan to blow someone off—let alone, her BFF—and especially not at a time like this.

Switching her attention to the large plastic bag that contained her cell phone, her purse, and her clothes, Macy thought about her mom: Luckily, Karen Wilson had driven Macy to the hospital, and she was going to stick around all day—she would be able to keep an eye on Macy's stuff.

Well, as soon as she got back from the cafeteria.

After watching her mom fidget with just about everything in

the room, pace back and forth across the small, sterile cubicle a half-dozen times, Macy had finally convinced Nervous-Nelly to go take a walk…get a cup of tea at the hospital diner. To put it bluntly, Karen had been driving Macy crazy. She needed a much more calming influence at a time like this—say, someone just like Jordan.

A cheeky, conspiratorial smile edged along the curves of her mouth, and her stomach did a nervous little flip as she switched her attention, yet again, to her handsome surgeon, Dr. Kyle Parker.

Talk about a calming influence!

Talk about a gorgeous, blue-eyed Adonis, with a headful of silky black hair, who had stared at her just a little too long, touched her just a little too gently, and pitched his voice just a little too intimately…for coincidence.

Talk about bedside manner…

There was no getting around it—Dr. Kyle Parker was interested. In Macy!

She shivered beneath the otherwise warm blanket and chuckled beneath her breath.

How had that happened?

When had that happened?

Her excitement was almost too great to contain.

And then she glanced downward and cringed. The hospital gown she was wearing was thin, green, and ugly: not to mention, she had a plastic bag on her head; she had forgotten to paint her toenails; and her breath was moderately questionable. After all, she hadn't been allowed to eat or drink anything since seven o'clock the night before, and she might have been too sparing with the toothpaste. Hell, she thought, feeling incredibly self-conscious, she'd be lucky if Dr. Parker still looked her way by the time this surgery was over—by the time he had seen pretty much *all* of what she had to offer. Ugh. Ugh. And ugh.

Still, she reasoned, preferring to be more positive, there *had* been something hard to name in his voice—a smooth, masculine drawl, something sensual, something implicit—as he'd cleared his throat and whispered, "If you need anything, Macy—*anything at all*—you just let me know, okay?"

She bit down on her bottom lip.

For whatever reason, Dr. Parker didn't seem to care about her toenails or the baggie on her head…

For whatever reason, the man was attracted to Macy!

She took a deep breath and glanced at the clock, a second time. She couldn't wait to tell Jordan about this recent twist of fate, *but where the hell was she?* No sooner had she conjured the thought than she heard a familiar voice outside the thick blue-and-white curtain: "Knock-knock. Can I come in?"

Jordan!

"Yes," Macy called, glancing toward the flimsy partition with excitement. "Come in." She practically wriggled like a child with a newfound toy, sitting straighter in the mechanical bed.

Jordan's elegant hand pulled back the curtains, and she sauntered in with a smile.

"Where have you been!" Macy demanded, and then her mouth dropped open and her eyes bulged out of her head.

Hell, she may have actually drooled…

Two positively breathtaking men—with ungodly perfect bodies, chiseled features, like Roman gods, and the swagger of Navy SEALs—followed Jordan into the cubicle. They were both wearing sunglasses—which was curious, since they were also indoors—and the heat and power that radiated around them almost made Macy leap from her bed (IV pole, be damned) and duck under the nearest partition.

"What the hell?" She spoke the thought aloud.

Jordan took a deep breath and smiled. "Sorry I'm late, Mace; and sorry I've been MIA." She glanced over her shoulder to regard the tallest of the two, the one with gorgeous dark-brown hair; broad, powerful shoulders; and thighs that looked like he could do squats while lifting an entire weight-bench. "This is Zane Saphyrius." She turned her attention to a divine masculine specimen with gorgeous dirty-blond locks. "And this is his partner, Axe." She swallowed nervously, and Macy knew right away that there was something serious going on, in spite of Jordan's valiant attempt at casualness. "Remember the other day when I mentioned that there was something happening at work—something creepy that came up that I had to take care of?"

"Yeah," Macy said, her voice registering her hesitation.

"Well," Jordan explained, "turns out that thing had a slight element of danger attached to it, so I now have a couple of body-guards." She quickly held up her hand to dispel any fears. "But don't worry. I'm fine. Truly, I am. I'm just going to be hanging out with Mutt and Jeff for a while." She crooked her thumb at the Navy SEALs, and the dark-haired man's savagely beautiful mouth turned down into a frown.

Whoa, Macy thought, getting the distinct impression that he didn't find Jordan's comment funny—in the least. And as for the dirty blond? He looked like he could stop an oncoming truck with the palm of his hand, wrench the bolts out of the tires while he whistled, and then chew on them for distraction, without breaking a tooth.

Okay, Macy surmised: *So why are you lying to me, Jordan? And what are you leaving out?* But now was not the time, or the place, to confront her. "So is that why you haven't returned any of my calls?" she asked, trying desperately to keep her eyes fixed on Jordan.

It wasn't an easy task...

Jordan winced, and the look of apology that flashed through her eyes was truly painful to witness. "Oh my God, Macy. I am so, so sorry." She dropped her head in shame. "And I told you I would be there if you needed me. To call me anytime..."

"Hey," Macy said, pitching her voice in a no-nonsense tone. "If you've been in trouble...*in danger*...then no worries, Jordan. It's okay. *Seriously.* I'm just glad you're safe." She raised her eyebrows in question. *What the heck was going on?*

Jordan shook her head. "I'll tell you more about it later. Honestly, I will. Right now, I just want to hear more about you. How are you feeling? How are you doing? I see you've already got your IV—did it hurt going in?" She made an unpleasant face, scrunching up her nose. "I know how much you hate needles."

And then she quickly changed the subject. "Are you ready for the surgery—to be rid of the unwanted cargo?" She winked, clearly trying to cheer Macy up.

Macy hesitated to answer.

She wasn't sure she wanted to change the subject so quickly, and Jordan was clearly nervous—all over the map, in fact—changing subjects way too rapidly. But *Mutt and Jeff*, as Jordan had so affectionately called them, were looking distinctly out of place, their large, intimidating bodies filling up the tiny cubicle; their deep, even breaths sucking all the oxygen out of the room; and their curious, covert sunglasses making them look like high-strung spies.

She needed to calm this crew.

Restore some normalcy to the room if she could.

"Well," she said, with an airy breath, "you look beautiful as always." Her eyes swept over Jordan's summer dress. "Breezy, stylish, and ready for the day."

The dark-haired male glanced at Jordan, and despite the concealing shades, Macy shivered inside. That look. That heat. That obvious...possession. There was nothing professional—or strictly protective—in that glance.

What. The. Hell. Was. Going. On?

She smiled and patted the side of the bed. "Come. Sit beside me." She giggled. "Hold my hand." She wished she could tell her bestie all about the fine Doctor Parker, but the conversation would have to wait. "Maybe we can watch some TV until it's time for my sleepy meds."

Jordan nodded, seeming relieved by the offer. She strolled across the room, took a seat on the edge of the bed, and grasped Macy's hand, gripping it far too tight for the situation.

Hmm.

As the bodyguards found two chairs and dragged them toward the back of the space, Macy began to feel more and more on edge.

She couldn't pinpoint the reason or identify the origin—her best friend being in danger, notwithstanding—but there was just something almost fatalistic in the room.

A sense of looming dread—or impending doom.

That feeling people get when the hairs on the back of the neck stand up because they sense they're in mortal danger. For lack of a better comparison: the recognition of prey in the presence of a predator.

Macy squeezed Jordan's hand in return.

It was no longer clear who was comforting whom.

⤎

Jordan felt like a total jerk.

Other than a short text here and there, on Saturday, saying "how are you" and "I'm okay," she hadn't been there for Macy over the weekend, and now, she was making matters worse.

What had she been thinking?

Or course, she also knew the drill—what Zane would do eventually.

At some point, before the day was over, probably in Macy's recovery room, he would make some feeble excuse to saunter to the side of her bed, place his hand on the top of her forehead—or remove his shades to reveal his otherworldly, hypnotic eyes—and implant whatever impressions, memories, or story that he chose: Macy would wake up from her surgery forgetting that she had ever seen the Dragyr: Zane and Axe. She would buy—hook, line, and sinker—the story that Jordan had taken a couple weeks off to reboot and recharge, beginning Wednesday, after her jury selection on Tuesday. And then, slowly, over time, Zane would help Jordan explain things to Macy, leaving out anything that was too hard to digest, replacing truth with fantasy when necessary, and filling in the holes with things that Macy would automatically believe—because Zane had told her to believe them.

What kind of friendship was that?

Was it even fair to continue, going forward?

Jordan sighed, feeling the full weight of her fate upon her shoulders, understanding, yet again, just how dire her circumstances were, how desperately she needed to find an out-clause.

Licking her bottom lip, she thought about her cell phone,

tucked safely away in her purse, and prayed that there had been a strong Wi-Fi signal in the hospital parking lot before the three of them had entered the building. She had scripted a text to Dan before they'd left the lair—earlier, while she was still in the bathroom—and she had subsequently placed it on "auto send, then delete" just to be safe.

In other words, as long as her cell was working properly, the message would go through the moment the device came in contact with a signal, and then the text would be promptly erased.

In truth, Dan could be reading the message right now:

Hi there. I know I'm breaking all the rules—the rules I insisted on you keeping. Not only did I send an email on Friday night, but now I'm sending this. The truth is, I need your help, and I don't know anyone else I can turn to. I have jury selection in Judge Stanley's court on Tuesday. Division B-9 at 10 AM. I will be there a half hour early, and I will leave a letter addressed to you with his clerk. Please pick it up before 10 AM, leave the courthouse, then read it—this will give you time to digest the contents and to choose a course of action. Please do NOT do anything while I'm in court. I know this makes no sense right now, but it will. I promise. Oh, and one more thing—AND IT'S VERY IMPORTANT—do not try to contact me before you read the letter. Do not try to find me, speak to me, or approach me in any way! Just pick up the letter, follow my instructions, and everything will be clear.

I know this sounds crazy, but I'm counting on you, Dan.

That's all I can say for now.

J

Chapter Twenty

J ORDAN, ZANE, AND Axe sat outside, beneath the shade of an umbrella, in the Exploratory Medical Center's café, sipping caffeinated drinks, discussing the world of the Dragyr, and waiting for Macy's surgery to be over. It was 9:15 AM; the three of them had been talking for an hour; and now, as a semi-comfortable silence settled between them, Jordan replayed the earlier conversations...

So far, they had touched on three interesting subjects: telepathy, human servants, and how the Dragyr moved in and out of human society without being detected. Obviously, on the first subject—the matter of reading minds—Jordan had listened intently. She had wanted to know where she stood.

After all, during her very first encounter with Zane, when he had taken her blood at the mall, he had been able to read her thoughts...quite directly. And ever since, he'd described them as projections—if they were especially loud, he could hear them—but what about the thoughts that were slightly less...overt?

Needless to say, Jordan desired a more specific explanation—she needed to know how far the dragyri's powers went—could Zane see right through her deception?

Unfortunately, Mr. Saphyrius had chosen to skirt all around the subject—perhaps he didn't want her to know, to grasp *everything* he could do—or perhaps he was hiding a few cards of his own, playing his own careful hand…

Either way, he had only elaborated on the specific powers of ESP, the science behind how it worked, yet during that elaboration, something unrelated—yet interesting—had come up: In a nutshell, Jordan would soon possess the powers of telepathy, herself. She would possess the ability to forge a mutual connection, mind to mind, with any of the immortal Dragyr. The moment her conversion was over, the ability would simply emerge.

The revelation had been unsettling, at best, and she had shifted back and forth in her seat. In fact, every impulse in her body at the time had wanted to get up and run. *Why?* Well, the answer was pretty straightforward: Zane had unwittingly opened the topic of Jordan's *rebirth*…

Being made immortal in the temple.

And that was a topic she'd wanted to keep closed, at least until she was forced to face it.

It was just too horrifying.

Too imminent.

Too incredible…

Too terrible to even imagine.

Not to mention, there was no way she was having that conversation in front of Axe: When and *if* she and Zane discussed that subject, they needed to be alone.

To Axe's credit, the blond-haired dragyri had tried (and failed) to come to her rescue, chiming in about another omniscient power she would also receive post-conversion: the ability to speak and understand all of the world's languages.

Yes, all of them.

He had insisted that the knowledge would just magically appear, the moment she was fully converted. Unfortunately for Axe, he hadn't understood that the topic of conversion was off limits. Just like that, it had happened again—they'd gone back to the subject of *rebirth*. Like the persistent monster in a child's dark closet, it just seemed to hover…and linger…and persist.

Thankfully, the conversation had quickly meandered to the

last two original topics: the presence of human servants in Dragons Domain, and how the Dragyr moved in and out of human society without being easily detected.

Earlier, at breakfast, Jace had made a comment about human cooks and maids, and the reference had left Jordan curious. According to Zane, there was a human sect—a secret religion, of sorts—that served the Temple of Seven. On occasion, some of these servants were brought into The Pantheon and allowed to stay for a time—they served the dragyri in their various lairs; they assisted the gods in the temple; and they played various roles in sacred rites, serving the entire domain. When their time was up, they were simply sent back, escorted to earth through the portal, with the most sensitive—or revealing—memories scrubbed.

And all of it was by consent.

According to Axe, they could help Jordan now with any number of tasks: They could go shopping or banking or run various earthly errands, all on Jordan's behalf. They could retrieve items from her condo—more shoes, more clothes, a computer—and if there was anything she wanted, needed, or simply desired, the humans could procure it for her.

Apparently, the Dragyr had many earthly holdings—houses, hotels, real-estate investments, and businesses of every kind—and the faithful humans served as employees at most of them.

It had been a cornucopia of new information, and Jordan had processed it the best she could—but truth be told, she didn't know how she felt about any of it: the idea of having servants, the idea of the Temple of Seven, or the persistent idea of spending an immortal lifetime with Zane…

Now, as she absently stirred some sugar from the bottom of a glass of iced tea, as she watched the granules float upward, refusing to dissolve in the drink, she noticed that most of the ice had melted, and she fidgeted with her spoon.

"Jordan. *Jordan!*"

She heard her name being called by Zane, as if from a very great distance, and she immediately lifted her head. Both he and

Axe were staring at her like she was from another planet, which, in truth, she kind of was…at least from another dimension.

Had she been zoned out that entire time?

"Yeah," she said. "I'm here. *I'm here.*"

"What were you thinking about, dragyra?" Zane asked.

Jordan shook her head. She glanced at Axe, rather than Zane, who for all intents and purposes looked like he'd rather be any-where else—he must have felt like a loathsome third wheel—and she decided not to answer.

Again, it was all too new, and the information overload was a bit overwhelming.

Before Zane could press her any further, there was a commo-tion in the cafe: Karen Wilson, Macy's mom, carrying a tray full of fruit, muffins, and crackers, and rapidly heading their way. She was calling Jordan in a boisterous tone, and trying to wave one hand without dropping the platter.

"Jordan! Jordan, honey! Oh, there you are." She stumbled up to the table, almost tripping over Axe's leg; slammed the tray down with a clamor, spilling some of her juice; and brushed her hair frenetically out of her eyes. "Whew!" she exclaimed. "I never thought I'd find you." And then, without awaiting a reply, she turned her attention to Zane. "You must be one of Jordan's *very special protectors.*" She gave him a conspiratorial wink. "I popped in to see Macy one last time before they wheeled her into surgery, but you guys were already gone. Just the same, she told me *all* about your terrible…*clandestine*…predicament." She looked inordinately pleased with herself as she shifted her gaze to Axe. "And you, young man: You need to keep your legs forward and under the table. I could have tripped and fallen to my death."

Axe jolted in surprise, his thick upper lip turning up in a scowl, and Jordan closed her eyes and cringed. *Yes, Karen Wilson is eccentric, but please, Lord: Don't let him flash his fangs….* Grateful that she didn't have to explain the dragyris' presence, she spoke in a rather loud tone of her own. "How are you, Karen? It's so nice to see you."

Karen pulled out the last remaining chair, plopped her rear

in the empty seat, and rested both of her elbows on the table like she was utterly exhausted. "Oh, I'm fine, dear, just worried sick about Macy—you know how I get." She leaned back in her chair and brushed some crumbs off her brightly colored blouse. "How are you, Jordan? That's just terrible that someone has caused you so much distress." She eyed Zane and Axe conspicuously, then immediately changed the subject. "But you seem to be doing well in spite of things—my gosh, that's a lovely dress! You look just like a spring flower."

Jordan's heart warmed at the disjointed compliment. "Thank you, Karen. I *am* doing well. Just here to show Macy my support." What else could she say? I've just been abducted by an immortal dragon. I'm scared to death. And you have no idea what—or who—you just interrupted?

Not hardly.

Karen nodded ardently, demonstrating her appreciation for Jordan's support. She took her plate off the tray, tugged it a little closer, and took a long, slow drink of her orange juice. And then she seemed to notice, for the first time, that nobody else was eating. "Oh my, how rude of me," she fussed. "Would you like a muffin, Jordan? I have two—they're banana-nut!"

"Oh, no thank you," Jordan said. "I ate earlier. I'm just having tea."

Karen frowned and glanced around the table, stopping to take a good hard look at Axe and Zane. "What about you boys? You must like banana-nut?"

Jordan laughed involuntarily, the sound coming out as a bark.
You boys?
Oh, man, talk about missing the mark.

Axe drew back his head like a bee had just darted toward his nose, and Zane furrowed his brow into a frown. "No, thank you," Zane mumbled, sounding a tad bit surly. "I'm fine with caffeine."

Karen paid it no mind. "Oh, don't be silly." She waved a dismissive hand, reached for a plastic knife, and promptly cut one of the muffins in half. Then placing each half on a separate, flimsy napkin, she dragged one half in front of Zane, the other in front of

Axe, and harrumphed. "There. A piece for both of you. You need to keep up your strength." She glanced at the mid-morning sun. "And you both need to stay hydrated, as well—you should drink something other than soda."

Jordan laughed again, only this time, she joined in the banter. "You're gonna need more than that," she mocked, repeating Zane's words from breakfast, while pointing at his Coke. The subtle dig gave her infinite satisfaction. And then she had the oddest thought…

What if she just spilled the beans?

Told Karen Wilson everything?

Could her best friend's mother somehow help, create a distraction, or aid in Jordan's rescue? Did she really have to wait on Dan? Why was she sitting there in a public place, with someone she knew—and actually trusted—allowing the whole dystopian scenario to play out, when she could simply cry for help?

Zane emitted a low, almost inaudible growl, the sound coming from deep in his throat, and Jordan started. *I am doing my best not to read your mind, dragyra*—he spoke in her head! *But your emotions—your impulses—are still leaking out. Take caution, angel. This is not a game.*

Jordan sank back in her chair.

What was she thinking?

No, she could not ask for help, and especially not from Macy's mother.

The flighty woman would abruptly freak out; Zane or Axe would take control of her mind; and last, but not least, Jordan would destroy any trust she had built with Zane—she might even lose the privilege to travel back and forth through the portal, albeit escorted by two fearsome beings.

She felt, more than she saw, Zane's deep sapphire eyes scrutinizing her from beneath his dark sunglasses, and a shiver rose up her spine: How would Karen Wilson react to Zane's intense dragon-irises—to sapphire orbs that should have been white? How would Jordan react if she saw them right now, and they were angry, disappointed…or critical?

Discomfited by the question, she reached for her purse, which was sitting on the table, grasped the leather opening in her closed fist, and yanked it onto her lap, leaning over the bag protectively.

Zanaikeyros moved like the wind, so quickly that he seemed like a blur.

He reached for her arm, pulled her out of her chair, and began to lead her away from the table. "Excuse us," he said, ignoring Karen's audible gasp. "We'll be right back."

A few heads turned as Jordan shuffled to keep up with him, but a quick compulsion from Zane made them mind their own business. Jordan glanced over her shoulder to check on Macy's mom—she was afraid of what the woman might do.

There was no need to worry.

Axe had taken off his glasses, and Karen was staring blankly into his black-and-sapphire orbs, her own eyes quickly glazing over from compulsion.

It was just that simple, Jordan thought.

Zane and Axe were just that powerful.

And she was just that screwed…

She yanked her arm free as they came to a halt near a willow tree, shading them from the sun, and she squared her chin at Zane. "What the hell are you doing?" she snapped, feeling her anger rise.

"Forgive me, dragyra; did I harm you?" Despite his intensity, his voice was thick with concern, and his eyes swept over her arm, searching for signs of a bruise.

The sudden shift in tack caught Jordan off guard, and she frowned apologetically. Yes, he looked angry…or perhaps he was worried…but his touch had not been brutal. Zane hadn't marked her skin. "My arm is fine," she said softly. "What is this about?"

Zane took a slow, deep breath and reached for her hand. "What is in your purse, dragyra?"

Jordan pulled her hand away. "What?"

The tip of his nose twitched in annoyance. "You heard me. What is in that purse?"

"I already told you, the map, a page from the atlas—"

"No," Zane argued. "You lied."

His words landed like a ton of bricks—it didn't matter that they were true—Jordan felt insulted, cornered, and disrespected. "How dare you," she whispered, her own nostrils beginning to flare. "After everything you have put me through."

Zanaikeyros shook his head and removed his sunglasses, allowing her to see his eyes. "You misunderstand my words, my angel. I did not say that *you* are a liar—I have seen your soul, and you are not—but you have chosen to deceive me in this matter because you feel as if you must. And I have done my level best not to invade your mind, not to search your purse, not to push the issue…at least this once. But even with that effort, I already know that you are planning something…reaching out to someone…hoping to escape our fate. And I would be remiss to let it go. What's in your purse, dragyra? Who did you text on your phone?"

Jordan swallowed her fear and held Zane's gaze.

Fine, he wanted the truth?

He was all about honesty?

Then she would give him some truth of her own.

"Unless you force me, I am not going to tell you. Unless you read my mind, you are not going to know." She pushed through her dread and gathered more courage. "You are doing what you have to, Zane, and so am I—why is that so hard to understand? Why can't you allow me one simple dignity? Did you really think I would just come with you, follow you into a whole new world—go along to get along—and never once complain or fight back? Did you really think you could take me from my life and insert me into yours?" She crossed her arms over her middle. "I don't want this, Zanaikeyros. I'm sorry, but I don't want you. I want to go back to my life as I've always known it, and I will try anything…do anything…say whatever I have to in order to make that happen. So yes, I lied to you."

The hurt in his eyes was visceral, but to his credit, he didn't lash out. Rather, he continued to stare at her, circumspectly, his own shadowy pupils scanning left and right as he peered deeper…and deeper…into her soul. When he finally uttered a reply, his voice sounded hoarse, like broken glass. "I do understand, dragyra," he slowly bit out. "And I care more than you will ever know about how all of this affects you, how you feel, and what you want. And I would do anything to shoulder this burden for you, to make the change and the adjustment easier, but I cannot." He took a small step back, and his countenance softened. "I will not destroy your dignity, Jordan. I will not rifle through your purse. And I will not steal your phone. But understand me clearly when I say this to you: *I will never let you go.* You are mine now, my dragyra, and the world you once knew is no more. If you bring other humans into this, they may get hurt. I am not a human male—my dragon is not merciful—and I will fight to the death for what is mine. Decide not rashly, my angel. You are playing a very, very dangerous game."

Jordan gulped and took an unwitting step back of her own.

She nodded her head in understanding and held his discomforting stare. "Very well," she whispered. "Is there anything else?"

He snickered and shook his head in disappointment. And then he raised his hand, caressed her jaw with the backs of his finger, and then traced her lower lip with the pad of his thumb—oddly enough, it almost felt like he was testing her mettle, appraising her inner strength. "So brave. So defiant. So beautiful." He sighed. "Just one more thing."

Jordan raised her brows.

"I would also die to protect you, Jordan, just as I will live for you, now…and all the days of my life. And if you'll let me—someday, somehow—I promise, I will love you forever."

Despite her stubborn, iron will, Jordan staggered to the side, and she had to steady her balance: both physically and emotionally.

She was still reeling from his confession—he'd known what she was up to all along—and she was stunned by his dragon's threat. This male absolutely believed she *belonged* to him, and he'd meant every word he'd said: He would never let her go.

And now…now…she was also spinning from his surprising pledge of affection, his promise to love her forever. By all that was holy, the dragyri was impossible to gauge.

He was fearsome, dominant, and tender…all at the same time.

He was terrifying, beautiful, and savage…all at once.

But most of all, he was telling the truth.

It was written all over his face.

Jordan licked her bottom lip—it suddenly felt dry—and she slowly sauntered past him. "Karen and Axe are waiting."

Chapter Twenty-one

D R. KYLE PARKER tightened his grip around the heavy base of the elegant flower arrangement as he entered Macy's recovery room. His patient had come through the surgery with ease; he had managed to remove the entire mass, and as expected, the growth was benign. In addition, Macy had come out of the anesthesia quickly, her vital signs were good, and she had already had a small cup of cranberry juice and a cracker.

Model patient in every way.

Routine surgery, and all went well.

Now, he had to make the most of his good fortune: the fact that the flower shop had delivered the arrangement to the main post-op desk, and he had an opportunity to deliver it himself. As the door to the recovery room swung closed behind him, he headed to the nearest counter, set down the vase, and turned his back on his patient so he could reach into his lab coat pocket, retrieve the ruby-and-gold beetle—strange how the item had just appeared on his nightstand that morning; he had no memory of buying it, but he must have—and clip it to the stem by the card.

Get well soon, beautiful ~ Dr. P.

That was all the card said, and yes, it was definitely crossing a line, but the surgeon didn't care. He wanted to make intimate inroads with Macy Wilson, and the urge—the need to make it happen—was like a hunger he could not resist. He spun around, feeling a bit uneasy, and reached for her chart, even as she eyed the flowers hesitantly.

"Are those for me?" she asked, with a croak in her voice, probably a result of the anesthesia.

"They are," Dr. Parker answered in his usual professional voice.

Macy's face lit up as she stared at the opulent arrangement of pale green-and-violet lilies, purple-and-white roses, and gorgeous scatterings of baby's breath. "Must have been my mom," she commented. "Wow. I can't believe she did that."

Dr. Parker flashed a wickedly sexy grin, set down the chart, then picked up the flowers. He brought them to the side of the bed and lowered them so she could read the card.

"Thank you," she said, sounding more than a little embarrassed by his blatant attention. She reached for the card and read it; then her jaw dropped open. Her eyes grew wide with astonishment, and her face flushed a bright shade of red. She shifted nervously in the bed. "From you?"

He nodded.

Her tongue snaked out to lick her lips. "W…Why?"

He smiled at her again, only this time it was warm and inviting. "Because you are my favorite patient, and I want you to get well soon."

She lowered her gaze into her lap, like a teenager, hiding her blush, and tucked a lock of hair behind her ears. "I don't know what to say." She read the card a second time and literally squirmed in the bed.

Good.

This was excellent.

The woman was very interested—her conquest would be easy.

And then she saw the pin and gasped. "What is this?"

"Take a look," he said, lowering the arrangement even further.

She plucked the jeweled beetle off the stem and placed it in the palm of her hand, studying it carefully. "Is this…is this real?"

"The gold?" he said. "The rubies? Yes, dear, they are."

She shook her head in confusion. "I...I don't know what to say. I mean...why would you do this? Really?"

Well, she had just thrown the door wide open, and Dr. Parker had every intention of walking through it. "I think you know," he said in a rich, deep voice as he held her stare, intently, with his own.

Macy gulped. "I...I..." She blushed again. "Thank you."

He nodded as if it were no big deal, placed the flowers on the bedside table, and then returned to the edge of the bed. "Can I call you sometime, Macy? Not as your doctor, but as your friend?" The corner of his mouth turned up in what he knew was a wolfish grin.

She seemed to have trouble breathing, and once again, she smoothed her hair. "I'd like that," she whispered, hardly able to conceal her delight.

He stepped forward, removed the beetle from her palm, and placed it back on the stem; and then he took her hand in his and squeezed it, in a slow, gentle caress. "You'll be hearing from me soon," he said softly. "Very soon." And then he gestured toward her chart. "As you know, everything went well with your surgery; you should be a hundred percent in no time, and the tumor should not return. So I think that aspect of our relationship is over." He gestured toward the flower arrangement, bent forward to tap the head of the beetle, and winked. "But here's to new beginnings."

Macy couldn't speak.

She was positively dumbstruck.

And that was just fine with Dr. Parker—no point in pushing it too far. He gave her a professional nod and sauntered out of the room.

Mission accomplished.

◈

Salem Thorne waited and waited...and waited.

For Jordan Anderson to enter Macy's room.

Dr. Parker had already done his part, and now it was up to Salem to find a way into the dragyra's purse.

When the human female finally made an appearance, the beetle was positively stunned: She walked in with two dragyri mercenaries, and one was a Genesis Son! His father's scent was all over him, seeping from his pores, practically oozing from his DNA.

So *this* was Zanaikeyros Saphyrius, the sapphire dragon's offspring.

It was remarkable to see him in person, and for a moment, Salem had to collect his wits—every impulse in his demon heart wanted to shift, right then and there, take on the immortal dragyri, and slaughter him in Macy's room.

He could hardly contain the desire to attack.

But—and it was a very important *but*—he couldn't be that foolish.

He needed to remain steady…and calm. He needed to bide his time: A son of a dragon was not an easy creature to destroy, and the fact that Zanaikeyros had a second warrior with him made the odds nearly slim to none. The three of them would wreak havoc in the human hospital, draw a host of unwanted attention, and in the end, Salem Thorne would be mincemeat, a ground-up patty of demon sludge. The dual Dragyr were too formidable to approach… just yet.

So he observed the trio instead.

He crawled down the stem in the flower arrangement, perhaps a centimeter or two, careful to remain undetected, and he watched as the human female hugged her friend and asked a host of irritating questions: *How are you? How do you feel? What did the doctor say about the tumor?*

Blah, blah, blah.

Did anybody care?

He made careful note of the tension in the dragyra's shoulders and the metaphorical elephant in the middle of the room: There was something almost palpable coursing back and forth between Jordan, the conquest, and Zane, the conqueror, something Salem couldn't quite place.

Anger?

Distrust?

Pent-up carnal energy?

What was going on between those two?

If defensiveness and possession were a cologne, then Zanaikeyros Saphyrius had drenched himself in half a bottle earlier that morning. Alternatively, if fear, apprehension, and edginess were a perfume, then Jordan Anderson was wearing the entire flask.

Yet…

There was something else in the air.

Something pervasive and undeniable.

Pheromones?

Erotic tension?

An undeniable attraction between the two!

They were drawn to each other like moths to a flame, no doubt as a result of their *fated* hearts, and the spark beneath the flame was highly combustible, ready to flare at the slightest provocation.

Hmm.

How very interesting.

So Jordan thought she hated Zane and was resisting all his advances, even as her soul was seeking his. And Zane was responding like an instinctual animal, the primal beast that he was—he was marking her, dominating their interaction, and corralling her like a hunter.

No matter.

The love story was their personal problem.

Defeating the enemy, spying on the same, and getting a foothold inside Dragons Domain was Salem's primary—and only—goal.

Jordan took a seat on the side of Macy's bed, forcing her friend to scoot over, and Salem saw his chance: He knew his body was beginning to glow, and he tried to tamp it down as he sent impulse after impulse directly into Macy's brain, targeting the firing neurons: *Get Jordan's purse. Set it next to your flowers. Turn the front pocket facing the ruby pendant. Do it quickly. Do it now.*

"Oh, my gosh, is that a new purse?" Macy asked Jordan.

Yes! Salem thought.

Jordan glanced at her handbag, and once again, a strange, unidentifiable energy sparked between the female and Zane. "No,"

Jordan said, shrugging one shoulder. "You've seen this bag a thousand times."

Macy crinkled her brow. "No I haven't!" she insisted. "I swear that's new. It's gorgeous. Let me see it."

Jordan giggled at Macy's enthusiasm, and handed her the purse. "Same ole bag," she said as Macy held it up and admired the attractive, soft leather. She played with a zipper or two, appeared to count the pockets, and then turned up her lip in a frown. "I guess you're right," she said. "Hmm. It just looked different to me for some reason." And then she set it down on the bedside table, with the lower leather pocket open and facing the pin.

Good girl, Macy, Salem said in his head.

Jordan eyed the pocketbook sideways, as if she was about to grab it and take it back, and Salem sent a subtle but undeniable fog into the room to distract her: It wasn't anything visible, and it wasn't strong enough to qualify as a compulsion—nothing like what he had just done with Macy, which was more personal—lest one of the Dragyr sense the errant energy they were also exposed to and respond.

Zane's spine stiffened.

The second male glanced around the room.

And Jordan forgot about the purse.

So they had all felt something, but no one had made a move toward the bag.

Salem didn't waste any time.

He crawled across the table, as slowly as he could, and creeped his way up Jordan's purse, ducking quickly into the stiff front pocket.

Done and done.

"When will I see you again?" he heard Macy ask.

Jordan paused for a bit—maybe she was giving her friend a hug—and then her voice turned noticeably hollow. "I can't say for sure, Mace. I still have jury selection on Tuesday, but I'm going to have to lie low for a while, just until the…threat…is sorted out."

Macy groaned like she was pouting. "Whoever it is that's after you? The reason for your bodyguards?"

Jordan chuckled insincerely, and Salem knew she was trying to appease her friend. "I wouldn't go that far," she said. "I wouldn't say that someone's actually after me, just that I need to play it safe. It's…it's a threat, and we need to take it seriously. But honestly, I'm fine."

Macy lowered her voice and murmured, "And so are *they*." She was obviously referring to the Dragyr. "You lucky, lucky girl. I've never seen anything like them. Holy…*shit*."

Jordan didn't answer, so maybe she just shrugged, winked, or smiled—who knew? But it sounded like Macy leaned in closer. "Well, call me when you can. I have to tell you all about my doc-tor—Kyle Parker—the hottie that did my surgery. He also gave me those flowers."

Macy probably glanced at the opulent bouquet because Jordan lowered her voice. "I saw them," she whispered in collusion, "but I didn't want to ask anything personal in front of the men." Whatever signals or winks they exchanged, Macy didn't press the issue of the flowers—*thank the pagan king*. "Just so you know," she murmured, "he asked me out on a date—well, he asked if he could call. I think he's got it bad…for me." She giggled conspiratorially, and Jordan asked her something in return, but at that point, Salem was no longer listening.

He was burrowing into the farthest recesses of Jordan's purse, the dark, lowest corner of the front pocket, and making himself as still as the night.

He would reawaken his senses soon…

From the Sapphire Lair in Dragons Domain.

Oh, great pagans of darkness, Lord Drakkar would be so pleased.

Chapter Twenty-two

LATER THAT NIGHT, in Dragons Domain, Zane took Jordan on a walk beneath the waterfall. The tension between them had been ebbing and flowing all day, and he wanted to offer her a retreat, a way to relax and let go...a place where she might feel comfortable, or at least a little more at home.

Lords knew he was at his wits' end.

The permeating roar of the water drowned out most of his thoughts as he led her along a narrow, rocky trail behind the falls, to a beautiful ledge where they could look out at the cliffs. Taking a seat on a smooth, naturally polished stone, he patted the shelf beside him. "Here," he said softly, "sit."

Jordan hesitated for a moment before taking the seat. She absently reached behind her neck, gathered her long, auburn hair into a cluster, and twisted it into a loose knot, apparently to avoid the splash.

"It's beautiful, no?" he said.

She nodded. "It is." And then she shivered.

"Are you cold?" He reached out to feel the top of her arm—he was capable of raising her temperature with his touch if needed.

"No," she muttered. "I'm fine, just..." Her voice trailed off.

"Just what?" he asked.

Her body tensed. "Just still a little off balance."

He nodded, demonstrating his understanding. Of course, she was a little off balance—who wouldn't be? "About earlier, our conversation—"

"No," she interrupted, holding up her hand to stop him. "There's no need to revisit it. You said what you meant, and so did I." She let her head fall back, stretching, as if she were releasing some tension in her neck, and then she folded her hands in her lap. "Tell me about the temple, Zane. It's eating me alive. Not knowing, that is."

Zane let out a slow, exhausted breath. So much for making things better, for getting his dragyra to relax. "We have time, Jordan," he said in a muted tone. "Not a lot, but we have time."

"We have six days," she amended. "Don't you think I ought to know before then?"

He sat quietly, pondering her words. Of course she had every right to know. That really wasn't the issue. The problem was the scope of the matter, the ferocity of the dragon lords, the reality of what conversion meant.

"I'm not..." He swept his hand through his partially dampened hair and forced himself to start again. "I'm not sure how to tell you, how to describe it. I've never done this before." He flashed a crooked grin and a hopeful glance. "You're my first—and last—dragyra, you know."

Jordan met his gaze, and her stunning hazel eyes flickered with a dim light of compassion. Still, she stuck to her guns. "What do you mean by *rebirth*? Is that...is it literal?" She visibly cringed.

He looked off into the distance, staring beyond the falls at the highland terrain before them, noting how all the trees were sprouting new leaves, how all the flowers were in full bloom, how the very soil around them seemed to pulse with new life. "It is." There was no point in mincing words.

She took a sharp, stuttered breath and exhaled slowly. "I see." She swallowed hard and raised her chin. "Am I going to be...going to be...do you have to kill me, Zane?"

He virtually recoiled at the word, drawing back in surprise. "No!" he insisted. "I mean, nothing that sadistic."

She blinked several times as if she couldn't comprehend his answer. "Then how am I supposed to be *reborn* if I don't first have to die?"

Zane clenched both hands into fists—there was simply no subtle or easy way around this. He stood up, paced around the semi-dark space, and then turned to face her directly, dropping to his knees at her feet. "Jordan…" He took both of her hands in his and tightened his grip, lest she pull them away as usual. "The *rebirth* is as much symbolic as it is literal." He knew he looked anguished, if not desperate—hell, he felt like a fish out of water. *Blessed Pantheon*, he was lying to her when she'd asked for the truth. He shut his eyes, gathered his courage, and started to explain it again. "Your death—as you put it—will be to a mortal body: to sickness, to frailty, to your strictly human decline. Your *rebirth* will be to immortality, to the Dragons Pantheon, to newfound wisdom and many of the powers that come with that enlightenment. It happens in a moment, in the blink of an eye…once the flames are extinguished."

Jordan jolted. Her back stiffened, she sat upright, and her complexion turned a sickly shade of green. "*Once the flames are extinguished?* What *flames*, Zane?"

He closed his eyes again, and this time he kept them shut. "In the Temple of Seven, there's a dais that faces the seven thrones of the dragon lords. You will be adorned in a beautiful gown, just like any wedding, and asked to kneel on the dais. I'll be right there with you." He rushed those last six words. "I will wrap my body around yours. Yes, the dragons will cleanse-away your human origins with mystical fire, *but*"—he placed a heavy emphasis on the word—"but I will be there to absorb the majority of the flames, the majority of the pain."

He swallowed hard, opened his eyes, and commanded her gaze with his own. "Jordan, the cleansing portion of the ceremony takes about thirty seconds, during which time, your mortality will…come to an end. But immediately after that happens, within seconds—an instant, really—the lords will gather their cumulative healing and transformational power, a silver-blue fire that soothes, repairs, and reforms, and reanimate you as their own... an immortal dragyra." Before she could reply or, worse, pass out, he pushed ahead, still holding her gaze. "Again, it will take about thirty seconds for the reanimation, and you will be made whole: perfect, without blemish, without illness, without vulnerability like you had before. The transformation will be over, and you will be reborn."

He left out the fact that the entire *rebirth* would begin with orange-and-red fire, and that it would hurt like a bitch—for him—his skin would blister, and his bones would start to melt from the effort it would require to shield her from the worst of the flames. And yes, she would feel a brief moment of agony, too—but only a flash—and then the flames would turn silver as the gods began to sanitize and cleanse her soul, finally becoming silver-blue in the final act of restoration.

When she spoke next, she was trembling so hard that her teeth chattered in her mouth. "W...w...which of the seven gods is going to do this to me...t...to us?" She bit down hard and forced herself to speak more calmly. "Breathe fire over the dais, that is? Will it be Lord Saphyrius?"

Zane shook his head. "All seven," he whispered. "The Pantheon must act as one."

In an instant so terrifying Zane would never forget it, Jordan yanked her hands out of his, stood up like she was perfectly calm, and sidestepped around him. She took three quick steps toward the rushing falls, and then, without preamble or hesitation, she leaped off the ledge, throwing her very mortal body into the roaring cascade.

Zane gasped in shock and horror.

And then he flew into action.

Moving with all the supernatural speed of his kind, he called upon his primordial dragon. Huge sapphire-and-chestnut-brown wings shot forth from his back, and he dived into the turbulent water.

He must have been going a hundred miles per hour as he sped downward, desperate to get beneath his dragyra; shot back up through the thick of the falls; and latched both arms tightly around her waist. He flew back through the torrent, into the crevice, and dragged her to the back of the ravine.

His heart was pounding in his chest.

His breaths were coming in ragged gasps.

And his own broad, muscular shoulders were trembling with shock.

"Are you insane?" he rasped, cradling her head against his chest and holding her even tighter. "By all the gods, Jordan—what were you thinking?"

She couldn't answer.

She didn't even try.

She simply began to sob into his chest, like a child coming apart, her streaming tears blending seamlessly into the cold, drenching water.

Zane didn't try to stop her.

She needed to let it out.

She needed to release all that terror and angst, and he had been unforgivably remiss to underestimate the depth of her pain. Of her horror. *Dear gods of The Pantheon, he had almost lost her.*

"I swear to you, Jordan," he breathed huskily in her ear, even as he retracted his wings, "I will be there with you...every step of the way...every second of the *rebirth*. And I *will* shield you from all that I can. The worst of it will only last for a moment. Angel," he beseeched her, "I'm terrified, too. I will be the one who is burned by the fire; I will be the one who feels all the pain, all the heat, whose body is scorched and blistered. I will be the one who endures all thirty seconds...for you...for us. And I swear on the sacred stone of my maker that I will not fail you in that task. I will shield you, Jordan. On my honor as a dragyri, I swear it."

She continued to cry for what seemed like an eternity, her body too limp to hold itself up, and then she slowly found her footing and pulled away.

There was no way—no way—he was letting her go. He grasped both wrists in an iron clasp and searched her eyes for proof of lucidity.

She cleared her throat with a hollow sound. "How bad will it get, Zane, for me?"

He searched his heart for the truest answer. "By the time that moment comes, the final three seconds before…expiration: It will pass so quickly it will hardly be felt or remembered."

She shook her head and tried again. "How bad?"

"You will feel it, love, for just that instant."

She nodded faintly, as if coming to terms with the truth. "And the rest? The other fifty-seven seconds?"

Zane sighed in relief. *This*, at least, he could tell her without cringing. "I have been told by other dragyra that the first twenty-seven seconds are uncomfortable and frightening. It is not unusual for a female to panic—it's loud, it's powerful, it's consuming. But not because of any pain. The next three seconds, when the fire is the hottest, when some of it breaks through, it is as I have told you, but it passes very quickly. And then, when the healing begins, during the last thirty seconds, it's supposed to feel like a cooling balm, one of the most pleasurable sensations you have ever felt—soothing, empowering, invigorating." He chuckled, albeit weak and insincerely. "Believe it or not, I have been told that the ecstasy, the euphoria of those last thirty seconds is so intense, so divine, that if it were a drug, we could sell it at a premium. The temporary… discomfort…is worth the sacrifice just to experience the indescribable high." His voice thickened with the intensity of his conviction. "I wouldn't lie to you, Jordan. That is what I've been told, and there has never been an exception."

She peeked at him through tear-drenched lashes, and her beautiful eyes looked pained, but alert. And then her eyebrows furrowed. "Does the healing fire, the last thirty seconds, restore you, too? Or will you continue to suffer?"

Zane drew back in surprise, his mouth growing suddenly dry. "I…I'll be fine, angel." He tried again. "The silver-blue fire will heal me, too—I will not continue to suffer." He was stunned that she had even considered his suffering.

She nodded slowly, and then she sighed. "So, basically, I really shouldn't tick you off between now and then, should I?"

He knew it was her feeble attempt at a joke, a way to try to ease the tension, albeit dismal, but it wasn't funny—not in the least. "Don't even think like that," he admonished her. "There is nothing—*absolutely nothing*—you could ever say or do that would make me withdraw my protection from you. I would be less than a male, less than a dragyri—I would be unworthy to draw another breath..." His voice trailed off, and he had to take a moment to subdue his inner fire. "I will shield you, angel. Of that you can be sure. I am not a virgin to the ways of the gods, to the Temple of Seven, or to the scourge of fire. I have served and protected The Pantheon for a thousand years. And now...I also serve you."

This time, it was Jordan who drew back in surprise, her soft hazel eyes growing dark with intensity: Had something he said finally broken through?

Zanaikeyros held his breath.

She stared at him acutely, like she was scrutinizing his face, like she had never laid eyes on him before. Her gaze swept over his brow, then down the straight ridge of his nose, and back and forth across the high, rugged angles and deep, furrowed planes of his cheekbones. And then she studied his mouth—was she searching for a hint of bestial fangs, or somehow measuring his sincerity?

Her mouth parted in the barest hint of a cautious smile, and Zane's heart slammed in his chest. "I'm sorry," she whispered faintly. "That I jumped into the falls, and that you have to endure so much agony...on my behalf. I know this is awful for you, too."

Her words were plainly...staggering.

Heartfelt.

Compassionate.

And so unexpected.

In the midst of her terror and forced captivity, she had stopped to think of him.

Zane cupped her face with exquisite gentleness, staring into her eyes. "I said it earlier, and I meant it then: I would move heaven and earth for you, Jordan. As much as you are mine, I am yours. We are truly in this together, and I won't let you down."

She shivered, and in that instant, Zane knew that his words

had struck a chord. She was hearing him now—*listening*—turning the meaning of his declarations over in her head. She was seeing him as the warrior he was, and gods be merciful, just perhaps, she was seeing him as a male.

His gaze dropped down to her mouth, to the soft, full lips that were still shivering, ever so slightly, with angst; and he knew he had to seize this moment.

The timing was wrong, the impulse was wild and erratic, and Jordan was anything but...ready. Yet and still, she was standing there, so close to his heart, so vulnerable, exposed, and raw. His dragon could do no less than try to comfort her. Try to show her. Reach to slowly...carefully...claim her.

He bent his head, so slowly that it almost seemed like an illusion, and then he breathed her name as his lips found hers and met them with a seal: soft, pliant, gentle as a lamb. He slowly drew her in, coaxing with tenderness, entreating with kindness, inviting with a wisp of smoke and fire.

She froze, refusing to kiss him back, but declining to push him away, and that's when he deepened the kiss, taunting her mouth with his tongue...then his teeth: just a gentle nudge, a casual swipe, a barely discernable nip.

Her mouth opened, and she kissed him back: not thinking, not resisting, not fighting for position. Just being in the moment with him.

Zane led her beyond the waterfall, beyond her fear, beyond her fragile caution, deep into the pleasure of a dragyri's passion—letting her taste the fire on his tongue—and then he pulled back, slowly—oh, so carefully—allowing the moment to linger.

There were times when words were inadequate, and this was one of those moments.

There was no need to *think* it, turn it over in their heads, analyze some far-reaching meaning. There was only the lingering sensation of their sweet exchange and the beginnings of a deeper connection.

Thank you, my dragyra, he spoke inside her mind, and then he rested his forehead against hers, and the two of them embraced the inner stillness, inside the underbelly of the churning falls, together.

❧

Salem Thorne backed deeper into the crevice of the damp, cavernous ledge as Zane and Jordan kissed. Well, he thought, with more than just a little disgust, that was not how he would have handled it.

Helpless maiden…

Captured, and alone…

There was nothing she could do, and nowhere she could go…

Shit, she'd be on her back, lying in the dirt, and her thighs would be wrapped around his hips, whether she wanted them there or not—to hell with whether she ever came around or got over it.

He thought about the stupid, dramatic scene that had preceded the short episode of intimacy, and he snickered. The dumb wench had actually thrown herself over the falls, ready to take a long, dangerous plunge to her death, and Zane had come to her rescue, like some sort of reptilian, comic-book superhero.

Wasn't that just quaint.

It had taken every ounce of self-control that Salem possessed not to shift into demon form and ambush them both when they returned to the ledge. He most certainly would have had the advantage of surprise.

But—and this was a point he would do well not to forget—he was traveling in the elusive Dragons Domain now, and Zane was one telepathic shout, one clairvoyant broadcast, away from seven formidable lairs inhabited by dozens of savage Dragyr. Salem could not elude them, outlast them, or best them in a battle, not in their own terrain.

Not as one against so many.

No, he had to play it smart.

Choose his enemy—choose his war—and strike when the iron was hot.

So far, he had made no mistakes: He had crawled out of

Jordan's purse the moment they'd arrived through the portal, hidden behind a nearby rock, and waited to watch…and follow.

At a very intelligent—and safe—distance.

He had not made any noise, and he had not caused a commotion. He had no intentions of being stupid, or suicidal. And as he'd ticked off his options, one by one—how to make the most of this fortuitous situation—a few things had become immediately clear: No matter how long he hid, in waiting, in the back of a sacred lair, he would not be able to take a dragyri out—he would not get a clean shot at a Genesis Son.

He would not get his demonic claws on Zane.

Everything in this cursed realm was so obviously interconnected: The sounds were interwoven with the sights—waves of visible energy danced through a braided tapestry, all matter waltzing as one—and even the oxygen dovetailed with the geography, everything pulsing in sync.

In perfect harmony.

Hells glorious minions, even the silence was a symphony of sorts—a dozen particles of electromagnetic energy all projecting their intrinsic, quantum thoughts, like a community of ESP: One dark, disharmonious vibration from him, and the entire Garden of Eden might ignite.

It was the weirdest thing he'd ever seen.

And without knowing how he knew, he was absolutely certain that everything—absolutely all of it—emanated from the Temple of Seven. So yeah, that was the last thing he intended to do: broadcast his presence to seven dragon gods who could take him out with a wink and a nod.

If Salem Thorne hoped to remain undetected, he had to watch his P's and Q's very, *very* carefully. His immediate efforts would be better spent recording his various impressions, taking some mental images, and broadcasting all of it back to the Pagan Underworld, sharing it with Lord Drakkar.

But in time—and oh, there would come a time—he would have an opportunity to make his move…

He chuckled inside, thinking about his dumb, demon luck,

how Jordan Anderson had just given him the eventual solution. Of course he couldn't confront—and defeat—a powerful, immortal dragyri, and of course, he had no intentions of alerting—and confronting—the gods.

But then he didn't have to, did he?

Not in order to take Zane out.

All he had to do was confront—and destroy—one helpless human female.

Taking out Jordan would have the same effect, as Lord Saphyrius would be forced to remove Zane's amulet.

If Salem could only exercise patience, continue to follow Zane and Jordan around, he would only need a second, an instant, to strike—one opportune moment to shift into demon form and seize the female's heart. She would be no match for his cunning. Her death would be instant. And Zane...well, his goose would be cooked. And that, as they say, would be that.

Point. Set. And match.

Salem Thorne slinked further into the shadows, sickened by the ongoing display of intimacy before him, the ludicrous vulnerability taking place beneath the falls. *Enjoy it while you can, Zanaikeyros,* he thought. *This piteous moment of endearment will soon be your last.*

Chapter Twenty-three

LATER THAT NIGHT, as Jordan got dressed for bed in Zane's modern, luxurious bathroom, she thought about the letter she had written to Dan—the letter she would pass to him through Judge Stanley's clerk tomorrow—and she thought about that kiss.

That sweet, sensuous, skillful kiss.

That primal, perfect, pleasurable…kiss.

The steam from her recent shower filled the space with warmth, and she sighed: Truly, Zane Saphyrius had a raging, deeply rooted fire burning just beneath the surface, and not because he was an immortal dragyri—but because his passion was intrinsic, his hunger was essential, and his primal desire was so deeply ingrained.

Jordan had felt that kiss all the way down to her toes, and it still made her weak in the knees, over three hours later.

She stepped into her nightgown, pulled it up to her shoulders, and then rubbed the palm of her hand in a circle over the massive antique-framed mirror in order to clear the fog. She took a step back, regarded her reflection, and cringed: Her eyes looked markedly tired—the orbits beneath her lower lashes seemed hollow, plus her lids seemed heavy—and her overall complexion was as pale as the dragon moon. She stared into her weary, elusive gaze and tried to search her soul: What should she do?

What should she do?

Should she tear up the letter she had written to Dan and just try—somehow, someway—to accept her fate, or should she fight for all she was worth? Time was running out—she might not have another opportunity—and she honestly didn't know which course of action made the most sense. On one hand, if she chose to fight on and resist, the odds were against her—she would be placing Dan, and anyone he recruited, in grave danger, exposing them to a deadly predator; and she would never forgive herself if someone got hurt.

Or worse…

But on the other hand, she had always done it alone: struggled alone, triumphed alone, survived alone. And she wasn't quite ready to give that up. She wasn't ready to be a dragon's consort—or whatever the term for it was.

She took a slow, deep breath and tried to recall the letter, word for word, in her mind:

Dear Dan,

I know I have insisted on maintaining silence between us, so this must come as a surprise, but I'm in trouble. Real trouble. And I desperately need your help…

Unfortunately, you will need to trust me implicitly in order to figure this out. I can only hope that you still have faith in me, that you remember my sanity—know I've never been crazy—and you still care enough to act swiftly, definitely, and on my behalf. Since there's no easy way to say this, I will just jump in with the truth: Last week, I was confronted by a man who is very powerful and connected. Without getting into too many details, he took me from my apartment, brought me into his world, and I have been "with" him ever since. He has no intentions of letting me go, and I have no clear avenue of escape. Yes, he has allowed me to show up at work and other places, but he is always close at hand, watching me…guarding me. Making sure I don't escape.

God, this sounds crazy, even to me, but it's true.

And here's the thing: You cannot confront this guy on your own; there's no way you will win. Believe me—nothing is as it seems. He has the power to obliterate you and everyone around you in the space of a heartbeat. (Think about confronting a trained assassin who possesses a hidden gun, or a bomb. Think about the entire room, or building, being wired to detonate if he goes down. Then think about all the people around you, who look like they're not involved, being there as his backup. THEN TIMES THAT BY TEN. And that is what you are up against. What I am up against.) Anything less than a full-scale intervention— quick, targeted, and efficient—will fail. And if you are foolish enough to dismiss my warning, or to shrug off my analogy as overly dramatic, then you will die. And so will many others.

I chose to contact you, rather than someone else, because you are the only person I know who a) might believe me, and b) might be capable of putting a tactical team together to get me out of this mess. Dan, do not confront him. Do not go for the arrest. Just. Get. ME. Out. And remove me to a safe, protected location…without looking back.

Only me.

Anything else will be suicide.

You have about two hours, maybe three at the most, before my jury selection concludes, and then it will be too late. Resist the urge to act impulsively, to try to see his face, or to come back into the courthouse and confront him. Curiosity is not your friend.

Time is ticking, Dan.

Please trust me…please believe me…please help me.

Jordan

Jordan shivered at the sheer intensity of the note, wondering what Dan would do. Every instinct in his body would want to rush in and save her immediately, identify and confront Zane right there on the spot, but hopefully, he would heed her warning.

She knew Zane and Axe—or whoever he brought with them tomorrow—could easily overpower a building full of humans, manipulate their minds, make child's play of any human weapons, but—and she was really counting on this exception—it would take a lot of time and attention to control something as organic and crowded as a busy courthouse, all the way down to the bailiffs, security guards, and armed officials at the front doors. Jordan was betting on the fact that the Dragyr also preferred to lie low, to remain undetected—they didn't care to be on the nightly human news, destroying a seven-story building.

Bottom line: They couldn't be in all places, in all the courtrooms, and on all the floors of the District Plaza at once.

She sighed, feeling curiously small and ashamed: It was a truly shitty thing to do, and it made her furious that she might feel guilty, even for a moment, about choosing to fight for her life. Just the same, she had seen the sincerity deep in Zane's eyes; she had felt his terror when she had leaped over the falls; and she had tasted his longing...for her...in his kiss. And she knew, perhaps for the first time since she'd met him, that this wasn't a game; it wasn't an act; and the stakes were incredibly high. But she couldn't think about that now—all the things that Zane had told her—not only about the conversion, but how irreversible it was.

If she entered that temple on Sunday, there would be no turning back.

She shuddered and reached for a thick terrycloth robe hanging on an ornate sapphire hook by the bathroom door. And then she shrugged into the garment, tightened the belt around her waist, and raised the collar to her chin in an effort to conceal her neck.

Truly, it was like she was hiding...

From Zane.

And from herself.

From what she knew she was capable of doing—whatever it took to win her freedom.

✦

Zane drew back the covers and waited—practically holding his breath—as Jordan came out of the bathroom, padded across the floor, and made her way toward the large wood-and-iron bed.

The energy that had been coming from that bathroom was distressing, unnerving, and alarming at best, and he didn't know how she would react to the fact that he was lying in the bed, waiting to greet her, that he had no intentions of spending another night in an armchair that reclined, no matter how comfortable the cushions.

Not to get it twisted: He knew better than to make a move on Jordan, to try to take their connection to another level, physically—she wasn't ready, and that was putting it mildly—and he certainly had no intentions of trying to *feed*, to reanimate his fire, though the impulse when he was around her was all-consuming. Just the same, he also knew that his presence, being next to her, was more imperative than ever.

His dragyra was frightened.

She felt alone.

And she was struggling with a major, heavy decision....

More than likely, it had everything to do with what was hidden in her purse, and he was taking a major risk by not following through, taking control of the situation before it got out of hand. But in the end, he wanted her to keep her dignity—he wanted to gain her trust. And right now, he wanted her to feel his nearness: to know that he was there...with her...beside her...and for her. She could reach out to him as a friend and a partner.

As she rounded the corner of the platform and approached the edge of the bed, the side of the mattress she had slept on since Sunday night, her eyes grew wide, she froze in her tracks, and she stared at him like he had donned his bestial scales.

"Shh, dragyra," he whispered in a soothing, gentle voice. "I am not here to take advantage. I only want to lie beside you." He shrugged, unsure if she could see it in the dimly lit space. "And honestly, I need to get some sleep." He patted the mattress beside him and crooked his fingers, ushering her forward. "Come. Lie down. Trust me."

She lowered her head and shut her eyes, almost as if those last two words had somehow shamed her. Ah, so it had come to that—she was still going to try to escape their fate. More than likely tomorrow, after they crossed through the portal…

He buried the hurt that welled in his chest and watched her like a hawk as she shrugged out of the robe, dropped it on the floor, and climbed into bed: slowly—tentatively—and with great reservation. He waited until her slender frame sank into the mattress, her hair fanned out on her pillow, and she seemed to find a comfortable position on her side, her back blatantly turned toward him. And then he snuggled up beside her, careful to keep his hips—or anything else untoward—from touching her curves as he wrapped a strong, enveloping arm around her waist.

She immediately stiffened, but he didn't care.

Her arms were crossed over her chest, her fists tucked beneath her chin, and he intentionally slid his fingers over her wrist and gently clutched her hand, interlocking his fingers with hers. Her breath quickened, and he squeezed her hand. "Listen to your heart, Jordan," he whispered softly. He knew he wasn't playing fair—he was consciously invoking their shared, singular flame, magnifying the flicker in his mind's eye, and coaxing it to burn brighter with his voice. "Follow what it's telling you, dragyra. You know me. You recognize…this. You are free to be at peace."

Jordan exhaled, like half of her was fighting it, while the other half was being drawn into the glow.

"That's it, angel," he rasped, releasing her hand so he could stroke her side, massage her shoulders, and then her neck. "Relax, baby. I'm right here."

He smelled—or sensed—more than he saw, the single tear welling out of her eye and trailing down her cheek, and his heart surged with compassion. What must this be like for her? To feel the truth in his words? To know the connection in her soul? To get, on a level that was far from conscious, the fact that her life was tethered to his—that he was, in fact, the other half of her soul—her greatest need? Yet to have her mind reject it, to have her body rebel...to be torn in such opposite directions?

"Let go, dragyra of mine." He spoke the words in Dragonese, allowing the lyrical, ancient language to wash over her like a cooling wave. "Give yourself up to the truth in your heart. Free your mind from your human restraints. Come home. *Be home.* Know that you are home."

He knew she didn't understand a word he was saying, at least not with her ears, but she was listening acutely, and something else was happening: Her body temperature was rising, and her heartbeat was slowing. Whether she understood it or not, it was the beginning of an offering: her human body offering its essence and heat to Zane's dragon, preparing itself to connect through the intimate act of *feeding*.

His fangs began to throb in his mouth, and he consciously overrode the impulse—buried the desire deep inside. Now was not the time, or the place—she didn't even know what she was doing—but his soul took solace in the physical reaction, and his inner dragon stirred, even as his amulet began to softly glow.

"That's it, dragyra mea—*dragyra of mine,*" he continued to soothe her in Dragonese. "You are safe within my care."

As the dragon moon shone through the sparkling windows of the Sapphire Lair, casting a brilliant shadow over Zane—*and Jordan's*—bed, and the cool night air swept through the room on a gentle breeze, Zanaikeyros Saphyrius continued to speak to Jordan in his native, primordial tongue: He told her about his childhood; he told her about his precarious life; and he told her how long he had waited...for her.

Until at last, the woman in his arms, who was listening so raptly, fell asleep.

Chapter Twenty-four

Tuesday ~ 9:45 AM

D AN SUMMERS CLUTCHED the unopened letter in his hand so tightly that his knuckles turned white as he exited through the back door of Judge Stanley's chambers, division B-9, and headed down the hall toward the courtroom plaza's elevators.

It took every ounce of self-control he had ever possessed—and a host of reserve he did not—to restrain the impulse to turn in the opposite direction, head down the hall to the main courtroom door, and march straight to the prosecutor's table: to walk straight up to Jordan and confront her.

What in the name of heaven was going on!

First, Jordan had sent him an email, late Friday night, telling him about some creepy perpetrator who had confronted her in the Two Forks Mall garage, letting him know that she had given the freak Dan's address. Fine, it hadn't amounted to anything—at least not with Jordan—but a two-bit gangster had been murdered in that same garage, on that same night, under some very questionable—and gruesome—circumstances.

Still, Dan had kept his distance.

He had not contacted Jordan…

Not even when his friend at dispatch had told him Saturday

morning about another late-night call that had come in on Friday night: a possible domestic disturbance at Jordan's freakin' address!

Once again, the incident was cancelled, and he'd let it go.

But then, she had sent him the most cryptic, disturbing text he had ever received on Monday, telling him about this even more bizarre letter: *I need your help...go to Judge Stanley's office and pick up a letter from his clerk. Do not try to contact me...etc., etc.*

What. The. Devil. Was. Going. On.

Just what kind of trouble had Jordan gotten into?

This was *Jordan Anderson*: stubborn, brave, one hundred percent independent, Jordan Anderson, the woman who had told him she never wanted to see him again, and no, they could not be friends. Other than when their paths crossed at work—which was seldom, as he worked on a different floor, primarily litigating appeals—he was supposed to look the other way, pass any necessary messages through clerks, and deal directly with one of her team members on the rare occasion that they were working a related case.

He had done all of that.

Even when it was inconvenient...

Now, as Dan stepped into the elevator and tapped the button to Level One—pressing it way too hard, at least three or four times—he was still surprised that Jordan had reached out to him... and in such a mysterious way. He stared at the standard white envelope still clutched in his hand, and appraised the cursive characters in his name, Jordan's familiar handwriting: Were the letters different, did they betray distress, had she written it under duress? "Screw it," he bit out beneath his breath as he tore the envelope open. He wasn't a blasted handwriting expert. And he couldn't wait to find out.

He yanked the letter out of the envelope and summarily began to read...

Dear Dan...

His eyes moved from line to line with a fury, sometimes backtracking to retrace the last word or to reread the last sentence. His heart began to slam in his chest, and his palms began to sweat as he continued to fly through the disturbing paragraphs.

And then his mouth dropped open.

He took me from my apartment, brought me into his world, and I have been "with" him ever since. He has no intentions of letting me go, and I have no clear avenue of escape.

Dan swept a trembling hand through his hair and clenched a handful of locks in his fist, above his neck. He began to pace in tight circles around the elevator as he continued to read even faster. "Oh, shit…oh, shit…*oh, shit.*"

His eyes came to the last line—*please trust me…please believe me…please help me*—he took three steps backward and virtually slammed into the elevator wall, slinking against it to support his weight.

He needed to catch his breath.

This guy—whoever he was—had Jordan.

She was free to move back and forth through her life—*what the hell?*—but she was doing it under duress…as a captive.

None of it made any sense, and he only knew one thing—he would kill the son of a bitch! He would grab the nearest armed security guard, march right into that courtroom, and yank Jordan out of there, away from that desk. And if that bastard dared to make a move, he would snatch the security guard's weapon and litter the scumbag's body with holes.

Consequences be damned.

He started to hit the ninth floor button, to return to courtroom B-9, when his common sense kicked in.

Wait.

No!

What had Jordan said?

You cannot confront this guy on your own; there's no way you will win. Believe me—nothing is as it seems. He has the power to obliterate you and everyone around you in the space of a heartbeat.

Dan repeated the pertinent words: "Nothing is as it seems." This was pure, unadulterated madness, but he couldn't take the risk: not with Jordan's life, and not with the lives of all the innocent civilians in the building. Hell, this was an active hostage situation. He needed the assistance of a special response team, perhaps ATF or SWAT. Hell's bells, did he need a bomb squad, too—did he need to clear the building and have it swept for explosives?

No.

Hell no.

That would only tip the bastard off, and he might slip away. Jordan might be lost.

Dan needed to assemble a highly tactical team who could strike hard, fast, and with targeted precision…

He stuffed the letter back in the envelope, dropped his head in his hands, and closed his eyes.

He needed to think this through.

⁓

Drakkar Hades strolled along the gothic castle battlements, gazing down at the moat several stories below, and for the first time in centuries, he thought about the past.

The ancient, primordial past.

A time before creation, fourteen billion years before the universe as we know it existed.

He thought about the swirling mass of evolving, kinetic energy in its most basic form, the black hole full of hot, dense, burning gas—energy that rotated, fed on itself, then expanded—until that critical moment happened, and the quantum fluctuation expanded.

Poppycock! he thought, revising the accepted version of ancient history. It didn't expand—it exploded! He should know; he was there.

The mass that would one day yield the seven dragon lords and the most powerful king of all the pagan realm had divided out of that mass due to conflicting consciousness. Everything—*absolutely everything*—had been there in its most basic, thought-impulse form: love, hate, desire, sin, joy, purity, hope, and destruction.

Everything that encompassed light and shadow had coexisted in that ancient mass.

And then, somehow along the way, the impulses had developed consciousness, and the consciousness had developed minds, and Lord Drakkar Hades had garnered a clear, distinct impression of the Self.

Of *his*…self.

And he had known from that first moment of inception that he was different from the rest. That all the errant, destructive, divisive vibrations were more pleasing than the rest—that he could feed on them, feed from them, and create an army, unto itself, that gave rise to the darkness and voice to the shadows.

That he could be the Chosen One, albeit self-appointed: Father of the pagan realm.

And at the same time, almost simultaneously, seven other conscious energies had emerged, ranging from a step above his own dark shadow, to the highest form of light. It had been—and still remained—unacceptable: Any trace of light was too stark, too bright, too foul to retain within the mass.

Darkness needed to escape.

It needed to break out.

The quantum fluctuation needed to explode so its individual vitalities could be free…and untainted.

And *that* was truly how it had happened: how Drakkar Hades and the seven dragon lords had burst forth from their own cosmic "Big Bang" and into the unformed universe, where they began to create their own dimensions as powerful, original lords.

The demon-shade sighed. He stopped strolling and leaned against a dark gray parapet, exquisitely adorned with a beautiful medieval sword—there was a witch's pentacle etched into the pommel; a reversed numerical seven inscribed in gold below the cross guard; and the tail of the *seven* was outlined in permanent blood, extending along the length of the blade. He crossed his long, spindly arms across his sunken chest and licked his reedy lips as he brought his attention back to the present day and time: the state of the worlds right now.

As Father of the pagan realm, he ruled the underworld with an iron fist, and the Temple of Seven ruled the higher domain. And now—*and now*—after all these millennia, he had a chance to strike back at his original kin, the brothers who had been born that fateful day: Lord Dragos, Lord Ethyron, Lord Saphyrius, Lord Amarkyus, Lord Onyhanzian, Lord Cytarius, and Lord Topenzi.

He had a chance to alter the state of their domain, a chance to destroy one of their cherished Genesis Sons.

He sharpened his long, pointed nail on the side of the parapet and stared at the thick, murky haze that permeated the underworld's sky. Now that Salem Thorne was safely sequestered away, ensconced in Dragons Domain, Lord Drakkar Hades needed to alter his plan—there was no point in using Dr. Kyle Parker and his newfound love interest, Macy Wilson, to try to get to Zane when Salem could strike directly at Jordan himself. The ancient demon had already transmitted his plan, and Drakkar had quickly agreed—"By any means necessary," he had told his wicked servant. "Take the female down at your first opportunity."

As for Salem's previous work, the thorough and effective compulsion he had placed in Kyle Parker's mind, Drakkar had no intentions of pulling it back: One never knew how things might turn out; it was always prudent to have a plan B. If for some ungodly reason Salem failed to get to Jordan, then at least the backup avenue was still in place; and besides, Lord Hades was known to have a plan C—or in this case, a D—up his sleeve from time to time. Things he didn't share with his counselor...

He sighed, feeling a bit of melancholy and monotony right now—things never moved as quickly as he hoped. Still, all was on schedule, plans were unfolding, and he had lived for fourteen billion years—he could certainly exercise a modicum of patience for a few more days...see what panned out.

Chapter Twenty-five

District Courtroom ~ 1:00 PM

ZANE SAT IN the back of the courtroom in a hard wooden pew, trying to get comfortable on the stiff, unforgiving wood. There were a dozen or so spectators scattered about the audience, including Zane's lair-mate Leviathon, since Axe had been busy and unable to come. Both Zane and Levi had been approached by the bailiff the moment they had walked through the doors, and asked to remove their shades—apparently, sunglasses and hats weren't allowed in the courtroom.

On first impulse, Zane had bristled—*the hell they aren't*—and considered searing a quick compulsion into the bailiff's mind, but on second thought, he had taken off the sunglasses, because all the other spectators would notice them, too—and then he would have to control them all. As it stood, both he and Levi had to throw up a soft, energetic barricade in place of the glasses, shield their eyes with a mental distortion—like a faint, hazy fog—so if other humans glanced in their direction, they would only get a dim impression of their otherworldly peepers.

Those damn sapphire irises that stood out like bright red paint on a pure white canvas.

So far, the morning had been mostly uneventful. Jordan and her partner, along with the defendant's defense attorneys—three middle-aged white males with cheap blue suits—had taken turns questioning potential jurors and letting the judge know if they were acceptable or not.

While slow and monotonous, the process had also been somewhat fascinating, at least in so far as it revealed more about Jordan's mind, her analytical abilities, and her legal skill. She was tough, and she was smart. In almost every instance, when Zane could read the human's soul, delve into their mind, and retrieve their true motivation, Jordan also hit the nail on the head. She knew who they were, what they were really about, and any preconceptions about the defendant in the case.

Only Jordan did it from experience. She read their body language, listened to their speech, saw beneath their facades. There was one guy, however, a forty-something dad Jordan had missed: He had a misogynist bent the size of Texas, which made him biased against the People's case, against the pretty female attorney, but he hid it beneath a soft, self-effacing demeanor.

Still, all and all, she was incredibly skilled at her craft.

"How do you feel about minority-owned businesses? Do you have any preconceptions or internal biases?" A defense attorney was questioning potential juror number fifty-two when all of a sudden, the air in the courtroom turned…frosty.

Zane swiveled his head to the side and met Levi's corresponding stare—so his lair-mate had felt it too, a shift in the energy that wasn't based on actual temperature or a sudden change in the climate, but a *feeling* of malaise.

What the hell? Zane thought.

He sat forward in the pew, all five senses seeking outward, on hyper-alert.

And that's when the mayhem ensued: The courtroom audience gasped, Jordan spun around at her table, and the bailiff crowded the judge as the main doors to the courtroom, along with the back door to the judge's chambers, swung open with a clattering bang.

An entry team of five amped-up, brawny men, each carrying his own submachine gun—three strapped with concussion grenades—stormed into the courtroom: two from the main doorway;

two from the judge's chambers; and one from the jury-room door. At the same time, a tall black male and his short Asian partner both took positions on opposite sides of the wall, each pointing deadly sniper rifles right at the courtroom audience.

"Everyone get down!" the point-man for the team of five shouted, as two other tactical watchdogs, those who had entered through the main courtroom doors, rushed down the center aisle, dashed past the courtroom bar, and headed straight for the plaintiff's table—coming way too close to Jordan.

Zane shot up in his seat, primed for a fight and ready to deflect anything that came his way, even as both snipers adjusted their rifles and aimed their barrels in his direction. A bright beam of glowing red light illuminated over his chest, even as a second beam—that he could feel, not see—appeared over the space between his eyes. His top lip twitched, his fangs descended, and he began to snarl…

So these humans wanted to play…

Before he could lunge or retreat, a tall, handsome man in his early thirties, wearing a charcoal-gray suit, with meticulously groomed brown hair, stepped forward in the doorway, and Zane knew in an instant that this was the guy who had been throwing off all that shade: the thick, disturbing vibration that Zane and Levi had originally felt.

This man wasn't just pumped with adrenaline; this man was summarily, personally, and intrinsically pissed off. And he had been staring like a hawk at Jordan before shifting that hate-filled gaze to Zane.

Shit, Zane thought, immediately putting two and two together: So none of this had anything to do with Jordan's case or the jury selection. It had nothing to do with the defendant. It was all about Jordan and Zane.

She had somehow gotten an SOS out to her human friends.

Zane swallowed his fury and instantly went dark—perhaps *light* was a more accurate term—the dragyri went invisible.

And then he prepared to lunge, right across the courtroom, land on the plaintiff's table, and grab Jordan by the waist—he would bust through the ninth-floor, bulletproof glass if he had to and take her out through the window.

His biceps twitched.

His pectoral muscles jerked.

And the ribbed, satiny wings nestled inside of his back began to expand behind his shoulder blades, preparing to open on command.

Whoa, brother! Levi's telepathic intrusion was about as subtle as a cannonball leaving the muzzle as it slammed into his head. *Don't do anything stupid, Zane. There are a lot of unknown variables going on in this scene: You can block bullets, but Jordan can't; you can pass through walls, but your dragyra cannot—the broken glass could eviscerate her. You can see and breathe through smoke or gas, but she could be adversely affected. The only way out of this may be to take a few lives—and I'm with you, if that's what it comes to—but these guys, their souls; they're not tainted, Zane. We will have to violate law.*

You think I give a flying shit, Zane roared in Levi's mind, spinning around to face him. He immediately realized that Levi had gone *light's out*, too, shrouded in invisibility with him, but it didn't matter: not one ounce. He could track the dragyri's primordial heartbeat. He could zoom in on the blood rushing in the dragyri's veins. *Lord Saphyrius will understand,* he snarled, sounding as mad as he felt. *Lord Saphyrius will have my back!*

His dragon was growing increasingly agitated, and he sidestepped out of the lasers' crosshairs, now that the snipers could no longer see him. Then he dropped down low, hunched his back, and his dragon began to snarl. His fingers curled inward as his claws began to grow, and a subtle wisp of smoke coalesced at the exhale of his breath.

Two powerful arms encircled him from behind. "Zane!" This time Levi growled in his ear. "Call back your beast, brother! You don't want to do this."

A red haze of madness began to swirl about Zane's head as two team members—these dudes were obviously SWAT—snatched Jordan by both arms, yanked her out of her seat, and began to drag her down the aisle, all the while running backward. At the same time, two other armed guards created a barricade in front of them—shielding them with their bodies and their weapons, sweeping the rifles side to side—as they took the rear retreat.

"Be still," Levi whispered in Dragonese. "Stay with my voice. She's not in any danger." He tightened his hold around Zane's trembling shoulders. "Breathe, brother…just breathe." The male was working so hard to restrain Zane's temper that a soft white light began to glow around his arms. "Let's follow them instead, see where they take her. They will move her to someplace far more secluded, and then *we* will have the tactical advantage. Besides, at this juncture, we need to know who they are, how much they know, how many we need to neutralize. No need to blaze this place, my brother. There's nowhere they can go; there's no place they can hide; there is nothing they can do to stop us. Comprende?"

What the heck?

Had Levi just switched to Spanish?

Zane closed his eyes and inhaled deeply, sniffing out two distinct aromas: Jordan's initial terror—*and then relief*—and that bastard's overwhelming stench of triumph.

The guy in the tailored suit…

The one with the well-groomed hair…

Zane would never, ever forget that scent.

And innocent soul or not—he would gnaw on the human's spine like a dog with a bone—chew it down to the marrow.

Levi whistled low beneath his breath, clearly tuned into Zane's thoughts. *We can evaluate that possibility later,* he said telepathically, this time. *But right now—*right now—*I need you to be one hundred percent—focused, alert, and fully present—so we can trail these guys… and Jordan. You with me?* Zane?

Zanaikeyros reined in his dragon.

He called back the beast.

And he slowly nodded his head, even though he knew Levi couldn't see it.

"Thank you," he grunted, almost unintelligibly, regaining his sense of composure. And then he shuddered at the territorial ferocity of his own inner dragon—never in all his years had he possessed such a primal impulse, such a savage, possessive desire to kill.

This *claiming* was truly a deeply ingrained, all-pervasive drive.

And Levi Saphyrius had just saved an entire courthouse full of humans from an unimaginable slaughter.

Chapter Twenty-six

ONCE THEY HAD made it out of the courtroom, Jordan did not need any encouragement to keep up with the men. She ran as fast as her legs would carry her, dove into the service elevator, right next to Dan, and descended along with the tactical crew of five to the basement floor of the plaza. The doors immediately opened into a parking garage, where a dark blue van was waiting.

The engine was already running.

The side door was already open.

And the driver's seat was already manned.

Jordan didn't hesitate. She scrambled into the hollowed-out vehicle—Dan was right on her heels—and scooted along the floor to make room for the tactical crew members. "Where are we going?" she panted, watching anxiously as the last of the five slammed the door shut.

"An empty, gated estate, about five miles away," Dan huffed, as clearly winded as Jordan. "It belongs to a federal judge who's received a lot of death threats—he has a bunker in his basement, and it's a virtual vault."

Jordan nodded, still catching her breath.

In a matter of minutes, they were speeding out of the garage, with the tires screeching behind them. They headed north, away from the courthouse, and turned in to a narrow back alley.

Jordan pulled her knees to her chest, brushed her hair out of her eyes, and tried to clear her mind. She was grateful that there weren't any windows in the back of the van—she could only peer through the front windshield—otherwise, she would constantly watch for Zane.

As the realization of what had just happened—what she had just done—slowly sank in, she felt like she might be sick.

Holy Saint Barbara, protect me from harm...

What had she set into motion?

What had she done to Zane?

The dragyri would never be defeated by the likes of Jordan, Dan, and a handful of human warriors—he would never be out-maneuvered by their pitiful, inferior tactics. Holy hell, both Zane and Levi had simply vanished in the middle of the fray—simply rendered themselves invisible in the middle of the gallery—but not before Zane's eyes had begun to glow, and his fangs had extended into sharp, bestial points. Not before those sapphire eyes had regis-tered rage and madness...and absolute determination.

God save them all, Zane's dragon was pissed!

And what must he think of her now?

Her teeth began to chatter, and she started to rock back and forth on the floor of the van, appreciating the fact that she was finally losing it: For the first time, since all of this had happened, Jordan was *this close* to flipping her lid, relinquishing her sanity for good. And it wasn't just the fear—the terror of it all. It was the deep, gnawing, inexplicable guilt, an emotion that was mounting—and spreading—like a radiating pain, traveling outward through her torso from the center of her chest.

Either that, or she was about to have a heart attack.

Damn, it felt like someone had just impaled her with a spike.

As she placed her hand over her heart, trying to measure the erratic beats, the van pulled out of the alley, crossed three lanes of traffic, and darted onto the on-ramp of the freeway. She let go of her heart and held onto a metal ring sticking up through a torn piece of carpet, dissecting the vehicle's floor.

And the nausea swelled.

It roiled in her stomach.

As wave after wave of vertigo assailed her.

She could only describe the feeling—the rising illness—as being in shock, but not the kind of shock that left the mind empty and blank, or the senses unaware. If anything, this was the opposite condition: Her mind was anything but empty, and her senses were *acutely* on board—registering the fact that she had just lost something...*left something*...incredibly important behind.

Something wholly fundamental to her well-being.

For lack of a better explanation, Jordan felt like a wolf who had been caught in a snare for days: desperate, hungry, and dying inside. In her panic and her angst, she had chewed through her leg to escape—she had severed a part of her body in a reckless grasp for her freedom—and only now was she beginning to feel the pain.

None of it made any sense.

She didn't care what happened to Zane—did she?

And all that cryptic talk about death and dying—that had just been hyperbole, right?

Zane would be fine without her, perhaps a little lonely, but fine.

So then why was this...*sensation*...so great?

Physical, spiritual, almost existential.

And completely unexpected.

"Jordan. *Jordan!*" Dan's voice was growing harsh with urgency. "Snap out of it, Anderson!"

She blinked three times. "W... w...what?" she asked. Had he been speaking to her for a while?

"What the hell is going on?" he practically shouted, brandishing her letter in his hand. "Who was that guy, and what's been happening? Jordan, you need to start talking, and fast! I don't know what we're up against. I don't know how to protect you, other than to take you to this bunker. You need to help me out—because this letter? It doesn't make any sense."

Jordan nodded her head and licked her lips, suddenly feeling self-conscious. Every head in the van had turned in her direction, and every ear had just perked up. *Shit. Just shit.* She hadn't thought this through, and she certainly hadn't thought about sharing any part of her ordeal with anyone other than Dan.

Putting anyone else at risk.

This wasn't the time, and it wasn't the place, regardless of the urgent situation. Maybe she could just tell him—

"Jordan!" Her name again.

She cringed.

"Jordan." He spoke softer now. "Sweetie…"

She dropped her head in her hands and dug her fingernails into her hair.

Oh God; oh, God; oh, God…

What. Had. She. Done.

⁓

Zanaikeyros stood in the underground garage, his feet a shoulder's width apart; his arms crossed over his chest; his sapphire-gold eyes closed as he maintained the deep psychic trance—as he tracked Jordan Anderson's blood like a homing pigeon, following the roadways, accessing her speed, feeling for the bodies—and heat—all around her.

Seven men.

One of them, the driver.

One of them, the dude in the charcoal-gray suit, the attorney.

His name was—

Dan Summers.

She was in a hollowed-out van, speeding toward the interstate, and she was virtually quaking with fear. Sick with regret. Or maybe regret was not the right word: She was feeling the truth of their connection…and now, their separation.

Her dragyra soul was weeping, whether she understood it or not.

He took snapshot after snapshot in his mind's eye, memorializing the images and the map as a series of pictures in his neocortex—transferable impressions that he could pass on to his lair-mates, a GPS that any of them could follow.

Speaking of his sapphire brothers: One by one, he could feel them surrounding him as they transported into the courtroom plaza garage: first Axe, then Jace, then finally Nakai. Levi was already there.

The dark blue van stopped in front of a gated estate. The iron doors swung open, and it pulled into a long, curved drive before snaking its way toward the back of the compound. Zane zoomed in on an address affixed to a brick-and-mortar post, next to five parallel wooden garage doors. The four iron block letters inscribed into the column were plain and easy to read: 6958. He didn't need to know the name of the street or the subdivision, and he didn't need to know the name of its owner—he had the map. He had the directions. And he also had his backup, the brothers of his lair.

He opened his eyes and banked his fire—suppressed his dragon's rage.

"This shit has already made the human news," Nakai said, without preamble, shifting his powerful muscles beneath the frame of his duster.

Zane eyed each of his brothers in turn: Indeed, they were all wearing their knee-length leathers, in the middle of June. That meant they were conspicuous as hell and packing a hidden arsenal: assault rifles, handguns, and their favorite medieval weapons, of every class and variety. "What is the news saying?" he grunted.

Nakai shifted restlessly. "Just speculation. You know the drill: report it first, then explore the facts. *Terror in a district courtroom*"—he mimicked—"a lone gunman; no, an escaped prisoner; possibly a terrorist attack—they're all over the map."

Zane nodded.

At least that much was good: The humans were far from putting two and two together, and they never would. One less thing to worry about.

"Where is she?" Jace intoned, his deep, resonant voice no-nonsense.

Zane wondered if the dragyri had his Katar. "In a van," he

snarled. "She was in a van." He softened his voice—no need to take it out on his brothers. "Now she's at a house—a fairly large estate. My guess is they have a safe room or some sort of hideaway built in. Probably a shit-ton of security, too."

Axeviathon nodded. "And who's she with?"

Zane visibly bristled. He rolled his neck on his shoulders, popping it three times to release some more tension. "Looks like, uh, a SWAT team, whoever drove the van, and her ex-lover, another attorney. Some guy named Dan. I think he masterminded the getaway."

Levi took a cautious step back. His deep, melodious voice dropped into a soothing, silken purr. "You good?"

Zane's nose twitched in an effort to restrain a guttural snarl, and his top lip drew back. "Yeah," he lied. "I'm good."

Axe looked him up and down, apparently assessing Zane's state of mind for himself. "We don't need to go all nuclear on everyone who's there, Zane. No need to kill them all—"

Zane leveled a hate-filled glare at his lair-mate, and this time, he snarled overtly.

Axe held up both hands. "Hey, don't get it twisted—we're going to get her back."

"But we need to wait for nightfall," Nakai chimed in, always logical in nature. "Too much news already." The winged cross on his left temple seemed to shift, as if in flight, as he furrowed his brows in determination.

Zane took a fresh appraisal of all the males, realizing how quickly they'd come to assist him—how serious they were about getting it done. "Thanks for coming," he offered, sincerely. "I know all of you were busy."

There wasn't a single reply.

Where else would they be?

The rejoinder was implied…

"Well," Levi finally said, eyeing the empty garage. "The one thing we don't need is a handful of humans laying eyes on a lairful of dragyri males, amped up, packing, and throwing off heat. We need to find someplace to lie low until sundown." He narrowed his indigo-sapphire eyes. "What say you, Zane?"

Zane nodded. "As long as that place is within a hundred yards of my dragyra, I'm fine."

Levi started to object, and Axe reached out a hand to dissuade him. "Works for me," he said, "but you know the routine: We need to have a plan—quick, in and out—wait for the cover of darkness, and minimize human involvement—as well as fatalities—as much as possible." He turned his attention to Levi and Zane. "I don't suppose one of you had a chance to read the humans' souls? The SWAT team?"

Levi nodded. "I didn't catch the guy in the suit...Dan... but the team, there was nothing discernably foul." He hesitated. "Although...one of the hot-heads beats his wife."

Jace frowned. "That's cause enough for me."

Axe grunted. "Look, we're talking about Zane's dragyra here— five days out from the temple. The dragon lords will understand if there isn't a soul left standing. Just the same, let's do what we came to do—bring Jordan home and try to minimize the fallout. Are we all in agreement: this waits until nightfall?"

Again, the group stood silent, turning their collective attention to Zane.

Zanaikeyros inclined his head. "Yeah...whatever...bring on the fucking moon."

Chapter Twenty-seven

LATER THAT NIGHT, just before sundown, Jordan huddled beneath the soft cotton blanket Dan had given her and clutched the mug of hot chamomile tea in her hands, grateful for his kindness and hospitality.

So far, so good.

Nothing had happened.

She sipped her tea, glanced around the underground bunker, and shivered. It was truly a sight to behold: The entrance was framed by a five-inch-thick, solid steel door, with a ten-gauge outer panel and a twelve-gauge inner plate. There was a biometric lock on the outside of the hatch, next to a five-spoked, polished handle; and there were twenty-two-bolts, spanning all three sides, keeping the door in place. To quote one of the members of the SWAT team, who had long since gone home, along with the van's unnamed driver, not even King Kong was getting through that door.

Inside the narrow chamber, the judge had everything a person could need to sustain a protracted stay: bunkbeds lined with fresh, clean linens; a galley-style kitchen, heavily stocked with canned goods; and even a miniature bathroom, with a stand-up shower and a tiny commode.

For all intents and purposes, Jordan and Dan were sequestered inside a small, slender apartment, fortified like Fort Knox, and they even had a flat-screen television to watch and a small leather couch to sit on.

So why was she still so jittery?

And why did her heart hurt so much?

"Feeling any better?" Dan asked, seeming to read her mind.

Jordan shrugged. There was no real way to answer that question—*correction*; there was no honest way to reply. So far, she had managed to evade most of his cross-examination, at least those questions that would expose Zane as a dragon—*a dragyri*—and The Pantheon as his home. There was just no way Dan would buy it, and if she told him the truth—the whole truth, and nothing but the truth—he would think she had gone insane. And instead of hiding out inside a comfortable basement bunker, she might find herself locked up in a padded room.

But there was more than that going on, something Jordan could not explain: She still felt disloyal—disjointed—like she was somehow dishonoring Zane.

And none of it made any sense.

So she'd danced around the root of the subject for the last six hours, pirouetting like a ballerina on a backlit stage, giving Dan half-hearted answers, outright lies, and clever, nonsensical diversions—partly for herself, and partly...for Zane.

"He's stronger than anyone I've ever seen..."

That hadn't gone over so well.

"He's connected to a virtual empire of...criminals..."

What the hell did that even mean?

"And he has access to resources beyond your imagining..."

Yeah: fire, telekinesis, and wings.

"Taking him on would be like taking on an army, a foreign government, or the head of the mob..."

Ever tried to wrestle a seventy-pound python with one hand tied behind your back and one foot chopped off?

There had been so very little she could reveal.

Needless to say, Dan had grown increasingly frustrated, and Jordan had grown increasingly withdrawn.

"But why couldn't you get away?" he'd repeated. "Why didn't

you call someone? Don't you think we could have arrested him, stopped him? Wouldn't that have been the safer play? What are you still so afraid of, Jordan? You're sitting in a vault."

Although playing dumb was not Jordan's strong suit, she had met each question with a small variation of the same explanation, coupled with an exasperated sigh: "It's impossible to explain. I just can't explain it. I'm sorry—I wish I could explain…"

And eventually, as she'd hoped, Dan had stopped asking the difficult questions.

He had also sent the SWAT team and the driver home, replacing them with a private guard of seven highly skilled—and heavily armed—men. He believed the private security team, along with the judge's state-of-the-art security system, would be more than enough to keep them safe…just so long as they remained in the bunker.

Jordan knew better.

And it was all her fault—the entire quandary.

Unless she could tell him the truth, what did she expect?

"So, how do you feel about leaving here in a couple of days and going to a safe house?" Dan asked, glancing at her steaming hot tea. "Drink some more, Jordan; you need to stay hydrated."

Jordan did as he asked.

"Do you think you need a new identity, something along the lines of witness protection, or will lying low for a while be enough?"

"No," Jordan exhaled. "It won't be enough, but neither will changing my name."

Dan rubbed his tired eyes. "Sweetie, we've been over this… again and again…what aren't you telling me, baby? It isn't like you to be this shaken up—and not to look for viable solutions." He leaned forward, beside her, on the couch. "For heaven's sake, you act like this man is a god."

Jordan ignored the distinct hint of jealousy in Dan's increasingly frustrated voice. It was unbecoming at best, and that had nothing to do with her predicament. "Dan," she moaned, realizing she was whining. "I just…I just…" She sighed. "I'm sorry I got you involved in this mess. It was so unfair."

He took immediate umbrage to her words. "Well, I'm not,"

he retorted. "I'm sorry this bastard has you so distraught. I'm sorry that you don't feel like you can tell me the truth—the whole truth. But I'm not sorry that you reached out to me for help. And I'm not sorry that we're finally talking, or that you're finally here—with me, alone—that you trusted me enough to take a chance."

Jordan stared at him, long and hard: the weary lines in his once-smooth brow, the small brown mole above his upper lip; his immaculate, thick brown hair that now had some gray around the edges…just along his temples. He was only thirty-two, and she couldn't help but wonder: Had he aged because of her?

"How have you been?" she asked.

The question was a mere whisper, but he let out a deep, lamenting groan, almost as if he had been waiting forever for her to ask that simple question. "Miserable," he mumbled.

She closed her eyes. "I'm sorry, Dan. I just couldn't—"

"No." He held up his hand. "I know what I did. I know how deeply I hurt you. I'm just glad that you called."

She chuckled halfheartedly. "That I sent you a cryptic letter, you mean."

"Yeah," he amended. "I guess that's a bit more accurate." And then he reached into his jacket pocket and retrieved Jordan's letter for the second time, setting it conspicuously down on her lap. "Tell me more about this, Jordan. C'mon. I need to know every detail. You say this is the same man, this Zane, who confronted you at the mall. You say he took you from your apartment and brought you *into his world*—what exactly does that mean? What did he do to you, Jordan?" When she didn't answer, he frowned. "You said he has no intentions of letting you go, yet he allowed you to go back and forth to work, to the hospital to see Macy—how does that work, butterfly? Where is his world? How did he control you from a distance, corral you from across the room? How did he keep you from running away?"

Jordan winced at the familiar, affectionate term, *butterfly*. He probably thought she hadn't heard it, but she had—it was the term he used to call her following the first time they'd made love, a reference to the litany of soft, gentle kisses she had planted on his nose…just like a little butterfly. And right now—*God help her*—for reasons she couldn't explain, all she could remember was another tender kiss—another primal, sensuous, smoky kiss—beneath the sonorous drone of a waterfall.

"Damnit, Jordan," he interrupted her reflection. "We've been at this for half a day, and I've listened to everything you've said. I've given you all the time in the world to feel comfortable…to trust… and I haven't pushed the issue, but you're smarter than this. You understand the stakes. Baby, I have to—"

"Quit calling me baby."

"What?"

"Don't call me that," she repeated. "And don't call me sweetie or butterfly, either. Do you think I wanted to reach out to you, Dan? Do you think I felt like I had any other choice? I was cornered, okay? I was lost, and I was scared. And most of all…*most of all*…I didn't think it through."

He looked thoroughly exasperated. "Okay," he murmured, "I understand that, but just the same—*you* reached out to *me*, so I need you to think about this: I'm going to have to explain to the police chief why I demanded the use of the SWAT team, why we ransacked a district court, and why we went in with snipers and grenades at the ready. Not only do I have to justify the expense, but I have to appease the judge, *both judges*. We are using Moran's home while he's away on vacation, and I'm going to need to pacify the press…and try not to lose my job. It's worth it to me, Jordan— you're worth it to me—but you have to give me something more. You have to tell me the truth."

"He's a dragon," Jordan blurted. To hell with it; she was out of pirouettes.

"Excuse me?" Dan said.

"He's a dragon," Jordan repeated. A terrifying, power-ful…exquisite beast, she thought, but she kept that to herself. "Technically, it's called a dragyri, but the point is this: Zane isn't human. And he's not from our world. His *world* is in another dimension, a domain beyond a portal, and the danger…the power…the imminent threat is the fact that he can move things with his mind; he can move faster than your eye can track; he can probably stop bullets; and he can sure as hell set you, or me, or this bunker on fire." She lowered her eyes and glanced at the floor, feeling instantly ashamed—Zane would never set her on fire, and she knew that, deep in her heart.

What had he said, time and time again?

"I will never...ever...harm you."

She shuddered and pressed on. "He believes I'm his mate"—dear God, was it true?—"or something incredibly archaic like that...*his fated, his chosen*...like these gods, his dragon lords, chose me to be with him before I was born, and he isn't going to let me go."

She sat forward on the edge of the couch, trying to get the image of that glowing white flame—the one Zane had alighted on the tip of her finger, from a droplet of Jordan's blood—out of her mind—and out of her memory—as she eyed Dan circumspectly. "And there's more." She set down her mug on a tiny metal end table, placing the letter beside it. "You want the whole truth, Dan?"

What was she doing?

What would Zane think?

How could she betray him like this?

Her heart felt as if it were collapsing inward, even as she rebuked her conscience—it was her life, her safety, her sanity at stake!

She had every right to protect it.

"That night in the parking garage, he drank my blood. That's why he can track me. That's *how* he can track me." She suddenly felt sick to her stomach: The dragyri's fangs *had* hurt her, and that drugging pull, the way he had fed, it had felt so primal, so shocking, so intrusive...he had left a trail of frost on her skin in his wake.

Perhaps there was a difference between *hurt* and *harm*...

She shook her head to dislodge the thoughts.

"And the text, the one you told me about, from your friend at dispatch? It wasn't a false alarm. Alonzo Diaz—do you remember him?—he was a sexual predator that the Second Judicial District put away, about five years back, when I first started working in the

DA's office—before you and I started dating. Well, he broke into my apartment that night and attacked me, and Zane killed him." *He saved my life*, she thought. "He set him on fire, slit his throat with a claw, and tore off his head with his hands. That is who we are up against, Dan. That is who I am running from."

And that was the final nail in her spiritual coffin.

Whatever flame might have once burned inside, it had surely gone out—Jordan Anderson felt empty, cold, and almost absent of life; and she resented the hell out of Zane for the feeling.

He had no right to affect her this way.

She barely even knew him.

Dan's nose twitched several times, and his eyes seemed to pale in vibrancy, but other than that, there was no immediate reaction.

No shock and disbelief.

No obvious fear for her sanity.

No ranting and raving, and no harsh criticism for the self-ish, costly game she had played with the state's valuable, limited resources.

Jordan scooted back on the couch…

What the hell? Why wasn't Dan reacting?

And that's when her ex got moving.

He jumped to his feet, tore off his expensive, tailored jacket, and removed the cufflink from his lower left sleeve, exposing his inner wrist. "Hand me that knife," he barked at her, gestur-ing toward a nearby set of cutlery situated on the galley counter, and looking back at the bunker door. "Hurry, Jordan. Hand me that knife."

"What are you doing?" Jordan asked, rising tentatively from her seat.

"Something I should have done hours ago," he said, staring once again at the bunker door, his eyes growing wider with alarm. "Your dragon is not the only one who is connected, Jordan—he isn't the only one with powerful friends." He thrust his chin in the direction of the knives, trying to make her rush.

"Then you believe me?" she asked, incredulous, taking several steps toward the stainless steel counter.

Dan shook his head. "I don't know what to believe, Jordan. It sounds pretty far-fetched, but I've seen many strange things in my life, and I know there are forces in play…forces we don't always hear about…talk about. Things that go bump in the night."

Jordan reached for the nearest carving knife, removed it from the block, and quickly strolled back to Dan, extending the implement handle-first. "What kind of forces?" she asked, feeling more than a little uneasy. "Have you seen monsters—or dragons—beings like Zane?"

Dan frowned. "Have I seen flying green reptiles with snouts and horns? No, I can't say that I have." And then he sighed. "But…"

"But?"

"But if we had stayed together—you and I—there are things I would have shown you, things I would have told you, people I would have wanted you to meet…in time. We never got that far." He took the knife by the handle, rotated it sixty degrees, and to Jordan's utter shock and horror, began to carve a deep, bloody gash in his forearm.

Jordan gasped aloud as she watched Dan Summers, a man she had once been in love with, continue to slice an insignia in his arm. And as the image took shape, she slowly backed away: It was a witch's pentacle on the pommel of a sword, with a reversed numerical seven carved just below the cross, etched into—and extending down—the full length of the blade.

She recoiled and took three generous steps back, appalled by both the occultist insignia and the ensuing sight of Dan's blood—bright crimson rivulets dripping down his wrist, snaking along his palm, and soaking the length of his fingers.

He tightened his fist, grimacing at the pain.

"You would have shown me *what*?" she muttered, still staring numbly at the grisly design. "Told me what? Introduced me to whom?"

Dan grunted as he dipped two fingers, from the opposite hand, into the blood now pooling in his palm, squatted down, and began to draw the same disturbing diagram on the bunker floor. "A better way to live," he said evenly. "Why I've never lost a case. The fact that we don't have to exist like helpless sheep, powerless, waiting to be victims. I would've introduced you to…to…" The ceiling above their heads began to creak, and his pained expression grew more tense. "There are thousands of us, Jordan—*tens of thousands*—judges like Theodore Moran, generals, senators; hell, even the local manager at the bank. We're everywhere, and we're not alone." He completed the diagram on the floor, dipped his fingers back into his blood, and stepped toward her, extending his forefinger toward her forehead. He was prepared to draw another sign—presumably the same one as before—*on Jordan.*

Right between her eyes.

Jordan drew back and slapped his hand away. "Stop it!" she shouted. "You're scaring me, Dan!"

His expression looked more desperate than dangerous as he held up his bloody hand in a placating gesture and began to plead with his eyes. "It's for protection, Jordan. Nothing else. Please, trust me on this."

She was just about to argue—to vehemently protest—to give him the third degree, when a deep, resonant voice—a familiar haunting rasp—resounded inside her head: *Dragyra, back away! Do not let him paint you.*

Chapter Twenty-eight

RECONNAISSANCE MATTERED.

Collecting information, knowing the enemy's whereabouts, and enumerating each individual adversary in order to gain a tactical advantage...mattered.

And that's why Zane didn't object when his lair-mates asked him to stay outside, to take the post closest to the back of the estate, beneath a thick row of oak trees, where he could watch and listen.

Axe had already shorted out the state-of-the-art security system, and there was nothing as simple as cutting a few wires to it. He had manipulated the electrical impulses streaming through the cables; he had literally sent his own kinetic energy into the intricate grid, read each complex pathway in order to grasp the setup, and altered the sensitive connections with his mind.

The alarms would not go off.

Nakai, on the other hand, had rendered himself invisible and simply walked the entire property—including the interior of the house—sending blueprints, the various positions of the seven guards, and information about potential obstructions back to the remaining Dragyr.

And that's how they'd formulated their plan...

The mansion itself was a ranch-level home, built as a basic rectangle, with only three entrances: the front foyer, the back vestibule, and a side door on the east that entered through the last port, within the five-car garage. Once inside the house, there were a series of long, dimly lit halls. The first hall led to the kitchen and a great room; the second hall led to a series of offices, libraries, and bedrooms—including to a central staircase that led to the basement, which then led down to the bunker—and the back hall, flanked the entire house, leading to the other main arteries. In a nutshell, there was one guard positioned at the front entrance—Axe would take care of him; two guards on the far east and west ends of the opening hall—they would have to split these sentries; and two guards on either side of the staircase that led to the underground bunker. In short, Jace would take both guards in the west—the one in the hall and the one by the stairway—and Levi would neutralize the humans in the east. Beyond that, there were only two more sentinels to contend with: a large burly bastard right outside the bunker hatch, and a heavily armed guard patrolling the back vestibule. Nakai would take the former, and Zane would handle the latter.

Once all the humans were removed from the equation, Zane could proceed through the back door, skirt along the main artery to the center hall, and head down the narrow stairway.

He could enter the bunker.

And that's how he'd found himself waiting, as the golden sun waned in a serene purple sky, hiding behind a thick gathering of trees, watching the back-door sentry, all the while knowing he was less than a hundred yards, as the crow flies, from the rear of the bunker, and listening, with his preternatural hearing…

Zooming in on every single word spoken between Dan and Jordan—*sweetie, baby, butterfly*—he was about to go insane. Especially when the conversation turned ominous and threatening…dire and just plain weird.

Give me a knife—what the hell was that all about?

A better way to live…why I've never lost a case…there are thousands of us, Jordan, tens of thousands…we're everywhere, and we're not alone.

Even without the benefit of his sight, Zane's keen, predatory mind was calculating a dozen clues per second: the peculiar, faraway cast in Dan's voice; the subtle but unmistakable grunts of pain—he was cutting himself with that knife; and the sudden emergence of three far more telling, detectable scents…

First, a coppery mixture of sweat, blood, and Lysol: *Was he smearing his blood on the floor?* The chemical reaction was far too distinct—it indicated three separate compounds.

Next, a sudden rise in cortisol—Jordan's fear was notably spiking.

And last, the faintness hint of sulfur permeating the air—this could only mean one thing: the burgeoning presence of a demon or a shade…maybe both.

Stop it! Jordan shouted. *You're scaring me, Dan!*

It's for protection…trust me.

Zane had heard all he needed to hear: The well-groomed attorney was cutting himself with a knife—on purpose—to evoke protection from the Pagan Horde. He was opening himself up to intercession—*and gods damn his ignorant recklessness*—he was trying to mark Jordan as well.

Zane wanted to scorch the guard at the back door, smash through the first-story wall, and tunnel right through the floor, into that bunker, without waiting for any backup, but he couldn't do it just yet…

Not yet.

Dan's actions had altered the dynamics for everyone, and they could have extremely dire consequences.

He shoved hard at Jordan's mind, inserting an imperious compulsion: *Dragyra, back away! Do not let him paint you.* And then he turned his telepathic attention on the brothers of his lair: *Axe, Levi, Jace—check in! Nakai, are you standing next to the bunker?*

What's up? Nakai replied immediately, and Zane could feel the presence of the other three, tuned in to the urgent connection.

Five minutes until sundown, that's what's up, but I don't think we can wait. Dan, the human Jordan is with, is a card-carrying member of the Cult of Hades; he worships Lord Drakkar. What's worse? He just carved up his body in that bunker, and he's trying to paint Jordan, too.

Son of a bitch, Axe snarled.

Exactly, Zane said. *He's inviting the pagans to the party.* He paused to catch his breath. *He also said something that set my teeth on edge—'there are thousands of us, Jordan, tens of thousands. Judges like Theodore Moran.'*

Isn't this Judge Theodore's estate? Nakai asked, ever the logical one.

You got it, Zane replied, biting down on his tongue, even as his dragon began to stir and smoke wafted freely from his nostrils.

Then we must assume Judge Theodore's home is filled with occultist, channeling objects, Nakai added, *things that make it easier for the pagans to appear. I'm sorry, Zane, I didn't pay any attention to the furniture or art.*

Doesn't matter, Zane snorted. *What's sticking in my craw is this: Why did the human send the SWAT team home and replace them with a private team?*

Levi dipped into that ever-present reservoir of calm, and spoke in a placid voice: *Because he wanted backup of a different sort, the kind that shares his philosophy.*

He wanted other members of the cult, Axe barked.

Safe to assume that, Zane said. *I'm definitely getting a strong odor of sulfur coming from the bunker; what about you, Nakai?*

Me, too, he answered. *From both the bunker and around this outside guard.*

Same here, Jace said.

Same, said Axe.

*Now that you mention it…*Levi chimed in. *Okay,* he said, turning back to strategy, *so we might be dealing with both pagans and humans before the night is over. Zane, you stick with the plan—get Jordan out. That's it. That's all. The rest of us, we'll handle our business.*

Should we call for another lair? Jace asked.

Hell no! Axe snarled. *It's been too long, as it is, since my beast was allowed to roam free. I say, stoke the demon fires…and let's play.*

⁙

The sun disappeared beneath the western horizon, yielding to the night, as Zane crept up to the back porch, sidled up to the guard, and snatched him by the back of the head, grasping a fistful of hair and shimmering into full view. As anticipated, the six-foot-six hulk of a man jolted at the sudden appearance of the dragyri, slid his pointer finger onto the trigger-pull of his AK-47, and pressed the muzzle into the center of Zane's stomach.

He never had a chance to get off a shot.

The dragyri extended his claws along the back of the sentinel's scalp, grasped all the flesh at the nape of his neck—presumably where his Cult of Hades tattoo would be stamped—and ripped the flesh from his head, disconnecting him from the pagan underworld.

The guard shouted in agony, even as Zane slid his bloody hand along the front of the man's throat, grasped his trachea, and squeezed, dropping him to the ground. As he snapped the assault rifle in two, then stepped over the unconscious body, he hoped the guy would not bleed out, die before he had a chance to change his wicked ways—maybe give Catholicism a try—but that wasn't Zane's concern.

Jordan was.

He busted through the solid back door, hightailed it into the house, and sprinted down the outer hallway on his way to the inner theater...to the top of the bunker staircase. As he ran, he could hear his brothers taking down their prey: the ear-piercing blast of Axe's HK45 going *bang!* into a human skull—the guard must have been pure evil; the barely discernable hum of Jace's Katar slicing its way through someone's flesh—who knew if he was silencing the human for good, or just taking him out temporarily; and the harsh, flesh-on-flesh blows coming from Levi's fists as the dragyri pummeled his quarry, preferring to fight with his powerful hands, unless and until something else was necessary.

And then the stench of sulfur began to rain down in the mansion like a torrent of wind and hail, permeating every nook and cranny and closet. The shadow-walkers were ascending from the underworld.

Zane grit his teeth.

Every instinct in his body told him to go to his lair-mates' aid, but they would have to fend off the enemy themselves. Zane didn't have a moment to waste. Dan wasn't just reaching out to the underworld for assistance—thanks to his affinity for flesh-and-blood art, the fool had opened himself up to possession.

Zane rounded the hallway and shot to the top of the stairs, just as Jace, to his right, and Levi, on his left, took out two more human guards, then spun around to face a trio of slinking, translucent shadows emerging from the walls. Zane kept his focus straight ahead, bounding down the stairs in one lithe leap and shooting past Nakai, who had the heel of his boot on a human's throat, while emptying an M4 carbine into the torso of a shade.

Holy spirits of fire; this shit was getting deep!

And while the judge's estate was secluded, ensconced behind a wall, it might be hard to hide a shadow-dragyri war. "Screw it!" Zane shouted as he approached the stainless steel vault and glanced over his shoulder at Nakai. "The Diamond Lair has the night off. Call 'em if you need 'em." He planted both fists around the solid steel wheel and tried to crank it through the locks—he didn't have time to listen and discern, to feel for an encoded password.

The disk came off the door.

"Damnit," he snarled, stepping back and balling up his fists.

He coated his hand with scales, hardened the individual layers, and began to punch in rapid succession, like a horizontal jackhammer, throwing all of his supernatural strength into every caustic blow. The outer panel creaked and groaned, and the inner plate folded inward—but the son of a bitch still held.

Zane took three giant steps backward, called on his inner fire, and hurled a bright orange flame at the center of the door, torching his way through the metal. When the entire panel began to glow a pale yellow-red, he leaped into the air and drop-kicked it open. The hatch flew off the frame—large steel bolts scattering in every direction—even as Zane rushed to get in front of all the debris, and keep it from hitting Jordan.

His dragyra was perched on the floor, behind Dan, her body quaking with fright. There was one streak of blood—drawn from her forehead and along her nose—but thank the gods, she had not been painted with the entire insignia.

Her eyes grew wide and her jaw fell slack as she met Zane's seeking gaze and scooted frantically backward. And that's when Dan began to convulse, his body taken over by a pagan.

Chapter Twenty-nine

JORDAN WATCHED IN absolute horror as the door to the bunker flew open, and thick, iron spikes scattered in her direction. She threw up both hands to cover her face, but the reaction wasn't necessary.

Zane was there in an instant.

Blocking the bolts, shielding her body, hovering over her cowering form in a rage.

His enigmatic gold-blue eyes were glowing in his skull; his upper lip was pulled back in a snarl; and his fangs had descended from the roof of his mouth, making him look like a human jackal. He spun around to face Dan, and his biceps visibly contracted.

He was going to tear Dan's head off.

Despite her terror and confusion, Jordan shot to her feet and tried to dive between them. "No! Zane, don't!" The air left her body in a whoosh as he caught her momentum with an open palm, stopped her trajectory, and shoved her onto the couch.

It was the first time he had ever laid hands on her in an aggressive fashion, and she landed with a thud, quickly sat up, and prepared to try again.

She could not let Zane kill Dan.

No matter what her ex-lover had done, he was there because

she had pleaded with him for help—begged him to come to her rescue.

A spine-tingling hiss reverberated throughout the bunker as Dan's neck began to undulate like a snake's.

What the hell?

The assistant district attorney suddenly stood a whole foot taller, and he held his arms out to the side. "Good evening, son of dragons."

Whose voice was that?

It was foreign, ancient, and dripping with evil.

"Do you have a name, shadow-walker?" Zane bit out.

Dan smiled like a fiend, and his gums were bleeding, his teeth were jagged, and his tongue had a fork in the tip.

Jordan screamed.

"Stay back, dragyra!" Zane commanded. "This is not your lover anymore." His words were as acidic as his tone.

Her lover…

Dan was not her lover, not anymore. What did Zane think was going on? She knew that his dragon was wholly possessive, instinctively territorial, and in this moment, he was also innately savage. "It's not what you think," she muttered.

"No," Zane argued. "It's not what *you* think, dragyra. Your friend is a member of the Cult of Hades. He worships a pagan king by the name of Drakkar—the sworn enemy of the seven dragon lords: their estranged, primordial sibling—and he has invited Lord Drakkar's sycophants, his shadow-walkers, to join us this night."

Dan bowed at the waist, and affixed his now blood-red eyes on Zane. "Names…names…what's in a name: Zanaikeyros, child of Saphyrius." He laughed like an escaped lunatic. "But if you insist on knowing the identity of the one who will silence your soul, you may call me Traylyn Zerachi, born in the time of Romulus Augustus, the infamous Roman emperor—I have waited many lifetimes to make the acquaintance of a Genesis Son."

Zane took a cautious step back, almost as if the creature's age had impressed him, and he dropped low into a defensive stance, raised both arms at his sides, and extended his claws, pointing forward. "Your shadow is strong," he observed. "But not strong enough."

In the blink of an eye, ten red flames shot from the tips of Zane's fingers, each one crisscrossing the next like an X and gathering power at the intersection. The potent amalgamation struck the shadow—it struck Dan—right in the heart.

The attorney howled and flew backward, slamming violently into the bunker wall. And then his chest rose outward like an inflatable balloon, leaking some kind of dark green sludge. The goo dripped on the tile floor, sizzled and popped, and then Dan's chest reversed and contracted, inverting in the opposite direction. His breastplate closed, and he took a long, orgasmic, deep breath. *"Ahhhh…"* He shivered, as if in ecstasy. "You are powerful, Zane Saphyrus. This pairing—our romance—will be exquisite."

Zane didn't reply to the taunt.

He dove forward, rotated into a half summersault, and soared upward to the bunker ceiling. Then he took three steps along the roof and came crashing down, landing behind the shadow-walker. Just as he had done that night in Jordan's apartment, he reached around the pagan's shoulder, ripped into his throat, and opened a spout of arterial spray.

Dan's hands shot up to his windpipe, and he began to choke on the blood, gurgling like a broken spigot. His demonic red eyes faded back to deep brown, and his face grew pale and ashen.

Jordan pushed to her knees, still on the couch, and clutched her hair in her hands, trembling. "Oh, God… Oh, no… Oh, please! You're killing him, Zane. You're destroying Dan." A plaintive sob escaped her throat—this was all happening much too quickly. She didn't have time to process—she only knew that murder was wrong, and even the worst of souls could find redemption. Surely Dan was not without his saving graces. He prosecuted criminals for a living, for heaven's sake! There had to be something…something redeemable…something Zane could do. "Please, dragyri," she pleaded breathlessly. "Please, don't kill him like this—not even for me. He has a brother, he has a mom, he has a life that makes a difference…even if he's lost his way."

The feral shout—the angry roar—that emanated from Zane's throat would stay with Jordan forever. She would never forget that sound as he glared at her with unconcealed rage and abject disappointment stamped into his predatory features. "You would die for him? You would risk my life…and yours…so he could live?"

"Not for him," she argued. "For what's right! *For justice.* I don't believe in execution without a trial. I believe each soul is innocent…until proven guilty."

Zane's laughter was purely sardonic. "Oh, my dragyra—I adore you so, but you have so very much to learn. The innocent are innocent. The guilty are guilty. One does not need a human trial when one can see into the soul. And one does not toy with a shadow-walker."

Jordan gulped.

She knew they were in grave danger.

She knew that whatever was animating Dan Summers' body, it was evil to its core. Still, she didn't want him to die. She just couldn't watch it happen. She straightened her shoulders and raised her chin. "I am human, Zane. If you despise us all so much, then you also despise me."

His eyes closed briefly, and he angled his head in annoyance. Then he dipped down into a squat, reached inside his boot, and retrieved an archaic stiletto, the handle carved into the shape of a dragon. With infinite precision and lightning quick speed, he rose to his full, intimidating height, grasped the attorney by the scalp, and sliced something away from the nape of his neck, the bloody flesh plopping on the ground. Then he drove his fist through Dan's heaving back, and pulled something macabre out of him—it looked like a shadowy spine, a dark, inky impression of thirty-three vertebrae: cervical, thoracic, lumbar—sacral and coccygeal.

Dan's body slumped to the ground, face first, seemingly absent of life, as Zane snapped the shadowy backbone in two, tossed both halves across the bunker, and knelt over the unconscious torso. His mouth opened wider than any mouth should, and a searing, oscillating, silver-blue flame bathed Dan's skull and his back in fire.

Then Zane tossed him over like a carcass of meat, and bathed his throat in the same.

The assistant district attorney sputtered.

He jackknifed off the floor and screamed.

And then he panted like a fish out of water, trying to catch his breath.

Zane met Jordan's gaze with a steely stare of his own, and he nodded before scanning the floor for the spine. "We need to get out of here, and fast!" he barked. "You need to go back through the portal with one of my brothers."

Before she could scramble off the couch or reply, there was a harrowing squeal in the bunker—a high-pitched wail, like a siren—and then all of a sudden, the separate halves of the shadowy spine began to slither across the tiles. They moved faster than Jordan's eyes could track—the two separate ends came together…

They merged.

And then they rose like a ghost from a shallow grave, transforming into a hulking tower of darkness, hatred, and rage…

A living, breathing shadow.

Jordan inhaled sharply, fearing she might lose her dinner, and her heart sank in her chest—the shadow was stretching to the ceiling, filling out the bunker, and lumbering slowly forward.

Toward Zane.

And the entire predicament, this newfound threat, was all Jordan's fault.

In the time it had taken Zane to heal Dan, the dragyri could have scorched the vertebrae, and Jordan and Zane could have escaped.

He hadn't had a second to spare.

For all intents and purposes, Dan had been dead, and Zane had chosen to reanimate Jordan's ex-lover instead of extinguishing the threat.

Now, he was facing a monster.

⁓

Zane knew they were out of time.

He would never get Jordan up the stairs, away from the perilous shadow, and into the portal, to safety. And he no longer had a window of opportunity to take her to one of his brothers while he stayed and fought the pagan.

The shadow-walker was too strong.

Too intent on annihilation.

Zane leaped across the bunker, placing his immortal body between Jordan and the shade, and he thanked the gods of the sacred stones that he had been born a Genesis Son. "Father!" he shouted, shaking the bunker. "My lord, I need your assistance!"

He felt Lord Saphyrius stir, but he didn't have time to listen…

Or to wait.

The shadow-walker had taken on a loosely human form, and it dove across the bunker at Zane, crashing into the center of the dragyri's torso. Zane's ribs exploded inward, breaking in his chest, and he gasped in pain, fighting for breath, all the while trying to shove his assailant backward. The bastard felt like a five-ton truck—he just kept coming, and coming…and coming. The dance of arms, of claws, and fists was like an industrial fan spinning at inhuman velocity: strike, block, stab, retreat…on and on, they tangled.

Zane grasped the shade by the forearm and broke it; the shadow countered by crushing Zane's hand. Zane slammed his forehead into the shadow's bony brow; the reptilian frontal lobe gave way, and the creature retaliated by spewing acidic goo—trying to spray Zane in the eyes.

He missed by the width of a human hair.

The pagan grunted, drew back his unbroken arm, and quickly plunged it forward, tunneling through Zane's exposed chest. He snatched Zane's heart and began to tug, trying to wrench it free from the dragyri's thorax. Zane latched on to the shadow's spindly wrist and held it in a vise grip of his own. He drew on his limited breath—his broken ribs were impeding his lungs—and exhaled a long, continuous flame, trying to melt the pagan's face off…force him to let go of his heart.

And that's when he felt the power of the dragon lord swelling within his breast.

Reach for your amulet, my son! The thunderous command was imperious, but holy shit—was Lord Saphyrius crazy? The pagan still had Zane's heart! If he let go, it would all be over.

Trust me, dragyri!

Marshaling all the preternatural speed of his kind, Zane released the pagan's wrist and clutched at his amulet. The sapphire glowed in an instant. Zane's ribs knitted together, and a force like a raging tornado exploded outward.

Rising like an ancient serpent from the sea, Zane let out a feral roar and lunged forward. His jaw went lax, his throat filled with fire, and his neck grew a dozen inches longer. He struck like a viper, inhaling the pagan's head and closing his jaws around it. Then he whipped his head from side to side, sending pieces of the pagan flying—serrating the shadow's body with his treacherous teeth.

Zane continued to pounce on the remnants.

He let go of the pagan's crushed skull and seared it to ash. Then he wandered from body part to body part, slinking throughout the room, scorching anything that was left.

A dazzling blue beam of light shot forth from Zane's amulet, cascaded upward into an arc, and curved backward, entering his body through his throat. It snaked through his veins, saturated his muscles, and meandered through the collagen in his bones. And just like that, his ribs were healed, his hand was repaired, and his forehead was whole.

His heart beat with new vitality as he rose from the floor and spun around, searching the room for Jordan while reclaiming his aboriginal form. "Angel," he called out, listening for her heartbeat.

She was hiding on the floor, crouched behind the couch, and peeking around the arm. Her eyes were as wide as saucers; her mouth was hanging open; and she looked like she had just seen a ghost.

"Are you okay?" he asked, covering the distance between them in seconds.

She jerked back, threw up her hands, and cowered before him.

"Do not be afraid," he murmured. "I will never harm you, angel—you know this."

She gulped, tried to speak, and grunted something incoherent.

Zane angled his head to the side and tried to offer a smile, however faint, to reassure her.

She shook her head back and forth to clear her bewilderment. "I thought…" The words came out as a croak, and she had to try again. "I thought you weren't a shifter."

Zane softened his voice. "I'm not, baby girl." Then he held out his hand to help her up. "Come, dragyra, we need to get out of here."

She stared at his palm like he was an executioner inviting her to take a trip to the gallows, and then she slowly marshaled her courage and clasped the proffered offering. "What about Dan?" she asked, glancing across the floor at the crumpled, unconscious body.

"He will live," Zane said, "but you're right…"

He released her hand, sauntered across the floor, and knelt in front of the body, cupping Dan's head in his hands. "When you awaken, you will remember nothing! The last time you saw Jordan"—he dipped into her mind—"was in passing, at work. You haven't spoken to her since. There was no letter." He scanned the bunker, eyed the missive on a tiny metal end table, and drew it into his hand, using telekinesis. And then he scorched it into cinders. "There was no text"—he found Dan's cell phone in Dan's jacket pocket and crushed it in the palm of his hand—"and you are no longer in love with Jordan. You don't know why you're here; you don't know what happened; and you no longer worship the Cult of Hades. Return to your life and make it worthwhile." He started to stand up, but remembered one last thing. "Oh, and you will be asked a lot of questions: about the courthouse, about Judge Moran, about Jordan Anderson. You don't know, you don't remember, and frankly, you no longer care enough to investigate."

There was no need to wake the human up to check for the strength of the compulsion, or to make sure the directives would hold. Zane's entire essence was still imbued with the power of Lord Saphyrius—the human would be lucky if his entire mind wasn't scrubbed, and empty, by the time he awakened.

He'd be lucky if he could still speak and walk.

But Zane was not going to share that with Jordan—he had done everything he could.

Just then, a pair of loud, heavy boots beat down the stairs and stomped to the edge of the doorway, and Axe Saphyrius peered through the decimated hatch. "Everything copasetic in here?" he grumbled.

Zane scrubbed his hand over his face and glanced around the room, taking in the massive destruction. "It's over—that's what matters."

Axe glanced at him sideways and frowned.

"What?" Zane asked.

"You're glowing…kind of blue."

Zane shrugged. "I had to reach out to my maker."

Axe whistled low, beneath his breath, and eyed the bunker a second time, paying special attention to the piles of slag and the inky stains of pagan blood. "Damn," he muttered. "Well, all right, then…" He swept his gaze over Jordan. "She okay?"

"I'm fine," Jordan said curtly. She sounded a tad bit miffed that Axe had asked Zane, instead of her.

Oh, well…

It had been a *really* long night—she would have to get over that infraction.

Axe nodded.

"What about the scene outside?" Zane asked. "How many pagans are we talking?"

Axe sniffed and grunted and rotated his shoulders, releasing a boat-load of tension. "Uh, that would be a zero at this juncture." He smiled, and the light-hearted gesture looked curiously odd on his harsh, masculine features. "The Diamond Lair showed up," he explained. "Jace has a broken leg; Levi is missing a hand; and last I checked, Nakai's entrails were still on the front lawn, but the pagans are either gone or dead, and Ghost is blazing Nakai back together."

"Ghost?" Zane asked, incredulous.

"Yeah," Axe chuckled. "He ripped two pagans apart in the grass, crouched down to eat them, and almost took a chunk out of Nakai. I think he feels guilty—well, as much as Ghost can."

Zane grimaced, and Jordan swayed on her feet. "Catch her!" Zane barked.

Axe moved with a quickness, slipping his palm along the small of Jordan's back, and slowly tipping her upright. He waited for her to catch her breath. "You good?"

Zane stepped in before she could answer, taking his dragyra in his arms, lifting her off her feet, and holding her like a child—tenderly, against his chest. "Well, I hate to skip out on the clean-up, but Jordan needs to rest. I'm gonna take her back through the portal."

Axe nodded again. "Not a problem, brother. I'll walk you outside. Nice to see you both in one piece."

Chapter Thirty

JORDAN SANK DEEP into the hot, bubbling water in Zane's private hot tub, outside on his secluded deck, and tried to let the warmth and the jets take her away. The moon was shining especially bright, and the deep blue sky was littered with glistening stars. Yet and still, her mind was still spinning...reeling...as she grappled with all that had happened over the past twenty-four hours: her decision to go forward with the letter to Dan, and all that ensued afterward.

As always, Zane was close by, refusing to let her out of his sight, but even though he had slipped into a pair of swimming trunks at the same time she'd put on her suit, he had not joined her in the water.

At least not yet.

For now, he stood several yards away on the deck, leaning against the rail and watching the magnificent waterfall—he seemed to be lost in a myriad of thoughts of his own.

Jordan sighed, wondering what he was thinking. He had been so quiet ever since they returned through the portal, nearly three hours ago. He had made sure she had a shower, something to eat, and he had checked her for any injuries—despite the violent night, she was more or less fit as a fiddle—and then he'd given her some space, at least within a dozen yards or so.

Now, as she soaked in the tub, alone, wrestling with her emotions and her thoughts, she knew that she had to face the inevitable—she had to face her fears head-on. She wasn't going to escape. Dan had been her last great hope, and that had been an ill-conceived, desperate grasp at freedom to begin with. It was time to regroup, and the way Jordan saw it, sometimes knowledge was power. The more facts she knew, the more she could process…the better chance she stood at surviving.

And along those lines, there was an inconvenient truth she could no longer afford to deny: She needed Zane. To stay safe. To stay alive. This world he had brought her into was filled with living nightmares and terrible creatures, things she couldn't even imagine in her wildest dreams: pagans, demons, shadow-walkers, and feral dragyri, like the one named Ghost. Hell, she reasoned, even the actress in the famous classical film *King Kong* had eventually turned to the ape when faced with all the terrifying monsters on the other side of the wall. She had sucked it up and hedged her bets—she had wanted to survive.

Jordan frowned.

Turned to the ape…

Glancing at Zane, she took in his broad, muscular shoulders, his proud warrior's bearing, and his striking good looks, the way the gentle breeze rustled all that chestnut-brown hair, fanning it in and out of his sapphire-gold eyes—those terrifying, glorious dragon eyes—and she knew he was anything but an ape. She drew a slow, deep breath, mustered her courage, and hit the button on the panel that controlled the jets.

Silence.

Except for the waterfall.

"Zane." The word wasn't spoken very loud, but he heard her just the same. He pushed off the railing and turned to face her, both of his eyebrows cocked. "Can we talk?" she asked, her stomach clenched into knots.

He nodded solemnly and strolled across the deck.

Good Lord, it was like inviting a potential hurricane onto the shore.

He stopped at the edge of the tub, glanced at the steaming water, and engaged her eyes. "May I?"

She gulped and then nodded, tucking her knees out of the way so he could climb in without touching her.

The water sloshed as he made his entry, and much to her relief, he took a seat in a corner chair, opposite the lounger, once again giving her some much-needed space. "What is it, dragyra?" he finally asked, once his large, towering frame had settled.

Jordan swept her hand through the water, back and forth, as a paltry distraction. "You're angry with me, aren't you?"

His placid stare was like the calm beneath a storm: dormant, beautiful, and eerily deceptive. "I'm not angry, dragyra," he said evenly. "I'm relieved. I'm disappointed. And I'm concerned."

Good gracious, she thought. Would he always be that blunt? She stilled her hands and cleared her throat. "Relieved that I'm okay, that you and your lair-mates are going to be all right, but disappointed because I betrayed you, because Jace, Levi, and Nakai got hurt...because you almost got killed. And concerned... because?"

He leaned forward, bracing his elbows on his knees, to regard her straightaway. "Because starting tomorrow, we only have four more days, and you are no closer to me now than you were in that parking garage...you are not trying...and I don't know how."

The candidness of his words struck her like an anvil, and in that particular, guileless moment, he looked like the loneliest male on the planet—*the loneliest male beyond the portal*—as lost as Jordan felt. She closed her eyes and steadied her breath. "I am sorry that I placed your brothers in danger," she whispered, hoping he could hear her over the ambient rush of the falls. "I'm sorry that you had to fight that...that shadow thing...and I'm also sorry about Dan, the way that affected you. I had to try, Zane. I had to." She opened her eyes and waited as he slowly nodded his head.

"I know you did, Jordan. And that's why I didn't search your purse, look for the letter. That's why I let the whole unholy spectacle play out." She started to object, to explain her actions, but he waved his wrist in a gentle arc, indicating that he really wasn't stuck on the details. "You weren't entirely honest with me," he said plainly, "and I haven't been entirely honest with you, either. Perhaps we should start there…"

Jordan's heart fluttered in her chest, and it immediately beat faster. Oh, shit—what hadn't he told her? And how bad was it? She bit her lower lip and searched his eyes, almost too afraid to listen.

He shook his head, slid out of the seat, and crossed the tub with graceful ease, taking a seat in the bench beside her, then reaching for her hand.

She let him take it.

She was too unsteady to object.

"Nothing nefarious, dragyra," he assured her. "Just careful omissions, here and there." He rotated his thumb in a gentle circle, along the center of her palm. "You wrote that letter to Dan while I was at the temple, correct?"

She nodded and looked away, staring at the water.

He squeezed her hand. "In truth, you could have emailed him or called him, although the dragon lords would have known—they would have felt it."

She frowned. "But I thought you said my cell phone wouldn't work here—I checked it, and there was never a signal. And as for Wi-Fi, I figured that was the same kind of thing. The dragyri speak telepathically; you don't have any use for those things."

Zane offered her a half-hearted smile. "We rarely use those things with each other, at least not on this side of the portal, but we do conduct a lot of business with the human realm—not everything can be made or acquired in The Pantheon." He watched as a small swell of water rolled over their linked fingers and cast a pale red shadow beneath the surface, projecting from the underwater lights. "On the back of the desk, in our suite, there was a sapphire paperweight—did you see it? It's a round, palm-sized object with a flat, level base."

Jordan thought about the layout of the desk and the few items she had seen. "Yes," she said softly. "It was sitting in the corner."

Zane inclined his head. "If you place your hand over the top of the globe and grasp it, the stone will warm to your touch, and then it will begin to glow. Every radio frequency or wave used in the human realm can be duplicated and harnessed—recreated and captured—in that sapphire stone. It was easily manufactured by the gods. Should you choose to communicate through a human device, you need only to invoke the sapphire sphere. There are several on every floor of the lair: one on each desk, and a larger one on the accent tables at the end of each communal hall."

Jordan swallowed any potential protest and chuckled insincerely. "That would have been nice to know."

"Yeah," Zane teased her. "You would've called every agency you could think of: the FBI, the CIA, heck, the White House—am I right?" In spite of his momentary levity, he understood the gravity of the situation and pressed on without awaiting an answer. "Point being: I withheld the entire truth, at least initially, because our connection was too…uncertain." He tempered his voice, and his dragon eyes narrowed. "And I withheld the entire truth about something else as well."

She held his gaze without wavering. "About what?"

"The temple. The consecration. The full stakes involved."

Oh. Shit.

She braced herself for the worst—if he was going to tell her something awful, something unthinkable, she wanted to suppress any potential hysterical reaction.

"Do you remember that night in your apartment when I told you I would not let you die, nor would I relinquish my life to make this easier?"

She nodded.

"What did you think that meant?"

"I don't really know," she answered honestly. "That you weren't going to let anyone—or anything—kill me, and that you weren't going to allow me to risk your life, or your safety, either." She cringed. "I know I almost got you killed, Zane—I just…I just don't know what to say. I had to do what I did. It was—"

"No," he interrupted, once again squeezing her hand. "We can speak more about that later, if you wish. Right now, I'm referring to something else."

She stared at him blankly, feeling a bit like a child being chastised by a teacher. "Okay."

"Jordan, there are consequences for failing to bring one's dragyra to the temple on the tenth day of the claiming."

If not for the warm, calming water, she would have visibly shivered. "Like what?"

He lowered his voice instinctively. "If you fail to show up, you will…perish…in your sleep that night. And I…I will have my amulet removed by Lord Saphyrius."

Jordan shot up in her seat, recoiling. She wrenched her hand free of his and held it up in question. "What do you mean by perish?"

He frowned. *"Perish."*

She shook her head in disbelief, and then her eyes shot to his amulet, resting so conspicuously on his naked chest: The uneven natural stone was exquisite, priceless…ominous. "What happens if he removes your amulet?"

Zane glanced away, and his silence shook her soul.

"Zane, what happens?"

He showed no emotion whatsoever. "My existence will be no more." And then, as if he was reading a fictional page from an ancient text, he went on to tell her about the seven white clay mountains—the Garden of Grace—and how the statues were the souls of the Dragyr's dead, immortalized as gemstones forever. He reminded her, yet again, about the life-force imbued in the sacred stones, making it clearer this time that, for all intents and purposes, the gemstone was the equivalent of a human soul—once it was gone, the body was no longer animated.

Jordan felt faint.

She felt disoriented and sick to her stomach.

This was insane.

Unthinkable.

Utterly…and absolutely…horrific.

After several protracted moments had passed—she would process the bulk of it later; they still had four more days—she asked him, "Has anyone ever done that? I mean, a human woman refusing to enter the Temple?"

Zane's countenance changed, and his features grew strained. "Yeah. It's happened."

He rolled his shoulders in an unconscious gesture, trying his best to relax, and for the second time since she'd met him, Jordan caught a faraway look in his eyes—she had seen that look before, that night in her living room when he had crouched in front of the sofa and taken a drop of her blood. "Zane..." She spoke softly. "That night, when you asked me about my family, whether or not I had a lot of relatives, I told you about my parents...about my grandmother passing away." She sighed. "You had this really distant look in your eyes, the same one you have now. What is that about, Zane? Who did you lose?"

Zane stirred restlessly in the tub, sending several waves of water rippling across the surface, and then he slowly shook his head, dismissing the subject.

"Am I the only one who has to be vulnerable?" she asked. "The only one who is constantly exposed and off-balance?"

Zane blinked his sapphire-gold eyes; his tongue snaked out to lick his lips; and his features looked positive ashen...like he had just seen a shade. "Jaquar."

A single word.

"Who?" Jordan asked. She leaned in, toward him. "Zane, who is—*who was*—Jaquar?"

Zanaikeyros slowly exhaled. He brushed his hand through his hair and hung his head, trying to hide his eyes. "Jaquariaz Saphyrius," he whispered, gradually raising his chin. "He was one of the original forty-nine hatchlings. We were born...we emerged... on the same day, at the same time: January 7, 1016. So, I guess we were a lot like twins." His forehead creased into a frown, and the light in his eyes grew dim. "I don't think we spent a day apart in seven hundred years. He was more than a brother to me—he was my closest friend."

His nose twitched in anger, and his voice grew hoarse. "His dragyra could not be persuaded to enter the temple. She just didn't want any part of this life. She was attached to her human identity and zealous about her religion—she saw Jaquar as some sort of evil spirit, and nothing could dissuade her." Like a candle blown out in the night, the dim, lingering flicker in Zane's pupils extinguished: a total eclipse of his soul. His voice was utterly hollow as he spoke his next words. "And that was a shame—for her—because Jaquariaz was, actually, the most honorable, genuine, and incorruptible male I've ever known. She missed out on a lifetime of happiness."

Jordan let Zane's words linger for several heartbeats. Finally, when she spoke, she treaded very carefully. "Jaquar is on the mountain?"

Zane nodded and looked away.

An animal in a nearby tree hooted, and it sounded very much like an owl, perhaps a little larger, more resonant...more mysterious. And in that moment, something struck Jordan deep in her soul, something she hadn't been aware of before: It was as if the fog all around her suddenly lifted, and the sky grew unexpectedly clear—like a downpour of rain had suddenly abated, and the mist was instantly gone. For whatever reason, Jordan could see the entire horizon beyond her immediate view. She could see Zanaikeyros Saphyrius as he truly was, and she could see a crystal-clear portion of his ancient heart.

The Dragyr was a mercenary, to be sure.

He was as savage as he was handsome; as dominant as he was strong.

He was clear-headed, determined, and ruthless when he had to be.

But he was also eternally alone.

Zane had never had a mother to hold him, kiss him, or tuck him into bed. And he had never known a father in any real sense of the word. His *maker* was a dragon lord who demanded his obedience, rescued him when he was in trouble, but would just as soon punish him—harshly, brutally, and without mercy—if it came down to it. The dragyri had never had a sister or a brother, outside of Jaquar and his lair-mates.

And he had never had a wife...or kids.

He was a soldier for the Temple of Seven.

A hired gun...

A supernatural killer.

Who had always known war, and fire, and blood.

He hunted like a predator to feed his inner flame, to reanimate his essence, and the act was as impersonal as it was, ironically, intimate. He was a primordial, detached soul following his master's orders and hoping to survive—*for what?* To live another day? Another century? Another millennium?

All of it...alone.

Despite all her inner turmoil—her personal angst and her dread—she would have had to be unfeeling—cold and entirely heartless—to not feel some compassion for this solitary male.

"I'm sorry, Zane." She said it, and she meant it.

He nodded. "Yeah. So am I."

She didn't want to push the subject, dig any deeper into an open wound, but she had to know, to understand: "So, it's true, then? A female can't be forced to enter the temple?"

Zane met her seeking gaze, and his demeanor seemed much more calm. "It's a matter of degrees," he amended. "She has to enter the temple of her own volition—that is the decree. Whether that means her own decision, wish, or desire is up to debate. It is not unheard of for a gentler male to try to win his female's heart... in only ten days...to insist upon obtaining her desire." He leaned back in the smooth, rounded chair and crossed his arms in front of his chest. "But it is also not unheard of for a harder male, a more determined male, to take matters into his own ruthless hands: Friends, loved ones, and even children—nieces, nephews, and wards—have been held hostage and used as leverage. Threats have been made against entire villages and clans...potential retaliation from other members of the lair if the female does not acquiesce. At the end of the day, she has to walk across that threshold on her own. She doesn't necessarily have to want it. Or to like it."

Jordan gasped.

She glared at Zane as if he had just grown horns, hoping to

find the truth in his eyes—which kind of male was he? The former, or the latter?

But what she saw in those golden pupils was a solid, unyielding wall, an impenetrable fortress built by a male who was just as afraid—and determined—as she was: a dragyri warrior who had lost his best friend to this cruel, unforgiving world that he hadn't chosen, either.

She swallowed her distrust and tried to reach out…just a bit. "What do you want from me, Zane?" She practically held her breath, waiting for his answer, and for a moment, it looked like he could go either way: retreat into his hardened shell, or reach out and try to connect.

He stirred restlessly in his seat, still clinging to her hand, and then he made his decision. "I want you to try, Jordan," he said earnestly. "I don't know if love is possible in such a short time, although I have seen it happen. And I don't know if there's anything I can say or do to deepen the bond between us—in the limited time we have left. But I do know that if you keep resisting, hiding, running, there won't be a chance for either of us. Your fate is unwanted—I get that—but is it a fate worse than death? Only you can decide. I want you to try to open your heart, try to open your mind, try to let me in, dragyra. See what might happen… between us." He grasped her hand in his—took it back—and she was curiously relieved. "I just need you to try with me, Jordan."

Jordan listened to his words.

She took them in, thought about them, and refused to run and hide.

And that determination, that desire to survive brought them both back—full circle—to the previous events of the day, to the giant gray elephant sitting in the middle of the tub: the assistant district attorney, and Jordan's attempt to escape. There could be no trying, no attempt to understand, no bridge built between them unless and until they cleared the air.

"Dan," she ventured bravely. "What I did, by reaching out to Dan—how does that affect things? How did that affect you?"

Zane felt the shift in Jordan.

He felt it in himself.

After nearly retreating from the situation, she had managed to draw him out—they had somehow made a connection and, although it was tentative at best, he didn't want to ruin it by discussing her ex-lover.

Not now.

Not when they were right on the verge of a breakthrough.

Yet and still, they had to see this through.

He sighed. "From this moment forward, only truth between us?" He posed it as a question, waiting for her assent.

Jordan hesitated—clearly thinking it over—and then she nodded her head. Her gorgeous hazel eyes shone like twin jewels in the moonlight, and every instinct in his body wanted to reach out… to touch her…to draw her in for a kiss. But it was much too soon. Much too aggressive.

His dragyra wasn't ready, so he made another calculation…

He released her hand, slid out of the seat, and sidled up behind her on the lounge, gently inching her forward. Her shoulders tensed, and she looked back at him with unease—but she didn't try to stop him. As he'd calculated, her body was buoyant in the water, and it floated toward the surface, just long enough for him to slide beneath her, behind her, and to tug her back into his lap. Straddling her hips with his legs, he wrapped his massive, muscular arms around her shoulders and he drew her to his chest. Her head fell back against his shoulder, and he nuzzled her neck, beneath her ear. "This is better for me," he rasped. "Having you in my arms. I want you to feel safe, Jordan. I want you to feel protected. I want you to feel my heart as we talk—to know that it beats for you, despite your earlier betrayal. I want you to feel the strength of my commitment."

She shivered, and then she gulped—and Zane suppressed a smile.

Gods knew, he was pushing her beyond the limit, but they were running out of time.

Slowly—oh, so cautiously—she finally let her body relax and

settle into the frame of his. She placed both of her elegant hands on his arms, but a mosquito buzzing by would have made her jump out of the water—she was that on edge.

Zane chuckled to himself…

Good thing they didn't have mosquitos in Dragons Domain.

"Now then," he spoke into her ear. "Your ex-lover…Dan. The man you reached out to. Why, Jordan? Why did you choose him?"

She shivered again, and he brushed his hands over her arms, knowing the chill wasn't caused by the night—hell, the water was 102 degrees.

She gradually settled down. "It wasn't what you're thinking."

"I'm not thinking anything," he said. "At least, I'm not pre-judging. Why did you seek his assistance above all others?"

She grew quiet for a moment. "Logistics."

He smiled.

"First, he was the only person I knew with that many connections and resources…the only one I thought could pull it off. And, beyond that, he was the only person I was certain I could reach with a letter, since I didn't have any other means of communicating." She paused. "Or so I thought." There wasn't any anger in her voice, just candid acknowledgment.

Zane nodded, knowing she could feel the subtle shift in his chin—then he took the opportunity to nuzzle her beautiful hair. "I believe you. I do. So you no longer desire this male—you no longer share his love?"

If her body had grown any stiffer, she would have floated away as a block of wood. He sent a gentle pulse of serenity streaming into her torso, using the tips of his fingers—it wasn't really cheating; he just wanted to help her out.

She sighed. "I stopped desiring Dan when I found out he was married. It took a little longer to fall out of love."

A feral growl rose in Zane's chest, and he had to keep it from escaping. He felt his fangs press against his gums and immediately constrained them. "He hurt you…" It was a simple but loaded statement.

"Deeply," Jordan replied.

This time, it was Zane who tensed, but only for a moment. "I'm sorry," he whispered, telling his beast to heel: *We cannot kill the human...at least not this night.* He banked his inner fire and extinguished the spark of rage.

And then Jordan croaked a timid question: "Why did you do it, Zane? Why did you spare Dan's life...even knowing that the shadow would grow stronger, and you might get hurt. Why did you take that risk?"

Well, hell...

His dragon stirred again.

And a part of him wanted to lie, but he couldn't. "There are some things," he began, "that you will never fully comprehend, being human—not even when you're made immortal. But trust me when I say to you that as a living dragyri, I wanted to eviscerate his heart. Every impulse in my body was humming with the need to destroy that man, and it cost me, far more deeply than you know, to restrain it. As it is, I will need to *feed*...very soon, to replenish what was lost." He modulated his voice, afraid of sounding too barbaric. "But when you spoke to me in the bunker about your values, about your beliefs, how deeply you revere the human concept of justice, it struck me...who you are...why you are an attorney, and why that need runs so deep."

Jordan started to sit up and turn around, but his arms prevented the movement. Instead, she tilted her head to the side, listening intently.

"Your life has been harsh and sometimes unfair, but you are, first and foremost, a survivor. In my observation, the injustice you prosecute is your own—your tragedy, your struggles, and your loss—and the need for a verdict that is just is your own need for a sense of balance...for a sense of fairness. If in the end, the guilty are punished and the innocent are set free, then there is hope that the scales can be balanced, that tragedy will not always be your lot. We all need something to believe in, Jordan, a way to make sense of our lives." He sighed. "And I also caught a glimpse of Dan's soul... before he joined the Cult. He grew up in a very rough neighborhood; he was no stranger to crime, but unlike you, he wasn't, foremost, a survivor—he became a conman of sorts, a manipulator of people and facts. He learned how to get what he wanted by reading and influencing others. It is true that he chose the law in order to right the wrongs of his past, but his chief motivation was to be on the winning team…always on the winning side…and that's what exposed his soul to the pagans. His desire to land on top. His ability to overlook whoever fell to the bottom."

Jordan grew inscrutably still, inwardly and outwardly, and Zane didn't have to read her thoughts to know what she was thinking—that's what Dan had done with her, hiding the fact that he was married. He had found something "winning" to latch onto—something he had wanted more than his current life and marriage—and he had reached out to take it, consequences be damned.

"Angel of mine," he continued. "I did what I did in that bunker for you, but also for me." A cool breeze stirred all around them, creating a light, crystal mist over the hot tub, and Zane concealed a shiver of his own—he didn't know if he could say the rest.

"How so?" she asked. And there was the lawyer again—always going straight to the heart of the matter.

Zane consulted the truth in his heart. "I did it because I wanted to give you something of true value. I did it because of the pain in your eyes. I did it because I wanted to please you; I wanted you to think more highly of me; and I wanted to win your trust. I did it, almost on an impulse, because I wanted you…to want me as well. And I had to betray everything I am—as a dragyri, as a warrior—in order to do it."

Jordan cleared her throat. "You let Dan live because you wanted me to…like you?"

Zane started, taken aback by her bluntness.

That was not what he'd said—was it?

He chuckled, deep and low in his throat. "Baby, my lair-mates are going to pull my man card for this."

She softened her voice. "Well, you don't have a man card—you have a *male* card, so I guess your secret is safe."

He smiled in retort, and then his tone turned deathly serious. "Jordan, I want you to know my true heart. I do. I allowed Dan to live because we are so very close to our date with the temple—and yes, because I already care deeply for you. You are the most stunning, intelligent, and desirable woman I have ever known, and I want you—by all the gods, I want you. But angel, don't get it twisted." He purposefully tempered his voice. "I am not Jaquar, and I intend to claim you by any means necessary." He paused for the breadth of one heartbeat. "Yet and still, if you would only try… Just north of the Diamond Lair, there is a white sandy beach in a beautiful cove. At night, when the sun sets and the dragon moon rises, there's fire in the water—the waves are like flames, undulating in the sea, in brilliant cascades of emerald, amethyst, and topaz… all the hues of the sacred stones. It will take your breath away, dragyra. Let me take you there, tomorrow night. Walk in the sands with me. Give me a chance to glimpse your heart." Despite his determination not to push too far, he dropped his head and placed a tender kiss against the slope of her throat, just above her carotid artery—and his dragon stirred.

He needed to feed, and he would do it soon, perhaps later on in the week. What he would not do is ask for something so intimate, so personal and primordial…of Jordan.

Not right now.

She just wasn't ready.

His fangs throbbed, and he nicked her skin, swirling his tongue over the small droplet of blood before cooling the abrasion with a thin blue flame. His beast growled, yet he kept his composure. "What say you, dragyra," he nearly groaned. "Will you try with me? Will you go to the cove?"

He expected Jordan to bolt.

To jump from the lounger, hurtle the waist-high panel, and take off running along the deck, but as she often did, his dragyra surprised him.

She sat up slowly, turned around, and met his hungry gaze. "Your dragon is close to the surface, isn't he—because of what I did, what I asked of you earlier?" She smiled faintly, and there wasn't a star in the sky that could match her beauty. "Thank you, Zane. For hearing me in that bunker…for seeing me in that bunker…for

saving Dan when you didn't have to. Thank you for wanting me…
to want you. It might be a place to start." She reached out with a
tentative hand and shyly cupped his cheek, brushing her elegant
thumb against his strong, angular jaw. Then she leaned slowly
forward and pressed a soft, chaste kiss on his mouth, quickly pulling away. "I will try, dragyri, although I can't make any promises.
I'm horrified, terrified, and beyond confused. But you tried for me,
and I will try for you." She paused, allowing her words to settle,
and then she flashed a shy, girlish smile. "Do you mind if I text
Macy—let her know that I'm still alive? She has to have seen the
news by now."

Chapter Thirty-one

THE DARK, INKY beetle slinked into the shadows on the outdoor portico of the third floor of the Sapphire Lair, hunkering down behind an ornate iron post in the railing.

Zane's words: *As it is, I will need to feed…very soon, to replenish what was lost.*

Well, thank the dark hosts, Salem thought. He was beginning to believe the dragyri would never leave his female's side. There had not been one opportunity—not one—to get to Jordan Anderson since the two had come back through the portal.

And just what the hell was that!

Twelve pagans dead in the last five days: first, Rafael, Malandrix, and Alexian on Friday night. Then eight more shadow-walkers at the judge's estate, not to mention the illustrious Traylyn Zerachi, slain by Zanaikeyros himself, with a bit of help from Lord Saphyrius.

Lord Hades was beside himself with fury, and Salem couldn't blame him. This was not what he had envisioned for his beloved horde. Furthermore, he was so despondent at the loss of his familial puppets that he had considered ordering Salem out of Dragons Domain, demanding that the demon come home before complet-ing his nefarious mission: to destroy Zanaikeyros' mate. Salem had objected, as respectfully as he could, swearing that he could get to her before Sunday, before she entered that temple. But now, he wasn't sure.

Zane was sticking to her side like glue.

Yet and still, he had to feed, and he had to feed soon.

That meant he would have to leave Jordan's side to hunt and corner his prey—he would have to go back through the portal, taking a member of the Sapphire Lair with him. Yes, Salem had paid careful attention to every spoken word—he knew everything going on in The Pantheon, including last Sunday's decree that the Genesis Sons had to travel in pairs: Levi and Axe had discussed it.

Unfortunately, what he didn't know was when Zanaikeyros would hunt. Would he go this night, while Jordan slept, or would he slip out in the morning? The Sapphire Lair was teeming with powerful Dragyr—every single male was home—and sleeping or not, he couldn't risk an attack on Jordan against such powerful odds.

He had to corner her alone!

Scurrying down the iron post, then dropping to the second-floor deck, beneath Zane's, Salem made his decision. There was no point in hanging out all night, playing the incessant *what-if* game. He would travel beyond the Diamond Lair while he still had time. He would scope out the northernmost region of Dragons Domain and try to find these white sandy beaches. He would need to shift into his natural demon form to cover so much ground—he would need to fly beneath the cover of darkness—and pray, all the while, that none of the dragon lords were out, in their primordial, bestial forms, soaring beneath the dragon moon.

If they were, then his goose was cooked.

They would scent him in an instant.

Still, he had to risk it.

And if luck—or the power of Lord Hades—was on his side, then by sundown tomorrow, he would be waiting for Jordan and Zane in their glorious private cove. And if Zane continued to hover about his female like a swarm of mosquitos over a murky pond, then perhaps Salem would be brave enough to take another risk:

to strike at the couple while they were still together, knowing there wouldn't be any backup.

It would only take one swipe…one lunge…to take down the mortal female.

⟡

Macy Wilson fumbled with her remote control, trying to find a better movie on cable: something sweet and romantic…and titillating.

Something that reminded her of Dr. Kyle Parker.

She giggled beneath the sheets of her bed, fluffing the pillow behind her.

The day had been both awful and wonderful, respectively: On one hand, there had been the terrible news from the courtroom—Jordan's courtroom—about some insane terrorist or escaped prisoner who had taken the courtroom hostage, only to be disarmed by SWAT. The details kept changing, the story kept evolving, yet they insisted that no one had been hurt. Macy had been beside herself with worry. On the other hand, she had gotten a call from Dr. Parker, which had conversely lifted her spirits. He wanted to come by her apartment on Friday night and make her a candlelit dinner.

A candlelit dinner!

It was almost too good to be true.

Granted, she was more than just a little bit loopy from her post-op medications—her four-hour doses of Vicodin and Tylenol—but she would have been just as giddy if she'd been totally sober. And as for Jordan's plight? Well, Macy had received a text, around 12:45 AM, saying everything was fine: Jordan was still taking a couple weeks off, as intended—she still needed some time to reboot and recharge, and she would get in touch with Macy off and on, but not that often—she just needed some time and some space…

She had apologized for not texting sooner—apparently, there had been a lot of confusion and commotion following the dust-up in the courtroom—but she had insisted that everything was fine. She was safe. And she had told Macy not to waste any energy being worried.

While it wasn't exactly unicorns and roses, it was enough to allay Macy's fears…

At least for the time being.

At least her BFF was safe.

Now, as she snuggled beneath her warm, cozy covers, luxuriating in the soft, downy sheets, she turned her full attention to Dr. Parker...and this coming Friday night. What would she wear? What would he be wearing? How should she style her hair...and do her makeup? Would the surgeon be wearing jeans or slacks? Would she get a glimpse at his arms or his chest?

Would he bring her a bottle of wine?

Oh, well, probably not, considering the Vicodin, but she would probably be done with it by then. In fact, Dr. Parker had said she'd be up and running in a couple of days, albeit at a slower pace, or he wouldn't have asked her on a date so soon. It was a benefit of laparoscopic surgery—no large incisions or damaged layers to heal.

Both affirmations gave her enormous confidence.

As she toggled through the line-up of late-night movies, she settled on a chick flick that immediately caught her eye: *Dancing with Doctor Right*.

Perfect.

Just perfect.

Chapter Thirty-two

Wednesday night - twilight

ZANE LOOKED LIKE a bronzed statue of the Greek god Adonis as he strolled across the white sandy beach in his faded blue jeans and no shirt. His hair was wet and mussed from sea-spray, having been splashed earlier as he stood on the edge of an outcropping; his skin was as fine as a baby's, both golden and smooth; and the crystal-clear ocean reflected off his golden pupils like beams of starlight, twinkling in the sapphire-blue sky.

Despite herself, Jordan had to catch her breath—the male was positively magnificent.

And that was only half of the revelation.

Much to Jordan's surprise—and dare she say, intrigue—Zane Saphyrius knew how to let his hair down. He actually knew how to laugh and to play.

Caught up in the magic and serenity of the beautiful cove, he had pointed out a school of brightly colored angelfish swimming on the edge of the outcropping; he had encouraged her to help him search for giant seashells, each one a brilliant rainbow color; and he had coaxed her out of her obscure, defensive shell in order to build a sand castle.

He hadn't bombarded her with questions, and he hadn't pressured her to talk.

He hadn't invaded her personal space—well, at least not that much—and he hadn't made her feel like a captive bird quaking in his primitive palm.

In fact, as the afternoon had progressed, and their hands had been busy—whether collecting shells, or molding sand into ramparts and towers—their conversation had begun to flow, almost in an easy nature: Zane had mentioned playing football on that same beach as a teenager—*a dragyri playing football of all things!*—and Jordan had confessed to being a tomboy at the same impressionable age. Zane had revealed that he'd tried to play the piano, but despite being the son of a god, he had failed at it miserably. Laughing at the thought of those large, rugged fingers plunking away at a piano, Jordan had admitted that she'd tried the flute, the clarinet, and even the trombone in grade school. For some mysterious reason, Zane could not stop laughing at the thought of Jordan wrestling with a six- to eight-pound instrument, her cheeks puffed out, her right arm extended—he'd said he would have paid good money to watch her try. And in an unexpected moment of levity, she had punched him in the arm.

She had actually initiated physical contact.

Now, as she stood on the edge of the shore, staring out at the ocean, waiting for the sun to go down, if she were totally honest, then she had to admit, she felt like a child on the Fourth of July, waiting to see the fireworks: eager, enthralled, and bubbling with anticipation.

How had he done it?

How had he made her forget her fears?

How had she become so absorbed in the moment?

He stood beside her, like the protective male he was, gazing out at the water, and then he confidently reached out, took her hand in his, and squeezed it.

She let him.

"Do you see how the waves are picking up?" he asked, that deep, sonorous voice playing like musical vibrations across her skin.

She nodded and stretched her neck to see further...

Off in the distance, about a hundred yards away, a string of aqua-blue waves were capping in a high, curved swell, the peaks dotted with ethereal white foam, and inside the deepest arc of the wave, a subtle prism was emerging: an underbelly of crystal, emerald, sapphire, amethyst, onyx, citrine, and topaz. As the colors grew more vivid, more stark, their molecular structure changed, and they began to dance in the air, forming rainbow-like gases. The gases expanded, upward, in combustible zones, and just like that, they turned to fire. Spectacular flames shot out of the waves: dancing in, without, and above the water.

Jordan gasped and squeezed Zane's hand, barely realizing she was doing it. "Oh my gosh!" she exclaimed. "That's impossible. That's amazing. That's spectacular!" She wanted to squeal like a child—she had never seen anything like it.

Zane smiled with masculine abandon, and pointed just beyond the striking swell. "Watch closely," he told her. "Fix your eyes beyond the wall of flames."

She sucked in air and her eyes grew wide, even as she rose to her tippy toes.

Zane laughed aloud, released her hand, and sidled up behind her. Then he wrapped both hands along the curve of her waist, hefted her up in the air, and set her on his brawny shoulders. "Keep watching," he said.

As awkward as it felt to be lifted like a child and placed on a grown male's shoulders, Jordan also felt a curious tingle running up and down her spine.

She liked it.

All of it.

The closeness, the contact, and his body beneath her.

The realization was surprising.

But before she could go into analytical mode, the most amazing thing began to happen: Just beyond the wall of undulating flames still cascading toward the shoreline, several powerful geysers began to shoot out of the water, creating magnificent lofty towers—prisms of light, explosions of fire, fountains of vibrant eruptions that fell back into the ocean like a waterfall—*a fire fall*—of color. She leaned forward, knowing Zane would never let her fall off his shoulders, and brought both hands to her cheeks. "Oh, my gosh, Zane." She glanced down at him. "This is freakin' amazing!" She looked back into the water. "Why do you ever do anything else? Why do you ever go anywhere else? If I lived here, I would never leave this spot. I would be here for every single sunset! Holy shit—I would give anything to have access to something like this. It's…it's totally beyond comprehension—there's nothing like it on earth!" The moment the words left her mouth, she realized what she had said, and she stiffened.

Zane removed her from his shoulders, set her down in front of him, and wrapped his arms around her, pulling her back against his chest.

"I just meant…" she muttered, feeling awkward.

"I know what you meant, dragyra." He tightened his hold around her, pressing his chest against her back and nuzzling her ear with affection. "It's okay to be enraptured, angel." He nipped the back of her earlobe with his teeth, then kissed the delicate flesh behind it. "And it's okay to like what is happening…between us."

She shivered, still staring at the water.

He placed both hands on her shoulders and massaged them as they both continued to watch the supernatural show, and then he slid his fingers into her hair, at the nape of her neck, and lifted it away from her shoulders. He bent his head and kissed her, right at the top of her spine—right below the edge of her hairline—and her knees grew unstable and weak.

She drew in a sharp breath of air and wriggled nervously.

He pulled back, splayed his fingers, and then placed them on her chest, just above her breasts, before sliding his hand upward to her throat, where he grasped it softly, then kneaded the taut, tense muscles.

She shuddered. "Zane, I can't." The words were a soft, plaintive whisper.

"Can't what, dragyra?" he rasped, kissing her again in the exact same spot before trailing his lips down to her ear…down her neck…and along the curve of her shoulder. His hand slid lower, to her stomach, and rested on her lower belly.

She felt dizzy, light-headed, and faint. "I can't...I can't...feel this," she breathed heavily.

"I see," Zane whispered. He placed the fingertips of both hands on her shoulders, raked his fingernails along her skin—so gently that he gave her goose bumps—and then he slid both shoulder straps, the strings of her summer dress, slowly, down her arms.

"Zane!" she protested, even as her neck arched and her head lulled backward. Holy hell, her chest was rising and falling from labored breathing—and anticipation.

She needed to stop this before it went too far.

And now.

Zane planted a sensual, seductive kiss right where her neck met her shoulder, and Jordan knew she was done for. Her teeth chattered from the trepidation, but her body came alive.

Apparently sensing both desires warring within her, Zane, being the predator he was, went in for the kill. He slid both hands along the curve of her bare shoulders, down her arms, and onto her waist—and then he slid them up to her breasts, felt the weight beneath them, and cupped them in the palms of his hands. He let out a deep, erotic, almost feral groan, and Jordan's shudder became a tremor.

Then just like that he scooped her up into his arms, laid her down in the sand, and blanketed her body with his.

She gulped, staring up at him like a startled child.

He studied her expression like a majestic hawk. "Do you fear me, dragyra?"

She bit her bottom lip, even as she arched beneath him. "A little...yes." She could barely speak.

He nodded. "I want you, Jordan, and you want me, too." He let his gaze sweep over her, appreciating her feminine curves from head to toe, ever so slowly, before meeting her eyes again. His sapphire-golden orbs were practically glowing with intensity: deepening, darkening, brimming with sensuality. His dragon purred, and Jordan shifted nervously beneath him.

And then he kissed her.

Softly at first: a slow, tender meeting of their lips.

But then, more firmly, exploring the contours of her mouth: first, her upper lip—he tasted it, savored it…relished it. Then, her lower lip—he bit it softly and swirled his tongue along the delicate silhouette. And finally, the corners of her mouth—he explored each side in turn, lingering…discovering.

Enjoying.

And then the kiss became ardent, seeking—enticing—as he skillfully teased her senseless with his tongue.

Good lord, the man was like molten lava, encasing her body in heat. He was passion, fire, and animal hunger, all wrapped up in one. Whether it was fear, or release—or arousal, restrained—Jordan would never know. She only knew that two unwitting tears began to roll down her cheeks.

Zane was so completely in tune to her responses. "It's okay, angel," he whispered, kissing the first tear away. "I've got you, baby, and I won't let you fall—trust me, trust this, trust your body." He tasted the second tear on his tongue, and then he did something so unexpected, it captured—and awakened—her heart. He pulled back, braced his powerful body on his elbows, and simply stared into her eyes: He studied every feature on her face, every soft angle and curve, every detail, indentation, and plane. And he sighed with appreciation. "By all the gods, you are the most beautiful creature I have ever seen. I want to love you, Jordan: I want to please you, consume you, taste your soul." He lowered his mouth to her neck, and she felt the subtle scrape of fangs along the length of her jugular. And heaven help her, because the single flame that burned between them, the one he had always described, ignited in an instant, and her body flooded with need.

She wanted Zane to bite her.

And he did.

His fangs sank deep, and the momentary shock—the temporary sensation of pain—was quickly chased away with a swirl of his tongue. He made a seal above the puncture and began to draw her heat—and probably her blood—and she felt her skin grow cooler…

Icy, frosty, and cold…

As he fed.

But then he withdrew his canines and coated the frost with heat, even as he healed the wound and reversed the leeching with a soft, beguiling flame.

She shifted her hips beneath him, trying to restrain the impulse to writhe.

He chuckled softly beneath his breath, and then he devoured her throat like the animal he was: kissing, tasting, nipping… claiming.

Jordan slid her fingers into his gorgeous, silky hair, tightened her fist around a handful of tresses, and tugged him away from her neck. "Kiss me," she demanded, and his entire upper body shook.

He lowered his mouth to hers and took her to heaven with his lips, his teeth, and his tongue.

His hands began to search her body—to tantalize, tease, and incite—and she found herself squirming beneath him, rising to meet his touch, offering her breasts, and raising her thighs to his hips.

He tugged the front of her dress down to her waist and covered her nipples with a growl; and then his tongue created some sort of magic—she hadn't even known was possible—as he tantalized her mounds. By the time he finished tasting, suckling, and flicking the peaks between his teeth, she was reaching for the top of his jeans.

He didn't hesitate to oblige her. "Shiiiiiit, mea dragyra." He began to murmur in Dragonese…

And she smiled.

There was nothing clumsy about his execution as everything happened at once: He removed his pants, her dress, and her bikinis—and sidled between her hips, his enormous arousal, both hard and smooth, pressing against her entrance. "I need your permission, baby," he grunted between his teeth. "Say yes, mea dragyra… for the sake of the gods…please…say yes."

Jordan hesitated, but only for an instant.

He was larger than any male she had ever known, and she wasn't sure if he'd fit.

Yet his body was trembling with the need to enter hers, and his chest was heaving with desire. She knew she was wet; she knew she was ready; but she didn't know what it meant.

He rocked his pelvis against her peak in a slow, undulating motion, and she gave in. "Yes…yes…*yes*."

He thrust inside her, burying his sex to the hilt, and she braced against the sudden burn. "Relax, angel, your body was made for mine," he coaxed, and she held her hips still as she stretched. Oh… lords of fire…he felt like solid steel encased in glorious satin: thick, throbbing, and perfect. She began to rock her hips, and he followed suit, pumping with even thrusts. As she slowly relaxed more and more, he let her dictate the intensity—their pace, their fervor, their passion—until nothing existed in that glorious cove other than their two sweating bodies.

As warm waves filled with dragon's fire washed over their skin, pleasure washed over her body. Harder, faster, in and out, he moved like a seasoned lover, until just like the waves in the magnificent sea, their passion rose to a crescendo.

Jordan's head fell back, and her lips parted softly in a torturous, wordless cry as she dug her nails into Zane's strong back and hurtled over the edge of ecstasy.

He released his seed at the same exquisite moment, and his expression was beyond description: savage, masculine…beautiful.

When, finally, the last, lingering tremors of their coupling had subsided, Zane reached up to stroke her cheek. "Are you okay?" he whispered.

She brushed her fingers over his and nodded.

He kissed her once more—lovingly, tenderly—before rolling onto his back and drawing her body with him. "Stay with me forever, Jordan. Make this world your home. Not for the temple, not for the lords, not because you have to…but because you want to, you need to, because you desire what we can have. Give me the chance to love you."

Jordan rolled over on top of Zane's chest and stared tenderly into his eyes.

There was nothing—absolutely nothing—manipulative, insincere, or deceitful in his words. He was being honest, raw, and vulnerable. And that, above all else, vanquished her resistant heart. She didn't know what the future would hold—heaven help her, she didn't even know if she could go through with the conversion, but she did know that Zane Saphyrius was one in a million, and maybe—just maybe—what she feared the most would turn out to be her life's greatest blessing.

She laid her head on his chest and listened to the rhythm of his heart.

It was beating in time with hers.

⮞

Salem Thorne scurried down from a jagged ledge on a rocky out-cropping, still in beetle form. He was disgusted by the lovey-dovey, seductive nonsense he'd just witnessed on the beach; impressed as hell by the Dragons Fire in the sea; and more than just a little sexually frustrated by the entire night's events—oh, how he'd wanted to shift into pagan form and stroke himself to the stimulus of Jordan's perfect tits.

But whatever.

He could always do that later.

Hell, maybe he'd make love to her corpse.

Right now, the dewy-eyed couple was vulnerable, exposed, and unaware—lying like a couple of sun-bathing seals on an open beach; only, they were cloaked beneath the cover of darkness, *moon-bathing* beneath the stars.

In other words, opportunity was knocking.

And loudly.

Salem needed to strike swiftly while the iron was hot.

Hmm.

Was that considered mixing one's metaphors?

Who gave a shit? he thought.

Zane would never be more exposed…unprepared…or unsus-pecting; and Jordan was spread out like a naked centerfold on top of him—she didn't have a care in the world. Salem could scuttle across the beach, tunnel beneath the sands, and emerge in one lithe leap, taking his demon form…

He could strike before they knew he was there.

In fact, he could extract the dragyra's heart from behind and shove it down Zanaikeyros' throat…

And wouldn't that just be divine?

His beetle made a high-pitched hissing sound, and he snickered deep inside: While it wouldn't be quite the rapturous release the tramp had just given Zane, it would still be positively orgasmic.

Chapter Thirty-three

A T THE DIAMOND Lair, beneath the deep blue sky, Ghostaniaz Dragos wandered onto his private balcony. Built like a five-star, upscale condominium on the ocean's shore, the structure offered each member of Lord Dragos' clan their own modern living space—an entire floor of contemporary, luxurious living—which led out to a private terrace and sat directly above an identical verandah beneath it. The promenades were lavishly appointed with outdoor kitchenettes, comfortable seating areas, and narrow, winding swimming pools that looked as if they stretched out into the horizon and joined the peaceful dragon sky. Needless to say, Ghost spent as much time as he could outdoors, often trying to clear his head. Or quiet his dragon.

This night, as he strolled to the edge of the balcony, he repeatedly sniffed the air.

He couldn't help it—something smelled wrong—something smelled foul.

Something was not as it seemed.

A deep, feral growl rumbled in his throat as he tried to lock onto the scent: to taste it, feel it, discern the disturbance. It was decidedly hard to place, and maybe that was because it was an alien, peculiar smell, even as it was oddly familiar.

He wrinkled his nose and snarled.

The chemicals in the pool wafted all around him, as did the various flora in the ocean below. But this—this stark, peculiar, *internal* fetor—it resonated, as if from his blood. And that didn't make any sense: How could a smell be both outside in the air and also seeping from his pores?

His inner beast stirred, immediately angry, and he threw back his head and grunted, allowing the monster to emerge more fully. Granted, it was always a gamble to provoke his beast—his dragon was so carnal and savage—once the creature took hold, it was impossible to determine where Ghost's life began and the dragon's life ended.

But oh well—who gave a shit.

Ghost was no stranger to madness.

In fact, he preferred carnal savagery to sanity—he was what his father had made him.

He stretched his arms and arched his back, commanding his serpent to take over—willing the dragon to track the peculiar scent and identify its curious origins.

Ah…

So…

Yeah, that was it…

At the judge's estate on Tuesday night, Ghost's beast, as always, had dined on his quarry—he had consumed the heart of a pagan. Though the meat had been rancid and the soul, profane, it hadn't mattered one bit to the dragyri. His dragon had been mindless and feral.

And now, whatever had been swirling around in Ghost's polluted veins, blending with his native platelets, was also hovering in Dragons Domain. The shit was literally *both*: within and without. It was concurrently all around him *and* inside his body.

Right now.

Right here.

But that didn't make sense—unless there was a pagan in Dragons Domain.

And that was simply impossible.

They could never open the portal.

He started to turn around, to go back inside, but his heathen wouldn't let him.

Instead, he crouched low to the ground, released his fangs and claws, and slowly lumbered forward, hopping to the top of the terrace. Then he growled, sniffed again, and bent his head to listen.

And that's when the rage exploded.

Bounding over the ledge, he released his leathery, phantom-blue wings and headed in a familiar direction: toward the private cove, filled with white sandy beaches, where he was absolutely sure he would find a pagan.

∽

Salem Thorne was a heartbeat away from succeeding in his perilous mission. Zane was half asleep, and Jordan was out of it, luxuriating in the dragyri's closeness.

He could hardly contain his anticipation.

Just one more inch.

Just one quick shift.

And his demon would be right on top of them.

He shook a handful of pebbled sand off his head, extended his antennae, and tunneled upward, commanding his demon to transition.

The extended antennae gave way to crescent horns; the thorax became a skeleton; and his two front legs became long, powerful arms, extending into two clawed hands. He dug the heels of his hooves deep into the sand as he lunged forward at Jordan—he was hoping to tear her throat out with his teeth, even as he wrenched her heart from her pericardium—and skewered her back with his talons.

The crushing blow to the back of his skull, from a fist that felt like a wrecking ball, sent Salem sailing through the air, high above the amorous couple, and into an oncoming tide.

What the devil!

He twisted like a cat, springing to his feet, prepared to meet his assailant, only to find two dragyri males wading into the water: Zanaikeyros—who was naked and *pissed*—and another formidable male who looked feral. The second dragyri was impossible to place—his features were so savage and twisted that Salem couldn't match his likeness to any of the portraits he had seen hanging in the pagan library. He only knew that the male's irises were diamond, and that meant he was the progeny of the lair ruled by Dragos.

He hissed at both dragyri, and the Dragyr roared, sounding like a pair of T. rex, and that's when Zane hurled a bolt of red fire at Salem's chest, and the second mercenary lunged at his throat. The blaze engulfed Salem's torso, even as a pair of saber-sized fangs tore at his vulnerable jugular. Unholy hell, he could not go down this easily.

Snatching the second male by the shoulders, even as the dragyri remained latched to Salem's throat, Salem dipped beneath the water to extinguish the agonizing fire, and took the dragyri with him.

Zane dove beneath the surface and struck Salem between the eyes, his orbital sockets collapsing.

Shit, shit, and more shit!

He was blind!

Salem writhed and bucked, trying to dislodge the feral warrior from his throat and boot Zane further away. His right hoof made contact with Zane's forehead and drove the dragyri backward. Swallowing an unwanted gulp of salty water, Salem went for the kill—he had to strike fast. He swiped and slashed and stabbed with his claws, filleting the feral dragyri's flesh, even as he released his urine to infuse the water with acid.

The second dragyri released Salem's throat, and Salem kneed him in the gonads.

Zane was coming at him again—Salem could feel the shift in the water—so he used his organ as a stingray: Isolating and transforming that singular part of his body back into beetle form, he infused the barbed penis with poison. *Hell, fire, and brimstone*, he couldn't see, but he could still hump if he had to.

Apparently, Zane was unimpressed.

He drove his hand between Salem's legs and ripped the organ from his pelvis.

And that's when the second, feral dragyri tore into Salem's abdomen and started removing his intestines.

Great Father of the pagan realm, Salem was going to die.

Right here. Right now. Right in the Dragon Sea…

He reached wildly and blindly for anything he could latch onto, and his skeletal fist caught purchase of the second dragyri's amulet. He yanked with everything he had—tugged and pulled and wrenched with every ounce of supernatural power he possessed—but the amulet would not give way.

"Son of a bitch!" he tried to scream, but he only gulped more water. His lungs were burning like lava—they felt like they were on fire.

And then he heard the most awesome, terrifying sound he had ever perceived in his countless lifetimes: the sound of wings, the size of a ship, beating in the air above the ocean. A dragon screeched, and the vibration shook the waters like a gale-force wind, parting the sea all around them. And then he felt an enormous compression in the air as a high-pressure area was created in front of him. Great Lord Drakkar, the dragon was swooping down, presumably to clutch Salem in its talons.

The torture, the agony, the suffering he would endure if he was captured by a dragon lord was beyond what he could imagine. He would rather take his own life and end it now than become the captive of an ancient serpent.

But how?

How would he do it?

Before he could answer the question, the compression rose to a crescendo—he felt Zane and the second dragyri draw back, and his rib cage was impaled by an enormous cluster of talons. The pain was beyond comprehension.

Mindless, terrified, and grasping at straws, Salem held on for dear life to the second dragyri's amulet—he would make the primordial god take a dragyri son with him, and he would try with all his might to kill the bastard while they soared through the air like wounded carrion. Most likely on their way to the temple.

Salem would not die without a victory!

And that's when he heard the sonic *boom!*

And light assailed his vision.

Another opening in the atmosphere channeled through the sacred amulet.

A gargantuan, inky-black hand with razor-sharp chiseled claws reached through the tear in dimensions, snatched Salem by the throat, and tugged him violently forward, causing the dragon's talons to rip like blades through his flesh.

He screamed like a banshee, assailed by the ungodly pain, and then he let go of the amulet, dropped his arms to the sides, and sighed in blessed relief.

He knew this dark, evil presence.

It had gifted him with his pagan life.

Lord Hades had punched through the portal, using Salem's physical connection to the dragyri's amulet—and while the king wasn't able to enter Dragons Domain, he was able to pull Salem out.

"Thank you, most venerable father," Salem breathed.

And then he passed out.

Chapter Thirty-four

ZANE SCRAMBLED FROM the shoreline and sprinted to his dragyra, desperate to see that she was okay. "Jordan!" he shouted, forgetting he was naked as he dropped to his knees in front of her. "Baby," he whispered anxiously, cupping her face in his hands. "Are you all right? Did the demon hurt you?"

She was trembling, her eyes were open wide with shock, but she didn't appear to be hurt. In fact, her clothes were on—she had managed to get dressed—and Zane couldn't smell any blood. "I'm…I'm okay," she murmured. "He never even touched me." She glanced down at her lap and shuddered. "At least I don't think he touched me."

Zane ran his hands all over her body to check her smaller frame for injuries, then he closed his eyes to listen to her heart and took a moment to check her pulse. When he was certain that she hadn't been injured, he drew her into his arms and held her like his life depended on the contact: which, honestly, it kind of did. "I'm sorry, angel. I'm so, so sorry. This has never happened before. A pagan has *never* entered this realm."

Jordan nodded, her skin as pale as the moonlight, and then she pointed a drooping finger toward the apex of the beach, and stuttered: "Y…y…you might want to put some clothes on."

Zane glanced over his shoulder to check the scene for himself:

Lord Dragos was standing like a raptor on the beach in his magnificent dragon form, and he was showering Ghost Dragos, who was curled up beneath him like a baby, in silver-blue flames.

So the dragon lord did care whether Ghost lived or died…

Hmm…that was interesting.

Zane glanced down at his own naked body and appraised his various wounds—he was pretty sure he had a hoofmark on his forehead; there were lacerations all over his torso, plus acid burns on his pecs and his abs; and his right hand was swollen with poison, but not enough to matter. He could heal all of his wounds himself, with the exception of any bruises on his brow. But yeah, he should probably get dressed.

He reached for his form-fitting boxers and jeans, and quickly slid them onto his torso. Then he stood to his full, proud height and helped Jordan up.

"What do we do?" she asked nervously, her voice still trembling.

Zane shook his head. "Nothing. Not when it comes to Lord Dragos. Just stand here and wait…and avert your eyes. If he wants us, he'll let us know."

She nodded faintly. "And what about the dragyri—the one on the beach. Who is he?"

"That's Ghost," Zane said softly. "Do you remember him from the bunker? He's the one Axe told us about, the one who almost took a bite out of Nakai."

Jordan grimaced as she thought it over, and then she slowly inclined her head. "Uh, yeah, I remember. I remember thinking, *What an animal*, but then that animal just saved our lives and took a beating doing it." She averted her gaze, looking pained and ashamed, and then she stared at his still-naked chest—at all the scrapes and cuts and dark, maroon scars, the various burns from the demon's acid. "Zane, you're hurt." She glanced at his hand—it was swollen like a bright red blowfish. She turned her attention to his forehead and winced. "Oh my gosh, dragyri, that looks awful. Shouldn't you go get healed yourself?" She gestured toward Lord Dragos.

Zane chuckled, low and deep, a cynical snicker in his throat—um, that was never going to happen. Not even if he was on death's door, which he wasn't. "I'm fine, angel. I can heal most of the wounds myself. If there's anything else I need, my lair-mates will take care of it."

She wrinkled up her brow. "But then why does he need the dragon—why does *Ghost* need Lord Dragos to heal him?"

Zane stared a second time at the odd paternal scenario playing out on the sands, and he let the question fully sink in...until, finally, it occurred to him: "Ghost doesn't need Lord Dragos to heal—Lord Dragos *needs* to heal Ghost. Ghostaniaz is his Genesis Son."

Jordan shifted her weight and frowned. "Well then, why isn't Lord Saphyrius here? Isn't he worried about you?"

"Believe me," Zane reassured her, "he's watching. He's just not as...possessive...over his lair as Lord Dragos." He hoped the fearsome dragon was too busy to pay attention. "I will probably spend the majority of the day tomorrow in the temple, along with Ghost. The gods are going to want to sort this out."

Jordan nodded. "Figure out how the demon got into The Pantheon—find out how he escaped?"

She shuddered, and Zane smiled.

He couldn't help it.

His dragyra was truly an angel—a bright, beautiful, perceptive miracle—and she'd learned so much, so very quickly.

She didn't miss a trick.

Lord Dragos snorted possessively in the distance, and Zane reached out to take Jordan's hand. "Be still, dragyra. Say nothing more. Let the dragon attend to his son."

As those ominous words lingered, Zane and Jordan linked their fingers and watched from a distance as the savage dragon nuzzled the male with his snout, dragged him to his feet with his talons, and then flipped him onto his back with one wing.

With a thunderous roar that shook the beach, the dragon released a ferocious ring of fire. Then the onyx serpent took three giant steps, bounding across the sand, and leapt into the air, where he spread his wings and circled high above them, heading back toward the Onyx Lair.

Chapter Thirty-five
Friday – 8:00 PM

S ECURE IN THE knowledge that Jordan was with Levi, Nakai, and Jace, safe in the Sapphire Lair, Zane glanced at the apartment door in front of him—13B—and nodded silently at Axe.

As expected, Zane had spent the entire day on Friday sequestered in the temple with Ghost and the dragon lords, debriefing the gods on the incident at the beach, brainstorming along with them about how the demon got into Dragons Domain, and listening as the all-powerful dragons discussed the mystics and science of Lord Hades Drakkar punching his fist through the portal in order to retrieve one of his own. They knew he'd used the power of Ghost's amulet, but they were surprised that he'd possessed the magic to do so.

Meanwhile, Jordan had been forced to go to the Topaz Lair to meet with Misty Collins, Tiberius' dragyra mate, without Zane present: With only three days left until Jordan's *rebirth* at the temple, it had been time to procure her dress (an enchanted gown that would not burn—a fact Zane hadn't shared with Jordan); the jewels that would adorn her hair; and to go through the basic pre-liminaries of the upcoming ceremony—all things that were usually done with another dragyra.

Zane had hated to leave her alone with Misty.

At the least, he would have liked to wait outside Misty's bedroom door, to have made sure Jordan knew he was there—always there—but when the dragon lords called, the dragyri jumped.

There were simply no *ands, ifs, or buts* about it.

The *Four Principle Laws*...and all that.

And there was something else—something that demanded Zane's attention—something that had come out during the debriefing with Ghost in the temple: When the feral dragyri had latched onto the demon's throat in the Dragon Sea, he had swallowed several chunks of the pagan's flesh, and in doing so, he had also absorbed a handful of *Salem's* most recent memories—the fact that he had entered the domain as a beetle, concealed in Jordan's purse; the fact that he was on a mission from Lord Hades to destroy a Genesis Son, in this case, by trying to murder Jordan; and the fact that he had placed a powerful compulsion into the mind of a vulnerable surgeon, ordering him to use and seduce Jordan's best friend.

On the advice of Lord Topenzi, the dragons had dipped Ghostaniaz into the pearlescent waters of the Oracle Pool, and since they finally knew what they were looking for, they had been able to see a little more: the fact that Dr. Kyle Parker would be at Macy's apartment on Friday night at seven o'clock to make her a candlelit dinner.

To begin the process of seduction.

Normally, the dragon lords would not have given two hoots about human affairs, not even those peripherally connected to a dragyra or a dragyri, but this was decidedly different—it was personal—every maniacal plan Lord Drakkar had hatched had been designed with a singular purpose: to destroy a Genesis Son.

To one day...somehow...get to a dragon lord's original offspring.

And that could not go unanswered.

Lord Saphyrius had ordered Zane and Axe to show up at Macy's apartment, remove the doctor's right hand, then stamp it with the official seal from the Temple of Seven and place it in a box of chocolates. The box was to be wrapped in Christmas paper and delivered to a local bank on Fifteenth Street—King's Castle

Credit Union, where the manager, a lifelong member of the Cult of Hades, would read the card and make sure that it got to the horde: *For Drak; the best-laid plans of mice and pagans often go astray!*

Axe inclined his head at Zane, letting the dragyri know he was ready, and with one swift chop of his battleaxe, Zane hacked a fist-sized hole in the center of Macy's front door, reached through the cavity to unlock the deadbolt, and the two ruthless Dragyr stormed inside.

❦

Macy Wilson stood in front of her bathroom mirror, checking her hair and makeup for the fifth or sixth time—she had excused herself from the table, yet again, to try to catch her breath.

Oh. My. Gosh.

Doctor Parker had brought her a dozen long-stemmed red roses and an expensive bottle of wine. He had lit two candles on her small glass kitchen table and even pulled out her chair before he'd presented her with the gourmet lasagna and tossed Caesar salad that the surgeon had prepared from scratch.

And thank God, all the saints, as well as good fortune, he hadn't noticed—or said anything—about the fact that she wasn't wearing his pin: that beautiful, expensive, ruby-and-gold beetle.

The one that Macy had lost!

She gritted her teeth and snarled at herself in the mirror—it still didn't make any sense. How could she have been so careless? How could she have lost something that was so very dear to her heart?

She wanted to kick herself a dozen times over.

Running her fingers through her hair one last time and smoothing her reapplied lipstick, she told herself to forget it—let it go—this night was too beautiful, too important to ruin. And then she drew back her shoulders, tried to calm her nerves, and headed back to the romantic table.

"Everything all right?" Kyle asked her, eyeing her like she was covered in whipped cream.

"Everything's perfect," Macy replied, gracefully taking her seat.

The aroma of the lasagna wafted up from the table as Kyle poured her a glass of red wine. "You haven't taken any painkillers today, have you?" he asked. And wasn't that just so sweet…

"Nope." Macy smiled. Then she lifted her crystal glass and clinked it against his.

"To new beginnings," he drawled in that deep, sexy voice, and Macy shivered from head to toe.

Just then, there was a huge clamor and an explosion of wood in the front hallway—it sounded like someone had just driven a sledgehammer through Macy's front door. Doctor Kyle jumped up from his chair, dropping his wineglass in alarm, and Macy suppressed a squeal. Her heart began to race like she had just run a marathon, and she instinctively reached for a knife.

"You won't be needing the utensil, darling." A sonorous voice rang out in the dining room, the words coming from a tall, gorgeous blond with strange sapphire eyes. "Sit down."

Macy dropped the knife and planted her rear in her seat, her mouth dropping open in horror and surprise. The blond was accompanied by a dark-haired male who looked as deadly as he did, savage. And for some odd reason—in that stark, terrifying moment—Macy's thoughts turned squarely to Jordan. She thought about her recent surgery and her recovery room…images from that morning.

But it didn't make any sense, and her mind filled with cotton.

Whatever thought, or memory, or impression she'd almost had slipped beyond her reach as the déjà vu passed.

The gorgeous blond stepped up to Dr. Parker and extended his right hand in greeting. "Dr. Kyle Parker?" he said, as casual as the day was long.

Kyle's features were a mask of rage, terror, and indecision, and Macy could see in his eyes that he was deciding between fight and flight—whether or not to throw an offensive punch or to duck—but the perfunctory greeting had thrown him off-balance. "Yes?" he muttered warily.

"Nice to meet you. I'm Axe."

The doctor stared at Axe's hand like he had just grown it from a test tube, and then he reluctantly took it and began to shake.

The blond tightened his grip around Kyle's palm, tugged the doctor's arm forward, and in the blink of an eye—less than that, really—the dark-haired male twirled a blade through his fingers, caught the dragon-shaped handle, and sliced through Dr. Parker's wrist, dissecting it at the radius.

He cut his hand clear off.

And then he stuffed it in his pocket. "We'll stamp it when we get back to the lair."

Macy gasped and began to hyperventilate.

She tried to scream, but the sound would not escape.

"Shh," the blond guy whispered, spinning around to face her. He placed his forefinger over his lips. "Relax, sweetheart. Just relax. Look into my eyes."

Macy met his heated gaze, and her own pupils must have expanded in shock because his jet-black pupils had grown as narrow as a cat's. As she fell into his gaze, leaned forward, and gaped in wonder, he began to speak a bunch of distant-sounding words: "You're not afraid; you will remember nothing; you have no interest whatsoever in Doctor Kyle Parker." And all the while, through her peripheral vision, she saw the other male doing something that defied common sense—something that defied logic, reason, and science.

He cauterized Dr. Parker's stump with a silver fire.

A flame that shot forth from his mouth!

And then the flame turned silver-blue, and he used it to clean up the mess: to remove the blood from the table and the carpet, to erase the splatter from Dr. Parker's shirt. And then he reached into the clean breast-pocket of his duster, removed several large stacks of what looked like hundred-dollar bills, and dropped them on the table.

"Get your door fixed, honey," the blond stranger said. Then he turned his attention on the surgeon. "And, you; invest that shit wisely. You won't be operating on humans anymore."

Dr. Kyle looked like he was going into shock.

He brought the stump up to his face and recoiled, but before he could faint or shout—or lapse into hysterics—the dark-haired male cupped his cheeks, seared his gaze into Kyle's, and began to speak in a soft, hypnotic tone.

The doctor nodded, and nodded…and nodded.

And then just like that, the strangers were gone.

Macy sank into her seat and blinked her eyes, several times in a row. What the hell was going on here? She stared at her kitchen table, at the lasagna and the spilled red wine staining the ivory cloth, and she frowned. "Dr. Parker?" What was her surgeon doing in Macy's apartment?

He was standing there like a deer caught in someone's headlights, holding his trembling right arm, and his hand was missing!

Holy hell…

But yeah, that was right—he had lost it in a hunting accident, just the other day.

Hadn't she heard that somewhere?

But then why wasn't it wrapped in bandages?

Why wasn't he still in the hospital?

Her mind went blank, and the questions simply…vanished.

As cruel as it seemed, Macy didn't care.

Dr. Parker shuffled toward the table and began collecting several stacks of cash. Again, that seemed really odd, but Macy wasn't concerned. "Would you like a bag?" she asked.

Dr. Parker nodded blankly. "Yes, um, I think I would."

Macy rose from her seat to go fetch one. "Well, thank you for the house call," she found herself saying, "but honestly, I think you should be home in bed, taking care of yourself."

Dr. Parker cleared his throat. "Yes," he said, the word coming out as a croak. "*Yes*," he tried again, more firmly. "I believe I will do just that. Um, don't forget to get your door fixed."

Macy stared past the living room to the front foyer and frowned. Angling her head to the side, she harrumphed. "Yeah. I'll call someone right now."

Chapter Thirty-six
Saturday ~ The Garden of Grace

JORDAN STOOD SOLEMNLY before the beautiful but haunting marker—the sapphire statue of a powerful, breathtaking male—the final likeness of Jaquar Saphyrius.

Wait, that wasn't true.

It wasn't Jaquar's likeness; it was all that remained of his soul.

And as the dragon sun shone brilliantly down on the white clay mountains, reflecting light off the sacred ravine where Jaquar's final sculpture had been erected, words eluded her—what in heaven's name could she say?

She glanced askance at Zane, who looked both reverent and tortured, and she reached out to take his hand. The gesture was easy now. Not only had they made love Wednesday night, but they had been intimate three more times since then. They had talked; they had shared stories about their pasts—childhood dreams, adolescent heartaches, and adult mishaps—and they had slept in each other's arms.

The choice to visit the Garden of Grace had been Jordan's—she'd needed to see the final resting place of the Dragyr for herself. She'd needed to understand the full implications of failing to enter the temple. She'd needed to know—honestly, unceremoniously, and viscerally—what would become of Zane if she didn't have the courage to go through with the consecration. And the dragyri had agreed to take her, reluctantly, but he had agreed.

Now, as she stood beside the strong, powerful Genesis Son of the Sapphire Lair, witnessing his inner turmoil—and his ultimate vulnerability—her heart sank in her chest, and she found it hard to breathe. She squeezed his hand, knowing that whatever she was feeling, his experience, in this moment, was worse. "Are you okay, dragyri?" she asked, turning to face him more directly.

He bit down on his lower lip. "This is not a place I care to hang out."

The words fell like a mallet striking stone, echoing through the mountains. Indeed, this was not a place he would want to hang out—not now, and certainly not forever.

Jordan shivered and tugged on his hand, backing away from the statue…

From Zane's best friend.

There was no need to linger—the outing had produced the desired effect.

"Come," she said, "let's go stand over there." She pointed at a brilliant cluster of bloodred and white osiria bushes that Zane had said, earlier, were always in bloom, and meandered in that direction.

He trailed beside her in silence, and when they stopped to talk some more, Jordan noticed that his eyes were not only distant; they were glassy with moisture, filled with all the tears he would never cry.

She released his hand and reached up to cup his cheek. "I've made a decision," she whispered.

His eyes met hers, but he didn't speak.

She looked away—it was just too sensitive a subject to face head-on. She was doing the best that she could. "I will not…I cannot…leave you to this fate, Zane." She fought back some tears of her own. "Dying in my sleep, that's one thing. Knowing that you…" She glanced over her shoulder at the sapphire statue—the one they had just walked away from—and shook her head with regret. "Last night, you saved my best friend from a horrible doctor—and from a tremendous amount of heartache—I just wish that I could've saved yours. That someone, somehow, could've rescued Jaquar." She quickly changed the subject, knowing that it was way too delicate. "But it's not just that. It's everything, Zane. Everything you've said and done since the day that I met you—it's everything you are." She placed her hand over her heart and tried to steady her voice. "It's everything I know…and feel…in here. I'm terrified, Zane. I'm so totally and unbelievably scared that I don't even know how to breathe—I would honestly rather die than have to manage this much fear, but I can't…I won't…I will not let Lord Saphyrius remove your amulet. Not ever. *I promise*."

Zane cupped her face in his hands, caressed her cheeks with his thumbs, and searched her eyes for…something.

Maybe confidence.

Maybe sincerity.

He wouldn't find either one—

She was balancing on a wire.

"Promise me," she continued, "that you will always be here, that you will take good care of my heart…that you will never hurt me like Dan did. Promise me that you'll give me the time and the space that I need to adjust to your world—and that you won't abandon me, like my parents, like my nana. I know it wasn't their fault, but I don't want to be left alone…not ever again." Her legs were trembling from the brutally honest confession.

"Oh, dragyra," Zane breathed tenderly, his eyes suddenly filled with wonder. A single tear escaped the corner of his eye, and he glanced away, trying to conceal his raw emotion. "I have waited a lifetime to know you, to have you, to be with you, Jordan, and I will never let you fall. I will never break your heart or betray you—it isn't in my DNA. Don't you understand: I was born loving you, angel. I have loved you all my life."

She grasped his wrists and held them, much too tightly, as her tears began to fall. She couldn't return the declaration—she couldn't speak those words—just yet.

Not now.

Not here.

Not until she was absolutely sure.

But there wasn't a question in her mind that a powerful bond—yes, perhaps even a powerful love—was rapidly growing between them.

She drew inward, encapsulating her mounting feelings—she didn't want to fall apart. "Zane," she whispered softly, needing to talk brass tacks. "What I need from you right now is to go over the ceremony…the consecration…every single detail." She tried to stiffen her shoulders, but she knew they were visibly shaking. "I don't want to leave anything to chance. I know that Misty told me everything I need to know, but I want to hear it from you: everything we have to do, every place we have to stand—or kneel—what to expect from the gods. I need you to walk me through the consecration, step by terrifying step. Do you think you can do that?"

He bent his neck, allowing his forehead to rest against hers. "If that is what you need, dragyra, then of course, I can give you that. It's the least that I can do. We can even rehearse each element—go through the motions—if it doesn't terrify you too much. It's up to you. Let me know as we proceed…how to make it easier. If you need to back off, if you want to continue. Let me know what you need, okay?"

Jordan nodded, but her knees felt faint.

Dear God in heaven, was she really going to do this?

Was she really going to walk into that temple—*tomorrow*—and face the seven dragon lords?

Was she really going to submit to *rebirth*…by fire?

"I…I…" The words wouldn't come. She was too consumed with terror. "Just hold me, Zane." She was about to come apart.

As his arms enfolded her back, his wings expanded, seamlessly, and he wrapped her up in a warm satin cocoon, cradling her against his chest. "I've got you, angel. Just breathe. *Just breathe.* I promise you—I will never let you go."

Chapter Thirty-seven
Sunday ~ Temple of Seven

WHEN MISTY COLLINS-TOPENZI, Tiberius' mate, dropped Jordan off at the temple steps—exactly at 7 PM—Zane's heart lodged in his throat.

She was positively stunning.

A vision from beyond.

Her hair was swept up into a loose chignon and plaited with a string of sapphires. Her neck was adorned with an intricate, braided choker, sparkling with all seven sacred jewels; and her gown looked like something out of fairy-tale tome: layers of satin embroidered with silk threads; dozens of sapphire-charmeuse roses, each flower encircled by a translucent chiffon bow; and a bodice so adorned in beadwork and lace that it appeared timeless, even ancient. Jordan looked like a princess, and there was nothing excessive about her enchanted ensemble: It was elegant, regal, and graceful.

Just like the woman who wore it.

But then, there were her eyes: glazed over with shock, absent of joy, and stark with reflection of terror in their depths.

Zane stepped forward and took her gloved hand, even as Misty whispered something in her ear, hugged her from behind, and quickly retreated...not looking back. "Look at me, dragyra," he commanded softly.

Her eyes darted to his.

"That's it. Look right at me and listen." He squeezed her hand in an unyielding grip. "A journey of a thousand miles begins with a single step—no one is asking you to embrace the entire journey in *this* particular moment. I am only asking for a single step: the next, solitary step. That's all you have to do. That's all you have to take: one step at a time, dragyra—it is all the bravery that's required. From this second forward, we do what we practiced. We take… just… one… more… step…together."

Jordan nodded frantically, and Zane knew she was at her wits' end. If he pushed her in any way—if he made her think, or feel, or go too deep inside—her valor would be lost. He needed to lead her, exactly as he was doing, one courageous step at a time.

And so they walked up the temple stairs—slowly, and together—one marble stair at a time; traversed the outer platform; and entered into the foyer, beneath the high, arched doorframe, where they approached the sacred, cleansing fountain.

The echo of Jordan's elegant shoes against the diamond foyer floor was unnerving to his dragyra, and he had to stop, yet again, to calm her nerves. "You're doing great," he reassured her. "We're already to the fountain. Look at me, dragyra—tell me what comes next."

She blinked through tear-stained lashes and her lips began to quiver. "We have to go inside—"

"No," he interrupted. "You're getting too far ahead of yourself. What are you going to look at?"

She sniffed and bit down on her lower lip. "I'm going to look at you."

"That's right," he whispered. "And what is the next *single* step?"

She looked down at her opulent shoes and stared at the light-reflecting deck, pointing six inches in front of them toward the edge of the ornamental rug, the one that sat beneath the fountain. "I need to walk to the rug."

His heart lifted. "That's right, angel. You need to take another step. Lift your foot…now move it forward…now place it back down, right here." He bent to kiss her on the temple. "You're doing amazing, Jordan. Stay with my voice. Look only at me."

She wrung her hands together, and her shoulders tensed. "Okay," she breathed quietly. "Okay."

"One more?" he asked, systematically taking her to the fountain, where he placed her hands in his and dipped both sets into the water. As the undulating current began to swirl around their fingers, and the lords began to draw from their heat, he nuzzled her ear with his nose. "Be at ease, angel. That's just your body losing a little of its warmth—it'll pass quickly. Just breathe."

She took a slow, deep breath and waited as Zane blew the frost from her fingers and heated them up with radiant smoke. By all the gods, this woman was a miracle—she was already halfway there. Drying their hands on a satin cloth—he wasn't about to ask her to shake them out—he led her forward, one step at a time, until they reached the massive sanctuary doors.

And that's when his own courage waned.

That was when he remembered Jaquar, and he felt the weight of his amulet bearing down on his chest: Jordan had to enter the temple of her own volition, and for a moment, he just wasn't sure...

He released her hand, pried open the heavy stone doors, and stood to the side, waiting for his dragyra to cross the threshold...to enter the Temple of Seven.

Jordan stared at the doorway and blanched. She swallowed several times, almost convulsively, and her teeth began to chatter. She looked at Zane; then she looked inside the sanctuary; then she looked back at the open foyer behind them.

He held his breath.

She exhaled loudly, then shook out her hands, seeking to dispel some tension. "I'm trying," she muttered in desperation.

"I know you are, dragyra."

What else could he say?

She lifted her right foot, extended it toward the doorway, then quickly pulled it back. "Zane, I'm so sorry."

The air left his body.

"I just...I just can't..."

He closed his eyes and shuddered, refusing to feel the knife in his heart—of course she couldn't do it...it was too much to ask.

She tugged on a lone, loose spiral of her auburn hair, looking anxious, frustrated, and totally lost. "I just can't…remember… what day you were born." She yanked on her hair again. "Isn't that silly? What a crazy thought. We're about to be married—or consecrated—and I don't even know your birthday."

Zane closed his eyes and modulated his voice. "January 7, 1016."

She nodded. "Oh, yeah, that's right—you're a Capricorn."

He shrank back, opened his eyes, and stared at her blankly. *Dear gods of The Pantheon, she was losing her mind.* "Yep," he answered dumbly, "and so are you—January fifteenth, right?"

She started to chuckle, and then her laughter turned to tears. "We are so going to butt heads sometimes. You know that, right?"

He nodded, feeling desperate.

"Zanaikeyros?" She spoke his name with deliberation, pronouncing every syllable distinctly, and he raised his brows. "Catch me, okay?" With that, she took five brazen steps forward, strolled across the threshold, and entered the sanctuary, collapsing the moment her footfalls stopped.

He caught her in his arms and held her like he was trapped under water, and she was his last, dying breath. "Angel," he rasped into her ear. Then he bit out a barely audible curse beneath his breath. Unable to restrain the sudden flood of emotion, he choked back a flurry of tears. "Thank you, Jordan." There were no other words…

She clung to him with equal fervor. "I promised you, Zane. And I meant what I said. I could never let that happen."

He held her even tighter; took a series of long, deep breaths; then slowly pulled away, collecting his wits. "Holy Pantheon," he breathed. "Okay. Back to plan A, right? One step at a time."

She grasped for his hands and nodded. "I'm really losing my shit," she whispered.

"I know, angel." He couldn't help but chuckle, softly. "Just stay with me a little longer." He pointed toward the raised octagon dais in the center of the room, and then quickly stepped in front of her to block the foreboding, ominous stage from her view before she stared too long. "That's about thirty steps away. Hold onto my arm, and we'll count them down."

Jordan clung to his bicep, stared down at the ground, and walked with him in tandem, slowly counting aloud.

Thirty.

Twenty-nine.

Twenty-eight…

ઝ

Jordan knew better than to think, or to look, or to observe.

She knew better than to let herself feel anything more than the terror that was already rising like an ocean wave at high tide, sweeping away her reason. So she stared at the cluster of diamonds on the toes of her shoes until they reached the dais; then she stared at Zane's arm as they climbed the same. She didn't glance upward at the high coffered ceiling to see the gilded layers of jewels; she didn't try to behold the pearlescent pool of living waters; and she didn't take a gander at the supposedly magnificent glass floor, which Zane had warned would blind her temporarily from all the refracted light.

And she sure as hell didn't look forward at the seven ornamental thrones.

The way she saw it, she would have a lifetime to admire the temple, if she could somehow get through the *rebirth*.

Oh God, *the rebirth*…

No, no, no-no-no-no!

She couldn't go there.

One step…one choice…one moment at a time.

When the floors began to sway and the walls began to undulate—when the seven dragon lords took their respective thrones— plan A, plan B, and even plan C instantly flew out the window, and Jordan spun around to bolt. *Screw it! There was no way she could do this.*

Zane sidled up behind her and caught her by the waist, and by the firmness of his grasp, she knew what she was too terrified to articulate:

By any means necessary.

Isn't that what he had said?

He was loving, he was supportive, and he was doing his level best—but they had come too far to turn back, and he wasn't letting her go.

Not now.

Not ever.

She felt it in his touch.

And then she saw the two tethered loops bolted to the floor—*oh, God; Zane's body had been blocking them*—those were the handholds she was supposed to grasp when she kneeled before the fire. "No, Zane. No! No-no-no!" She backpedaled into his chest.

"Avert your eyes, dragyra," he whispered into her ear. "Be brave, my angel. I've got you."

The air around them began to heat like an oven, and she struggled to draw in breath.

And then, one by one, each dragon lord rose from his respective throne, starting with Lord Dragos, rising from the center diamond cathedra. "You may regard our eyes." His voice resounded like crackling thunder ricocheting throughout the great hall, and Jordan's knees literally knocked together beneath her luxuriant dress.

She lifted her eyes, and her stomach grew queasy.

The gods were in their amalgamated form—spectral prisms of light reflecting the hues of their primary stones—while their ferocious beasts shadowed them in silhouette. But no sooner than Jordan's eyes had regaled—and accepted—the first merciful visage, their dragons advanced to the forefront: The ghostly beasts, behind the ancient lords—within them, all around them, and enveloping them—donned their scales, released their pointed ears, and revealed their razor-sharp teeth. And now, it was their human counterparts becoming dim, masculine reflections that faded into the background as dark-gray wisps of smoke began to waft from their elongated snouts.

Oh no, oh no, oh no!

Jordan's legs gave way, and she staggered to the side.

Zane caught her by the waist and hauled her upright, steadying her body with his hands. "I'm right here—right behind you, dragyra. I've got you. I'm with you," he whispered in her ear, but she could feel his strong arms trembling.

Zanaikeyros was afraid.

For the first time since she'd known him, the male was consumed with dread; and didn't that just tell her everything he couldn't—or wouldn't—say.

"Kneel with me, angel," he murmured, and she literally gasped for breath.

"I can't…I can't…oh, God, Zane, I can't."

"Shh." He stroked her hair and rubbed her arms. "We're almost there, my love. Kneel." He grasped her by both hands and drew her down to the dais floor, even as he fell to one knee before his lords. "Count backward from three to one, angel. Do it. Do it right now."

Jordan felt like her throat was closing, and she struggled to croak out the words: "Three, two, one…"

"That's exactly it," he said. "That's all. Three seconds, dragyra. Be strong." And then, without warning or preamble, he placed his hands over hers, stroked each glove, and stretched out her arms, one at time, toward the secure, solid-steel rings. As he wrapped her fingers around the handholds, each hand in turn, she trembled like a captive bird, and tears of helplessness began to stream down her cheeks.

"Shh, baby, I know. Be brave for me, my love. Hold onto the rings, and don't let go." He tightened his hands along the small of her hips, feeling for her center of gravity, and then he shifted her body, a little to the left, and leaned heavily into her, pressing her torso forward, until she was crouched in a secure position.

She thought her bones might just rattle right out of her body, and she began to gasp for air—dear lord, was she hyperventilating?

"It's okay," Zane whispered again. "I've got you. Can you feel me? Concentrate on your breathing; listen for my heartbeat; let go of your thoughts. Don't think at all, Jordan. Just tune into me."

She tried desperately to do as he instructed, but her panic was getting the best of her, and then Lord Saphyrius ambled forward, away from his sapphire throne—apart from the other dragons— and his azure eyes began to glow in the pale light of the temple. He raised his giant serpentine head and fixed his gaze on Zanaikeyros. "My son."

The dragyri lowered his head in homage. "Father."

"We will hear your invocation now."

"What's happening? What's going on? What's going to happen next?" Jordan whimpered, although she already knew the answers.

Zane tightened his arms around her. "Be brave," he whispered one last time, and then he cleared his throat, released his wings, and enfolded Jordan in their satin—crushing her beautiful dress—as he encased her body, one final time, in a cocoon made of silk.

In a timeless address to his primordial masters, he raised his voice, and his words echoed throughout the sanctuary, rising to the cathedral ceilings and beyond…

"Great dragon lords, from the world beyond;

fathers of mystery, keepers of time;

I bring to you this mortal soul.

Born of fire, bathed in light;

to guard by day and watch by night;

to live, and love, and breathe as one,

the fated of a dragon's son—

be gentle with her soul.

Through sacred smoke and healing fire;

a flesh- and blood-renewing pyre;

I give my life, with one desire—

reanimate her soul.

Great dragon lords of the sacred stones;

from the Temple of Seven, from your honored thrones;

renew my dragyra, and bless the Sapphire Lair."

Jordan wanted to get up and run.

She just couldn't do this.

Heaven knew, she adored Zanaikeyros, but this was beyond reconciliation. She started to wriggle back and forth, to fight against the dragyri's heavy presence, but he only leaned harder against her, clasped his hands over hers—over the infernal rings—and tightened his satiny wings all around her, until they felt like the vest of a straightjacket.

And then she heard a distant purr.

It sounded like the tremolo of a lion.

And then it rose to a crescendo and filled the cathedral, roaring like an oncoming train.

The blaze that struck the dais was like nothing Jordan had ever experienced or imagined—the sound, the feel, and the fury—it was like a battering ram slamming through a living room wall.

It was terrifying.

It was savage.

And it was brutal, without constraint.

Jordan screamed, but the sound was drowned out by the fire.

All around her—to the left, to the right, above, and below— she was suddenly engulfed in flames.

"No. No! Noooooooooo!" she cried, bucking, twisting, and struggling. Through the corners of her eyes, she could see the seven mystical dragons as fire shot forth from their throats. The flames coalesced—and then they mingled—they became a centralized conflagration: permeating the dais, exploding like living lightning, and landing with finite precision.

She was about to pass out from fright, so she fixed her eyes on Zane's strong hands—still looped over hers on the handholds—and she began to count backward: "Thirty, twenty-nine, twenty-eight, twenty-seven—"

Her counting was abruptly cut off by an ear-shattering bellow—Zanaikeyros crying out in pain!

Oh gods, oh, gods, oh gods…

The sound was so full of anguish and torment that it shook the dais beneath them.

Jordan's heart seized in her chest, and she gasped for air, twisting to glance behind her. "Zane…"

He sounded like he was dying.

"Zane!"

The air filled with the stench of his burning flesh, and the heat—the sheer, unrelenting temperature—felt all-consuming. The dragyri's head jerked back on his shoulders, and his mouth contorted in trauma. He arched his back; his thighs began to tremble; and he started to writhe like an animal.

They were torturing him beyond reason.

"Zane! Zane! *Zane!*" She wanted to reach out and soothe him. "No!" she shouted angrily at the gods, consumed with wild fury.

This wasn't right!

It wasn't fair!

And still, he wouldn't stop shouting.

Someone, make him stop!

Oh, please, just make it stop!

His wings were melting, his bones were disintegrating, and his hands were sticking to her gloves—yet and still, the male held on.

He bent forward, forming an arc above her.

He used his head like a shield to protect her.

And he tightened his arms—what was left of his wings—all around her torso, even as he pressed tighter against her back, his now-hollow chest heaving from the effort…

And the agony.

And then, out of nowhere, the fire broke through.

Zane could no longer contain it.

A pain so acute, so unbearable—so unholy—punched the breath out of Jordan's body. It struck her like a hammer bearing down on an anvil, and she prayed to any deity that would listen—*just kill me*!

Please, have mercy, and just kill me.

She jackknifed and screamed, bucked and shrieked, out of her mind with agony, and then—just like that—there was silence.

Darkness.

Stillness.

The complete absence of being.

It wasn't a sensation—because there was no consciousness—it was more like simply ceasing to be…anything.

Alive.

Aware.

Asleep.

There was simply and absolutely…

Nothing.

And then she heard a sharp but distant *pop*, and an even fainter sound, like music—maybe a harp or a cello—rushing through her consciousness like an ambient stream; and light began to radiate all around her. First silver, then blue, then a resplendent combination of the two, and her body felt like it was floating.

Ah, and then…

And then…

It felt like a pure awakening.

The lightness in her head was intoxicating, her body tingled with ecstasy, and her spirit felt powerful—*invincible*—alive.

And Jordan knew she was perfect.

She was free.

There was no pain. There was no worry. There was no guilt, or shame, or regret—there was only the nirvana that swept her away: serenity, joy, and peace.

All her life she had sought this perfection—just a moment, just an instant, just a glimpse—and she wanted to remain there forever. She didn't need to eat, or think, or *do*—not anything—ever again.

She just wanted to bathe in this light.

Forever.

"Oh gods, please, let me stay in this grace. If this is dying, I'm no longer afraid."

Zane stirred behind her, threatening to pull her out of her reverie; and truth be told—in that blissful moment—he was the only soul in the universe that could. She felt him take a huge gulp of breath, and then his chest expanded; his body stopped trembling; and he slowly retracted his wings.

Jordan turned around, ever so slowly, and reached for his handsome face. She cupped his strong, angular jaw in her fingers, ran her thumb along his bottom lip, and began to weep, uncontrollably.

She couldn't help it.

She was drowning in clarity.

Greater love hath no man than he would lay down his life for a friend…

And Zane had sacrificed everything—to shield her, to protect her, to bear the brunt of the pain…to spare her from the worst of the dragons' flames.

If she lived a thousand years, she would love this male until her dying breath. Only now did she truly understand what this mating had cost him—from the very first moment, when he had claimed her in that garage.

Out of the corner of her eye, she caught a sudden glimpse of a brilliant sparkling light, a prism of effervescence gleaming from the fourth finger of her left hand. And like the glow of the moon on a dark, cloudy night, the light stood out on her finger, contrasted against the golden hues of Zane's flawless skin. She studied her hand absently, and then her eyes zeroed in on the ornament.

Great dragon lords, there was a dazzling, perfectly cut sapphire in the center of an antique ring encircling her wedding finger. The disk was fashioned in the shape of a dragon, and flowing, like planets around the sun—orbiting the flawless sapphire—were six immaculate gemstones: a diamond, an emerald, an amethyst, an onyx, a citrine, and a magnificent topaz.

"Zanaikeyros," she whispered lovingly, rubbing her thumbs along his skin. "Are you okay? Say something, dragyri; tell me you're no longer in pain."

He heaved a rugged sigh, and then he fixed those glorious sapphire-gold eyes on hers and smiled like an innocent child. And by all the gods, it was the most glorious sight she had ever seen. Her ring paled by comparison.

He was too exhausted to speak, so she crawled into his arms and held him like she would never let him go—because she wouldn't.

"I love you, Zane," she breathed into his ear. "I love you so very much—and I'm sorry I ever doubted you…" Her voice trailed off, and she giggled, actually laughed with merriment.

He tightened his arm around her back, nuzzled her neck with his nose, and pressed a warm, tender kiss into the hollow of her throat. "You were brave, dragyra. Brave and beautiful. And I love you, too. I will love you forever." His gorgeous mouth quirked up into a smile, and he stared at her glistening ring.

"Welcome to The Pantheon of Dragons."

Epilogue

AXEVIATHON SAPHYRIUS, BETTER known as Axe, strolled into the lobby of the King's Castle Credit Union around ten o'clock, Monday morning. A well-dressed brunette, who looked equal parts eager and insecure, greeted him at the front entrance with a smile and a nod.

"Good morning. How can we help you today?"

Axe spared her a sidelong glance and kept right on walking.

One, he didn't have the time, nor the desire, to deal with extraneous humans today; and two, he knew exactly where he was going: through the lobby, past the tellers, and down the long, narrow hall on the right—straight to the opulent office of the bank's newest manager, Warren Simmons.

Warren was a card-carrying member of the Cult of Hades, a faction of clueless humans who dabbled in the occult—or so they thought. In reality, they served a dangerous, supernatural god, and they didn't even know it.

Drakkar Hades.

King of the underworld and ruler of demons and shades.

Father of the Pagan Horde.

The ancient pagan had messed with the Temple of Seven. He had ticked off the dragon lords by trying to destroy an original dragyri son, Zane Saphyrius—Axe's lair-mate. And in doing so, the dark king had provoked the Seven's wrath. Not only had Drak sent Salem Thorne, a despicable, caustic demon, to try to slay Zane's new mate, but he had manipulated the female's best friend, Macy, by using her surgeon to take advantage of her vulnerable heart. In short, he had planned to use the women's friendship to one day get to Zane, and the doctor had just been a pawn: an accessible, pliant, easy-to-manipulate tool, due to a weakness in his character...

And a fissure in his soul.

Pagans were bottom-feeders at best.

No better than carp or vultures.

They fed on the souls—and the sins—of humans.

If the pagan was a shadow-walker (or a "shade"), he simply fed on the human's essence; he reanimated his immortal, skeletal carcass by devouring the person's spirit. But if he was a demon—and especially if he was ancient—then he fed on the human's sins: He encouraged them, milked them, caught them in the act, and grew stronger by association...

And proxy.

Salem had taken advantage of the surgeon's pride, his never-ending ambition to rise in the eyes of others, no matter the stakes or the costs, and Lord Drakkar Hades had hoped to use the not-so-fine doctor sometime in the future, in a manner as old as time. As Zane grew closer to his new dragyra, as her burgeoning role in The Pantheon was cemented, Drakkar had hoped to draw on her enduring friendship with Macy to sneak a wolf in sheep's clothing into Dragons Domain. Whether on Christmas, Valentine's Day, or some other uniquely human holiday, the pagan king was gambling on the certainty that a time would surely come when Macy would want to send her BFF a box of chocolates, or a bag stuffed with gifts—hell, a simple housewarming present would do.

And then Drakkar could use the doctor, and the doctor could use Macy...

The pretty, wrapped gifts would not contain delectable chocolates. They would not contain a snow globe or a bottle of fine wine. They would be the pagan substitute of a Trojan horse: ten, fifteen, maybe twenty ancient demons, all in beetle form, nestled snugly inside the packages, waiting to invade, shift, and attack. Drakkar was gambling on the fact that the doctor could get Drak's pagans through the portal—and into that foreign realm—that they could one day slip in, undetected, posing as harmless gifts. And then they could strike swiftly—and definitively—at The Pantheon of Dragons.

And that's why Axe was at the bank.

That's why he was carrying a large box of chocolates, stuffed with Dr. Kyle Parker's right hand, and wrapped in pretty gold paper, secured by a bloodred bow (truly, the bow had been dipped in blood), and the accompanying card was simple, elegant, and to the point: *For Drak; the best-laid plans of mice and pagans often go astray.*

The king would get the message.

A young African-American security guard rounded the corner in a rush and called out to Axe—the greeter must have tipped him off. Axeviathon spun around, lowered his shades, and gave the youngster a clear, up-close-and-personal view of his sapphire irises and his jet-black pupils, his otherworldly dragon eyes, and he smiled. "Go back to your post, son, and stay there." His words were laced with an implicit compulsion, and the human stopped dead in his tracks. He blinked three times, scanned the hallway in confusion, and immediately turned on his heels.

Good human, Axe thought.

He continued to saunter down the hallway to the last door on the right. Then he reached for the handle, turned it clockwise, and strolled into the room. Warren Simmons bolted upright, stepped back from his desk, and immediately reached for the fly on his pants. A skinny female *companion*, who didn't look a day over seventeen years old, reached for the sides of her skirt, yanked it into place, and shimmied off Warren's desk.

Both of them looked ashamed.

Axe snorted and shook his head.

Well, it didn't take a rocket scientist to figure out Warren's *sin of entry*, how he had exposed himself to the pagans.

So the man was a pedophile...

Disgusting, but whatever.

The Dragyr did not get involved in human affairs, at least not beyond any direct or interlocking business with The Pantheon.

They did their masters' bidding.

It wasn't an optional clause.

And that, as they say, was that.

As the short blonde female scurried around Axe and headed for the manager's door, Axe tapped her on the shoulder. "Sweetheart," he said in a husky voice, laced with lethal intention. "You never saw me, okay?"

Her light-green eyes grew cloudy, and she slowly nodded her head. "Yeah," she whispered, "okay."

"Oh, and one other thing."

She shifted back and forth, nervously, as she waited.

"This old piece of shit—the one you were about to get it on with, on the desk. That's finished. Find someone your own age."

She drew back in surprise, but she nodded. Then she hurried out of the room.

Warren's face flushed red. "Who the hell are you? And what makes you think you can just walk into my office without an appointment?" He reached for the intercom on his phone and grunted into the speaker: "Jackson? Jackson! Get in here."

Jackson must have been the African-American security guard, and if so, he wasn't coming. Axe's compulsion would hold—probably for the rest of the day. But just to be safe—and to make sure Warren didn't reach out to anyone else—he flicked his pinky in the direction of the intercom, sent a slender electrical flame through the air, and blew out the internal wiring. "Sit down," he barked.

Now, there was no point in going into Pantheon business with this pitiful Cult of Hades' sycophant. Truth be told, the low-level human had probably never even met Lord Drakkar, and he likely never would. He was just a pawn on a chessboard—a naïve, corruptible mind that the pagans could use until they were finished with him—until they had sucked all the anima out of him or left him on the sidewalk for dead. The leeching could take a day, a year, or a lifetime, depending on how much sin they consumed from Mr. Simmons—and at what rate they consumed it.

"You got a tattoo on the back of your neck?" Axe asked.

The human's eyes narrowed. He looked instantly guilty, and he reached up to scratch his nape. Yep, he was sporting a medieval sword with a witch's pentacle etched into the pommel, on the back of his neck. Sure as shit, he was. And that meant that somewhere in the underworld a demon was watching, listening, and tuning into Warren Simmons several times a day. They would read his distress, catch the disruption in his sin, and eventually come to investigate. Hopefully, the hand wouldn't stink too badly before they found the box of chocolates.

Axe figured he'd better speed things up.

He dropped the "gift" on Warren's desk, planted his forefinger in the center of the bow, and seared his gaze into Warren's. "You leave this right here until someone…important…comes to get it. You don't open it; you don't talk about it; you don't mention it until then. We copasetic on that?"

The man looked decidedly pissed off, like he wanted to rip Axe's head off—good luck with that one—but somewhere deep inside, where predators recognized prey and quarry hid from hunters, his common sense kicked in. "Yeah," he mumbled in a surly tone, "we're copasetic."

"Good," Axe said.

He was about to pull a disappearing act, simply vanish from the bank, when he thought better of it: He should make one last pass through the lobby, make sure nothing had gone wrong—make sure no humans had been tipped off—before he made his way back through the portal. His muscles bunched and contracted in the lithe, smooth gait of a hunter—it was the animal nature of a dragyri—as he sauntered out of the office, headed back down the hall, into the lobby, and quickly checked all human eyes for signs of awareness.

Convinced that everything was A-Okay, he passed by the last female teller—and his amulet heated up.

What the hell…

The timeless, heavy sapphire stone hanging around his neck—the one that linked his soul to The Pantheon and his life to Lord Saphyrius—suddenly singed his flesh, leaving a trail of smoke in the lobby.

His inner dragon drew to immediate attention.

He angled his body toward the nice-looking teller and regarded her *much more* closely.

Her beautiful, dark, amber eyes, which matched the color of her hair almost perfectly, began to glow inside her irises, and then, just for an instant, her pupils turned deep dark blue.

Sapphire.

Just like Axe's stone.

The precious gem seared a scar into his flesh, and in that moment, he knew…

Oh yeah, he knew…

And, holy hell, the realization was stunning.

He was staring at his *fated* dragyra.

His beast began to snarl as he took a step in her direction—just what the hell was she doing in King's Castle Credit Union?

TO BE CONTINUED IN BOOK TWO

AXEVIATHON ~
SON OF DRAGONS

Books by Tessa Dawn

(THE BLOOD CURSE SERIES)
Blood Genesis (prequel)
Blood Destiny
Blood Awakening
Blood Possession
Blood Shadows
Blood Redemption
Blood Father
Blood Vengeance
Blood Ecstasy
Blood Betrayal ~ Coming Soon

(OTHER TITLES)
Dragons Realm
Daywalker ~ The Beginning

(PANTHEON OF DRAGONS)
Zanaikeyros ~ Son of Dragons
Axeviathon ~ Son of Dragons (Coming Soon)

Join the Mailing List

(And never miss another new release!)
If you would like to receive an email notifying you of Tessa's
future releases,
please join the author's mailing list at

www.tessadawn.com/mailinglist

You can also find the author and her works at
www.TessaDawn.com

Get your FREE copy of

BLOOD GENESIS

(Prequel to Tessa Dawn's bestselling Blood Curse Series)

at
Amazon (kindle)
Barnes and Noble (nook)
KOBO
iTunes

About the Author

Tessa Dawn grew up in Colorado, where she developed a deep affinity for the Rocky Mountains. After graduating with a degree in psychology, she worked for several years in criminal justice and mental health before returning to get her master's degree in non-profit management.

Tessa began writing as a child and composed her first full-length novel at the age of eleven. By the time she graduated high school, she had a banker's box full of short stories and novels. Since then, she has published works as diverse as poetry, greeting cards, work-books for kids with autism, and academic curricula. Her Dark Fantasy/Gothic Romance novels represent her long-desired return to her creative-writing roots and her passionate flair for storytelling.

Tessa currently splits her time between the Colorado suburbs and mountains with her husband, two children, and "one very crazy cat." She hopes to one day move to the country where she can own horses and what she considers "the most beautiful creature ever created" — a German Shepherd.

Writing is her bliss.

CPSIA information can be obtained
at www.ICGtesting.com
Printed in the USA
BVOW08s1554121217

502602BV00001B/58/P